the snowball effect

HALEY CASS

For Monica - in the process of writing this, we've experienced a death, a wedding party, moving across multiple states while buying our first house together, and all I can really say is that there is no one else I'd rather be with in the craziness of life than you.

acknowledgments

This book truly would not have happened without the support of so many people in my life.

Mostly, though, this novel wouldn't have come to fruition without the support and excitement of all of my readers.

To everyone on my patreon - you really went with me on this journey, and I loved every second of it. I can't wait for the next project.

A very big, amazed, wondrous appreciation for Kermetris Hill, Ashleigh Barnett, Sarah Baker-Goldsmith, Nicola Lewis, Betsy Walker, RB, Carrie Totta, Base250, Miranda Hurley, Larissa Frank, Banban Cheng, Derek G, Bridget Ruane, Caroline Swift, Angie Bobinger, Cora Linehan, Lisa Sanchez, Emily Shinabery, Tiffany Sorrell, Macon Leigh, Carol Morales, Cole, Tiffany Wells, Kendall Hatfield, Eabha Buttimer, Courtney McCraney, Jennifer Reeves, Stella Johnson, Sue Reese, Liz Hendrick, Court Hanson-Miller, Haleigh Heyne, Briana Bradley, Bethany Wright, Natalie Hernandez, Cat Crittenden, Lexi Le, JC, Sophia Barrett, M Walter, Kylie Harris, Sarah de Kok, Danielle Seneca, Noelle Pinto, Amber Mitchell, Andy Howland, Camila Silva-Ta, Trevor Scott, Alice Wang, Jamie Baird, MC, Sarah Namias, Lia Perez, Nosferatu, Chance McGinn, Q, Melanie Reber, Merle M, Kayla Bhadra, Lisa Tillery, Rachel, Leah Martines, Kirsty Hogg, Mary Ann Bosworth, Joanne, Amarilis Aranguren, Stephanie Leeth, Sophie, Hanna Baptist, Pearl Goodbread, Tina Meade, Joy Herbert, Dianna Norman, Alicia Perez, Amelia Tomson, Taylor Carr, Natassia Leverington, Bridgette Marie, Allixandra Castiglione, Susan Hiler, Cherry Young, Kristine Friling, Rachel Russell, and Bukola Jimoh.

TWO YEARS AGO

Liquid Burns Are No Joke

Would Regan Gallagher say working at a coffee shop was "her calling," so-to-speak? Not exactly. Was it what she wanted to do for the rest of her life? Definitely not.

But it happened to be something she was really fucking good at. Maybe it was the frenetic pace during rush hours, never dipping into a boring lull or letting Regan get too distracted. Maybe it was the freedom she was granted during the slower hours – especially now that she was an assistant manager – that allowed her to get hands-on with multiple aspects of the cafe, indulging her curious nature. Maybe it was simply the scent of caffeine that fueled her coffee-addicted can-do spirit.

Whatever it was, Regan had been working at Topped Off for five years, and she was something of a one-woman show at the moment.

Topped Off rarely experienced *true* emptiness – it was a 24-hour hipster shop in the heart of New York University's Manhattan campus, serving some quality grounds. They had a revolving door nearly constantly, with students holing up at tables and booths throughout the night. It was more likely to be busy than not.

Usually, though, Regan wasn't the only person working during finals week. In fact, as the person who made the schedule, she made it a point never to put *anyone* as the only barista manning the front of the store during this time.

Today, though, she was the ringleader and entertainment all-in-one, and she just might *kill* Rochelle and Pat for both calling out sick today. Regan was no dummy; she knew they'd gone out the night before and had gotten blasted. The "sickness" they were enduring today was undoubtedly alcohol-related.

"I deserve a medal for this," she said, swiping her arm over her forehead to brush away any strands that had escaped her ponytail in the three hours since she'd had time to redo her hair. "Gold, too, because I fucking *killed* that."

Really, she did. She'd just handled the never-ending morning line of stress-addled nerds single-handedly. After she prepared this drink, she was going to call Jacklyn out from the kitchen and have her cover so Regan could take her well-deserved fifteen-minute break.

The drink in question that she was prepping was... questionable. Even to her own palette.

Regan considered herself a rather daring coffee drinker – whatever batshit-sounding specialty orders came down from corporate, Regan tried them all herself. It was somewhat of a special activity here. When the monthly specials list was received at the beginning of every month, everyone would gather around to try them. In particular, as the main event, Regan would assemble a small size of every single special, then go down the line and try them all. Even the one that had both lemonade *and* pumpkin spice in it.

In Regan's humble opinion, the taste testers – or whoever the hell came up with the flavors at their northeast-based chain – had no fear. Occasionally, when they sent down the recipes for some of those wild flavor combinations, she wondered if they even had taste buds.

She gave the final pump of liquid sugar before finishing with the caramel drizzle over the top, unable to hold back her grimace. But she worked quickly because the girl who'd placed this order of a "steaming hot extra-large dark roast, two shots of espresso, four shots of chai, five pumps of liquid sugar, finished with caramel – keep them coming" had preemptively tipped Regan a hundred bucks, before she'd made herself at home in one of the back booths next to the windows, two hours ago.

Topped Off didn't typically provide table service, either, but when this woman had wordlessly flashed another hundred at Regan as a promise of an additional tip... well, Regan was going to provide table-side delivery.

As she hustled out from behind the counter, she frowned down at the cup as she tried to snap the lid on.

"This fucking thing," she muttered. The most recent shipment of lids for their large hot cups weren't snapping onto the cups quite right, and –

Regan gasped in surprise as she bumped into someone, hot coffee leading the way.

A cold terror slid through her veins, and she swore she watched the next few seconds play out in slow motion. As the shitty, malfunctioning lid popped right off, and the literally steaming hot liquid dumped from over the lip of the cup down the woman's shirt.

"Shit!" She shouted in the middle of the packed café because she was a professional. "Oh, god! Fuck!"

While she was yelling, the other woman grit her jaw, grimacing deeply in pain. Which made a ton of sense.

That drink had been hot; the bit that had splattered on Regan's fingers had hurt, even. So she could only imagine how it felt all over this woman's chest.

Her very ample chest that was only a couple inches lower than eye level for Regan, who was level with this woman's strong jaw.

And this woman's pale blue long-sleeved button-up had already been form-fitting, but it was utterly soaked through, now, clinging to the woman like a second skin. Regan could clearly see her bra and how hard her nipples were.

Fuck, *those* must be burning, too! Regan's own nipples were so sensitive that she'd have probably been in tears if hot coffee had been poured on them.

Out of pure reflex, she dropped the cup and reached out, grabbing both sides of the woman's shirt so she could rip it open, trying to get some cool air on her.

Regan would be the first person to say that sometimes her... impulsivity got ahead of her. But *this* was the right decision; she knew it was.

She could hear the scattering of buttons over the wooden floors, and she could feel the stares of most of the patrons. Which wasn't shocking, first because Regan had dumped coffee on her, and now because, like, *seriously*, this woman had breasts to die for.

"What the *fuck* are you doing?" The woman finally spoke. Rather, growled.

"Helping!" Regan shouted back, laser-focused on the task at hand.

She grabbed the woman's hand and started to pull her toward the employee break room, barely pausing as she shouted, "Jackie! I have an emergency! Please come cover the front!"

Without another second to waste, she tugged the woman into the back room, her thoughts racing. They had to check her for burns; everyone thought that the warning on the McDonald's cup was funny, but liquid burns were no joke! Then–

Before Regan could lead the woman to one of the chairs at the break table, the woman yanked her hand out from Regan's, repeating, "What the *fuck* are you doing?!"

This time, it wasn't a quiet hiss, but a demanding shout.

It didn't bother Regan, though. This was a stressful situation, and stress begot yelling from time to time. Especially if she was hurt.

Regan turned, leaning in closer to inspect the skin of the woman's chest, where the majority of the liquid had made direct contact. Though the smooth, pale skin was pink from the heat of the coffee, it didn't appear to be blistering or have any other lasting repercussions. She lowered her gaze, looking at the woman's gently rounded stomach, which was also blushing from the heat, but –

The woman jerked her arms across herself as she repeated in a low, dangerous voice, "I don't want to ask again: What. The fuck. Are you doing?"

Satisfied that the woman wouldn't endure any serious burns, the relief that slid through Regan was swift and immense. God, that could have been terrible. As it was, it seemed like a ruined shirt was the only victim!

Turning on her heel, she pulled her unlocked locker open and started rooting through it. She definitely had a sweatshirt somewhere in here. "I saw this totally gross video once about this guy who spilled boiling water on his legs, and basically, he ended up with these sick burns because his pants had clung the hot liquid onto his skin, right? And the doctors had said the burns would have been way less severe if he hadn't had the pants on."

She shuddered from the visual; she could still clearly see in her mind's eye of the burns. God, that had been so disgustingly awful. They really had been so lucky just now.

Oh – there it was! Her sweatshirt.

"Got it!" She cried out triumphantly, pulling it out from where it was nestled between her cosmetics bag and spare rain jacket.

Her very well-loved, soft, blue and gray Brandeis sweatshirt – from the single year of college that she'd attended – that she kept here for when the air conditioning was turned up too high.

She turned to give it to the woman, finally taking a good look at her in a non-clinical way.

She had a long, graceful neck and a very strong jaw that led down to that expanse of soft-looking skin of her chest. She had a light smattering of freckles that stood out starkly against the pink irritation, and Regan's gaze, again, was drawn to her white lacy bra that was very much on display now. It seemed to only be slightly dampened, though, which was great. Because, unlike the sweatshirt, Regan most definitely did not have a bra lurking in her locker that would be able to accommodate this woman's band or cup size.

"My eyes are up here," the woman grit out.

Summoned, Regan snapped her own eyes up to meet them. The eyes in question were an icy blue, which was the only way Regan could imagine to describe them.

"I see that," she agreed, as she felt twin chills at the base of her spine and the pit of her stomach from the look she received, which fascinated her on a whole other level. *That* was a new experience for her!

The woman's hair – caught between a dark blonde and a light brown – had been spared from the coffee fiasco, pulled up into an elegant braided twist, which added to her *previously* professional look with the button-up and the well-fitted black pants.

"What the hell is the matter with you?" The woman demanded to know before she crossed her arms tighter and then grimaced in disgust at – what Regan guessed was – the wet stickiness of the coffee that still soaked the material.

"I mean, adult-identified ADHD. But I don't really like to look at it as something that's wrong with me."

The set of the crazily strong jaw and an entirely unamused sigh told Regan that this woman did not find any levity here. Which was a shame because Regan was usually pretty good with levity.

She stared into the woman's eyes, hoping that her deeply apologetic feelings were mirrored there. "I'm just – it's been totally hectic here, and I didn't look before I turned around, which was a really dumb rookie mistake, and I didn't see you. I swear, I didn't mean to–"

"No, I got how you spilled the coffee. What I don't get is where the hell you get off, ripping my shirt off at all, let alone in front of fifty people!"

"It was more like twenty people, tops, and I thought you were going to have third-degree burns!" She gesticulated wildly, a curl of remorse about the shirt incident sliding through her stomach; that was how it always happened. She acted first, and then everything else came later. "I'm sorry! I wasn't thinking."

"Yeah, clearly," the woman snapped in her low, clear voice. "Do you ever?"

"Well. Ouch." She cradled her sweatshirt in her arms and leaned back on her heels.

"Not only do I have my first meeting with my advisor with a coffee-soaked and stained shirt, but one that doesn't have any fucking buttons," the woman absolutely fumed.

"Oh!" Thankfully reminded of what she'd been doing, Regan pushed her sweatshirt toward the woman. "Here. Take this. I mean, it's no fancy ironed button-up – you know, I didn't realize twenty-some-things owned irons anymore? I definitely don't – but it is from Brandeis, which is a, uh, really... good... school."

Her words came out slower as the woman whipped off her shirt entirely, her chest heaving in the white bra as she muttered unintelligible but clearly angry words under her breath. She grabbed Regan's sweat-shirt and jerked it on over her head.

"Well, thank god I like to buy my sweatshirts a couple of sizes bigger," she commented with an appreciative nod.

Regan liked to cuddle into that sweatshirt for comfort, and she bought it with that purpose in mind. So it sat baggy and low on her, ending at her mid-thighs. On this woman, conversely, it hugged her chest and sat flatteringly fittingly on her curved hips.

She only realized her words could be taken the wrong way when the woman's mouth fell open in offense, and she gave Regan a look that she could only explain as – this woman definitely thought she was legit out of her fucking mind; she was somewhat familiar with it.

"Unbelievable."

"Not that I'm, like, calling you fat," she quickly explained, shaking her head, before she thought for a second and wrinkled her nose at herself and added on, "Or that there is anything wrong with being fat, either, for that matter, I just meant, like, it fits well–"

The woman clearly did not want to stick around to hear the rest. She huffed out a breath and balled up her wet shirt in her fist as she cut Regan off, "I'm leaving now."

She strode to the door before pausing and took a noticeably deep breath. She squared her shoulders and it only then occurred to Regan that this woman was embarrassed to walk back out through the café full of people who'd seen her without her shirt.

"I'm really–" she started, stepping towards the woman. Who strode out of the back room without a backward glance as if propelled away by Regan's voice, "Sorry."

If she had given Regan a moment to speak, Regan would have offered her an exit through the back!

~

Regan had nearly forgotten about that terrible, no-good morning a month later.

The semester was re-starting after winter break, and business was picking back up at Topped Off, but that wasn't Regan's problem tonight! Because tonight, she was having a night in with her best friend/roommate, Sutton.

Sutton was on her way back from her first day of classes, officially halfway through her second year of grad school, and had texted Regan an hour ago to say:

> I hope you didn't order dinner already! I'm going to leave campus soon, but I've been hanging out for the afternoon with Dr. Woods' new teaching assistant and showing her the ropes. I invited her to have dinner with us if that's okay?

Regan's reminder alarm to order dinner had just gone off, so...

> You got me just in time. Hit me with the order. Can't wait to meet your new school friends, sunshine!

She'd just received their order and laid the spread out on their kitchen table when their apartment door opened. "And your fortunate timing continues, Sutton-lucky-Spencer!" She shouted, wiping her hands on her thighs as she moved to step through the doorway into their short front hall.

Only to stumble over her feet and come to a stop at the sight of the woman next to Sutton. Tall – just as tall as Sutton was, in fact – with familiar icy blue eyes.

Sutton grinned, bright and oblivious, as she nodded toward Regan. "Emma, this is my roommate, Regan." She gestured at the woman. "And this is Emma, my fellow teaching assistant."

Those icy blue eyes seemed to frost over as they widened, then narrowed. "We've met," she'd muttered darkly.

Even though it had been *weeks*, Emma's glare was just as sharp as it had been that day. Regan was fairly certain right then and there that they were not destined to be friends.

one

Emma Bordeaux yawned widely as she blinked her eyes open, staring up at her bedroom ceiling.

For the briefest of moments, her morning awakening was peaceful.

Waking up without the assistance of her alarm was incredibly rare. So rare, actually, that it was unheard of for her. Typically, her first alarm went off at six-thirty. Followed by her alarm at six-forty-five. Followed again by the alarm at six-fifty. And finally, the alarm that annoyed her enough to rouse her was her seven o'clock.

With that thought in mind, she rolled onto her side to tap the screen of her phone to check the time.

Only to frown, sitting up straighter in bed as her stomach sank.

Because her phone screen remained dark, even as she continued to tap on it, each touch more compulsive than the last.

"No. Nooo, no, no. Come *on*," she hissed, all semblance of her calm welcome into the world washed away in panic.

Was her phone broken?! It wasn't the newest model... all right, it was far from the newest model. But it had been working perfectly fucking fine last night! It had been at ten percent battery when she'd plugged in to charge before going to sleep.

She cut her gaze to the window as she threw the sheet away from her body, hopping out of bed. The sun was high in the sky, brightly shining into her room, and she could hear the sounds of the city, very much awake, muffled from the street below.

It didn't look or sound like it should when she rolled out of bed at seven.

Adrenaline-fueled panic coursed through her veins as she threw open her bedroom door and ran into the kitchen to check the clock over the stove.

Which did nothing to help, as the digital clock flashed the time back at her in blinking numbers that read 12:13.

She rushed back down the hallway to her bedroom, where the artful yet functional – and battery-operated – clock hung on the wall, and informed her that it was currently 8:02.

Even though she'd already been stressed, her stomach now tied in knots so tight, she thought she might be sick from them.

"Fuck," she swore under her breath, wheeling around so quickly she needed to brace her hand on the opposite wall to keep from falling in her haste.

Bathroom. She needed to get into the bathroom, brush her teeth and hair, and make herself as presentable as possible. She'd have to skip her morning shower, but that was... fine. What *wouldn't* be fine would be arriving even later to work than she already would be.

She'd only started at *Olly* three weeks ago, and she was pretty certain that Allegra Pantone, her boss, hadn't taken a special liking to her in that short time. Emma wasn't really sure if Allegra had ever taken a liking to anyone.

Reaching out, she tried to open the bathroom door, only to find that it was locked.

Which – *locked*? What the –?

"Regan? Are you in there?" She called out, hearing the desperation in her own voice.

Showing a vulnerability to anyone at any point in time made her feel uncomfortable, but she absolutely loathed displaying it to Regan even more.

However, desperate times called for desperate measures, and she banged on the door with her palm. "Hello? Regan?"

"This is she," Regan's smart-aleck voice replied from the other side of the door. "Who's asking?"

Ah. There it was, that sharp feeling of annoyance at Regan. Honestly, this was such a terrible morning she welcomed that feeling right about now.

She narrowed her eyes at the door, huffing out a breath. "Obviously Emma."

"I thought so. But since you asked if I was occupying the bathroom in our two-person apartment, I figured I would make sure that you were the person doing the asking."

Emma's foot started to tap against the hardwood floor as agitation, impatience, and anxiety twisted together inside of her. She took a deep breath before setting her jaw and letting go of the retort she normally would have said.

Instead, she asked, "Are you almost done in there?"

There was a beat before Regan responded, "Um... I guess I could be. Why?"

"Because I need to use the bathroom!" Really, she tried for patience.

But, *jesus*, she swore Regan Gallagher made it a point to be as irritating as possible. She couldn't say yes or no to a simple question, couldn't make anything easier.

Typical.

"Like, a pee-emergency?"

"Oh my god." Emma strove for control, dropping her forehead to the door jamb and closing her eyes. "No."

Though, now that Regan mentioned it, Emma was due for her morning pee.

"A little," she amended. "But I overslept, and I need to get ready for work literally as fast as humanly possible, okay?"

She jumped as the door, only inches from her face, suddenly swung open.

"Why didn't you just say that?" Regan asked, stepping out from where she stood in the doorway.

Emma wasted no time as she stepped past Regan, not even bothering to snap the door closed as she jammed her phone charger into the bathroom outlet, hoping it would work.

Relief rushed through her when her phone buzzed with a sign of life, even if the battery was completely dead.

Without wasting time, she immediately started brushing her teeth with one hand, using the other to open her side of the mirror to rifle through her toiletries.

If she got herself together in the next fifteen minutes, skipped her morning coffee, and arrived at her subway stop in record time – *and* if the subway didn't experience any delays – she could make it to work less than ten minutes late.

"You know, I don't think I've *ever* seen you so panicky." Regan's voice cut into her rushing thoughts.

Emma slid her gaze toward the doorway that Regan stood in, having not realized she was still there.

She ran her eyes over Regan, actually taking her in for the first time. Regan was wearing only a towel, wrapped snugly around her lithe body, knotted between her breasts, and her shoulder-length dark hair was thrown casually into a knot on the top of her head.

"Because I'm not," she muttered back around her toothbrush, turning away from Regan to spit into the sink and wash her mouth out.

"What's going on this morning, then?" Regan asked, making herself comfortable in the doorway. Instead of doing what Emma would classify as the normal thing, and *going away.*

It was what every other roommate Emma had lived with in her adult life would have done, anyway. And it was most definitely what Emma would prefer.

"My alarm didn't go off," she answered curtly as she quickly started tugging a brush through her hair. Typically, she kept it just below her shoulders, but it was several inches longer now; she'd been so busy in the last month that she hadn't had the time to get it cut. "Do you know why the stovetop clock isn't working?"

"Ohhhhh," Regan drew out, snapping her fingers. "Yes. I do."

Emma huffed impatiently, snapping her eyes up to meet Regan's in the mirror. As she could have predicted, Regan was wearing a shit-eating smile on her irritatingly perfectly full lips.

"And?" She grit out.

"And there was a power outage just after midnight. It's this crazy freaking heat wave; I can't believe you didn't wake up!" Regan tossed her hands in the air dramatically as if unable to even *fathom* it.

Emma continued staring at her in the mirror, wondering if Regan even understood the absurdity of her comment. "Why would I have woken up from a power outage?"

"Because! It was so hot," Regan explained, her eyebrows flying up high on her forehead as she stared at Emma like *Emma* was the insane one here. "The air conditioning shut off, obviously. I was laying on the kitchen floor with ice packs all over my body."

"Of course you were," she murmured, shaking her head.

The *dramatics*.

"It was, like, ninety degrees in here. Literally. For at least an hour before the power came back on, and then I could finally go to sleep."

"And yet, you didn't set the clock on the stove," she pointed out, unable to stop herself from rolling her eyes.

Because, of course, Regan had been awake and in the kitchen and hadn't taken it upon herself to set the clock again.

Regan looked uncharacteristically sheepish, then. "... that's a fair comment. Sorry. I forgot."

The apology sounded sincere, but it was the fact that Regan hadn't set the damn clock that was the root of Emma's perpetual irritation with her. Therefore, she ignored it.

"My phone was plugged in all night," she commented, gesturing down at her charging phone with her elbow as she quickly started braiding her hair over her shoulder. "Do you know why it didn't start charging again after the power came back on?"

Regan seemed to perk up, previous sheepishness forgotten, as she nodded. "Yeah, actually! So, obviously, the apartment is in good shape, even though the building is, like, a hundred years old." She fondly patted the wall next to her. "*But*, there's a little snag when the power goes out – everything we have plugged into the outlets in our bedrooms needs to be unplugged and then plugged in again before it starts working."

Emma could only stare at Regan with a confused, narrowed look.

Regan held up her hands as if anticipating Emma's bafflement. "I'm not an electrician, so I don't know how it works! But everything in the kitchen and living room turns back on like normal. It's just our bedroom outlets that are weird."

"This might have been useful information to have been told when I moved in," she pointedly said, arching an eyebrow as she snapped her hair tie to secure her braid.

This time, it was Regan who shot *her* an incredulous look. "First – like, yeah, I guess so. But secondly and most relevantly – you would have still been sleeping when the power came back on, and I'm not allowed in your room except in case of emergencies, in your own passionate words. So... how would you have charged your phone, even if you knew about the outlets?"

Emma pursed her lips, hating that she couldn't think of anything to say to counter that point.

She hated even more that Regan's dark eyes lit up with an obvious *gotcha*.

"Fine." Maybe Regan had a point; she supposed even a broken clock was right twice a day. Much like the clock over the stove right now. "Regardless, I have to go."

She unplugged her phone and started toward the door.

Regan didn't really move out of her way, only turning her body slightly so Emma couldn't avoid brushing by her. This was something Regan did frequently when they ran into each other in the hallway, and Emma always wondered what compelled her to not do the polite thing and scoot out of the way.

Emma did her best to give Regan her space whenever they passed one another, but the simple reality was that Manhattan apartments were not spacious, and Regan was, like, half Emma's size. Emma was at least five inches taller than Regan at five-foot-ten, and outweighed Regan by at least forty pounds. She didn't know if Regan was simply used to living with Sutton – a waif – or what, but it was yet another thing that *irked* her.

"Anyway, you're welcome. I paused as I was *literally* about to step into the shower," Regan called as Emma rushed back to her room.

This gave her pause, and Emma tossed Regan a look, once again taking in the whole towel situation. "Thank you. I appreciate it."

A bright, annoyingly luminescent smile slid over Regan's face. "Was that so hard?"

Emma stepped into her room without a verbal response and sharply shut the door.

~

"You're late," Brynn, Allegra's other assistant, commented as soon as Emma entered the open space their desks shared.

Emma dumped her bag onto her desk, immediately searching for Allegra in the glass-walled office next to them. "Is she here yet?"

"Today's your lucky day," Brynn informed her. "She texted early and said she was going to be taking a last-minute meeting over coffee."

Even though Emma had felt *far* from lucky this morning, the relief that flooded her veins was so heady that she could have passed out. "Thank god."

"Seems unlike you to be late," Brynn observed, arching her a sharp look. "Or have you just been on your best behavior for the last month?"

"The former," she was quick to answer. "Definitely the former."

She all but collapsed in her desk chair, feeling like she could finally breathe. She reveled in that for a few seconds before looking up and catching Brynn's amused look.

"Apparently, the outlets in my new apartment are tricky when there's a power outage, and my alarm didn't go off," she explained as she started unpacking her bag.

Brynn hummed in acknowledgment. "I guess you're lucky it was my day for Allegra's morning coffee, too. I know she ended up taking a meeting, but imagine if she'd texted you at seven-thirty to inform you, and you didn't answer!"

"Honestly? Yeah." Because Emma hadn't even *thought* about that and shuddered at the very idea.

She and Brynn were on a rotating schedule to fetch Allegra's food and drinks, and fortunately, Emma had been on duty yesterday.

Brynn was two years younger than Emma's twenty-nine and had already been Allegra's assistant for nearly a year. She'd gotten her foot in the door at *Olly*, the digital magazine they worked for, before she'd even finished her bachelor's degree because her aunt worked in the fashion department.

Emma had long accepted that there would be people like Brynn or Sutton who were able to have easier access in the world because of their connections. She could still appreciate that Brynn was good at the job – always prompt, polished, and organized, and she'd been very magnanimous in showing Emma the ropes, giving her insider information on Allegra and everyone else at *Olly*.

After Emma organized her desk for the morning, she blew her hair out of her eyes and looked across the small reception area to find that Brynn was watching her with an amused smile.

"Look, Allegra should be out for another twenty minutes. Why don't you go down to the cafeteria and grab a coffee? Gather your bearings a bit. We have an all-hands meeting for two hours this afternoon, so..." She trailed off forebodingly.

Emma winced, not needing Brynn to say anymore. Allegra was the editor of the human interest department – the fastest-growing area at *Olly*. And while Emma admired her boss for being an amazing writer, editor, and a woman who'd carved her place out in journalism for decades, Allegra did not take kindly to the writers she handpicked turning in sub-par work. And it was no secret Allegra had not been pleased with several pieces as of late.

This meeting was going to be a long one.

"Thanks. Want anything?" She asked, standing from her desk.

Brynn shook her head and gestured to her half-full iced coffee as she turned back to her computer.

As she made her way down to the third-floor café, Emma felt like she could breathe normally for the first time all day.

Having wanted to preserve the small amount of battery she'd accumulated before leaving the apartment, she hadn't really checked her phone on her commute other than scanning to see if Allegra had called or emailed.

But, as she started to take in all the notifications that had popped up since she'd turned her phone on, that *easy* feeling fled yet again.

By all accounts, Emma's life should have been in a great place right now.

Her grandmother had settled into Primrose Grove, an assisted living community in Astoria that she actually seemed to enjoy. Not a lot, but a little bit, and for now, *a little bit* was enough.

She'd finally graduated with her master's degree last month. She had landed a more-than-decently paying job at *Olly*. Assisting Doctor Magda Woods for the last two years while getting her graduate degree had been hard as hell, given that Woods loved to bust her ass, granting no favors and giving no slack. Ever. Not even when Emma had the flu.

But it had paid off when Woods met with Emma as graduation approached and granted Emma her stamp of approval. In the literary world in this city, Magda Woods's professional recommendation held a lot of weight. That referential phone call she'd made to Allegra had made all the difference to Emma getting this job.

She finally – *finally* – wasn't living with her three vampiric roommates in the apartment right next to the fucking subway in Jackson Heights anymore. No, she was living in Greenwich Village, in a cozy two-bedroom. It was, undoubtedly, the nicest place she'd *ever* lived in, quirky bedroom outlets or not.

Unfortunately, that apartment was shared with Regan Gallagher, so that really put a damper on things.

Forgetting to set the time after the power had gone out was *so* typical of Regan. Emma should have expected it.

While Emma hadn't *loved* her previous roommates and how they'd been jammed into their small apartment like sardines, she had appreciated that they all seemed to want to have the same level of involvement with her that she wanted with them – very, very little. They'd stayed out of her business and all adhered to their roommate agreement to a T.

Living with Regan couldn't be more different.

When Regan had approached her with the offer to move in, Emma had been baffled before she'd found herself laughing, certain that Regan was telling her a ridiculous, nonsensical joke.

But, no. She'd been serious.

Regan was near the very bottom of the list of people Emma would choose to live with, wedged firmly between the friendly-yet-unhygienic girl who sat next to Emma in their Shakespeare course and the smarmy know-it-all guy who worked at her favorite bookstore.

But when she was offered Sutton's bedroom, in a much safer, nicer, and more convenient neighborhood, for the same monthly price that she was paying for her last lease... well, Emma figured she could manage any roommate for that.

She debated daily if that was the truth.

The day Emma moved in, Regan overzealously knocked a box out of Emma's arms, resulting in it crashing to the floor. The box that had, naturally, contained one of her grandmother's porcelain hummingbird figurines that she'd given Emma when Emma had moved out. The figurine had, of course, shattered.

And things hadn't really improved since then.

Regan loved to sing loudly to herself while she cooked and cleaned. Hell, while she tied her shoes. She questioned Emma incessantly whenever they ran into one another, and if she wasn't peppering her with inane questions, she rambled about her own day with stories Emma didn't ask for. She was consistently banging around in the kitchen at all hours of the night.

She didn't stick to a bathroom schedule of any kind. In fact, her entire schedule was unpredictable to Emma. She knew Regan managed Topped Off, a coffeehouse, but there was no semblance of regularity or consistency in how she flitted about her days. It was highly disconcerting.

Like a lot of Regan's behaviors were.

Once, less than a week into Emma moving in, Regan had exuberantly thrown Emma's door open when she'd returned home from work at ten in the evening. Emma had startled, and barely managed to pull up the shorts she'd been changing into before bed to cover her ass before she'd whirled around to demand, "Is there an emergency or something?"

To which Regan had given Emma an absurdly confused look before answering, "... not that I know of? Why?"

"Because that is the *only* reason you should ever be opening my door without knocking," she'd snapped back, incredulously, before gesturing for Regan to get the fuck out.

So, while things on the home front were geographically the best they'd ever been, logistically, it was a nightmare.

And, as she stared dismally down at her phone, *somehow*, Regan didn't manage to be the most stressful thing in her life right now.

Not when she faced five texts and a missed call from Kimberly.

> HURRICANE KIMBERLY – 6:52 AM
>
> Good morning, Emma Bo Bemma!
>
> HURRICANE KIMBERLY – 7:27 AM
>
> Sorry for calling so early. I know you're probably getting ready for work at OLLY!!!
>
> HURRICANE KIMBERLY – 7:29 AM
>
> I was just trying to nail you down for a dinner confirmation sometime in the next few weeks before your schedule fills up again.
>
> HURRICANE KIMBERLY – 7:31 AM
>
> I'd just like really REALLY like to see you, soon. I miss you. And so do Everly and Eva!!
>
> HURRICANE KIMBERLY – 7:48 AM
>
> But I know you're busy. I'll try again in a bit!

Mixed in with those messages, unsurprisingly, was one from her grandmother.

> GRAM – 8:18 AM
>
> She's really trying, honey.

Emma rubbed intently at her temples upon reading her mother's texts. Miraculously, Kimberly always managed to give Emma the beginnings of a headache. It was like she was conditioned for it at this point. Pavlov's Migraine.

As if summoned by Emma's thoughts, her phone started buzzing in her hand – apparently, waiting for less than two hours was the "bit" of time Kimberly had meant.

She pursed her lips as she stood in line for her coffee, automatically hovering her thumb over the decline option.

One of the last things she wanted this morning was to talk to her mother, especially because upon the sight of her name, her stomach cramped with anxiety.

More than anything, Emma hated uncertainty and unfamiliarity, and Kimberly brought those feelings on in spades.

But the last thing she wanted to do in life was upset her grand-mother. Whose latest text of encouragement was only the most recent in her attempts to help bridge the gap between Emma and her mother.

With that in mind, she sighed, pressing a hand to her stomach where that anxious flutter was, and hovered her thumb over the answer icon. When she reasoned that Kimberly wouldn't give her texting/calling a rest until Emma answered her, she finally did so.

"Um. Hi," she greeted, feeling uncomfortable, as she always did, when interacting with Kimberly.

Like, what *was* the proper greeting to your unreliable and unpre-dictable mom that had sporadically been around throughout your child-hood before moving to Florida and starting a second family when she finally reached adult maturity levels, who was now – having moved back to New York – desperately trying to bond with you?

Emma would give anything for there to be a book about how to manage this situation. She'd yet to find one.

"Emma!" Her mother's voice shouted in her ear with both obvious delight and surprise. "Oh, wow! I finally got a hold of you! I'm so glad you're awake."

Emma gave the barista a flash of a polite smile and placed her coffee order before she stepped to the side to wait. "Yeah, well, you did call on a work morning."

"Oh, I know. And I know you're very busy and all. I just can't wait until you finally have some free time to come over for dinner and tell me all about your glamorous job?" There was an undeniable edge of hope in her mom's voice that tied Emma's stomach into knots for the second time before ten AM.

A few months ago, she'd agreed to have dinner with her mom, when Kimberly had reached out and said that she'd "be in town." Emma was used to having an uncomfortable meal with her mom once every year or two when she was in the city to visit.

When she'd made that agreement, she hadn't realized that her mom was *going to be in town* because she was literally moving here.

As soon as Emma had learned the whole picture, the anxiety was quick on its heels. Kimberly being *here*, attempting to try to actually be in Emma's life... that was *not* the same thing as a dinner every other year.

"It's not really glamorous," she said, side-stepping any comments about dinner, before she looked over her shoulder to make sure Allegra hadn't appeared in the café that she rarely ever stepped foot into. But, just in case.

When she confirmed the coast was clear, she continued, "I'm only an assistant. So. There's not much to tell."

That was a slight lie; Emma's days were incredibly busy, and something was always going on. Kimberly didn't need to know that, though.

"I'd love to hear the boring details, then," Kimberly readily responded as if anticipating Emma's not-so-subtle shut-down. "I figure things have been settling down enough for you to book a dinner, now that you've been there for almost a month?"

She rolled her lips together, holding in her sigh.

Emma had found an easy way to finagle her way out of dinner at first – it was the end of the semester, and she had a ton of work to finish as she ended her master's program. And then, for the past month, she'd had the reasoning that she was extremely busy at work as she found her footing at *Olly*. Unpredictable late hours and whatnot, even though the truth was that Emma typically would be able to have dinner most nights by seven.

Again, Kimberly didn't need to know that. Not before Emma felt *ready*. And she still just... had no idea when that would be.

"Your gram said that you've been doing so well," Kimberly added enthusiastically. "She said you told her you even got an official nod of approval from your stern boss!"

Emma dropped her head back on a silent groan. She knew that Kimberly was her gram's daughter and all, but was nothing sacred between the two of them, anymore?

If she wasn't jam-packed at work, what could she say now? Short of, *actually, I'm not ready to see you, and I don't exactly know why, but I also don't really want to put in the mental energy to figuring that out,* anyway?

Which she couldn't say – first, because her gram had already had two heart attacks in the last three years, and Emma refused to be a cause of any additional stress in her life.

Secondly – and infinitely more complicated – Emma didn't want to hurt Kimberly's feelings, either. God. Yeah, she *really* wished she could find that book.

"Uh... yeah, I mean, work *is* settling down, I guess." And it *was.* Allegra gave her a considering, thoughtful nod last week, when she'd overheard Emma discuss an article with one of the staff writers, who'd been waiting to see her.

Emma had ridden that high for days.

"The thing is, I'm still kind of swamped. Now that work is calming down, I have to switch gears to focus on my new living situation," she lied through her teeth.

Regan was chaos personified, but that would never change, and Emma would never get used to it.

"Oh, yeah! I haven't heard just about *anything* about this new apartment, other than that it's in the Village, right?" Kimberly asked eagerly.

Emma smiled at the barista as she accepted her coffee, bringing it over to the fixing station. "Yeah," she confirmed, drawing out the word as she tried to figure out what to add on. "It is. And it's, you know, it's a really new circumstance for me, because I'm not living with my old roommates or anything. This isn't like I was just moving in with some random strangers I found online. Regan is... different..."

She trailed off, and this time, it had less to do with her mother and more to do with the fact that she had no idea how to summarize the entirety of Regan and still keep this conversation as brief as possible.

Her mom gasped, the sound so jarring in her ear that Emma fumbled with the lid of her iced coffee. "I didn't know your new roommate wasn't *just* a roommate! You never mention your romantic partners!"

Dumbfounded, Emma nearly dropped her phone as she wracked her brain to think over what she'd just said, trying to figure out if her words alluded to Regan being anything more than what she was – that was, Emma's pathologically irritating housemate.

She didn't think so, but it wasn't crazy that Kimberly had made that leap. After all, when her mother was Emma's age, her life was consumed by her various love interests.

"I remember the first time I moved in with Johnny. Do you remember him?"

The dreamy quality of her mother's voice did absolutely *not* align with Emma's memories of Johnny, whom she absolutely did remember. He'd been her mom's most long-lasting and prevalent on-and-off boyfriend throughout Emma's early childhood. He'd also been an abusive alcoholic, resulting in Kimberly moving back to Gram's in tears.

"Sure do," she confirmed grimly.

"The first time we moved in together, it was so... encompassing. We were so wrapped up in each other and in making the apartment our little home. It's a big thing, moving in with someone like that."

Emma remembered very well how *wrapped up* in Johnny her mother had been. So wrapped up that Emma didn't recall her mother coming back to see her and Gram for weeks.

"Yeah," was all she said.

"I understand, Em. I really do. You should take some time now to revel in living with your Regan for a little while. I'll just keep reaching out, and when you're ready, we'll confirm dinner plans? You can bring Regan, too!" Kimberly readily added. "I'd *love* to meet her."

Emma couldn't hold back her scoff as she walked back toward the elevators. "I'll keep that in mind." Before her mother could say anything else, she cut in, "All right, I have to get to work. Have a good one."

"Bye! I love you!" Her mother managed to get in before Emma disconnected the call.

She shook her head as she rode the elevator back up to the twentieth floor. If her mother believed Regan was her girlfriend rather than just her roommate, Emma would gladly take that excuse as far as it would take her from making any dinner plans.

At the very least, she supposed she'd found the silver lining to her new living situation.

two

WHEN REGAN'S phone buzzed with a text, she stopped in the middle of the grocery store pasta aisle and snatched her phone from where she'd left it in the carriage.

Sutton had told her she was going to call today, and Regan was so excited to –

Oh.

> **AUDREY L. GALLAGHER – 10:00 AM**
>
> The dress fitting for my bridal shower is a week from Tuesday – Opal's Bridal Boutique in the West Village, at ten. Be there by nine forty-five.

Regan grimaced down at her phone. Her sister even *texted* on the hour.

For a few seconds, she debated not even answering; after all, Audrey wasn't looking for Regan's response. She never was. Not really.

Heaving a sigh, she typed back solely because she knew she wouldn't hear the end of it if she didn't.

REGAN – 10:01 AM

Yeah... you already sent this memo to me via email... twice... and it's in the Audrey and Armando wedding calendar that you added me to...

AUDREY L. GALLAGHER – 10:01 AM

And you didn't respond to them, did you?

REGAN – 10:01 AM

I didn't see anyone else respond with proof of receipt either???

AUDREY L. GALLAGHER – 10:02 AM

I know how often you've been reminded of the event, Regan. But I don't want you to mess this up. The entire wedding party is going to be there, and the last thing I need is for you to show up late with an asinine excuse.

Or worse, miss it completely, meaning it would fall to ME to reschedule you a fitting. Do you know how far out I had to book this appointment at Opal's? It's not a department store, Regan. We can't just show up whenever we feel like it.

Furthermore, I have far too much on my plate as it is. I don't need any additional stress, Regan.

She pulled a face. God, she hated how frequently her sister said her name. Like, there was no one else in this text thread; Regan knew she was the one being addressed here.

REGAN – 10:03 AM

... why are you talking to me like I've already fucked up? Shouldn't we at least wait for it to happen before I'm on the receiving end of your unfailing disappointment?

AUDREY L. GALLAGHER – 10:04 AM

That's the entire point, Regan. So that you DON'T fuck this up.

"*That's the entire point, Regan,*" she mimicked under her breath, giving the thumbs up to the message before tossing her phone back into the cart to continue shopping. Well, at this point, she might categorize it more as meandering...

Audrey would hate that response, which was somewhat satisfying.

She remembered – easily, as it was only four months ago – Sutton's older brother's wedding and how excited Sutton had been to be a bridesmaid for her future sister-in-law. Sutton's experience being in the wedding party for a family member had been so fun and exciting for her. Phone calls about the happily anticipated nuptials had been plentiful in their apartment, and Sutton had been swept up with it.

Regan's current experience with her sister was... different.

So, her family believed Regan was going to fuck up her sister's wedding before the day even happened – what else was new?

As Regan's phone rang, the sound coming through loud and clear from her earbuds signaling an incoming FaceTime, she didn't jump to answer it, as she would have only a few minutes ago. Going grocery shopping alone was already distressing enough for her – too many choices – the last thing she wanted was to have a video call with her sister.

She peeked down at her screen.

And gasped with excitement, Audrey and her irritating texts easily forgotten.

She'd strategically planned her shopping for work hours during the middle of the week to minimize crowds – ergo, to minimize the number of people that might get annoyed with her for needing to take her time browsing; she was indecisive at best and overwhelmed by all of the choices, even with her list, at worst – but she was especially glad now because she understood that it was somewhat ill-mannered to FaceTime while shopping.

But, while she recognized that, she could only speak to her best friend on a very limited schedule while Sutton was in Rome. So, she couldn't summon enough shits to give to not answer a public FaceTime.

Regan could already feel how widely she was grinning, even before she saw her little, grainy image in the bottom right of her screen.

She couldn't help it, though.

Nor could she help the excited, "Ahhh! Look at you! A sight to behold!" From escaping her at a decibel that was slightly louder than publicly appropriate.

Sutton smiled just as brightly back at her, even as she rolled her eyes. "Regan, I look exactly the same as I did the last time you saw me. A month ago."

"Pfft," she dismissed, leaning in and narrowing her eyes to *really* look at Sutton's image. The quality of her video connection in the back aisles of the grocery store wasn't great, so Sutton was a bit grainier than usual. "Let me do a visual sweep," she jokingly-but-not-jokingly commanded.

Sutton's smile dimmed slightly as she stared right into the camera. "Regan."

"Sutton," she parroted her tone. "Girl, you are halfway across the world! You've never been so far away from me for so long! Prove that you're whole, please."

Even though Sutton quietly protested, she *did* set her phone on a perch and took a step back, holding out both of her arms and doing a quick spin so Regan could inspect. The whole process only took three seconds, so Regan had figured Sutton would indulge her.

"You know, my *mom* doesn't even make me do this," Sutton grumbled as she settled back into the seat at her desk.

Satisfied, Regan shrugged. "Some might say I'm more protective over you than your mom." She cut her gaze to Sutton, warning, "But don't tell Katherine I said that."

Sutton laughed. "As if I would."

Regan would never say it to Katherine Spencer, either, because she respected, feared, and loved that woman too much to say anything that ran the slight risk of impugning her. But she did think it *was* the truth.

After all, while Sutton was closer to her mom than the average adult was, there were only so many things Sutton disclosed to her mom.

Regan, as her best friend, knew all of Sutton's stories. All of her truths, all of her heartbreaks.

Regan was the person who knew about every manipulative boyfriend, every date who didn't call, every person who took advantage of Sutton's giving nature over the years. Ever since they'd become

19

friends in the second grade, she took her duty as Sutton's closest confidante and fearless mouthpiece very seriously.

While she was so fucking proud of Sutton for obtaining her master's degree and getting into a prestigious internship in Italy for the remainder of the year, it didn't mean Regan didn't worry about her.

"Rome seems to agree with you," she noted, taking in the tan on Sutton's fair skin. "You have a lot of time out of the Archives for sightseeing?"

Sutton shrugged, pulling her legs up so that her feet were perched on her chair in front of her and she could rest her chin on her knees. "Not a ton, yet. I was just granted access to the oldest files on record last week," she reminded Regan, and her voice had an edge of undeniable excitement.

Regan smiled affectionately. "Such a fuckin' nerd."

Sutton flipped her off, even as she continued, "*But* – when we aren't working with the physical files – we're allowed to work in the courtyard. And it's so beautiful – filled with all these natural plants and..." She sighed, shaking her head. "It's great."

"Good. I'm happy for you." And she really, really was.

Regan jumped when someone pointedly coughed behind her, spinning around to face a middle-aged man. Who pointed at the rows of pasta behind Regan, annoyance clear on his face.

She grimaced. "Sorry!" Before she hopped out of the way.

When she looked back at her phone, Sutton was frowning. "Where are you? Are you at the store?"

Regan looked around once more, making sure that the aisle was still empty – other than that man, before turning her attention back to Sutton. "Sure am," she confirmed, holding back her frown.

Unsurprisingly, Sutton caught it, and she sat up at attention and leaned in to try to look closer at Regan. "Are you okay? What's up with you?"

As always, Regan had trouble lying in the face of that concern. "Uh..." she hedged. "Nothing's wrong."

"Tell me," Sutton flat-out commanded. "Come on."

Regan squeezed her eyes closed, leaning into the handles of the grocery cart as she admitted, "I *am* okay. It just – I..." She huffed out a breath. "I'm struggling a bit. With Emma."

There. She'd spoken the unsurprising truth that she'd been trying to tiptoe around with Sutton for the last few weeks.

As she predicted, at her words, Sutton's frown deepened, concern etching into her features. "Oh. I thought you said everything was okay? When I texted Emma the other day, she said it's all fine?"

"Well, for Emma, I'm sure it *is* fine!" Regan felt the words burst out of her, throwing a look over her shoulder at the man behind her. Good, he was gone, and she was alone.

"Do you want me to set up a call to try and mediate?" Sutton offered, biting at her bottom lip as she studied Regan. The little lines on her forehead formed, and because Regan knew her best friend so well, she knew that those only appeared when Sutton started to really stress. "I knew I shouldn't have so easily accepted Emma moving into my room while I'm gone. If I were thinking more clearly, I wouldn't have–"

Regan shook her head, groaning. "No, I don't, I..." She deliberately slowed down and made herself take a deep breath. "I don't want you to be stressing about this while you're literally in *Rome*, okay?"

And that was the utter truth.

Sutton had been so worried about how Regan would fare without her that she'd seriously considered not taking her spot in this elite European internship. She hadn't even *told* Regan she'd applied for it! Admittedly, Sutton had also been going through an intense heartbreak, so there were some other factors at play, and Regan didn't delude herself to a grander level of importance than she deserved.

But it didn't change that Sutton had sobbed in Regan's arms only four months ago, confessing about this internship and apologizing to Regan. Telling Regan that she didn't have to worry, that Sutton wouldn't go.

It had been somewhat of a wakeup call for Regan herself at that moment.

A wake-up call that while she would always be Sutton's best friend, one of the closest people to her in the world, she didn't ever want to be someone that held Sutton back. Especially not when Sutton was capable of so many things and had such a bright future ahead of her, while Regan... didn't.

So, even though she didn't want to say goodbye to Sutton for over six months, even though she didn't *want* to live with Emma Bordeaux – a woman whose dislike for Regan had never wavered in the last two years – Regan had womaned up and done what needed to be done.

She'd filled out Sutton's acceptance form and reached out to Emma to broker a deal. And she'd resolved right from the start that she would be a Big Fucking Girl and handle her roommate business with Emma without needing Sutton to stress about it.

"But, I know that you're only living with her because of my situation, and–"

Regan cut Sutton off with a sharp shake of her head. "Look, it really is... fine. Emma and I haven't killed each other. We haven't even gotten into a brawl."

"She'd kill you," Sutton deadpanned. "So, yes, I can see that you're telling me the truth due to the fact that you are alive."

Offense slid through her, and Regan's mouth fell open with it. "Excuse you! She may be bigger than me, but I think I have a much more scrappier spirit than she does!"

Sutton's silence, paired with her skeptical look, was *incredibly* insulting, and Regan reeled from it, gasping.

"Wooow. I can't believe you think Emma would take me in a fight!"

Sutton offered her a placating look. "You wouldn't go down without getting in some licks, I'm sure."

Regan sniffed.

"Before we go any further down this road, I sincerely hope that I will never have to find out how true these conjectures are."

"You won't," Regan assured her quickly and knew that at the very least, that was true.

Regan and Emma *both* were outspoken and solid in their own personalities, but they'd never gotten physical. Not even close.

She sighed, giving in to a question she'd been holding out from asking. But since they were on the topic... "Can you just, like, give me some pointers? How to woo Emma, maybe?"

Sutton choked out a surprised, incredulous laugh. "Excuse me?"

"In a friendly way! Emma liked you from day one, and she hated me. So, how do I do it? How do I get her to like me? Or at least tolerate me?"

She knew she sounded desperate, and she didn't even give a fuck.

Because the reality of her situation was that Regan was floundering at home with Emma. She'd been rapidly discovering about herself that she did not do well living in close quarters with someone that didn't even want to have a simple conversation with her.

She'd known it would be an uphill battle to get Emma to like her – at least, to stop *disliking* her – but, "Nothing I do works, Sutton. *Nothing*. And I really am trying."

She stepped back so Sutton could fully see her, holding up her hand as she counted on her fingers. "I tried to help her with her boxes when she moved in. But we had a, uh, miscommunication. And the box fell. And some stuff broke." She winced, holding up a second finger. "Every time I try to make casual conversation, just asking about her day or telling her about mine, she gives the shortest answers and goes to her room." She held up a third finger. "This morning, I was about to get in the shower – like, *literally*. Usually, I've been waiting until after she's left for the day, which I thought she already had. So, I was naked. I'd just put my hair up. And when she knocked and asked to use the bathroom, I put on a towel and let her!"

Emma had hardly even spared her a glance.

"Even then, she barely even *thanked* me."

Not that Regan needed Emma to kiss her ass in gratitude or anything, but a simple acknowledgment without Regan needing to ask for it would have been nice! Especially because, "I highly doubt she would have done the same thing for me had I asked her."

She stared challengingly at Sutton, daring her to disagree. They both knew it was the truth.

For her credit, Sutton didn't deny it. Instead, she let out a slow, deep breath and reached up to rub her fingers over her eyes.

"So, what do I do?" Regan beseeched.

For a few seconds, Sutton was quiet. But, even in this blurred video, Regan could recognize her thinking face.

"First," Sutton started slowly, "You should approach this knowing that you two may never be... friends."

Regan stared at Sutton in disbelief. "What a profound psychological insight. And very encouraging."

"Thank you. Secondly." Sutton rolled her lips as if searching for *how* to say her thoughts. "Look, you operate – on an average day – at least at a seven out of ten level of energy." She lifted her hand up next to her forehead. "Emma operates at a three." She lowered her hand to just under her chin. "She's very muted, very level. Even when she's emotional, her emotions are–"

"Level," Regan cut in, thoughtfully drawing out the word.

"Yes. Therefore, when you show up, in Emma's face, at a *seven* – even at six in the morning or after a long day of work – Emma will automatically want to, um... get away." Sutton winced. "I couldn't think of a more delicate way to say that."

Regan waved away the apology. "It's fine, I get it." She tapped her index finger against her lips in contemplation. "So, what you're saying is that I need to meet Emma where she's at. Vibe on her wavelength."

Sutton snapped her fingers triumphantly. "Yes! Exactly that. Start there."

Regan was pretty fucking pleased with herself as she heard Emma's key scrape in the lock of their apartment later that night.

She'd just finished plating her home-cooked dinner that she'd been working on for the last hour and a half. *Two* plates. Timing couldn't have been better. And, if she was being entirely honest, it looked objectively delicious.

Rather than do what she *wanted*, and rush to the kitchen doorway to announce her culinary triumphs, she drew in a long, deep breath through her nose. And simply stood next to the table, waiting for Emma to walk by the doorway.

She smiled brightly as Emma slowed to a stop, scanning her eyes over the kitchen before landing on Regan. "Hey!" She cleared her throat, reminding herself *level three*. "How was your day?"

Ignoring her question, Emma's gaze dipped to the kitchen table and landed on the dishes there. "Are you expecting company?" She reached up and pointed to the large calendar she'd put up on the side of the fridge when she'd moved in. "If you put your schedule up on there as I'd asked, then I would have made myself scarce when you're going to have people over. It's kind of the point of the shared calendar system."

Regan darted her eyes over to the calendar in question, noting Emma's small, neat handwriting on it that listed her work schedule. "Ah. Right. I keep meaning to do that."

And she *did*. Only then she'd forget.

Either way, she was on a mission and determined not to get distracted. Regan shook her head. "Either way – no. I'm not expecting anyone to come over. I had the day off and went to the grocery store by myself, and while I was there, I thought... why don't I make us dinner tonight?"

"With all of the pans in the cabinets, I see," Emma commented, sliding her gaze beyond Regan into their kitchen.

Where, admittedly, Regan's wreckage was on display. "The small size of the kitchen makes it look worse than it is," she promised. "I'll clean it up after we eat; it'll be fine."

After all, Regan had lived here for seven years – cleaning up after her cooking messes hardly took long at all.

Emma dubiously nodded, looking back at Regan.

Who did her best not to bounce up onto her tiptoes from the weight of the uncertainty of the unspoken dinner invitation. "I remember you telling Sutton how much you love Chinese food one night but never order it. Tonight, I made General Tso's chicken!"

She gestured to their plates, feeling very victorious. Especially when Emma's eyes lingered on their food – after living with Emma for nearly a month, Regan knew very well that Emma often came home after six or seven in the evening without having had time to eat anything since lunch.

Calmly, Regan pulled out her chair and sat before gesturing to the seat opposite her at the small table. "I had some extra time on my hands today. I promise you that having a meal with me doesn't mean I'm going to be giving you a homemade friendship bracelet."

Though, Regan had been absolutely *incredible* at making friendship bracelets back in the day. She bit back that fun fact.

"Good, because I've never really been one for friendship bracelets." Consideringly, Emma nodded. She carefully set her bag on the ground before walking toward the table.

Regan could feel her excitement mounting as Emma sat down across from her.

Be cool. Be cool.

She waited as Emma picked up her fork and poked curiously through the dish – which was, admittedly, very simple. Rice, broccoli, chicken, and sauce. Apparently, it passed inspection, though, and Emma took a bite.

No matter how much she silently chanted it to herself, Regan couldn't help the broad smile that overtook her face when she watched Emma's eyes slowly close as she chewed, a soft sound of enjoyment escaping her.

When Emma looked back up at her, Regan was still smiling. "Good?" She asked, as chill as possible.

"Delicious, actually," Emma answered after she swallowed, studying Regan carefully. "I feel like I haven't seen you cook that much since I moved in?" She held Regan's eyes as she deadpanned, "Other than whatever it is that you're doing in the kitchen at night when I can hear pans clanging together."

Regan shrugged, ignoring that last part, as she used her own fork to slide her food around as she answered, "Oh, that's because I kind of haven't done much actual cooking in the last few weeks?" She felt the ramble coming but couldn't tamp it down in time before it came spilling out, "The thing is, I really hate cooking meals for myself. It makes me so... sad. You know?"

Emma's simple, arched eyebrow reflected to Regan that no, she did not know.

"It's so much work," Regan explained, gesturing around the kitchen. "To get all of the ingredients and then spend all of the time prepping and cooking, and then the cleanup – all to, what? Sit here and have dinner *by myself* for twenty minutes?"

It was one of the things she was struggling with, in having Emma as a roommate.

Even though she wondered if she should stop her ramble – feeling like the vibe was a higher frequency than a three – Emma took another bite and seemed to be listening to her, giving Regan her famous thoughtful attention, so...

"But, maybe, if you like my cooking – I'd totally be happy to make something for the both of us a few times a week," she offered eagerly. "We could chat a bit and maybe start to wipe our slate clean? I think it could be good, you know. For the both of us. Since we're here together, and we used to have Sutton to hang out with, and now it's the two of us."

She stared expectantly at Emma, waiting for an answer.

Instead of giving her one, Emma stared down at her plate, her fork frozen in her hand as she started breathing more heavily. She sounded almost... pissed off?

Regan slumped down in her chair. What could she have possibly done *now*?! Like, honestly?

"Emm–"

"What did you put in this?" Emma demanded. She was breathing even heavier as she dropped her fork and looked up at Regan.

Regan blinked at her in confusion. "Huh? I told you what it was."

"Did you use some kind of nut?" Emma asked, putting her palms flat on the table.

"What? No. Why?" She was shaking her head before she remembered. "*Oh*, well, I did use almond flour to coat the chicken. We had a ton of excess at the café, and it was the wrong order, so I was able to get it for free, and... what is going on with you?" She asked, concern curling through her as she stared at Emma.

Whose breathing could only be defined as labored, now.

"I'm allergic to almonds." Emma's voice was tight, and she squeezed her eyes closed as her cheeks started to pink. "Regan, I know you *obviously* don't pay attention to anyone but yourself. But I'm going into anaphylaxis now, and I need you to get my EpiPen."

Regan's hands fell to her lap with a heavy thump as she stared, her blood rushing through her ears. Everything in the world turned motionless.

Before Emma took a loud, gasping breath and that shocked Regan's system back to the moment.

"What do I do!" She shouted as she jumped up, her chair clattering to the ground behind her.

Emma's breathing continued to labor – only *worse*, by the freaking second, it seemed.

"In my bag. Front... pocket," Emma managed, pointing weakly toward where she'd placed her bag in the doorway.

Regan couldn't feel her legs as she ran to it, dropping to the ground and frantically ripping through the front pockets until she found it.

"I got it!" She screamed in relieved triumph. She cradled it carefully as she scrambled back over to Emma.

Terror pounded through her at the red hives outbreaking over Emma's arms, chest, neck, and face and how audibly she seemed to be struggling for air.

"You – do it," Emma wheezed, weakly tapping at her thigh.

Regan didn't need to be told twice.

She thanked whatever higher power there might be for the fact that she'd had to take a first aid/CPR class when she'd done management training for the café and quickly took off the emergency cap before she stabbed the needle into Emma's thigh.

As she held the pen firmly to Emma, she stared up at her from the ground, feeling her heart racing as she watched for signs that it worked. It *had* to work.

After several seconds, Emma weakly waved her away. "Take it out. It's done."

Regan carefully did so, her hands holding steady until she dropped the EpiPen to the floor beside her. Only then did she start uncontrollably shaking, gasping for breaths, herself.

"Are you okay?" She sat up on her knees, reaching out to take Emma's hands in her own, squeezing intently. "You seem like you're breathing better. You're better?"

Emma's head was bowed, and she was covered in a cold sweat, but she nodded. "It worked," she confirmed quietly. "But I still need to go to the ER."

~

The nurse that had been tending to Emma since they'd arrived at the hospital three hours ago gave them both a small smile after she checked the nearly empty bags on an IV drip into Emma's arm. "Everything looks good here. Doctor Allen will be in to see you again soon, but then you'll be ready for discharge."

Emma nodded before readjusting her head on her pillow and closing her eyes. "Thanks," she whispered, sounding completely wrung out.

"Thank you *so* much, Sarita," Regan effused, finally feeling her own heart return to normal after getting that confirmation that everything really would be okay. She'd been on edge for *hours*, watching Emma for any sign of distress.

Emma hadn't seemed to enjoy it, but she'd also seemed to not have the energy to argue. Regan would take it.

They'd arrived via ambulance, so they'd thankfully been taken right back to a room. Since then, Emma had gotten all of her vitals checked several times, she'd been administered more epinephrine, and, in the last hour, she'd had both intravenous fluids and steroids.

But she'd been stable for the last two hours and was looking entirely normal, and Regan could have absolutely *melted* from relief. Honestly, she'd already cried several times, much to Emma's chagrin.

"I'm sorry, Emma. I'm *so* sorry," she apologized, her throat tight with emotion.

She'd been entirely responsible for this, and that bore heavily down on her. Every time she looked at Emma, whose cheeks had alternated between having an alarmingly ghostly pallor to abnormally pink hues, she'd felt her insides churn so much that she was glad she hadn't had time to eat anything at dinner, or it would have already made a reappearance. *She'd* done this.

They hadn't exchanged many words in the last few hours, which was fair. But given that Emma was cleared now, it finally felt like the appropriate time to really apologize. And Regan was *bursting* with remorse.

"So, killing me wasn't part of your plan tonight?" Emma asked, her eyes still closed as she laid her head back.

Regan wasn't sure if she was joking, but she gasped at the question anyway.

"No! God! What a terrible way to go about doing that. I'd be the only suspect!"

Emma blinked her eyes open, then and nailed Regan with an unamused look. Okay, apparently, Emma *hadn't* been joking.

Sobering, Regan intently shook her head. "No. I promise you, I had *no* idea that you were allergic to almonds! I made sure that I didn't use peanuts because that's what you're allergic to. So I thought, anyway," she mumbled, dropping her head down as she silently berated herself.

"I *am*," Emma confirmed, turning her head completely to look at Regan. Truthfully, she was kind of relieved to see that angry fire back; she'd take any sign of normal Emma right about now. "I'm allergic to peanuts *and* all tree nuts."

Contrite, Regan grasped at Emma's hospital sheet; she was fairly certain Emma wouldn't be receptive to Regan holding her hand for comfort. But, damn, *Regan* could really use the comfort. "Now that I know, I swear, I will rid the house of everything–"

"Did you even read the roommate contract I sent you when we decided to live together? That you agreed to?" Emma's irritation was clear, and Regan couldn't begrudge her that in this moment.

Guiltily, Regan shifted in her chair. "Um. Well. Not the *entire* thing," she hedged before her desperation got the best of her. "Emma, the contract was over six pages long, single-spaced!"

"Well, excuse me for thinking you could read at a second-grade level. I guess that *was* my mistake," Emma snapped.

"No! It's – I just mean..." She took a deep, stabilizing breath. "I thought that you would move in, and we could go over your contract *together*," she emphasized. "You know, like two adults sharing an apartment would usually do. Talk about the expectations and share the important facts about the apartment and each other. Like about the bedroom outlets. And deathly allergies."

Emma glared at her wordlessly.

And Regan's stomach turned in on itself all over again as she conceded, "But I should have read it. I really should have. I'm *sorry*. This is the last thing I would have ever done intentionally, and I really hope that despite whatever it is that you think of me, you know that."

Emma's strong jaw set, and she didn't speak for several seconds. And when she did, she ignored Regan's apology entirely.

"I need this to sink in for you: we are not friends. We don't need to be friends to live together. In fact, I haven't *ever* been friends with my roommates, and I lived with them for three years. I'm not a replacement for Sutton now that you don't have her at your beck and call every single day. You will live your life, and I will live my life, and even though we share a bathroom, those lives are *separate*. I think you'll find that way, we'll have far less chances of killing each other."

Her blue eyes glinted challengingly up at Regan, and she – for once – found herself powerless to disagree.

three

SHERYL BORDEAUX WAS A CARD SHARK.

It was something Emma had learned about her grandmother so long ago, it was simply ingrained knowledge at this point. Her gram hadn't pulled any punches when playing card games with Emma when she'd been too young to even shuffle, and she certainly didn't give anything away now that she was an adult.

Emma kept that in mind now, as she always did whenever they played cards. Some of her most frequent and fond memories were of sitting around her grandmother's card table in the small Brooklyn apartment that she'd been raised in, the same table they were playing around now.

She was *so* close to gin rummy, she could taste it. And it was so rare that she won against her grandmother; it was all the more exciting. Still, she maintained her poker face, acting as nonchalant as possible when her gram picked up a card from the deck.

Only for her façade to drop a moment later, when her grandmother triumphantly set down her own cards and declared, "Gin."

"Are you kidding me? I was so close!" Emma set her own cards down so that her gram could see exactly how close.

The smile that played around her grandmother's lips was fond and amused as she tutted at Emma. "Close only counts in horseshoes and–"

"Hand grenades. Yeah, yeah, I know," Emma finished with a grumble, unable to hold back her smile, though, as she gathered the cards in her hands. "You taught me that life lesson a long time ago."

"You have time for one more game?" Gram asked as she readjusted in her seat, leaning in with an undeniably hopeful glint in her eyes.

"Sure," Emma readily agreed, even though she didn't check the time first. With her new job, she'd only had the time to stop by and see her grandmother once a week, which weighed on her enough to never cut that visit short. She slowed her shuffling down, peering out the window.

Primrose Grove wasn't a palace by any means, but it was one of the nicer independent living facilities on the outskirts of the city. They'd been lucky to get her gram into a private room here at a *more* than fair price, given that her grandmother had worked with the mother of the facility director for decades.

As it stood, her grandmother had a small bedroom, living room, kitchenette, and bathroom, with a large window in the living area that overlooked the courtyard. And Emma couldn't be more grateful.

"Do you want to go for a little walk instead?" She suggested, keeping her voice light and conversational. "I could use one; sitting at the desk all week is killer on my back."

A little fib, given that her workspace included an adjustable standing desk. But what her grandmother didn't know wouldn't hurt her.

But if there was one thing Emma knew about her gram, it was that she'd do a lot of things for Emma that she wouldn't necessarily do for herself. Like agree to voluntarily go for a walk around Primrose.

Her grandmother watched her carefully before nodding. "Why not?"

Even though her gram was still a little slow to move, she'd stopped needing to use her walker in the last month. Even so, as they stepped out of her grandmother's suite and into the clean, well-maintained hallway, Emma subtly hovered an arm behind her.

"I know what you're doing," her grandmother whispered, turning her head to look up at Emma with a smart, sharp smile. It was the same smile she'd given Emma throughout her life whenever she'd caught her engaging in anything she shouldn't be doing. In fairness, it was a rarity, as Emma had always been a devout rule-follower.

"I don't know what you're talking about," she side-stepped, reluctantly dropping her arm back to her own side.

"The cardiologist said I'm *fine* to be walking on my own, honey. I've been doing my steps every day to make sure."

"Have you been doing any of those steps with any of the exercise groups here?" She asked, already knowing what the answer was.

"No," her gram muttered. "You know me; I like to keep to myself."

Emma knew that wasn't necessarily the case, but her heart ached with sympathy for her grandmother.

Her gram had always thrived on stability. She'd kept the same schedule for Emma's entire life, only deviating when life necessitated an emergency. She'd liked to talk to her small handful of friends who'd all lived in the building Emma had grown up in, she'd liked to go to her job as the head administrator at Rettol Academy, and she'd enjoyed indulging in her hobbies – cards, gardening, and knitting – during her free time.

When she'd had her first massive heart attack nearly four years ago, she'd been sixty-six, and while she'd eventually made a full recovery – thank *god* – her healing process had necessitated somewhat of a forced retirement. And with that forced retirement had come Sheryl's loss of ability to pay the rent in the apartment she'd lived in for nearly forty years, even when Emma had been paying her own portion of rent and bills.

She'd resolutely demanded that Emma, who'd already been working full-time to slowly put herself through undergrad with as little debt as possible, *not* quit school to take on more work.

Instead, they'd both left the apartment. Emma had found herself sharing her shitty little place with her roommates, and her gram had found a studio that she'd been *just* been able to afford.

And that had worked... for a little while. Her grandmother had adjusted to her new life – away from her social network, out of the job she'd had since she'd been in her twenties – but she'd managed.

Until four months ago, when she'd had her second heart attack.

This one had been even worse than the first, and she'd been in the hospital for nearly a month.

She'd vehemently resisted going to Primrose Grove, citing that she wasn't even old enough for "that place" yet.

This was somewhat true; her grandmother was only seventy, and she was one of the youngest residents here.

But Emma knew her grandmother. And she knew she'd been terrified of moving into a brand new locale, surrounded by brand new people and routines.

Emma had felt fucking terrible about it – she *still* did – but the reality was that her gram needed to live somewhere that had medical staff on-site, and Emma was far from a place in her life where she could afford to provide something like that for the woman who'd raised her.

She wished things were different, but they weren't. So mostly, she wished her grandmother, who'd never been comfortable pushing outside of her comfort zone, could somehow find a way to slip into making some friends. To find something that would make living here enjoyable.

"Maybe we could take a look at the events calendar when we swing through the lobby?" She suggested. "They might have something going on that you'd like?"

Gram hesitated ever so briefly before she shook her head. "I don't think so," she murmured before she cleared her throat and aimed a very direct look at Emma. "You know, little lady, I'd like to talk about *you* rather than *me* for a while. How about that?"

Emma couldn't help but scoff out a smile at the *little lady* nickname that her gram had used for her entire life. Even when Emma had hit her growth spurt at thirteen and stood a solid six inches taller than the short, slight older woman ever since. "What do you want to know?"

"First of all, I want to know how you're feeling. You keep looking at me like my health is in question, but *you* were in the hospital far more recently than I was!"

Emma's eyes rolled involuntarily as she thought about her almond flour-induced allergic reaction last week. "Yeah, I guess so," she grumbled, narrowing her eyes at Regan's total disregard for her roommate contract.

Like, who *said* they read a roommate contract, and said they agreed to abide by it, only to be a total fucking liar?!

She wished she could say she was shocked by it, but unfortunately, given that this was Regan she was dealing with, she wasn't.

Shaking her head, she grit her teeth, and looked at her grandmother. "But I'm one hundred percent okay, haven't had any other issues since that night. Good as new."

The one and *only* thing she would give to Regan was that she had insisted on handling all of Emma's hospital bills, including the ambulance. Emma hadn't wanted to call one, knowing the hefty charge she'd receive for it after the fact, and she'd been fairly certain that after her first epinephrine dose, she could reasonably take the subway to the closest hospital; it wasn't very far.

Regan had called the ambulance, anyway, gently keeping her hand on Emma's shoulder to keep her sitting at their kitchen table.

She supposed that paying exorbitant hospital fees to someone like Regan, who had a hefty trust fund to rely on, wasn't such a big deal.

Her gram studied her closely. "All right; I trust you to be able to take care of yourself."

Emma nodded, feeling that sense of pride at knowing she had her grams' trust. It had been something she'd felt honored by since she'd been a teenager.

As they turned another corner, Emma spotted the pair of women she'd hoped to find on their walk. As far as she'd seen, there were six other women who were under eighty, all of whom seemed to clique up in different permutations. Two of them seemed to always be chatty and in good spirits whenever Emma saw them – typically in the large, communal kitchen – and she'd been subtly trying to nudge Gram toward them for months, now.

She tilted her head toward them. "Oh, hey – have you chatted with those ladies yet? We could go over and see what they have going on?"

Her grandmother looked at them for several beats before she looked back at Emma and shook her head. "No, little lady, I don't think so. Not today."

Before Emma could even try to insist, her gram asked, "Have you made any plans with your mom yet? She said she may be coming by this evening."

Ugh, Emma felt the question land in her stomach like she'd swallowed a lead weight. She was immediately thankful she'd come to hang out with Gram early, so she could easily leave before the evening.

"Um... not yet," she answered honestly. Because she wasn't great at lying to her grandmother, and – mostly – because she knew Gram would find out the truth from Kimberly, anyway.

She stared straight ahead down the open, airy hallway as they turned a corner, starting the second half of the loop that would lead back to her grandmother's room. But she could feel Gram's eyes on her.

Emma knew how badly her gram wanted that reunion between Emma and her mom. She knew, clear as day, that her grandmother was so desperate for her daughter and granddaughter to forge this unbreakable bond, one that apparently Gram had managed to keep with Kimberly despite all of their issues over the years.

It was something Emma wished so badly to understand. How did her grandmother manage to so easily push through the hurt of Kimberly's abandonment? Was it different because Kimberly was her daughter, whereas she was Emma's mother? And, what went even deeper than the hurt – how was it not awkward? How did her grandmother know what to say to Kimberly?

How could she make their relationship seem totally... normal? That was what Emma was most desperate to know. *How?*

She wished she could ask. She wished that this topic hadn't become so prevalent in their lives, ever since Kimberly's grand return a few months ago.

Because Emma's inability to push through this barrier with her mom seemed to be the biggest disappointment she'd ever caused Gram. And seeing the disappointment on her grandmother's face when Emma had blurted out how she felt about Kimberly... well, she'd hated it. And she was resolutely not going to repeat it.

"She was here Thursday night, again," Gram mentioned, a small, hopeful grin playing on her lips. "She brought the girls, and we all went out to dinner. Just to the place down the street, but it really was so lovely. I think, maybe if you spend time with your sisters *and* your mom, you might find the girls provide a little conversational relief."

Even the mention of Emma's sisters made her stomach tie itself in knots, and she didn't have the heart to tell her grandmother that she honestly felt the exact opposite. "Uh, maybe."

Emma could feel her grandmother studying her profile as she quietly said, "You're always more than welcome to come to Thursday dinners if you want. I think it would be *great* to have us all together."

She could feel her throat tighten at her grandmother's words, at how hopeful and intent she sounded.

"Yeah, sometime," she agreed.

And, on some level, she meant it. But that didn't mean that the idea of making that a reality didn't make her feel nervous, clammy, and unready.

She heard her phone buzz in her pocket and was relieved for any excuse to check briefly out of this conversation.

Her gram nodded at her. "You should check it. It could be important."

REGAN FREAKING GALLAGHER – 2:31 PM

Hey! Just letting you know that it's BLAZING hot today – the power went out after you'd left but should be back on soon! Make sure you unplug and re-plug everything in your room!

Maybe she'd spoken too soon about that relief, after all. For a brief moment, she debated not answering before she grumbled to herself and sent off –

EMMA BORDEAUX – 2:32PM

Thanks for the update/reminder.

"And?" Her grandmother prompted.

Emma felt herself flush as she locked her phone before her grandmother could sneak a peek.

"Uh, it was just Brynn. You know, my coworker. But it's not urgent."

It was such a lie, but she didn't want to disclose the truth.

As far as her grandmother knew, she'd moved in with *her friend, Regan* – a stretch of the imagination – and that was how she liked to keep it. After her grandmother's first heart attack, when they'd had to move, Gram had very clearly felt terrible regarding Emma's living situation. And over time, she'd found that holding onto these little pieces of life and keeping everything – family, relationships, friendships – separate worked very well for her.

Even when she'd told her grandmother about how Regan had put her in the hospital last week, she'd been careful to keep her ire out of her voice.

"Oh, well, give me the work updates!" Gram encouraged excitedly.

That, Emma would happily do.

Emma made it home from Astoria by five, thankful that it seemed the air conditioning in their building had, indeed, kicked back on sometime in the last couple of hours.

She was *desperate* for this heat wave to come to an end. In the ten-minute walk to her building in the thick, muggy air, she was sweaty, uncomfortable, and wanted nothing more than to strip her sweat-soaked shirt off at the quickest opportunity.

"Regan?" She called out into the apartment, cautiously optimistic as she closed the door behind her.

She stilled, straining to keep an ear out to detect any signs of life from within. When there was no response to her shout, she nearly did a little victory dance. If she weren't still so freaking *hot*, she might have.

She didn't need to call out again, not when she was met with resounding silence. No music playing from behind Regan's closed bedroom door – loud enough that she could always hear it from anywhere in the apartment – and TV wasn't on in the living room, either.

Entirely unsurprisingly, Regan did not exist quietly. Ever. When she was home, Emma was very well aware of that fact.

Walking into the kitchen, she checked the calendar on the side of the fridge. The one that Regan had *finally* started to fill out in the last week, ever since she'd nearly murdered Emma.

Things had been better between them since then, Emma would admit. It took almost killing her, but Regan had started to actually adhere to the contract she'd apparently pretended to agree to weeks ago.

She'd given Emma a wide berth in the last six days, only making short, direct conversation when they incidentally run into one another. She'd made a point to text Emma a picture of everything that had *any* mention of nuts on the label in the trash the morning after the hospital trip. And she'd taken to writing her work schedule on their calendar.

The schedule in question informed Emma that Regan was working a double today. She wouldn't be off shift until ten, which meant she wouldn't be home until at *least* midnight, given that she typically seemed to like to hang out with her coworkers for a while after work.

Emma grinned brightly; it seemed she was able to experience a lucky break from time to time, after all.

With that knowledge, she reached down to tug off her T-shirt right there in the kitchen, relishing the feeling of the air-conditioned temperature directly on her body.

And with Regan at work tonight, Emma had the perfect opportunity to sit down and try to get some real writing done for the first time in a month. Maybe she could start to draft her latest book review!

During the week, Emma was so busy with Allegra's schedule that it was impossible to find the time and energy to do any writing of her own. And during the last few weekends, it seemed something had consistently popped up – first, she'd been unpacking from her move, the weekend after she'd taken her Gram to one of her physical therapy follow-ups and had spent the day with her, and last weekend she'd been recovering from her near-death experience.

She'd have a simple dinner first. She knew she had some chicken salad in the fridge that she'd had for lunch at work for the last few days...

Emma stopped short as soon as she opened the refrigerator. Because it was empty.

Not completely; condiments were still lining the door, and drinks were on the top shelf. But all of the actual *food* that had been in there was gone.

Squeezing her eyes tightly closed, she dropped her head back in annoyance as she shut the fridge.

Only to snap her head up a moment later as she heard the front door open and close in one quick motion before footsteps bounded down the short hallway leading to the archway of the kitchen. In several short moments, Regan came into her view, stumbling to a stop upon seeing Emma.

Regan's eyebrows lifted high on her forehead as her gaze slid down and focused below Emma's face. "Huh."

Confusion slid through her, but only for a few seconds before Emma realized that she was standing in the middle of their kitchen, topless.

Cheeks flaming with embarrassment, she tugged her balled-up T-shirt up over her chest and stomach. She recovered from her surprise enough to snap, "What are you doing here?"

"I live here," Regan answered, and Emma honestly wasn't sure if Regan was just stating a fact or if she was trying to be a smart aleck, but it still rankled.

Clinging to that annoyance – because it was better than embarrassment by a mile – she grit her teeth. "I'm all too aware of that. But you were supposed to be at work until ten."

The calendar to prove it was hanging on the fridge, right next to her!

Regan shrugged, still staring unrepentantly at Emma's chest in spite of the T-shirt Emma held up. "Right. Yeah. I *should* still be at work. Only, Topped Off – and, actually, that entire block – is experiencing a total blackout. Just like the one we had here. So, after an hour, I decided to shut down for the evening. God forbid people start crowding into our non-air-conditioned confined quarters, demanding caffeine from machines that aren't working." She shuddered. "Anyway. Here I am."

As she finished with her explanation, Regan lifted her gaze up again, and a mischievous smile took up residence on her face. "I definitely didn't think I'd be interrupting your... special alone time."

"You *aren't*," she bit out, even though Regan kind of definitely was. But not any sort of explicit alone time, as Regan was clearly implying. Pivoting away from that before Regan could run with it, she gestured at the refrigerator. "Where's my chicken salad?"

Regan's eyebrows furrowed in obvious confusion for several moments before something dawned on her. "Oh! I had to throw it out. And the other perishables we had in there. The power was off for a few hours, and I was worried that something smelled... not right? I couldn't determine what it was, but I didn't want to chance it."

Emma stared, feeling like she was on crazy pills. "So, you got rid of everything. Even *my* things."

Regan stared right back. "Obviously. I've already been responsible for you going to the hospital for food-related causes; I wasn't going to keep something in the fridge that could make you sick again."

Reaching up to rub her temples, Emma *tried* to breathe through her irritation.

Especially when Regan clapped her hands once, garnering her attention. The feeling Emma had in her stomach did not align with Regan's bright smile in any way.

"I think this calls for a roommate grocery-shopping trip!"

"I think not," Emma snarked right back.

"We have no real food," Regan astutely pointed out. "Even before I got rid of your chicken salad, you barely had anything in there. And *I* haven't gone shopping since the debacle last week, because I've been terrified to buy anything with the wrong ingredients; I don't want to bring anything in here that you could be allergic to."

There was something in Regan's tone that was both factual and beseeching, almost like it had been practiced. It was enough to raise Emma's suspicions about her chicken salad not *really* being off.

She narrowed her eyes. "Can't you just read the labels if you're so concerned?"

Regan's stupidly bright smile was guileless, her dark eyes wide. "Emma, I couldn't even properly read a roommate contract. You trust this noggin not to kill you by mistake?" She tapped her index finger against her own temple.

Emma wasn't an idiot; she had a very real hunch that she was being played into spending more time with Regan.

But on the other hand, she wasn't sure she *could* trust Regan to properly read food labels. Plus... Regan wasn't technically incorrect in saying that Emma really hadn't had anything else by way of groceries.

She let out a long-suffering sigh. "I'm only doing this because I actually need to go grocery shopping."

Regan's grin was far too wide, revealing her pearly white, perfectly straight teeth.

~

Was food really all that important?

Emma pondered that important philosophical question as she pushed the cart up and down the aisles at the store, following Regan. Who – surprise, surprise – seemed to like to talk through all of her choices before depositing things in the cart.

"I'm better with a list," Regan informed her, even though Emma didn't ask.

She hadn't commented on anything for over ten minutes as she held steadfastly onto the belief that her silence would make this experience go quicker.

Her lack of response hadn't seemed to hinder Regan in the least, though, as she continued to chatter their way down the next aisle.

"You know what I miss the most about living in a suburb? Like, back in Massachusetts, before I moved here?" Regan posed the question as if Emma could *possibly* know the answer as she maneuvered their carriage around a woman who was pondering pasta sauces.

"I'm aching to know." The sarcasm escaped her, breaking her quiet streak.

Regan continued, seemingly unaware of Emma's lack of sincerity. "The size of the grocery store aisles. Everything here is so cramped."

Emma turned to look at Regan as she registered her words. A question that she genuinely wanted the answer to formed in her mind, one that she couldn't help but ask. "Why did you even move here?"

It was a question she'd never really thought to voice. Granted, she'd tried her best not to think too deeply about Regan for the last two years. It had been something she'd actually avoided because – in spite of Emma's best efforts – Regan was an interesting person. Deeply irritating. But interesting.

Now that she'd voiced the question, she couldn't help but push for the answer. After all, it was too late to pretend she'd never asked. "I mean... you don't have a location-specific job." Regan could be a barista literally *anywhere*. "And you don't have any ambitions you're pursuing in Manhattan. Or any family here. You're not going to college here. You didn't even move here the year after high school, right?"

The more she spoke, the less sense Regan made to her.

Regan grew up in a wealthy family in Massachusetts, with everything she could possibly want available at her fingertips. And she'd just decided to move to Manhattan at nineteen, with no academic or career pursuits? She'd decided to move to one of the most expensive places in the country, away from her family, to work at... Topped Off?

Regan turned to look back at her, and – for once – she didn't have a quick, enthusiastic, glib response. Her full lips were quirked to the side, and there was the slightest crinkle between her eyebrows before she answered, "Sutton lived here."

Her words were thoughtfully spoken but didn't explain anything to Emma. If anything, they incited more confusion.

Incredulously, she turned to stare at Regan as they turned into a new aisle. And because she was so focused, she didn't even realize she'd bumped into someone else's cart until after the damage was done.

Jarred back into the moment, the apology was already falling from her lips, "I'm so sorry, I didn't–"

Abruptly, the words fell away as she realized exactly who she'd run into.

Felicity Hammond. Whose eyebrows lifted just as high as Emma's were on her own forehead, clearly surprised. "Emma. Hey."

"Uh... hey," she returned, shifting uncomfortably.

She hadn't seen Felicity in over two years. Not since she'd accepted a position for a doctoral program in Oregon and had then promptly broken up with Emma after having been together for five freaking years. After planning a future together, one they'd intended to really *start* after Emma finished grad school.

"Hey," Regan inserted herself into the moment, and Emma wasn't sure if she was more annoyed by that fact or grateful for it. "Sorry we bumped into you."

"It's – it's fine," Felicity cleared her throat, looking from Emma to

Regan. "Not a big deal." Her gaze slid back to Emma. "I'm surprised to see you here. Far from your own neighborhood...?" She trailed off, obviously waiting for an answer.

Emma shook herself out of it, gripping the carriage handle to center herself. "Yeah. This is my neighborhood now. I'm surprised to see *you* here since this is far from your neighborhood. In Portland."

She'd been determined not to show Felicity just *how* deeply cut she'd been by their breakup and, thus, had continued to follow her on all social media. Her lack of knowledge about Felicity's comings-and-goings in the last two years boiled down entirely to Emma's self-control at not looking at Felicity's socials.

It hadn't been easy that first year. But she'd done it. And, as her gaze meandered to Regan's profile before snapping back to Felicity, she resolutely didn't ever think about the coping mechanism she'd employed in those first few months.

Felicity smiled slightly, breathing out a chuckle. "I'm back for a few weeks to visit. Staying with my sister, so..."

Ah. Emma nodded. Of course, she remembered that Felicity's sister lived only four blocks away. She tapped her thumbs slightly against the handle, wondering what the hell was appropriate to say when you ran into the woman who broke your heart, accompanied by the roommate you only ended up living with *because* that plan for the future hadn't come to fruition.

A situation that was only made more complicated by how much she didn't want said roommate to ever be privy to this part of her life.

"Sisters, right?" Regan jumped in, looking between the two of them.

Looking, much to Emma's chagrin, entirely too interested in this awkward interaction.

Felicity nodded, giving a small, suspicious smile in Regan's direction. "Yeah, right." Her attention landed back on Emma. "Speaking of sisters, I should probably get back to Jan's."

"Yeah, you probably should," Emma agreed, curtly.

"My sister totally hates it when I run late," Regan added.

The reminder that Regan was *there* made Emma grip the handles of the carriage even tighter, and she started to walk blindly ahead. It didn't matter which aisle she went down, as long as it wasn't this one. Not only was seeing Felicity again at the bottom of her wishlist, but having that experience with Regan?

A nightmare.

"Maybe I'll see you around while I'm in town," Felicity added as they passed by one another.

Emma couldn't help but look at her despite her previous resolve to move staunchly ahead. "I doubt it," she returned.

Within the first few steps she took, she heard Regan let out a low whistle. "Oh my *god*, that was stone cold. I love it; it's really nice to see that part of your personality isn't strictly reserved for me."

Embarrassed irritation heating the back of her neck, Emma grit her teeth and didn't acknowledge that. "I need to grab bread. Why don't you go down the next few aisles yourself and meet me in the back?" She firmly suggested.

As she'd unfortunately predicted, Regan's hurried footsteps kept pace a step behind her. And with every step she took, she could feel Regan's stare boring into her.

It only made her will to ignore it even stronger.

"Sooo," Regan drew out, amusement gratingly clear in her tone. "Who the hell *was* that?!"

"No one. Never seen her before a day in my life," Emma dryly answered.

Regan huffed out a laugh. "Emma, the vibes were *vibing*. Hard. I'm not an idiot."

This time, Emma did turn to aim a pointed stare at Regan, arching her eyebrow.

Regan tossed her head back and laughed, reaching out to lightly push at Emma's shoulder. As if they were friends. "If you aren't going to tell me, I'm going to *have* to guess."

"You making conjectures about random people in the supermarket is your own business."

Regan hummed, the sound still entirely too entertained. Emma swore she could practically feel Regan skipping with glee.

Emma worked hard to maintain boundaries between all aspects of her life, and the Felicity part *did not* mesh with the Regan part. It went against everything inside of Emma. Those were two worlds that she liked to keep very separate in her mind.

"Well, my first guess is that this was some sort of *Pretty Woman* situation. You picked her up – oh, wait. No. I think she's a little older than you are. So, scratch that. *She* picked *you* up, and you two engaged in a torrid affair. Before things ended miserably because her shitty coworker hit on you." Regan paused, tilting her head up in thought before she shook it. "Nah, that one isn't really working for me."

"Really? It sounded very plausible to me."

"Okay! What about *Notting Hill*? You were at work one day, years ago. Just a normal gal, living your life. She's a celebrity..." Regan trailed off, shaking her head again. "Nope, that one doesn't work, either."

"And why is that?" Emma regretted that she'd asked the second the words left her mouth. It was like adding fuel to a gas fire.

Regan stared at her, incredulous. "Because if she was a celebrity, I would know who she is. Obviously. I was raised on tabloids. Celeb gossip is one of my favorite subjects."

"Right. *That's* what makes that plot impossible."

"Yup," Regan popped the *p* sound. "Oh! Okay – what about *The Proposal*?"

"You gave up on Julia Roberts plots so quickly," Emma remarked, steering the cart toward the very back of the store, where the freshly-baked bread was.

"You're not giving Julia right now." Regan studied her critically. "I guess you would have been Hugh Grant in that scenario. Either way–"

"Oh my *god*." The words burst from Emma's throat with a groan. "If I give you the most basic of information, can we stop with the movies?"

The satisfied smile on Regan's face told Emma that this had been exactly her plan all along. Emma hated that she was impressed. Or, if not impressed, she could somewhat appreciate that Regan had known she was being a shit, at the very least.

"Her name is Felicity. We were together. We broke up."

The six-word overview of her only *real* relationship felt like so little, like it wasn't nearly enough to describe what had transpired between them.

But it was also all she was willing to give Regan. Plus, brevity was the soul of wit and all that.

Regan gasped so loudly, so dramatically, Emma jumped. "You're into women?!"

"Keep your voice *down*," she hissed, looking over her shoulder. The last thing she wanted was for Regan's shout to carry and actually reach Felicity.

"Well, sorry!" Regan's tone and expression were anything but. She, thankfully, lowered her volume as she whisper-shouted, "I just – we've known each other for two years! How did I not know this information?"

"Probably because you know very little about me," she succinctly summed up.

"And whose fault is that?" Regan needled, tapping her finger insistently on Emma's shoulder.

Emma cut her a glare.

"Does *Sutton* know?" Regan asked, dropping her hand back to her side, tilting her head in thought. "Because she never mentioned it to me, either."

"No," Emma clarified. "Because Sutton never pries for information, and it was never relevant to bring up."

"Not relevant?!" Regan cried out, making Emma wince at the volume yet again as she tossed her arms into the air. "Sutton – *your friend* – went through her own sexual awakening crisis last year, and you said absolutely nothing! Nada! Zilch!"

"Her sexual awakening wasn't about me," Emma pointed out, baffled as to how that was relevant. "And I never went through any sort of crisis, so I don't really think our experiences were comparable."

And the truth was that Sutton never asked Emma for advice or expressed that she was actually in *crisis*, as Regan proclaimed. Sutton had talked to Emma about her burgeoning sexuality, but it had always felt to Emma that Sutton had appreciated Emma merely lending an ear rather than commentary. Which she was clearly getting from Regan.

Regan stared, clearly dumbfounded. "You are so... weird."

And Emma simply could not control how her mouth fell open in disbelief. "Pot calling the kettle black, in a major sort of way."

Regan was unrepentant. "Yeah, but at least I own it!" She jabbed herself in the chest with her thumb before doing the same to Emma. "You think you're normal!"

Good. God.

She reached out and grabbed her favorite sandwich rolls before turning on her heel. "On that note, I'm going to peruse the store at a *normal* pace. Less focus on me and more on grocery shopping, because we've had more than enough sharing time today."

four

WHEN SUTTON HAD LIVED in the room across from Regan's, the weekend mornings that she didn't have work were *fun*. They were times she looked forward to.

Mornings where she and Sutton could enjoy coffee together and decompress from the week, watch some television, enjoy one another's company. She hadn't had a cozy, pleasant weekend morning hanging out with her roommate in over a month.

Quite frankly, it was driving her crazy.

As she sat in the kitchen, thoughtfully sipping her coffee Sunday morning, she had to admit something to herself: this living situation was approaching DEFCON 1 levels.

The last week of living in uncomfortable timidity had put Regan on edge, and she wasn't quite sure how long she could continue living like this.

Not to be dramatic, but she was going *crazy*.

Getting Emma to go grocery shopping with her had been an unexpected and very welcome twist, but it had left Regan feeling more unsettled than anything.

Because running into Emma's... ex-girlfriend? Ex-lover? Ex-whatever had led to the only meaningful interaction Regan had shared with the person she'd lived with in what felt like forever. And she would only qualify it as meaningful because she'd learned something brand new about Emma.

But Emma hadn't even wanted to share it with her!

Emma was into women! Was she bi? A lesbian? Queer? Regan had no clue how she identified. She had no idea how the woman she literally shared a nine-hundred-square-foot apartment with identified her sexual orientation.

"It's so *weird*," she muttered, shaking her head as she paced across the kitchen.

Weird enough that she'd fixated on it all night, long after they'd returned home, and Emma had ducked into her bedroom. Weird enough that it sat uncomfortably in her stomach, and that feeling had woken Regan up at six o'clock.

Six o'clock! On a Sunday morning, when she didn't have to be at work until this afternoon!

That wasn't normal and she most definitely did not care for it.

Everything about their living situation made Regan desperate for change.

"Only, what can I do?" She asked herself, spinning on her heel to face the kitchen counter and the miniature French fruit tarts she'd made this morning.

The custard she'd made had set very nicely and was holding up impressively well under the fruit slices. The last time she'd attempted a classic French fruit tart, her shortbread had cracked, and her custard had been just a *little* too loose. That tester recipe had still gone over well at the café, but *these*... oh, she was sure these were going to do even better. Being awake so early this morning had been good for one thing, at least.

Carefully, she placed them inside their containers to put into the fridge. At least *something* was doing well, while she was floundering.

She had no problem admitting she didn't do well when left to her own devices for too long. When she didn't have *a person* to rely on. To quality spend time with and feel close to.

Not romantically; Regan's romantic endeavors that lasted longer than a couple weeks could be counted on one hand, and she'd very rarely ever felt truly connected to them. But... she needed to feel a connection to someone. Without it, she felt so untethered.

She'd always had a tether in Sutton. Even when Regan was at her most impulsive and chaotic moments – which, admittedly... there were quite a few of those times – Sutton was there for her. She was never too much for Sutton, even when Regan knew she exasperated her.

And she knew that she still had Sutton in her life, but having Sutton exist on a different continent, in a different time zone, was so very, very different than having her *here*.

While she hadn't thought living with Emma would be easy, she'd figured – for some now unknown reason – that they'd settle into a rhythm together.

"Five weeks later? No rhythm." She sighed, slumping against the counter.

Her self-talk was interrupted by a knock on the apartment door, and Regan snapped her head to face the direction of their entryway. Not that she could see the door from the kitchen, but still.

Head cocked to the side, she waited for several moments. Maybe she was hearing things? It wouldn't be the first time she'd mistakenly thought a knock on their neighbor's door was on her own.

After a beat, three more tentative knocks came. Even though they weren't sharp, demanding sounds, they were *definitely* on Regan's door.

She pushed herself off the counter to glance at the clock on the stove – 9:31. Okay, so she wasn't crazy. Someone was actually knocking on their door before ten in the morning. Given that Emma wasn't awake, it couldn't be for her.

"Besides, nothing's written on that precious calendar, so..." She muttered to herself, then placed her mug down on the counter before she headed for the door.

She peered through the peephole, her eyes landing on a woman standing on their doormat. The woman bounced where she stood, and she seemed... nervous? She had a small white bag in her hands and a large tote bag slung over her shoulder.

"Huh." She hummed to herself, pushing onto her tiptoes as she looked to the left and right of the woman – to her best ability, with the limited view – to ensure she was alone.

Regan had read many horror stories about young women living in apartments, far too many to take no precautions and open the door to a stranger, all willy-nilly.

But it was silent in the hallway, with no hint of another person. And Regan was nothing if not curious.

As the woman lifted her hand to knock again, Regan unlocked and opened the door.

The woman's hand that had been primed to knock dropped to her chest in surprise. "Oh! I didn't expect – hi! Good morning."

"Good morning to you, too," Regan greeted, taking the chance to peer her head out and look up and down the hallway to confirm that they were alone.

Once satisfied that they were, she dropped back to really look at the woman. She was several inches taller than Regan was and older – maybe in her mid-forties? She wore a short skirt, cut off at the thigh, and an animal print blouse with red lipstick. Her hair was obviously dyed, but Regan got the sneaking suspicion that the woman had chosen this muted blonde because it was close to her natural color.

There was something familiar about her, but Regan had no idea where they'd met, if they ever had. Topped Off, maybe? But, that would be weird.

"Are you a solicitor?" Regan couldn't help but ask, dipping her gaze down to the woman's large tote bag. Maybe it was filled with flyers or handouts or a sign-up sheet. "I gotta tell you, there are *very* few things I'll bite on these days."

Typically, their doorman caught anyone attempting door-to-door canvassing, but sometimes people slipped through the cracks. And Regan was very good at sending them on their way... unless they were selling something she was interested in.

The woman smiled, the corners of her blue eyes crinkling with it, as she let out a confused laugh. "A sol – no. No, I'm not. I'm just looking for Emma Bo Bemma? Er." She shook her head, pushing out a little laugh, "Emma Bordeaux. Is this the right apartment?"

Regan's eyes widened so far that she thought they might fall out of her head as she barked out a laugh. "I'm sorry. Did you say *Emma Bo Bemma*?"

She glanced over her shoulder just to see if Emma had heard those cursed words. Deep inside, Regan felt like Emma would have woken from the deepest of sleeps at being referred to in such an unserious way.

Nope, the coast was clear.

The woman's grin settled in, obvious affection in her expression. "I sure did. And you're... Regan?"

She was shocked at the idea that anyone in Emma's – Emma Bo Bemma's – life would know who she was, because Regan simply couldn't imagine Emma willingly offering that information. "Why, yes. Yes, I am. And you're...?"

"Kimberly." She offered her hand. "Kimberly Hayes. I'm Emma's mom."

Regan could literally hear the record scratch in her head, her hand going momentarily limp in that handshake. Maybe she'd misheard?!

"Her *mom*?" Yeah, she could hear how doubtful she was in her own tone, but... *this was Emma's mom*?

She seemed young. And she smiled a whole damn lot!

Regan hadn't thought much about where Emma had come from, but in this moment, she realized that she'd always assumed Emma came from a very straight-laced, organized background. Much like Emma herself was in everyday life. She'd assumed, honestly, that Emma had come from a family similar to Regan's own.

She eyed the woman – Kimberly – closer: maybe that was why she seemed so familiar. Her height, the icy hue of her eyes, the high, sharp slash of her cheekbones. Regan lived with the person who shared all of those characteristics!

Kimberly's smile faltered, becoming sheepish. "Yes. And I know Emma's been so incredibly busy lately, so I understand if she may not have told you very much about me. I'm sorry if I'm interrupting your morning together."

Regan slowly shook her head, laughing at the absurdity of that comment. "Uh, no, you're not interrupting *our morning together*."

Emma's mom really had a sense of humor, she'd give her that. She could only imagine what Emma told her family about living with Regan, especially after the allergy disaster.

"Emma's still in bed," Regan explained after a beat, when Kimberly didn't laugh at her own joke. "Given, you know, she's not exactly a morning person."

Not that Regan generally considered herself a morning person, either. She was more of a whatever-sleeping-schedule-fit-the-bill-that-day kind of person. But she definitely managed mornings better than Emma did.

Kimberly laughed, a light, tinkling sound. "Oh, that's always been Emma."

Regan found herself grinning out of the sheer curiosity of this woman, who didn't match Regan's vision of Emma's mother. At all. In any way. What a fascinating twist.

"Do you want to come in?" Regan offered, pulling the door open wider as she stepped back. "Sorry, I should have offered earlier."

"I'd love to!" Kimberly stepped into the entryway, peering around at the pictures on the walls before she looked apologetically at Regan. "I don't mean to be nosy. It's just..." She bit her lip, and those nerves Regan had thought she'd seen while watching Kimberly through the peephole became evident once again. "I'm sure you know this, but I've never really been in Emma's apartment. I just want to take everything in."

Regan's eyebrows lifted high on her forehead. Yeah, absolutely *fascinating*.

Before she could comment on that, Kimberly let out a self-deprecating laugh. "I mean, I've never met her romantic partners before either, which I'm *obviously* more excited about."

"You never met Felicity?" Regan asked, her interest notching up even higher.

Regan had always been a curious person. About most everything, but people in particular. And with how very little she actually knew about Emma being highlighted yesterday, she was voracious about learning as much as she could.

"No, I was living in Florida, as I'm sure Emma's told you, and..." She cleared her throat, looking embarrassed as she tucked her hair behind her ear. "Anyway, I'm so happy I get to meet you."

"Yeah, I'm utterly thrilled to meet you, too," Regan returned sincerely.

This was the most in-depth look she'd ever been offered into Emma's life, and she hadn't even done anything rude or invasive to get it!

"You're such a cutie pie; I can see why Emma's so excited about this new phase of your life together."

Regan stared, dumbfounded. "You said – Emma's excited?"

Emma had told her mom she was *excited* about them living together?! The very thought seemed unimaginable to Regan, but she wouldn't deny that it pleased her. Maybe, somehow, they were turning a corner? Had it been the grocery shopping adventure?

Kimberly scoffed, a wry smile on her lips. "Well, of course! And who wouldn't be? Graduating with her master's, getting a job at a big publication, and moving in with her girlfriend! Those are all amazing milestones, and I'm so happy for her."

Regan could only continue to stare, replaying Kimberly's last few comments.

I've never met her romantic partners before. You're such a cutie pie. Girlfriend.

Girlfriend.

Girlfriend?

"Girlfriend," Regan repeated, feeling like she was operating much slower than usual. She didn't typically feel like someone else easily pulled a *gotcha!* on her, but Kimberly came in swinging.

But Kimberly was, like, middle-aged, right? And older people sometimes used the word *girlfriend* to mean girls that were friends, she reasoned. Which still didn't quite fit her relationship with Emma, but –

Kimberly looked stricken, waving her hand in front of her. "Oh, I'm sorry. I guess I never really asked if that's what you two call one another. Is it better to say partner?"

"Partner," Regan repeated, still unable to comprehend. Because, no. It didn't seem like Kimberly meant to say girlfriend, as in girls who were friends. She seemed to really mean –

"Partners it is! I love how that's become such a mainstream reference for couples nowadays."

Yep. She really meant that Regan and Emma were *romantically involved.*

Regan stared, silently, for several more seconds. Finally, the sense of bafflement and the need to know what the fuck was going on kicked in, and she snapped out of it.

"Um... you know what? I'm just going to go wake Emma up for you. That *crazy* sleepyhead."

"Thank you. And let her know that I brought bagels!" Kimberly called after her, shaking the white bag in her hand.

"Sure!" Regan shouted over her shoulder as she rushed down the hallway toward Emma's bedroom.

The door across the hallway from Regan's own was firmly shut, as it always was, now. She'd gone from living with Sutton, who had lived in this very room with an open door ninety percent of the time, to living with someone who acted like her room held state secrets.

After Emma had bit her head off for opening her door a few days after she'd moved in, Regan respected her wishes to treat her room as a restricted area.

Until now. She granted herself permission to go into Emma's room under this circumstance.

She shot Kimberly, who'd watched her charge down the hallway like a crazy woman, a smile before swiftly opening Emma's door without so much as a knock.

"Oh, *honey*! Rise and shine!" She called out loud enough for Kimberly to hear her before closing the door with a sharp *snap*.

Emma groaned from where she lay in her bed.

She was entirely wrapped up in her covers, cocooned tightly in her comforter, so only her head poked out at the top. Kinda cute, all wrapped up like a burrito.

Regan looked around the room, momentarily distracted from her mission.

All of Sutton's belongings had been moved to storage, and Regan hadn't gotten to look around after Emma had settled in from her move. Not *really*.

Unsurprisingly, everything was neat and tidy. No clothing was on the floor or strewn over the desk chair or anything. The only furniture Emma had brought with her was her bed, a desk, and two bookshelves that were stuffed to the brim. Regan wasn't actually sure she'd ever seen so many books crammed onto shelves; did Emma know about kindles? Oh, and there was a tall plant next to the window. That was a nice touch.

Emma's sheets and pillowcases were a stone gray, and the duvet she was rolled up in like a burrito was a mint green. Cute neutrals.

She turned, taking in the room as a whole before her eyes landed on a *giant* calendar on the wall. Regan gasped loudly, immediately walking over to it.

"Regan? What are you doing in my room?" Emma's voice behind her was hoarse and raspy from sleep, and Regan found that she very much enjoyed the husky timbre of it.

"Emma, do you literally have every second of your life planned on this calendar?" Regan asked, gesturing to the poster board-size calendar next to her.

Every single day was written for the month, with Emma's clear and concise writing listing *everything* she did. Holy shit.

"Do you know that we have the internet? You could do this in a magic little app on your phone and have it with you all of the time."

"I like to have it written out where I can physically see it," Emma grunted back, seemingly too tired to be aware that she would typically be livid at Regan for barging into her room like this.

It seemed she was more awake by the second, though. She pushed herself onto her elbows to face Regan across the room. "Is there an emergency? Is the building on fire?"

There was a look on Emma's face, like she was torn between being preemptively annoyed with Regan for coming into her room and waking her up, and genuinely concerned there might be something horribly wrong.

Regan shrugged, dropping her hands to her waist. "You know, it's kind of hard to say."

Emma's expression could not be less amused. "Regan, I swear–"

"I guess," Regan swiftly cut in, sending Emma a *look*. "It all depends on what you call an emergency. See, there I was, minding my own business in our kitchen. Wearing my sleep shorts and ripped tank top – not fit for company, obviously." She gestured to herself. "Drinking my coffee. Contemplating life. The normal things people do on the weekend. When there was a knock on my door."

"Oh my *god*." Emma's words came out on a whine as she fell back onto her mattress, bringing her hands up to cover her face. "I'm going to choose to believe that there's not a fire out there, right? Please tell me you aren't keeping us in here because of a fire."

"No fire. Anyway," Regan cleared her throat, and... she didn't quite know at what point in the last couple of minutes her bafflement had mixed with entertainment, but she was highly entertained now. "Imagine my surprise when *your mom* knocks on the door."

All of Emma's agitation swiftly disappeared, as well as any lingering sleepiness. She sat straight up, her blanket slipping down to her waist as she stared wide-eyed at Regan. "What? My *mother* is here?"

Regan held up her hand. "No, no, the story isn't over. This part is really interesting: imagine my even bigger surprise when your mom tells me that you and I are in a relationship!"

There.

Satisfied, she crossed her arms and nodded at Emma. "Now it's your turn."

Emma didn't immediately launch into her usual commentary, however. Instead, her jaw went slack as those blue eyes widened even more. When she did speak, she didn't explain. She offered a murmur of, "Jesus fucking Christ."

"Did I miss somewhere in that contract that we're apparently dating?" Honestly, it was the only thing she could think of that made any sort of sense, even though it also didn't.

Emma glared. "Of course not."

"Hey, don't snap at me! I'm not the one who has any fucking *clue* what is going on!" Regan whisper-shouted, jerking her thumb over her shoulder at Emma's closed door. "It's not *my* mom that showed up before ten AM on a Sunday morning to blindside us!"

In fairness, Regan's mother had never shown up at her apartment in the entire seven years she'd lived here. Regardless, even though what she said was true, she hadn't expected Emma's response.

Because, typically, Emma was always just so... short with her.

In this moment, though, Emma deflated. Her typical agitation that she wore like a second skin during their interactions was gone, and her shoulders slumped as she bowed her head.

"You're right," she admitted, softly. "I'm sorry."

Regan's eyebrows flew high up on her forehead in surprise. "Wait. Can you repeat that?"

That might have been the most surprising thing to happen all morning! Which was saying quite a bit.

Those startlingly blue eyes narrowed at her again, but Emma still didn't respond angrily. "I *said*... I'm sorry," she repeated, with that vulnerable edge to her voice.

Emma brought her hands up and scrubbed them over her face, taking a deep breath and holding it, before slowly letting it out.

Finally, she looked back up at Regan. "Long story short: my mom got this idea in her head that we moved in together because we're in a relationship."

"Good thing I already found out that you're queer, or this would be doubly confusing," Regan quipped.

Emma stared at her for a few seconds before her lips ticked into the briefest of smiles. "Yeah, I guess so."

Regan's mouth dropped open as *shock* coursed through her.

Emma really must be out of her element if she was cracking a grin at one of Regan's jokes during what was obviously a stressful time!

"Can you make a long story a little bit longer? Because my brain is not computing this."

Emma's smile was gone as soon as it came. "Look, things with my mom are complicated, okay? It's really... complicated–"

"Wait – are you saying things with your mom are complicated?"

Emma shot her a dirty look as she trailed a hand through her sleep-tousled hair. "Given how *complicated* it is, I just went along with her supposition because it made things easier."

As she explained, her tone was something Regan had never heard from her, something raw and very real. Something, when it came to complicated family dynamics, Regan could very much understand.

It was also a side of herself that Emma *never* showed Regan, which made the exuberant ribbing she desperately wanted to give Emma dim. The impulse was undeniably still present but the prospect of teasing

Emma about it seemed remarkably less enjoyable when Emma was giving Regan a rare moment of true, unfiltered connection.

Instead, she – gently – teased, "Well, your situation with your mom must be dire if telling her that you're in a relationship with *me* was your best choice, huh?"

Emma swore under her breath, throwing her blanket off her as she said, "Clearly, right now, I am regretting it."

Regan watched with interest as Emma stood up with a huff, noting the black sleep shorts that just barely covered her incredibly impressive ass. Regan could do squats every day for months – she had – and never get an ass like Emma's, whose hips, butt, and thighs seemed to have first dibs on any weight she put on. Regan had no idea if Emma appreciated that as much as Regan did. But she should.

Emma didn't often hang out in the common areas of their apartment, so in the last few weeks, Regan hadn't really her in anything less than the bevy of gray, black, and blue professional outfits she wore – slacks and button-ups, a smattering of blazers.

Other than when she'd walked in and had seen Emma standing in the kitchen in her bra, that was. The red lace had surprised Regan – she'd have figured Emma for a much more neutral tone lingerie woman, if she wore lingerie at all.

"In my defense, I didn't expect that she'd ever show up here," Emma continued muttering, and Regan honestly didn't think these words were even meant for her. Especially not as Emma started rifling through her dresser, no longer paying Regan any attention. "Why the hell would I? I don't even know how she got our address!"

Utterly riveted by this rare look at Emma – while she wasn't focused on being pissed at Regan – she was unashamedly curious to hear even more.

Like... Emma had never given her address to her mother? She talked to her enough that her mom got the idea that *they were dating*, but she wasn't close enough with her mom to tell her where she lived?

Emma snatched a pair of joggers from her drawer, shaking her head. "Gram. Obviously. I just – *ugh*."

Regan's eyebrows raised high on her forehead with interest when Emma's hands went to the waistband of her shorts, clearly ready to pull them down. Only to lower again when Emma blew her hair out of her eyes and shot Regan a dark look. "Do you mind not staring at me while I change?"

Shrugging, Regan made a show of turning around and staring at the calendar again. "Well, for a second, I really didn't think you even remembered I was still here."

"And that meant you had permission to watch me strip?" Emma shot back, still lacking her usual Regan-inspired vigor.

"Hey, we're both women here. I've seen Sutton change a million times."

"And, for the millionth time, I'm not Sutton."

Oh my god, did Emma really write her twenty-minute nighttime routine in her calendar? Regan leaned in for a better look, and... yeah. She sure did.

As well as her reading block before sleep.

Wow. That kind of organization was both terrifying and impressive.

"I was also curious to know if you had cute red underwear to match your bra," Regan unthinkingly and honestly remarked, scanning her eyes over the details of Emma's day-to-day life that she normally wasn't privy to.

She could hear Emma pause. "I – just – you... that's none of your business."

Even though Emma couldn't see her face, Regan's mouth dropped open from the sheer shock of Emma not having the mental energy to zing back at her.

She never thought she'd see the day!

Clearly, it was because Emma had re-focused her attention back on the situation at hand. Man, Regan wondered what it was like to have a brain that could prioritize and execute so deftly.

"And, of course, she shows up at an ungodly hour, on a weekend!"

"Ehhh, I agree it's a little early to come calling without prior notice, but I wouldn't necessarily say after nine is *ungodly*."

"Whose side are you on?" Emma hissed.

Regan spun around, thrilled. "Wait. Do you want me to be on your side? I think this is a momentous occasion for us."

She could tell from Emma's glare that she took Regan's comment as teasing, but she'd been very serious.

Emma didn't verbally acknowledge her. "And now, not only do I miss out on my day to sleep in, but I also have to go out there and figure out how to tell her – in the most delicate way possible – that I lied to her about my relationship status to avoid spending time with her!"

Regan hadn't known what to expect from Emma beyond *it's complicated*, but... huh. Okay.

Maybe it was a relief to know that while Emma didn't seek out Regan's company, she seemed to slot higher on Emma's list of preferred company than her mom?

The flush on Emma's cheeks and the obvious stress riddling her expression pushed the words from Regan's mouth before she could even fully process them. "Why do you have to tell her that?"

Emma paused while combing her fingers through her soft, honey-colored hair, staring quizzically at Regan. "What?"

"Why do you have to tell her the truth?" Regan clarified.

Emma's hands fell heavily to her sides, the look in her eyes suspicious. "What are you saying?"

Tapping her fingers together in thought, Regan tilted her head to the side. "I don't know. What's the big deal if she thinks we're in a relationship if it helps you out? I don't care if she thinks that."

"You don't," Emma slowly repeated, staring at her. "You don't care... that my mom thinks we're in a relationship?"

Regan shook her head, trying to sort through her feelings on the matter to make sure she was telling the truth. But she wasn't getting that weird, gnawing feeling in her stomach like she did when she felt like she was doing something wrong. "It's not like I'm actually dating anyone." Which she imagined might be her biggest issue. "I'll just be having a bagel with a woman I barely know while calling you snookums."

Emma shuddered. "Do not."

Regan's grin crept over her face. "My little sweetie baby honey pie." She winked before making an exaggerated kissy face at Emma, taking a far stronger delight in it than even she'd imagined.

"I think I'd rather tell her the truth," Emma deadpanned.

"Your prerogative." She shrugged.

They stared at each other for several long moments before Emma let out a deep breath. "I cannot believe I'm saying this…"

Regan felt a buzz of anticipation slide through her, surprisingly potent.

It made sense, she reasoned, because – this was *bonding*! This was the dream!

"Regan, will you do me a favor and simply not disagree with the notion that we're dating while my mom is here?" Emma's blue eyes searched hers.

In them, Regan found that same rawness from minutes ago. The one that made her take this a little more seriously, as she agreed, "I'll do you one better, and make her believe without question that I'm besotted."

She offered Emma her hand to shake.

Emma stared at it before hesitantly sliding her warm, soft hand into Regan's. "I want it stated on the record that this is the most ludicrous situation I've ever gotten into."

"It's not for me," Regan informed her, lightly stroking her thumb over Emma's as she shook her hand. "But, in what I'm sure is the worst part for you, it's a situation in which you *need me*."

Emma leaned in closer, then, and Regan felt the tiny hairs on the back stand up with awareness, her shoulders snapping back at Emma's proximity. They'd *never* stood so close; she could feel Emma's warm breath on her cheek, as she murmured, "Believe it or not, that's actually not the worst part for me right now. So don't flatter yourself."

Emma dropped her hand and stepped back, brushing her hands through her hair as she quickly tied it up in a ponytail.

And Regan stared for a baffled, silent second before she regained normalcy; that was weird. "I'll do my very best not to flatter myself. But I do have to say that I'm sure your mom might be wondering what we're getting up to in *our bedroom*, since we're taking so much time." She fluttered her eyelashes, dramatically faux-swooning. "She probably thinks you're having your way with me this morning. Or, I guess, that I'm having my way with you. Since I came to wake you up and all."

Emma's gaze snapped to hers in disgruntled alarm, her cheeks turning pink as Regan laughed in amusement at the idea.

"Let's go," Emma directed, walking toward the door.

Regan dropped her swooning act as she diligently followed, still chuckling to herself.

They found Kimberly right where Regan had left her, in the archway that led into the kitchen. She was clutching the bag containing the bagels like it was a lifeline, and the smile that bloomed over her face when she laid eyes on Emma was so exuberant, Regan was sure that it supplemented the sun streaming in through the windows to illuminate the kitchen.

That was kinda sweet.

"There's my Emma Bo Bemma!" Kimberly dropped her other hand to the top of the paper bagel bag, looking as though she was trying to contain herself. Trying to stop herself from reaching out toward Emma, maybe?

Curiously, Regan shot Emma a side-long look. And she was entirely unsurprised to see how tense Emma was, a tight smile on her mouth. Almost like she didn't know if she really wanted to smile a little or if it was entirely forced. Her face couldn't decide.

"Mom. Hey," Emma greeted, stiltedly, before falling quiet again.

Quiet enough that Regan could start to feel the awkwardness settle into the air, like a heavy, physical presence.

Luckily for Emma, she had Regan. And Regan had never met an awkward silence that she couldn't dissipate.

She cleared her throat to capture both of their attentions rather than allow them to maintain the awkward eye contact they were making and then quickly dodging with one another. She scooted in close to Emma, in a far more familiar way than she'd ever act around Emma in any other situation.

In every day life, if she bumped her hip into Emma's before settling in so close that they were touching from hip to ankle, Emma would bite her head off. Probably.

Not this morning, though!

Because *right now*, they were in love.

"I didn't know I was in a relationship with one of the famous New York City Bo Bemma's!" She teased, angling her head up at Emma as she bit her bottom lip.

Kimberly laughed at her joke as Emma cut her a look. It was – surprisingly – not annoyed. Regan didn't think so, anyway.

She arched her eyebrows, darting her eyes to Kimberly and back to Emma's. "Don't worry, *honey*, you're my favorite Bo Bemma, no matter how many relatives of yours come calling for a visit."

All right, was Regan milking this?

Maybe a little bit.

She reached out, easily sliding her arm around Emma's waist, as the grin on her face wavered slightly in question. But Emma gamely accepted the embrace, even if she looked like she might be developing a jaw twitch.

Regan would count that as a win.

"Thanks, *babe*. You know how much I love it when you're so peppy and joke-y so early in the morning."

Emma's resounding sarcasm made Regan laugh, as Kimberly watched them with such warmth.

"Right – and since I'm sure we're both aware Emma isn't much of a morning person, why don't we go into the kitchen and grab a coffee?" Regan suggested, gesturing at the small round wooden table a few feet away.

"Best idea you've ever had," Emma murmured, relief evident as she stepped out of Regan's hold.

"I just brewed some before you knocked, Kimberly," she informed the woman, ushering her into one of the three seats clustered around the table. "I can grab some plates for the bagels?"

Kimberly pulled a chair out and perched in it as she carefully placed the bagels onto the table. Way too carefully for bagels, to be honest, but Regan got it – there was some emotionally charged shit happening here. She didn't know exactly what kind of emotionally charged shit, but sometimes people needed their emotional support bagels.

Kimberly shook her head, giving Regan a small, appreciative smile. "Um, I'll just take a coffee. The bagels are mostly for Emma – er, the two of you," she rushed to amend, lightly patting the paper bag. "There are four bagels in here. Two everything, since they're Emma's favorites. Remember how we'd go and get everything bagels with scallion cream cheese at that deli down the street from gram's apartment?"

There was so much hope in those words that Regan felt compelled to turn and look at Emma's response.

Emma stood facing the counter with her back to them, but Regan could still see the tense set of her shoulders. She also noted that Emma wasn't actually making a coffee but was merely... standing in front of it.

"Um, yeah," Emma agreed after a beat of quiet.

Kimberly's expression went from tentatively excited to downtrodden in seconds and *oof.* Regan stepped up next to Emma at the counter, nodding at the table, silently telling Emma to sit.

Emma frowned, shaking her head.

Regan nodded toward the table *more* insistently, jerking her thumb in Kimberly's direction. Managing the emotions for this woman she didn't know from a hole in the wall was not in her purview.

Emma's jaw twitched again before she relented, maneuvering around Regan to pull out one of the other chairs.

She quickly poured them both a mug, fixing Emma's with a dash of milk and a single pump of the syrup Regan kept on her antique metal serving tray. Not only did she love how it looked, but when it was no longer time for coffee, it was so easy to hide off the counter – Regan regarded it as one of her best decorative finds.

She turned around, placing Emma's coffee in front of her. "The way you like it." She put Kimberly's in front of her as well. "Dairies and sugars are right behind you."

"This is fine, thanks a bunch." Kimberly shot Regan a grateful smile.

She returned it with one of her own as she retrieved her coffee that she'd been drinking earlier. Blessed be, she needed this caffeine.

Admittedly, getting roped into these kinds of shenanigans did jazz her up a bit. Especially because she was curious as *hell* to know the backstory here.

Never in her life would she have expected this from *Emma*.

"Mm," Kimberly hummed brightly as she placed her mug on the table, her eyebrows raised. "This coffee is delicious!" She laughed, a light, tinkling sound, as she put her hand against her chest. "Believe me, I drink a lot of it – most of it not so good. What brand is it?"

Regan perked up, pride pushing through her. "It's my own blend, actually! It's a medium blend with Brazilian and Ethiopian coffee beans."

Kimberly sipped again, nodding effusively as she swallowed. "Well, you should be proud of this."

"I'm a barista by trade," Regan offered. "So, it's kind of my thing."

"She makes my favorite coffee. It's perfect every time," Emma supplied, sipping slowly on her own coffee. She spoke so casually and flippantly, but her words snagged all of Regan's attention.

She shifted to look at Emma in surprise, studying her profile. "Really?"

Emma turned to meet her gaze, looking confused at Regan's interest. "Yeah? I mean, I've gone to Topped Off for years; it's not like that's the only coffee shop near campus."

A pleased warmth slid through her at the compliment and Regan settled back in her chair. Well, then.

"That's so sweet," Kimberly's voice cut in, regaining their attention.

Regan watched Emma furrow her eyebrows as she looked at her mom. "So... what are you doing here?" Emma asked.

She'd have to hand it to Emma – she really cut straight to the point. She supposed there was something to say about that directness.

Honestly, it had always been Regan's favorite thing about Emma.

"Right!" Kimberly lit up, her posture straightening as she cleared her throat. "Well, I finally finished going through all the boxes we'd put in the basement after the move. You know, filled with the things we don't use day-to-day."

"Sure..."

Kimberly nodded as if thrilled by Emma's simple validation. "Yesterday morning, I found Mr. Cuddles." She leaned down to rummage through her tote bag before she emerged with a stuffed animal. A purple bear with a faded embroidered heart on the tummy, which she held up, looking both victorious and nervous. "I, um, I just remembered how much you loved him when you were little, and I thought it would be nice to give him back to you."

Regan slid her gaze to Emma, who sat shock-still for several long moments. From her side view, she could see the slight ticking of Emma's jaw, but other than that, she looked... frozen.

If Regan really was Emma's supportive girlfriend, she would do something here.

So, she did.

Leaning forward, she put her hand on Emma's knee and squeezed softly, sending Kimberly a delighted smile. "He's so cute!"

Which was true.

Mr. Cuddles was clearly well-loved, though also well-taken care of. He was in a much better state than Regan's favored childhood stuffed animals were. Or would be if they still existed outside of the landfill they'd likely ended up in when she'd turned ten, and her parents had thrown out her stuffed animals.

Kimberly looked relieved at Regan's response and offered Mr. Cuddles out to her. "He is! I, uh," she glanced at Emma. "I got him for Emma when she was two. She was so sick; she had a hundred-and-four-degree fever. It was terrible. She loved Mr. Cuddles, though, the second she got her hands on him."

Regan carefully took the bear with her free hand, squeezing Emma's knee again with the other.

"I can see why." She studied the well-kept companion; not even a patch of hair missing or anything. "I liked that you used a male pronoun, even though he was purple. Very ahead of your time."

"I've always been into equality," Emma seemed to finally find her voice.

Kimberly's phone vibrated where it sat on the table next to her, but she ignored it. "I brought it when I went to see your gram yesterday, but you'd already left when I arrived. I was trying to arrange it so we ran into one another, but..." She trailed off with a shrug and a forced laugh, wrapping her hands around her coffee mug. "I know how it is; it was a Saturday evening. You're young and in love. So, I just – I thought I could just drop it by before it gets lost in the shuffle at my house."

Regan settled Mr. Cuddles in her lap, sipping her coffee to hide her tickled smile at being called *young and in love*. And she just knew that while hearing that phrase to describe the two of them amused her, it made Emma want to shout the truth from the rooftop.

Only Emma didn't look aggrieved at all.

She looked very much like she wasn't sure what to say. And she definitely looked relieved when Kimberly's phone rang again, giving her a reason to encourage, "Why don't you answer it? It could be important."

Kimberly slid her gaze down to her phone screen before she sighed. "It's – I should be on my way to the shelter."

"What shelter?" Regan asked.

"The Culver Women's Shelter, on third? I'm the director there, and I have a few meetings today," she answered with a tentative smile, as she slid her gaze to Emma once more. "I just... I wanted to see you. Even if it was only for a few minutes."

"That's – I didn't realize you worked there. That's great," Emma murmured, her cheeks flushed as she looked away from her mom's gaze and down into her coffee. "But, yeah, I don't want you to miss the meetings on my account."

Regan's eyes widened. *Yikes!* Again, she sipped her coffee to hide her expression.

Kimberly nodded. "Right. Of course, you're right." She leaned conspiratorially toward Regan, a smile on her lips again. "Believe it or not, Emma has always been a stickler for never being late and sticking to the rules." She looked back at Emma, a smile screaming of hesitance and affection curling her lips. "I like that some things never change."

"Happy to help," Emma seemed to manage with something that resembled a smile. Kind of.

Regan realized her hand was still resting on Emma's knee and squeezed again. This one was entirely for real support, no teasing intended.

Kimberly stood, tugging her tote bag over her shoulder. "I really hope we can get together soon. Maybe the two of you can come over for dinner with Ted and the girls? If you're settled in here, that is."

"Oh, Emma's totally settled in here! Aren't you, sweetie?" Regan leaned toward Emma enough so she could rest her head against her shoulder.

Emma, in turn, dropped her hand on top of Regan's and squeezed a little too hard to be considered nice.

Kimberly lit up like a Christmas tree. "That's amazing! I'll set something up real soon!" Her phone started buzzing again as she clutched it tightly in her hand. "I should answer this. I love you, Emma! And it was *so* great to finally meet you, Regan."

"Yeah, it was so great to *finally* meet you, too!" Regan called out to her as she rushed out.

As soon as the apartment door shut behind her, Emma turned to Regan, eyes blazing. "*Why* would you agree to making dinner plans with her?"

Regan held her hand up, defensively. "Uh, excuse me? I don't recall hearing myself do that."

... did she? She tilted her head to the side, running through the last few minutes of interaction and – yeah, no. She hadn't mentioned anything about that.

Emma groaned, reaching up to pinch the bridge of her nose. "Sure, technically, you didn't do it in as many words. But to *Kimberly*, that was an agreement of epic proportions."

Regan stared incredulously. "I have a really good suggestion for you: next time you tell someone we're in a relationship, give me a cheat sheet or something so I can properly prepare myself! How should I know your mom's double-talk? I didn't even know she existed until thirty minutes ago."

She couldn't help but laugh at the absurdity of it all.

As she did, some of the fight also seemed to leave Emma's body. It had been fascinating, really, how she could quite literally *see* the tension lessen in Emma's shoulders as soon as Kimberly had left.

Hoping to continue with the lightening of the mood, she lifted Mr. Cuddles, holding him in front of her face as she called on the deepest voice she could summon. "Yeah, Emma, it's not Regan's fault. She was just trying to help reunite us. I missed you!"

Emma choked on a laugh, reaching up and taking Mr. Cuddles from Regan for the first time. "Oh my god, never do that again. That's not even what his voice sounds like."

Regan gaped, delighted. "You know you can't say that to me and then *not* demonstrate what his voice is supposed to sound like. Right? You can't."

Emma met her stare, clearly unintimidated. "Yes. I can, actually. Very easily."

"Emma! After I just did you such a huge favor!" Regan widened her eyes, fluttering her lashes, trying to appeal to Emma.

"Seriously, Regan..." Emma closed her eyes and nodded. "I really appreciate you doing that for me. Not enough to demonstrate Mr. Cuddles' voice for you, but... a lot."

That sincere tone came back into Emma's voice, and Regan felt like she was glowing with it.

God, this was so *good*. Right when she'd been lamenting about getting them to a good place, this had dropped in her lap!

Because she loved it when Emma was real-Emma with her. The same genuine tone that Emma used with Sutton and other people who weren't driving her crazy – Regan liked it. She could get used to this.

She was desperate for them to get to a place where they could get used to this.

"It was kinda fun," she admitted. "I love being on the inside of a good secret. A little scheme."

Emma rolled her eyes as she stood up. "Of course you do."

Regan watched Emma strut down the hall toward her bedroom, sipping triumphantly on her coffee; she felt like that had gone rather well.

Maybe the next time she lamented to the universe, she'd ask for a million dollars.

five

"I REFUSE to believe that this article was written, word-for-word, by Henry Cryer. I refuse to believe it because I refuse to believe that I was responsible for hiring someone who wrote *this*, and believed for a second it would have a chance of being published," Allegra fumed, aggressively tapping her well-manicured nail down on the hard copy of the article she was referencing.

Emma exchanged a quick look with Brynn as they sat in Allegra's office, and in the split-second of eye contact, she could tell they were both on the same page.

And that page read that it would be *shocking* if Henry was still gainfully employed in the near future.

A beat went by, and they both realized Allegra was staring at them expectantly. Emma's eyebrows inched up in surprise; she'd believed this rant had been somewhat rhetorical.

Brynn cleared her throat. "Do you think it was plagiarized? Written by AI? Or maybe he had an off week?"

Emma couldn't help but quietly scoff. "More like an off two months."

As soon as the words left her mouth, everything inside of her froze.

Allegra was a good boss. Honestly, she was a *really* good boss.

Demanding, worked long hours, sent both Brynn and Emma tasks on the weekends. But all of her past assistants had gone on to have meaningful careers in publishing. She allowed both Emma and Brynn to read every piece that made it to her desk, and she gave them space to critique and give their opinions.

Granted, it wasn't an editing circle, where everyone's thoughts mattered and had an equal voice. It was more of a test; at least, that was how Emma viewed it. Allegra would stare at her, direct and intense, as if measuring every word she said. She likely was.

But – until this moment – Emma generally had felt like she'd passed!

However, it was only after the words had left her mouth that she realized: her comment could very well sound like she was doubting Allegra's judgment where Henry was concerned. And Emma had already been at *Olly* long enough to know what happened when someone questioned Allegra's judgment.

She blamed Regan, she thought desperately. Blurting out whatever came to mind; she'd obviously been living with her for too long.

Out of the corner of her eye, she could see the high lift of Brynn's eyebrows in surprise at Emma's sardonic comment as well.

Keeping her composure, Emma sat with her shoulders straight, staring at her boss from across her desk. She could feel the stampeding of her heart in her chest.

Allegra quirked her head to the side as she stared back at Emma, giving her no visual indication of a response. Until – *there*. The slightest uptick of the side of her mouth as she hummed and dropped her gaze back to her open laptop. "You're quite right about that, Emma. It's been far too long since Henry's work has reflected the quality he was hired for."

She could have melted from relief.

"Brynn, I want you to collect Henry's work from the last three months. No, four. I want you to sum up any salient points made, then compare the work to samples of his work from the last two years since he was hired. I need a paper trail here. On my desk by tomorrow morning."

"Absolutely." Brynn was already tapping on her tablet, undoubtedly pulling up Henry's submissions.

"Emma," Allegra said, making Emma snap to attention.

"Yes?"

Allegra stared at her from over the top of her glasses. "You were selected for the Alton Writing Fellowship, correct?"

Emma gaped in surprise. "I was. Yes."

Her heart continued to pound in her chest, wondering where Allegra was going to go with this topic.

The Alton Writing Fellowship was one of the country's most competitive and coveted literary programs. Thousands of undergraduate and graduate students submitted portfolios, vying to fill one of only fifty spots. And each spot guaranteed a door into the literary world like no other for any aspiring writer. Tutelage and mentorship from well-known writers and editors, networking into the publishing world.

Emma had nearly fallen out of her chair in shock when she'd received her acceptance email four years ago.

Allegra sent her a critical stare. "You're my assistant. Why are you acting as though I would be unaware of your accomplishments?"

First and foremost, because Emma hadn't actually completed the fellowship.

She didn't say that, though.

Instead, as her cheeks burned, she cleared her throat and wracked her mind for the right response. Because she hadn't been aware that Allegra would have personally reviewed applications for her assistants? Because she wouldn't have thought Allegra would retain such a small detail from Emma's resume?

Neither answer sounded great.

"I apologize; I was just not expecting it to be brought up," she settled on.

God, she didn't think she'd had such an off day at work since she'd been hired.

She would admit, though, that she'd felt off-kilter since yesterday morning. Waking up first to Regan in her bedroom, quickly followed by the information that Kimberly was in their apartment, had made Emma feel so – *off*.

That feeling had continued throughout the day, no matter how much she'd tried to shake herself out of it.

Clearly, it had carried over.

"Right," Allegra drawled. "This year, I'm on the applicant review board. Given your experience, I figured you'd be my right-hand in the process. The submission deadline is today, and all those in my purview will be directed to you."

Emma nodded, perking up in excitement as she brought her tablet to life to start organizing her email files in preparation.

This was – by far – the biggest responsibility Allegra had given her since she'd started. And she was *ready*. She was so ready to prove herself she could taste it. It was how she'd always been.

"We have three weeks to decide who will move onto the interview rounds, so I do hope you're prepared for quite a bit of reading," Allegra continued, turning her attention back to her laptop once more.

Emma was already figuring out her color codes as she nodded, trying to bite back her smile; she didn't want to look like an insane person *thrilled* to have this responsibility dropped on her desk.

Even if that's exactly what she was.

"I'm always prepared for quite a bit of reading," Emma confirmed.

She *swore* she saw Allegra's lips tick up once more before she merely answered, "Good."

She was still riding that high as she left the office that evening.

Yes, it was seven in the evening by the time she was able to pack up.

Yes, the submitted portfolios had started rolling in an hour ago. There were already ninety-five emails in the Alton Fellowship email folder she'd created.

Yes, the disgusting heat wave *was* still wreaking havoc on everyone living in this densely populated concrete island.

Emma simply didn't care.

She fished her phone out of her back pocket as she felt it vibrating, her excitement only growing when she saw her grandmother's contact information reflected back at her.

"Hi, Gram," she answered, thrilled to share her updates.

After all, her grandmother was the one person who'd always been there to share in her triumphs and to support her in her failures. If there was one person who would understand Emma's elation at being entrusted with such a big project, she knew it was her gram. The same woman who'd taught her the value of working hard and being proud of a job well done.

"I'm sorry," her grandmother immediately apologized, forgoing a typical greeting.

Emma's swift stride toward the subway slowed. "You're... sorry?"

"I am," Gram confirmed. "I didn't want to interrupt you at work, and I know Mondays are busy for you; that's why I didn't call earlier. But I'm sorry, Emma. I had no *idea* your mom would go to your apartment without notice."

Though she'd been swept up in the craziness of her schedule, her grandmother's apology reminded her of yesterday's events.

It only slightly dimmed her excitement.

"Yeah," she responded, combing through the mix of emotions that were so easily recalled.

How jarring it had been to see Kimberly, amongst her belongings, in her home. Having coffee with her – *and Regan* – in their kitchen. Emma had been thrown into the situation that she'd been putting off for months, and Regan was there to witness it.

"I only gave her your address because she brought me to my cardiology follow-up a couple of weeks ago," her grandmother explained, sounding so earnest. "I'd wanted to add her to my emergency contact list, and it came up that she didn't have your information. It seemed like a good idea – her having all of your contact information – in case something ever happens and she needs to get a hold of you."

Emma reached up, rubbing her hand at her temples as she digested the explanation. "I get it," she finally said.

And she did.

She understood the connections her grandmother had made, and it wasn't as though Emma had ever instructed her gram not to give her information to Kimberly.

"And it's... fine," she added on after a minute, blowing out a deep breath.

Obviously, she hadn't been *pleased*, but it had – technically – been *fine*.

Kimberly hadn't stayed for long, and Regan... well, not only had Regan done her a solid favor, but she'd done it well.

Maybe a little too well. She supposed it wasn't a shock that Regan had been so comfortable acting so casually lovey-dovey toward Emma. Leaning into Emma as if she did it all of the time, dropping her hand to Emma's knee like it was a normal thing between them.

Honestly, Regan had been so casual about it that the action hadn't even registered to Emma as *abnormal*. It had been just as jarring as Kimberly's presence was to have realized that she had found some semblance of stability in Regan, however brief it had been.

"I'm so glad to hear that, Em. I really am." The relief in her grandmother's tone was palpable. "I heard all about it from Kimberly this afternoon."

Emma hummed under her breath as she turned onto the block where her subway stop was. Honestly, she had no idea what about the visit Kimberly could have said to Gram that had been so thrilling, given that she'd only been at their apartment for –

The horrifying realization dawned on Emma at the same time her grandmother started talking again.

"I'll admit, I was a little surprised to find out from your mom that Regan is your girlfriend!" Gram stated, sounding exactly that – surprised. "She said you two looked very sweet together."

Emma stopped walking right there, in the middle of the bustling sidewalk. "Uh."

It was all she could manage.

"I know you've been busy, of course. But... if you two live together, you must have been dating for a while. I'm not trying to pry, of course. I'm just – I suppose I just don't understand. Normally, when you have news about your personal life, you tell me. Or, I thought you did."

There it was: that slightly hurt tone that she could tell her grandmother was trying to hide so as not to make Emma feel badly.

The great news on that front was that Emma *didn't* feel guilty; she felt panicked.

"I do tell you." She couldn't help but state, as it was the truth.

She'd always told her grandma about her romantic life. Even though neither of them had ever been the type to be swept up in romantic fantasy, her grandmother had made it very clear to Emma throughout her adolescence that dating and sex weren't taboo discussions. That it was better to be frank and honest about emotional and physical health. It had clearly been a response on her grandmother's side to make sure Emma didn't end up as a pregnant teenager like her mother.

So, Emma had always been honest and open. Her grandmother had been the first person she'd confided in about her sexuality when she'd been fourteen. She'd been the person to comfort Emma through high school heartaches.

"I know I could sometimes be... harsh. About Felicity," her gram admitted ruefully. "In retrospect, I realize you haven't really discussed your romantic life with me since then."

Her grandmother *had* been somewhat harsh on the topic of Felicity. Gram had never liked Emma's ex; she'd thought Felicity was judgmental and elitist, that she hadn't prioritized Emma the way Emma had prioritized her. And her gram had never been one to pull punches, especially not when it came to how Emma was being treated.

"*You need to be with someone who treats you well,*" her grandmother had told her intently and often when she'd been with Felicity.

Emma had theorized – much like the teen pregnancy thing – it was because they'd both watched Kimberly make shitty, irresponsible dating choices for years, and Gram hadn't wanted to see history repeating.

Her grandmother's disapproval of Felicity had weighed heavily on Emma.

She'd lived her entire life wearing her grandmother's quiet stamp of approval with pride, and she hadn't quite known what to do, knowing that the person she'd fallen for would never have that same approval.

She'd also stayed in that relationship long enough to see that everything her grandmother had ever said about Felicity had been, unfortunately, accurate.

"I *haven't* told you anything about my dating life since Felicity," Emma echoed.

It was the truth – but it was only the truth because she hadn't had anything to say about her dating life in the last two years.

"I understand that, and what you do in your romantic life is your business," Gram stated, still with that hint of sadness in her voice. "I just wish I'd known. I've never missed one of your milestones, and living with a partner for the first time is a decent one."

"Um... I guess it is."

Emma wouldn't know; she'd never done it.

"But Kimberly said she was very friendly! Very pretty. Made an excellent cup of coffee."

"That's all true," Emma confirmed because Regan *was* friendly, pretty, and made the best coffee Emma had ever tasted. But, mostly, she was starting to feel a little overwhelmed.

More than a little.

"I know Astoria is a bit of a hike, but – now that the cat is out of the bag – I'd really like to meet the woman that's captured your heart."

Emma recognized that tone. That speculative tone told Emma that her grandmother very much wanted to meet Regan. Not only because she'd *captured Emma's heart*, but because she wanted to see if Regan measured up or if she was another Felicity.

She had to bite back the truth that wanted to come spilling from her mouth. It wasn't in her nature to deceive her grandmother, first and foremost. On top of that – she *wasn't* in a relationship with Regan fucking Gallagher!

But if she told her grandmother the truth, it would only bring about more questions: why would she have lied to her mother in the first place? Why would Emma, the woman Gram had done her best to raise as an honest person with integrity, have hidden behind such a silly untruth? Why in the world would she and Regan, as two grown adults, have furthered the act and gone along with it in person?

How was it, Emma wondered as she stared bleakly at the passing taxis, that this was the one time in her life where telling the truth seemed to only bring about *more* complications?

"Yeah," she settled on instead. "Sometime soon."

Oh, there it was. The pounding headache that Emma should have seen coming two minutes ago.

She had to end this before she found herself in a deeper hole. "Gram, I'm sorry, but I'm about to get on the subway. I have to run."

By the time she got home, that headache was well on its way to becoming a migraine.

She was frustrated with her mother for a whole host of reasons – for being responsible for the way their relationship was. For presuming that Regan was her girlfriend and making it so easy for Emma to go along with it. For showing up yesterday unannounced. For sharing every last detail with Gram like a game of telephone.

She was frustrated with her grandmother for always letting Kimberly come sweeping back into their lives. For giving Kimberly Emma's address. For being such an incredible presence in Emma's life that she felt sick whenever she disappointed her.

And most of all, right now, she was frustrated with herself for being a fucking *idiot* and getting herself into this mess.

Shutting the apartment door behind her with a sharp snap, she closed her eyes tightly when she heard Regan's music *blaring*.

The insistent, worsening pain behind her left eye throbbed at the volume, her frustration bubbling over.

Because she was frustrated with Regan, too. Perpetually.

She only had to take a few steps down the hall before coming to an abrupt stop in the doorway to the kitchen.

Her eye twitched.

A slew of ingredients, utensils, mixing bowls, and pans were strewn all over the counters, the disorder of it all pushing her over the edge.

Regan was singing – loudly – along to one of the pop songs from an old 3G album she had blasting from the small speaker perched on the windowsill as she stood at the sink.

"Do you *have* to listen to your music at a deafening volume?!" Emma had to shout to be heard. She honestly wasn't sure she would be, even then.

Regan perked up, though, looking over her shoulder. A bright smile slid into place as she reached out and tapped on her phone, lowering the volume. "Hey! You're home! I wondered when I'd see you;

you didn't answer my text about dinner. Or about how I have a surprise for you."

Yes, Regan *had* texted her to say she was in the mood to cook and wanted to know if Emma was craving anything. And had texted her *again* to say she had a little surprise and couldn't wait to show her.

But, "I was busy at work, and we didn't have dinner plans. We don't have dinner together," she stated plainly. "Other than the time you almost killed me. And given our track record, I wasn't expecting a surprise."

Regan waggled her finger in Emma's direction. "One day, you'll stop bringing that up; I was hoping today might be the one."

"Yeah, well, it's still pretty fresh," Emma retorted, crossing her arms tightly over her chest.

Whenever she felt overwhelmed, as she did now, feeling constricted – like everything was in her control – made her feel a little better.

Regan was undeterred. "I'd just thought we could have dinner together before inviting you out tonight. I'm going to Beth's – my coworker at Topped Off? You've met her tons of times – soon. It's going to be a super chill thing, just a hangout. I made some cupcakes. Anyway, they're going to fucking *die* when I tell them about yesterday with your mom."

"How about you *don't*?" Emma snapped, her frustration bleeding into her voice.

But she couldn't really care right now.

Regan tilted her head slowly as if having trouble computing her words. "Don't... what?"

"Don't go telling everyone you fucking know about my business! I told you my relationship with my mom is complicated; you witnessed it yourself." She flung her arm out, gesturing at the table between them. The scene of the crime. "You know that I don't want everyone that peripherally knows who I am to know my business. In fact, especially regarding yesterday, the *fewer* people that know, the better."

Regan shrugged, and the easiness of that shrug only irritated Emma further. "Okay? It was just an entertaining story."

Emma could literally feel herself hitting the breaking point as she glared incredulously at Regan. "It's not just an entertaining story; this is my life. *My* life with *my* mom. *My* grandmother calling me, trying to make plans to meet you, too. *I'm* the one who has to figure this all out, and it's really *not* entertaining."

Regan's mouth dropped open. "Your grandmother wants to meet me?!" She clapped her hands as if she were high-fiving herself. "Yes! Okay. You tell me where and when, and I will be girlfriend-ready."

Were they living on different planes of existence? Emma blinked at Regan, so utterly baffled as to how her statement could garner *that* reaction.

"The last thing. I want to do. Is introduce you. To my grandmother!"

Regan stared back at her, tossing her hands into the air. "Sorry, I just figured you weren't ready to clear up this *complicated* situation based on what happened yesterday."

"I'm not!" She shouted back before wincing. She brought her hand up to her temple, rubbing furiously as her migraine worsened. "But fooling Kimberly that you and I are together is one thing; my gram actually *knows* me. More than that, I had to manage the pressure of her disliking Felicity – well-educated, organized, responsible, ambitious Felicity – for years. I wouldn't even know where to begin to manage the flack I'd catch for being with you."

She dropped her head back with a groan. "And if I tell her we broke up, it will only invite more questions. Why are we still living together? Why would I move in with you if things were so unstable between us that we broke up within a month?"

It was her own fault. She knew that. For going along with Kimberly's dumb little assumption in the first place.

"*Why* did Kimberly even come over yesterday?" Emma muttered, shaking her head as she thought about Mr. Cuddles, now sitting on her bookshelf. "Why did you have to be awake and let her in?"

Thinking about her childhood bear made her stomach twist.

She hadn't understood at that moment that there would be any ramifications. She hadn't realized that one dumb little lie-by-omission could have such a snowball effect.

After she took a few moments to breathe in – deep breath in, slowly let it out – she looked back at Regan. Truthfully, she was shocked Regan hadn't said anything in the last thirty seconds.

It felt decidedly un-Regan.

So did the serious look on her face.

"Well, Kimberly *did* come over yesterday," Regan said, quietly. "And I was awake. And I did let her in. Because how the hell should I have known I wasn't supposed to? It's not like you gave me a list of acceptable visitors I should be on the lookout for. In fact, it's not like you voluntarily tell me anything, ever."

When Emma had muttered those words a minute ago, she hadn't actually been blaming Regan.

But Regan's uncharacteristically sharp tone made Emma feel even more defensive than she already had. It was an easily inspired feeling whenever she was around Regan already, let alone on a night like tonight.

Because – was Regan *crazy*?

Emma stared at her like she was. "Well, it's not like you've ever given me a reason to confide anything in you." Before Regan could even attempt to disagree, Emma continued, "Do you even realize that our relationship is the way it is because basically every interaction we've ever had one-on-one goes miserably wrong? Due to *you*?" She didn't even have to take a second to think before she was able to list the transgressions. "Spilling coffee all over me the literal day we really met. Followed immediately by you ripping my shirt in front of dozens of strangers–"

God, that memory still mortified her.

Regan narrowed her eyes. "I was trying to help you!"

Emma ignored that as easily as she had the day it happened. Whatever the intention was, the action had been insane.

And she had a whole laundry list more.

"I'm not even going to try to go through the last two years; I don't have to. All I have to do is recall the last few weeks. You lied about reading our roommate contract. Because of that, you sent me into anaphylactic shock. You broke my grandmother's antique porcelain hummingbirds the day I moved in. You constantly are in my business. And whenever we do spend any time together, I feel like I have to watch my back because – by your own admission – you were going to gossip about my life to your coworkers!"

When she was done, she simply stared. Waiting for Regan to attempt to refute the cold, hard facts.

Instead of the animated self-defense Emma anticipated – that she was ready for – Regan grew quiet. Quieter than Emma had ever borne witness to.

Regan crossed her own arms, withdrawing into herself in a way Emma had never seen. She cocked her head as she studied Emma closely, slowly shaking her head. "Do *you* even realize that all you just did was highlight that your bad attitude is why we've never been able to have a positive relationship?"

"*What?*" She couldn't have heard that correctly. There was no fucking way.

Regan didn't laugh, though, nor did she change her tune.

She stared at Emma, her dark eyes so... cold. Startlingly chilly.

"All I do with you is try. All I have *ever* done with you – for some stupid reason – is try. Especially since you moved in. And yeah, sometimes I mess up, or things don't go according to plan–"

"Sometimes?" She cut in because – really? *Sometimes?* Was Regan kidding her?

This time, Regan ignored her. She shook her head. "But you never try with me. You never give me the benefit of the doubt or try to see anything from my side. You decided who I was the day we met – over an *accident* – and that was it."

Regan studied Emma as if reading her for the first time, a frown etching into her face. "So, congratulations, Emma; you finally get exactly what you've wanted since you moved in. I'll stop texting you, stop trying to hang out with you. You wanted a roommate you barely have to speak to, and you finally got her. Because I am so done trying."

six

REGAN LIGHTLY DRUMMED her fingers against the polished wood arm of the chair she sat in as she looked around Opal's.

Unsurprisingly, her sister's bridal boutique was ritzy as hell; Regan had been a little nervous to sit on the chair she'd been directed toward when she'd arrived half an hour ago, wondering if it was some sort of antique that was designed for her to look but not touch.

As she heard her sister's voice talking animatedly to the same woman the had brought Regan into the showing room – Anita, a very bubbly shop assistant – she braced herself.

Regan *always* braced herself when preparing to spend time with her family. But today, after her fallout with Emma last night, she was extra antsy.

There was nothing like your roommate telling you that you were a directionless loser, only to spend the following morning with your sister, who believed the same thing. Regan was finding that she didn't have the same fire she normally summoned for her infrequent meetings with her family.

Audrey walked back into the ornate fitting room, cutting herself off mid-sentence when she laid eyes on Regan. "Regan. What are you doing here?" She asked, in her soft-spoken yet steely voice.

Regan stared back, wondering which one of them had lost their damn mind. "Um... it's the day we're getting fitted for our dresses? You told me to be here? It's on the calendar? You literally told me I better be here on time, or I was going to fuck up your entire wedding?"

Audrey opened her mouth to respond, before she seemed to remember they had company, and she turned to Anita. "Thanks so much for bringing me back; the rest of the party should be here any minute. Would you mind waiting for them?"

Her sister managed to have perfect manners and the nicest tone for everyone, it seemed, except for her. Typically, Regan would have probably commented on it. At the very least, rolled her eyes.

As it was, she simply breathed out a sigh, letting herself slump back against the chair, feeling so... lackluster. It was the only word that came to mind to describe this utter lack of energy or enjoyment in the little things right now.

Audrey turned back to face her, pursing her lips. "I know *why* you're here." She brought up her hand, rubbing her fingers over her temples, as if the very sight of Regan already stressed her out.

Normally, Regan would have taken some small satisfaction in that, given that she, too, was stressed out by Audrey. As it was, with Emma's words echoing through her mind, it just made her feel... badly.

Or *worse*, Regan supposed, given that she felt like shit already.

"But it's only nine-thirty, and the appointment is at ten. I told you that you didn't even have to be here until nine forty-five."

Regan shrugged. "And I figured I'd get here a little early. I assumed you'd be happy about it."

Mostly, Regan had *needed* to get out of the apartment. She'd left before seven, making sure to slip out before she'd see Emma getting ready for work. She'd first gone to Topped Off and baked another batch of the new recipe she'd tried out for cupcakes last night. The ones she'd wanted to share with Emma. Then she'd left as the morning shift changed over, not feeling up to conversation.

Audrey stared at Regan as though she were a little green alien, waving at her with a three-fingered hand. "You've never been this early to anything in your entire life."

Regan set her jaw, hearing Emma's words echo in her ears as she'd indirectly called Regan unorganized and irresponsible. "I've never been late to anything you've ever invited me to, either," she pointed out in her own defense.

Which was the truth.

Granted, Audrey had never invited her to anything, so there was also that. But Regan was so – so *sick* of being judged without even being given a real chance.

Her sister chewed on the inside of her lip as she stared at Regan as if she were a stranger and not someone who'd lived in the bedroom down the hall from hers for nearly eighteen years.

"Fine," Audrey finally settled on, shaking her head. "I'm not going to get into a ridiculous debate about this, today of all days."

"Great," Regan muttered, the word barely louder than a breath as she leaned back and stared up at the ceiling. "When is everyone else supposed to get here?"

"Why? Have somewhere better to be?" Her sister asked, in that *tone*. The tone she always made her way to when they talked.

Regan slid her gaze to meet Audrey's stare.

"Work," she replied shortly. "I have work after this." When Audrey lifted her eyebrows, Regan dropped a hand over her eyes. "Look, I also don't want to get into a ridiculous back and forth today, okay? Even though I'm not a high-powered public relations executive, I still have a job. Someone has to make you a coffee on your way to the office, right?"

It was as much fire as she could manage, but it seemed to do the trick. Audrey drew her lips into a tight line and turned to look at herself in one of the many dizzying full-length mirrors.

Regan wondered if her sister ever contemplated how wildly different they looked. With her long, pale blonde hair and pale green eyes, Audrey favored their mother as much as Regan favored their father's dark hair and eyes. They were as different in looks as they were in personality.

When she'd been little, Regan had wished desperately to look and be more like her sister. She vividly remembered begging her mom to dye her hair like Audrey's for her sixth birthday. But those wants had died a long time ago, when she'd realized she'd much rather be like herself – ADHD and all – than like her judgey, snobby family.

Which was why Emma's comments from last night shouldn't bother her.

Regan knew that. And Regan liked to believe that she had skin thick enough that one person's opinion of her wouldn't hold any true weight.

She'd been sworn at more times than she could count, in multiple languages – it was so beautiful, in a way, how much of a melting pot New York truly was – even had a few coffee cups thrown at her from angry customers with no sense of decency. And every time that happened, she'd walked away with an unmarred sense of self and a funny story.

Yet, here she was. In an undeniable funk ever since last night. When Emma had torn Regan apart in less than ten minutes. The worst part was that Emma hadn't even intended to be rude when she'd called Regan dumb, unorganized, irresponsible, and ambitionless.

Nope, she'd stated it so casually. As if she and Regan were both on the same page about those facts. As if they *were* just those – facts.

If Regan was being honest with herself, the fact that Audrey's dress fitting was this morning exacerbated everything. She was already on edge leading up to today, as she always was with Audrey, and to have Emma tell her that she thought of Regan the same way Regan's family did... it did hurt her feelings. A lot.

"So, how's your life with *Sutton?*" Audrey asked, using the same shitty tone she always used when she said Sutton's name.

Regan was almost grateful to be pulled out of her depressing thoughts. Almost. She scowled at the way Audrey referred to her best friend.

"It's fine," she answered. "I mean, Sutton's in Rome. But it's fine." She traced her index finger over one of the little golden lines that was imprinted into the wood of the armrest as she spoke.

"On a vacation with her congresswoman girlfriend, then?" Audrey pressed in that same voice.

Regan did a double-take at her sister's reflection, wondering how she'd even known about that. Since when did Audrey take any interest in Regan's life, of which Sutton was an extension? Audrey wasn't looking at her and was instead re-applying her already perfect lipstick. Regan hadn't even realized she'd broken out her cosmetics.

Then again, Regan reasoned with herself, Charlotte's coming out had been a fairly public moment. "Uh, no. She's been there for about two months; she's doing an internship, so she's going to be there for a while. Until the end of the year."

God, that felt like forever right about now. Regan's stomach was twisting with knots at the idea of going home to Emma, and they still had another five and a half months to go.

"Without you?" Audrey scoffed out a laugh, shaking her head as if she'd said something incredibly amusing, as she popped the cap back onto her lipstick.

Regan pulled a face at her sister's back. "Obviously, *without me*." She tapped her fingers against the armrest again, biting at the inside of her cheek. Waiting.

Waiting for whatever smart remark would come next, certain one was coming. When it came to her family, it always was.

Several moments beat by in quiet as Audrey rifled through the designer bag she had sitting on the chair next to her. When she did speak, that *tone* was gone. "Huh. And how's *that* going?"

Regan nearly fell out of her seat – literally, she gripped both armrests just in case – from the shocked confusion that rushed through her. Audrey asking her a follow-up question? About her *life*?!

Suspicion edged in, and Regan narrowed her eyes. "How's *what* going?"

"Not being attached at the hip with Sutton Spencer," Audrey clarified, scoffing slightly again.

Really, was Regan dreaming? Had she tripped on the way here and fallen into an alternate universe? Was Audrey actually asking how it was going? Or was she being bitchy?

When she remained silent, Audrey pressed, "Well?"

"Well, what?" She asked, feeling unbelievably dumb.

"I asked you a question..."

"I wasn't sure you really wanted an answer."

Audrey turned to look at her, one of her perfectly shaped eyebrows lifted. "Why would I ask a question and not expect an answer?"

"Because... you never ask me questions about my life?" Regan pointed out, her bafflement growing. What the *hell* was going on here?

When was Audrey going to pull out the rug and make a comment on Regan being Sutton's leech? Granted, that was their mom's preferred comment, but Audrey wouldn't be her sister if she didn't stand behind everything their parents preached.

"I'm your sister, Regan. I have some modicum of interest in your comings and goings." Her voice was sharp again. Sharp enough that it gave Regan some semblance of normalcy, even if her actual words didn't.

"Since *when?*" The words slipped out incredulously. She couldn't have stopped them if she tried. "You've never had any interest in my comings and goings! We don't even text."

"Because when I text you, I inevitably receive either a snarky response or that insipid thumbs-up emoji!"

Okay, here was the Audrey Regan knew. "Because you're always being judgmental and rude!"

She had the text thread to prove it, and she was about to grab her phone from her pocket to do just that when they heard Anita approaching.

"Perfectly on time," Anita announced as she walked into their fitting area. "All of your bridesmaids are here."

Even though Regan wasn't thrilled about the prospect of spending any time with Audrey's social cohorts, she found herself intensely relieved.

"Regan! Those cupcakes you made have already sold out!" Beth called to her as she diligently cleaned the display case full of their baked goods. "I can't believe you came in this morning to bake them, especially because you weren't scheduled to come in until noon?"

Regan glanced over to confirm that the cupcakes she'd made were, indeed, all gone.

"Yeah, I decided to come in early and get it done since everyone seemed to like the recipe so much last night," Regan answered, summoning as much enthusiasm as she could.

It wasn't much after the combination of her fight with Emma and her morning at Opal's.

But Beth accepted her words without a question. "I mean, it was a good call. I was just hoping there would be enough to grab another one before I head home later. My bad, though. I should have set one aside."

Regan normally would have teased Beth – *you've worked here for over a year now and haven't learned the basics of setting aside desserts from the afternoon stoner crowd?*

But she found she didn't really have it in her at the moment.

"Yeah," was all she said back before dropping her chin back into her hand with a sigh.

She half-heartedly wiped the counter space next to the cash register down with the cloth in her free hand, even though it was unnecessary, as she kept her workspace immaculate. Would she continue to garner as many tips as possible and enough positive comments from her regulars to maintain her *employee of the month* status for the twentieth time with a countertop full of crumbs and coffee stains?

Successful barista life meant never resting on her laurels.

She sighed again, mindlessly swiping the cloth over the counter, staring blankly down at the stainless steel as she did so.

"I'll take a large iced coffee, dark roast," a quiet yet commanding voice ordered. It was a voice that, though low in volume, cut through the general din of the café, demanding attention.

It was a voice Regan recognized.

She looked up from the countertop, where she'd apparently been so lost in her thoughts that she hadn't even registered the door to the café opening. And she looked right into Charlotte Thompson's honey brown eyes.

"Oh! Hey," she greeted, her lips quirking into the slightest of smiles. She automatically punched in Charlotte's order – same as she always ordered. Plain, no frills.

"Hey," Charlotte echoed, her eyebrows lifting slightly as she paid with her credit card.

Regan turned away from facing Charlotte, scooping ice into the cup before moving to the brewer. "So... how are you doing? How's life as a congresswoman?"

As she capped the coffee cup, she decided that she appreciated Charlotte getting a very simple order. Regan could tell a lot about someone from their coffee order, and Charlotte's was very straightforward. Strong and direct. Really, it was the first clue that she could potentially trust this woman with her best friend's heart.

Granted, it had been a long road with some bumps along the way before Regan had *fully* trusted that. But if Charlotte's coffee order had required more than two pumps of anything, Regan would have had to question her character.

Still, Regan typically gave Charlotte a little shit for never trying anything else or spicing up her order. She viewed it as part of their banter.

But today, she wasn't in the mood for jesting. Instead, she simply slid Charlotte's coffee across the counter.

"Busy. But good," Charlotte answered as she accepted her drink. "I just got back from two weeks in D.C."

Regan nodded. "Yeah, Sutton mentioned that in a text. That's cool."

"Yes, it is," Charlotte murmured, tapping her well-manicured fingertips against the top of her coffee lid as she stared at Regan with a measuring gaze.

Regan stared back, confused.

"Is that all?" Charlotte pressed. "You don't have any other commentaries or questions regarding my trip or my relationship? All you have to say is... cool?"

Her disbelief was blatant.

Which was fair, Regan could admit that. She would probably have a lot more to say any other day. Some teasing comments about Charlotte being a simp for Sutton, asking if she could still feel Sutton's love from Rome down in D.C., maybe. Asking how her first trip as an officially elected member of congress had gone. Had she witnessed anyone trying to steal the Declaration of Independence? The normal stuff.

Right now, Regan merely shrugged. "Yeah. It's cool."

Both of Charlotte's eyebrows lifted high onto her forehead. "All right."

Regan dropped her head back in her hand with another sigh,

watching out of her peripherals as Charlotte grabbed a straw at the station a few feet away.

She anticipated Charlotte would leave, which she normally did. Since she'd become a regular at Topped Off, she'd stop in a couple of times a week and grab a coffee but never linger.

This time, though, rather than strutting toward the door, she paused and gave Regan a look over her shoulder.

"All right," she repeated her words from a minute ago, rolling her shoulders back. This time, the words weren't a question but a statement. "I can't in good conscience leave this café until you've told me what is wrong. Sutton would never forgive me."

"Eh, she would." Regan waved her hand in the air. "She thinks you're basically perfect and knows you have a busy schedule."

Charlotte's eyes widened, concern etching over her features. Regan decided it was an interesting look because she didn't think she'd ever seen it before. Not directed at her, anyway. "Well, *that* deflection makes me even more certain this is a dire situation."

Charlotte's lips pursed as she cleared her throat and called out, "Beth?"

Beth, who just finished cleaning out the display case at the other end of the counter, looked up in obvious surprise at being addressed. Or, perhaps, surprised at being addressed *by Charlotte*. "Uh, me? Me-Beth?"

"I wasn't aware another was working here," Charlotte said with a charming smile. "It doesn't seem to be busy here at the moment. Would you mind very much if I borrowed Regan for a few minutes?"

Beth's eyebrows lifted even higher as she swung her gaze from Charlotte to Regan, then back. "Uh..." She focused on Regan, eyes wide and clearly asking for permission.

Which Regan granted with a shrug.

"Sure," Beth promptly answered, and it was very clear she was thrilled to be giving Charlotte the answer Charlotte wanted to hear. "It's the afternoon lull, so it should be fine."

"Wonderful." Charlotte turned her determined gaze back to Regan, tilting her head toward the nearest table. Though the motion was subtle, the unspoken order was crystal clear.

Regan had to wonder if Charlotte's elegant imperialism was something she was born with or had learned to master. Regardless, she followed her, pulling out a seat and plunking down into it.

Charlotte mirrored her with far more grace. She checked her watch on the inside of her wrist before shaking her hair back and looking directly across the table at Regan. "I have approximately twelve minutes I can spare before I'm egregiously late. I'd prefer if I didn't have to spend much more of it prying information out of you, but–"

Regan splayed her hands on the table, leaning forward as the words tumbled out of her. "Last night, Emma came home and told me everything she actually thinks about me, and none of it was good. Actually, it was all really bad. Like. Stupid and immature; she'd be embarrassed to even introduce me to her grandmother."

Charlotte's mouth snapped shut as she stared at Regan for several seconds. "Huh. That took far less than I'd anticipated, given your obviously glum state."

Leaning back with a shrug, Regan answered honestly, "I like to talk about my problems. If you're asking, I'm going to tell you."

Regan was far from a closed book and wasn't above demonstrating that. The reality was Regan didn't do well when silently stewing on something. In fact, she hated it.

So, even though *Charlotte Thompson* was an unexpected ear to open up to, Regan would take what she had. Right now, her options were limited.

"Plus, you have this... quality," Regan muttered, tilting her head to the side as she narrowed her eyes at Charlotte. "I kinda *want* to talk to you. How do you do that?" She demanded.

A small smile tugged at one side of Charlotte's mouth, even as she lifted her eyebrows. "It's a practiced skill."

Ah. Well, that answered several of Regan's questions about Stunning Charlotte.

"Can you teach me how to do it?" She asked curiously.

Especially right now. Maybe, if she could pry the truth from people in the easy way Charlotte could, she would never end up in situations like this one with Emma. Maybe she would have known *years ago* that Emma would never be able to see past their misunderstandings.

Charlotte's eyebrows raised even higher, the smile slowly dropping from her face. "I'm afraid it's not something I have a lesson plan for. I'm also afraid you're a little more forthright, where this requires a decent bit of subtlety."

She slowly nodded; that was fair feedback.

"Anyway," Charlotte crossed her legs, the look on her face all business as she re-focused her attention. "Did Emma say those exact words to you?"

Regan's lips twisted as she thought back to the night before. "No, not all of them," she admitted, quickly shrugging it off. "But it wasn't a hard leap to make."

Charlotte studied her intently. "I may be mistaken here, as I know I haven't spent much time with both you and Emma together. But from what I know, the news that Emma isn't your biggest fan isn't actually *news*. Correct?"

"Well, when you put it like that, it makes me feel a little stupid," Regan muttered because she really *did* feel a little stupid after Charlotte's comment.

Because, no, nothing Emma said should feel like it came out of nowhere. Emma had never once, in two years, made a friendly overture toward Regan. And yet...

"The thing is, I never believed she had such a low opinion of me," Regan explained, frowning. "I thought – I don't know. I mean, I knew that we were always on the wrong footing. But I never thought Emma believed I was such an inconsequential fuck up."

Saying it aloud demoralized her again, the words twisting her stomach painfully. She was glad she hadn't fixed herself a coffee because it would have been an absolute waste; she couldn't stomach anything right now.

"It's interesting," Charlotte's voice was low and thoughtful. "I never pegged you as a person that would care so much about what someone would think. Especially someone they aren't friends with."

Regan frowned even deeper, her stomach tying up in bigger, tighter knots. "I guess the humiliating thing is that I considered Emma to be friend-adjacent? Like. I know we weren't *friends*. I would never text her to go out for a drink or anything like that. But I'd always assumed we both had a baseline level of respect for one another? At this point, we've been in the same social circle for a couple of years, so..."

She trailed off, hunching in on herself.

That was the truth. There had been moments over the last couple of years where she and Emma had been out with Sutton, and they'd both laugh at the same comment that no one else found funny. Or they'd make eye contact and roll their eyes at something stupid. Regan didn't believe that made them *friends*, but she'd thought it made them... something.

What was more than that – what ate at her even more deeply – was what she wasn't telling Charlotte. What she couldn't tell Charlotte was that, even as an open book, there were certain chapters that she didn't allow anyone to read, and they all revolved around her family. Emma had unknowingly picked at a scab Regan had been carrying her entire life.

"Does Sutton know about this?" Charlotte asked, regaining Regan's attention.

Quickly, Regan shook her head. "No, she does not."

"I thought so," Charlotte quietly mused. "I believe this is something she'd want to know."

"No!" Regan quickly sat up, vehemently shaking her head as the ardent disagreement with that assessment flowed through her. "Look – Sutton is in Rome, working ten-hour days at this internship, and it's the first thing she's doing in her life that's entirely for herself. Okay? There's nothing she can do about this situation other than stress and wonder if she never should have left in the first place. I *don't* want that."

Which had been the reason Regan hadn't done what her instincts had been screaming at her to do – which was to turn to Sutton for comfort in the first place. She hadn't wanted to hang out with her coworkers last night after the fallout with Emma; she'd wanted to curl up in her bed and talk to her best friend, the one person who would understand why Emma's words cut so deeply.

But she couldn't do that. Because it was the middle of the night in Rome and Sutton was asleep, first and foremost. And Regan... she didn't want to be that person to Sutton. The person who held her back in any way.

She fixed Charlotte with a serious look, hoping that Charlotte could see that Regan meant business. "You aren't going to tell her about this, either. I'm confiding in *you* right now because you asked. If you go and tell Sutton, you'll be breaking girlfriend-of-best-friend code."

"Girlfriend-of-best-friend code," Charlotte drawled incredulously. "Now, why do I get the feeling you've just made that up?"

"No clue," Regan shot back. "Because it's totally real and super valid. Listen, keeping my confidence is a good thing. It proves you have stand-up character and that you *aren't* simply talking to me and offering me council to curry good favor with Sutton."

She arched a challenging eyebrow at Charlotte, knowing she had her.

Charlotte released a sigh seconds later, holding her hands up in a sign of defeat. "You obviously don't need me to teach you my methods of persuasion," she said dryly.

Regan grinned, bright and victorious. The burst of positivity felt so good, she soaked it up for the first time all day.

For several moments, Charlotte silently regarded her with a critical stare. Finally, she shrugged. "Fine. I will keep this between you and me – but if Sutton asks me if anything is wrong with you, I will not lie to her."

"I find these terms acceptable," Regan readily agreed.

After all, she wouldn't want her best friend to be dating someone that would lie to her.

"Furthermore, regarding your quandary with Emma..." Charlotte hummed under her breath. "I'll tell you a valuable piece of information my grandmother told me very early in my career."

Regan perked up, leaning in. "Advice straight from the horse's mouth?!"

Charlotte shot her a dour look. "You'd do well not to refer to my grandmother as a *horse*."

Regan *pfft*'d. "You know what I meant."

"Even so." Charlotte affixed her with a stern look – one Regan was unintimidated by – before she continued, "In my chosen aspiration, I've put myself in the line of fire for public opinion in spades. And people will *always* have an opinion."

All right, Regan was following what she was saying. Charlotte had publicly come out only a few months ago while running for Congress, so... yeah. Even if Regan hadn't read many of the comments about Charlotte on social media, she was aware that many people had something to say about her life choices.

"The trick to never letting that get to you is knowing that if someone doesn't truly know you, ninety-nine percent of the time? Their opinion says far more about *them* than it does about you. Or, in the words of my grandmother: judgments made in ignorance are better left ignored."

Slowly, Regan leaned back against the chair, letting the words take root in her mind.

It didn't make her feel better about what Emma said; her feelings were still hurt.

But she had to admit, the perspective *did* help shift her mindset a little bit.

She met Charlotte's gaze. "You know, I'm really glad you came in today."

"I suppose I am, as well. It's a good thing you make such a good cup of coffee," Charlotte acknowledged, toasting Regan as she held her cup up. "Or else I likely would never have returned after my first stop here."

"Oh, your first stop here when you stalked Jack Spencer?" Regan challenged, grinning with the words. It felt *so good* to finally not feel like she was in such a funk.

Charlotte's eyebrows furrowed as she narrowed her eyes over the lid of her coffee cup. She didn't hurry her sip along, though. Instead, she moved at her same, steady pace, leisurely lowering the cup as she cleared her throat. "I wouldn't quite call it stalking."

"What *would* you call it, then? When you find out a man's schedule and rush through the city to coincidentally run into him?"

"Wise business strategy," Charlotte answered simply. "Also, you and Sutton share far too much."

Regan gasped, placing a hand over her heart in offense. "That is simply not possible." She waved her hand as if wiping away that assertion. "Anyway, I think you would have returned after that even if my coffee was shit."

Charlotte stared back at her, pointedly arching an eyebrow at her. "You believe I would have returned to your coffee shop – twenty minutes out of the way of my typical commute – if your coffee was shit?" She echoed Regan's words with a deliberate slowness, obviously designed to make Regan doubt her own sanity. "Why, exactly, is that?"

She tapped on the table, giving herself a little drumroll, before she answered, "Because! You wanted to get into the beautifully high-waisted pants of one glorious creature by the name of Sutton Spencer. Who frequents this very coffee shop. Because, along with having the best coffee in the city, her best friend works here."

Regan pointed to herself with both thumbs triumphantly.

Charlotte chuckled, filled with both exasperation and amusement – Regan was familiar with the sound. "On that note, I think I've over-extended my break for the afternoon."

As Charlotte stood, Regan followed suit. Before Charlotte could leave, she reached out to touch her wrist and stop her. "Thanks for this," she said, seriously. "It really means a lot to me."

A small grin pulled at Charlotte's mouth as she tilted her head in acknowledgment. "What else is the girlfriend-of-your-best-friend for?"

"I've never been so glad that I helped you two get together – twice – than I am now."

Regan returned home that night with a sense of comfort from Charlotte/Elizabeth's sage wisdom.

She held on to it tightly and stumbled to a surprised stop when she found Emma sitting in the living room. "Weird seeing you sitting out here," she couldn't help but comment.

But it was the truth. Because Emma seemed to conveniently never hang out in their common spaces when Regan's schedule informed Emma that she would be home.

Emma offered her a tentative smile. "I mean, you were gone really early this morning, so."

Confused, Regan asked, "... So? I assumed you'd be happy about my absence."

That small smile fell from Emma's face completely. "Listen—"

Regan cut her off, determined to not be dragged back into the headspace she'd been in pre-Charlotte. "If you're going to make an apology to me that you obviously don't mean, then I don't want to hear it."

It went against *everything* inside of her to not try to hear Emma out, but she powered on, knowing she was doing the right thing for self-protection.

"Before I go to my room, I'm going to tell you the hard truth this time, okay?"

Emma's expression was very clearly dubious, but she nodded nonetheless.

Regan took a deep breath, staring Emma right in the eye. "Have you ever considered that the way you react to me isn't really *about me*? Like. Fine. I get it; I can be really chatty, and sometimes I act before I think, and sometimes I do the wrong thing. But – the stupid thing is? When push came to shove, I always would have had your back. And I thought you'd have had mine. Why, exactly, does it bother you so much that I'm not getting a graduate degree or pursuing a *serious career*? My ambitions, organization, and whatever else are none of your concern. I think those are *you* problems, Emma. Because they aren't mine."

As Emma blinked at her in surprise, Regan drew her shoulders back with a sense of pride.

Huh.

That felt pretty good. Good enough to spur her to dig into her bag, where she'd stashed the package that had arrived yesterday.

"Here." She tossed it, still in the bubble wrap, to Emma. "The *surprise* I'd wanted to give you."

With that, she turned and headed for her room.

seven

I ALWAYS WOULD HAVE HAD your back. And I thought you'd have mine.

I think those are you problems, Emma.

Regan's words continued to ring in Emma's ears days after she'd said them. They haunted her to the point of distraction.

After Regan had thrown that *ridiculous* accusation at her, she'd strutted right past where Emma had sat and smartly shut her bedroom door behind her. As if to say *case closed*.

The kicker of it all was that Emma had been waiting for Regan to discuss their... issue. While she hadn't been willing to apologize for what she'd said, she *had* been willing to apologize for how Regan had taken it.

However, her reaction after Regan's spiel the other night had changed everything.

First, she'd been annoyed all over again – now Regan was telling Emma what her problems were? She was telling Emma that her very legitimate issues with Regan *weren't* legitimate? Where the hell did she get off?!

And she'd intended to say as much to Regan!

Only, as the days passed, Emma was finding that Regan could maintain boundaries – as long as those boundaries meant sticking to her word about ignoring Emma.

Which *shouldn't* bother her! That was, perhaps, the most aggravating thing of all.

Every time Regan walked past her, or they ran into one another in their apartment, Emma was filled with an anticipation she couldn't quite understand. This *waiting* period for Regan to say or do something... Regan-like was terrible.

It was like walking on eggshells; somehow, Emma was finding that it made their living arrangement even worse.

At least, she told herself, she used to know what to expect from Regan. Annoyed or pestered as she was, she knew what was waiting for her when she got home. There was a sense of regularity and familiarity.

Now, who knew?!

If someone had asked Emma a week ago if she believed she'd prefer to live in a situation where Regan didn't attempt to connect with her, she would have agreed the affirmative without a second thought.

It turned out – annoyingly – that was an incorrect assumption.

And Emma hated being incorrect.

How was it that Emma had moved into an apartment with three total strangers that she barely spoke to for years, and it was a less awkward living situation than what she was currently experiencing? *How?*

Really, she wanted the universe to answer her.

Because, quite frankly, it wasn't fair.

That was the conclusion Emma had reached over the last few days as she'd cycled through her feelings.

It wasn't fair that she'd voiced her honest opinion about Regan – literally citing wrongdoings Regan had committed against her – only for *her* to end up feeling this gnawing sense of guilt afterward. Only to end up with every interaction filled with loud, unnatural silences.

Emma hadn't done anything wrong!

And yet, she was left feeling like she'd kicked a puppy. Unsure and careful in the aftermath.

This gnawing, shameful feeling had only gotten worse in the last few days.

Especially because she'd given in and opened the *surprise* Regan had tossed to her. Inside had been two small, delicate, beautifully ornate painted hummingbird figurines, carefully packaged in bubble wrap. Along with a note that Regan had clearly slid into the packaging after they'd been delivered –

I know these aren't the same ones I accidentally broke when you moved in, but they were the cutest ones I could find for a replacement. They're from a little shop in Alaska, isn't that cool! They custom-make every order, which is why these took a little while to come in.

I've decided to name them Thomasina (Thom) and Geri - the female Tom and Jerry, if you will. I think they're very representative of you and me.

(obviously, you're Tom)

Your favorite roommate, even though you can't admit it (yet),

Regan

And, fine. Regan replacing the hummingbirds that she broke was... sweet. Unsurprisingly sweet. But – she was only replacing them because she broke them in the first place!

She'd tried to thank Regan two days ago, only to be given a dismissive smile in response.

Everything about this situation was ridiculous and annoying, and, most bizarrely of all, it was starting to distract her at work.

Every time her phone buzzed and alerted her to a text message, as it just had, Emma felt compelled to check it right away.

Was it Regan? Was she going to be the one to break? Was she *finally* going to give Emma back some semblance of normalcy and ask if Emma wanted to do pedicures or have a movie night or something?

But Emma didn't even *want* to do those things! So, why was she anticipating the texts?

It was starting to make her feel crazy. Absolutely, entirely out of her mind.

Because, as Regan had promised, she was giving Emma exactly what she'd asked for multiple times. She was acting as a roommate and nothing more.

Her phone buzzed again in her desk drawer, and Emma – who had been diligently reading through the portfolios for the Alton Fellowship, because she only had a couple of weeks to weed through literal thousands of applicants – couldn't help how her hand twitched to check it.

Even though she resolutely never checked her personal texts when she was busy at work. Never.

"Oh my *god*, just answer it. Please," Brynn's exasperated encouragement reached Emma from a few feet away, where she sat at her own desk. "Please, answer it."

Emma felt herself blush – annoying – and she cleared her throat. "What?"

Brynn rolled her eyes but kept her voice hushed as they were both aware of Allegra's open office door. "Your phone."

"How can you hear it? It's on silent." Emma could barely hear when it vibrated, and she was right next to it.

"I *can't*," Brynn stressed, throwing her hands into the air. "But every single time you've gotten a text in the last few days, you lift your hand over the drawer your phone is in." Brynn mimicked Emma's hand, freezing it before she could open it the drawer. "And then you hesitate like this." She stared, with exaggerated intent, at the drawer. "Like, is this some sort of situation where someone offered you ten million dollars, but only if you press the button to kill someone, and that button is on your phone?"

Emma was not going to dignify that with a response. Instead, she dropped her hand into her lap, away from where it had been hovering next to the drawer handle. Caught.

Closing her eyes tightly, she debated whether to say anything, but the need to talk about the situation won out.

Quickly, she looked at Allegra through the glass wall and noted that she didn't seem perturbed by their quiet conversation.

She might as well go for it, she supposed. "I'm having some trouble with my–"

"Girlfriend," Brynn cut in, nodding sagely and looking remarkably more interested. "Go on."

Emma reeled back, shaking her head. "Uh, no. No, no."

Brynn leaned back, clearly surprised. "Really? I thought I got that sapphic vibe from you."

"I mean, yes, I date women." Not so much recently, but Emma had never discussed her dating life at work, and she sure as hell wasn't going to start now. "But – no. This is about my roommate." She couldn't help but frown as she questioned, "God, why does *everyone* assume that when Regan comes up?"

"Because," Brynn gestured to Emma's face with the pen she held in her hand. "That whole demeanor you have going on, all bothered under the collar and whatnot, doesn't read as *just a roommate* problems. Regardless, you have my attention."

"Yes, do go on," Allegra's clear, cutting tone startled them as she stood in her doorway, arms crossed.

Despite the glass walls, Emma had no idea when Allegra had stood and walked over toward them. Judging by Brynn's wide-eyed expression, she hadn't noticed, either.

Even more mortified than before, Emma wanted to shrink back into her seat and cover her face with her hands. She *didn't*, but only because a sense of self-preservation kept her sitting with perfect posture.

"I'm sorry, Allegra," she apologized, grateful her voice came out louder than a whisper. "I'll get back to work."

"Why stop on my account? You didn't seem to have reservations a moment ago when I could still hear you, only from several feet farther away."

Unsure of what her boss was getting at – was she being uncharacteristically sarcastic? Typically, Allegra was very direct – Emma couldn't help but squirm in her seat.

Allegra arched an eyebrow, dark gaze boring into her. "Well? Brynn and I are waiting for the conclusion to the conundrum that has had you distracted all week."

Emma wanted to *murder* Regan for being the root cause of this.

106

As her stomach tied in uncertain knots, she realized that *was* the root of her issue.

"Ah... right," Emma slowly began, darting her gaze to Brynn to check that she was reading the situation correctly and that Allegra genuinely wanted her to continue. Brynn, unhelpfully, looked just as unsure as Emma. "Well, my roommate and I have never really gotten along. Strictly speaking."

Allegra nodded, waving her on.

"Then why did you move in together in the first place?" Brynn cut in before she widened her eyes at Allegra. "Sorry to prolong the story. Emma told me she'd just moved in with this new roommate a few weeks ago."

"No, context is important. Do tell," Allegra... ordered?

Order or not, Emma felt compelled to answer, "We have a friend in common." It was the easiest, simplest explanation. "She's on a prolonged internship, and I didn't love my living situation, before."

"So, you asked to move in with your current roommate," Allegra asserted.

"No, actually. *She* asked *me* to move in," Emma corrected. "Because... well, because she knew how much I didn't enjoy my previous living arrangement."

As she finished the statement, she spoke slowly, as if hearing the words for the first time.

But – it was the truth.

Regan didn't *have* to ask Emma to move in while Sutton was away. Their apartment, in their neighborhood? She could have gotten a ton of applicants who would have paid far more than Emma was.

"And the problem is?" Allegra's exacting voice cut into her thoughts.

Emma blinked at her boss as her stomach sank even lower than it had already been.

"The problem is that I think I might have been the cause of several of our issues in ways I hadn't thought of before. Which means," she had to pause, accepting the truth as she was being faced with saying it aloud, "That I might have been wrong about *her*, too. And I was made aware of it because we had a–"

"Brawl," Brynn supplied, "Emotionally, anyway, given I see no bruises on your person."

"An altercation," Emma corrected, shooting Brynn a *what the fuck* look. "In which I think I finally crossed a line with her."

"I see. And now, she's making your living situation untenable?" Allegra asked.

Emma started to nod before she caught herself. "Not really. Not in a technical sense."

Because Regan *hadn't* attempted to make Emma leave the apartment or anything like that.

No. What was becoming distressingly uncomfortable, she realized at this very moment, was that living with this – this *pod person* version of Regan was starting to feel untenable.

"You have a simple solution, Emma," Allegra stated, pushing herself away from the doorway. "You have a journalism degree and want to pursue publishing as a career, correct?"

Skeptical as to how they correlated, Emma nodded in agreement.

"As such, you shouldn't be afraid of the truth. And pursuing the truth may often mean facing facts you're uncomfortable with – including facts such as realizing you were wrong." Allegra nodded once, firmly, as if she'd given Emma the keys to the kingdom. "What you do with truths once you face them, well, *that* is where the world gets interesting, isn't it?"

Maybe she *had* given Emma the keys.

"Now that we've worked through your problem – undoubtedly faster as a trio – I think you can decide what to do with your newfound truth *after* work, no?" Allegra lifted her eyebrows as she gave Emma and Brynn a look before turning to walk to her desk.

Emma would never let it be said that Allegra wasn't exceedingly fair. Or exceedingly correct.

Upon returning to the apartment, she knew that Regan wasn't scheduled to get home for another couple of hours.

She also knew that it was time to call in the big guns.

Because Allegra was right; it was time for Emma to figure out what to do post Regan's bombshells earlier this week.

Taking a deep breath as nerves tangled in her stomach, she sat on the side of her bed.

And called Sutton.

Emma eyed the time as the call started to ring; it would be a little after midnight in Rome. But it was also a Friday, so she was hoping Sutton might still be awake and up for a chat.

She was proven correct only seconds later, as Sutton picked up, "Emma! It's great to get a call from you!"

Emma sighed, taking some comfort in Sutton's genuine warmth. It was a quality Sutton had – this kindness to her that she'd always found so appealing. "Hey. Yeah, I'm sorry it's so late. I just got home from work."

"It's completely fine; I have a video date with Charlotte in half an hour, so I was still awake." Emma found the sweet, undeniable excitement in her voice even more comforting for some reason.

"That's great. I'm glad you two figured out a system." She meant that. Though she'd been skeptical of Charlotte's intentions, she was slowly coming around to her. After all, it had been Emma's couch Sutton had sought refuge on when Charlotte had broken her heart earlier this year. Emma wouldn't say she had many *protective* instincts, but she'd certainly felt protective when Sutton had shown up on her doorstep, looking utterly wrecked. "How is everything over there? I got your text the other day with the pictures of the first edition library."

The wonder mixed with envy in her tone was unavoidable. Because it was precisely what she felt every time Sutton shared her experience through pictures or social media posts. A raw desire to share in that experience, herself, and amazement for Sutton being able to be there.

Sutton laughed, sounding utterly exhilarated. "It's *beautiful*. I mean – the hours are nuts, and there are so many rules to follow, but it's... well, you know from our texts."

"Yeah." Despite the envy she felt, she found herself smiling slightly, as she often did with Sutton. Seeing Sutton, one of the only people Emma counted as a true friend, thriving was deeply satisfying, no matter what.

"I'm always happy to hear from you," Sutton started, her tone cautious. "But... you don't usually call, especially without texting first. Which – it's one hundred percent fine for you to do!" She was quick to assure – typical Sutton. "I just can't help but wonder if everything's okay?"

Ah, and there it was. Somehow, Sutton could be both incredibly obtuse and perceptive, depending on the situation. In this situation, it seemed perceptive won out.

Even though this was the entire reason Emma had called, she was hesitant. Unable to voice anything about Regan.

Because if there was one thing she knew to be certain about Sutton Spencer, it was that she deeply loved Regan Gallagher.

Something told Emma that while Sutton was casually dismissive/exasperated by her and Regan's usual bickering, she wasn't going to be pleased with Emma truly hurting Regan's feelings. And she found that she didn't want Sutton to be upset with her.

Something in her silence seemed to alarm Sutton. She took a sharp breath, all hint of light-heartedness falling away as she asked, "Is Regan okay?"

Emma pulled the phone away from her ear, staring at it incredulously. There was no way Sutton had heard her thoughts, right?

Or – more likely – Regan had already informed Sutton that this situation wasn't going well, and Sutton was asking this as a way to get Emma talking.

Before she could explain herself, Sutton was speaking again, her words tumbling quickly out of her mouth. "God, I've just been so busy this week, so I haven't even had time to think about it, but she hasn't called me in days! Not since last weekend. Emma, is she okay?" Sutton repeated, even more concerned than she'd been a minute ago.

Regan hadn't even called Sutton this week?! Fuck, if Emma needed further confirmation that she'd well and truly hurt Regan, there it was.

And, as she let out a defeated breath, she slumped in her bed. It did *not* feel good. Kicked puppy, to the max.

Still, "She's fine," she assured. Before doubt edged in, and she bit her bottom lip. "Physically, that is."

Sutton's worry clearly receded, "Whew. Okay. Good." There was only a moment's pause before she followed up. "Wait. *Physically?*"

Emma winced. "Yeah..."

Even though everything inside her did not want to tell Sutton what had played out between them, she did. She left out the fake dating part because she hadn't been exaggerating to Regan when she'd said the fewer people that knew about that humiliating lie, the better.

After relaying the events from earlier this week, she waited with her stomach tied in nerves.

For several beats, Sutton was quiet, and it was far from a companionable silence.

"I see." Was all Sutton said when she did speak.

Even though it was literally only two syllables, Emma realized that was all she needed to hear Sutton's anger. Because Sutton was not quick to anger – in fact, she wasn't sure she'd ever seen or heard Sutton truly *mad*.

It was even more jarring when she realized Sutton's newfound anger was directed at *her*. "I didn't mean it the way she took it," she defended, feeling unbelievably lame.

Sutton was quiet for several more beats before she drew in a long breath and then let it slowly out. "I believe you wouldn't intentionally be so mean," she allowed, and Emma was so grateful that the heat in her tone had cooled.

"But... Emma, Regan is my best friend," Sutton stated, her voice low and serious.

"I know," Emma agreed in confusion. Of course she knew that, though. Everyone with eyes knew that.

"Regan is my best friend," Sutton repeated intently. "I want you to think about that for a second. Because I know she can be... a lot," she settled on. "But, if you respect and trust me, I hope you understand that I would have never been Regan's best friend for two decades if she wasn't a good person. Maybe even the *best* person."

All right, Emma most definitely wasn't going to agree that Regan was *the best person* she knew, but that didn't mean that Sutton's words weren't twisting the knife in her stomach even deeper.

Ugh. Because somewhere inside, even when she was incredibly annoyed at Regan, she knew that Sutton was speaking the truth.

"I know," she quietly admitted.

And maybe that was why she'd been feeling so terrible, she realized, feeling that weight bearing down on her.

Because while she *had* been telling the truth and merely stating the facts about their interactions from her perspective the other night, she knew that Regan wasn't wrong. She'd known if she was forced to admit it to herself, that very night after Regan had quietly leveled with her, that she'd been so focused on her own tunnel vision, she'd deliberately never looked at anything from Regan's point of view.

Deep down, she *knew* Regan was never intentionally causing her harm.

She knew that Regan hadn't meant to spill the coffee on her the first time they'd met. She knew Regan hadn't intentionally broken her grandmother's hummingbirds. She definitely knew that Regan hadn't meant to send her to the hospital with her almond flour.

Regan was, at her core, someone who constantly *tried*. Just like she'd said. Every time something went disastrously wrong between them, it was because Regan was trying to do something kind. Trying to make her dinner, trying to help her move. Trying to "save Emma from third-degree burns" or whatever Regan had thought was happening with the coffee.

And now... now that Regan was actively refusing to let Emma smooth things over and move on, she'd had to spend days reckoning with the ugly truth that Regan was right.

Emma never gave Regan the benefit of the doubt. She never tried with her.

And, most distressingly, she found that she didn't want to be that person.

"*Please* believe me when I tell you – I've been trying to figure out how to make it up to her."

Granted, those attempts had mostly been spending time in their shared living spaces and hoping Regan would come to her and act normally. But Emma didn't know what else to do when Regan didn't seem interested in a simple apology!

"Why?" Sutton asked, surprising her.

"Why... what?"

"Why are you trying to make it up to her? Why are you trying to bring her back around when it sounds like you finally got what you wanted out of this living situation?" Sutton wasn't being mean or taunting; her tone was genuinely questioning.

Emma found, at that moment, that she didn't immediately have an answer.

"I mean, is it just because you feel guilty?" Sutton pressed. "Because, if so, you could just write Regan an apology note and go on with your day."

"I guess," she acknowledged. "Though, she doesn't seem to want an apology?"

"... So?" Sutton asked. "Emma, your entire relationship with Regan has never been based on what Regan wants. If you feel bad, and all *you* want from this situation is for her to know that you didn't mean what you said, then make the apology and move on."

Sutton's advice was sound. There was not a single incorrect component here.

And yet, Emma found that it wasn't sitting right with her. The idea was, alarmingly, very unappealing, which was why she hadn't done so already. "That doesn't feel like enough."

"But why?" Sutton pressed.

Had she taken some sort of interrogation lesson from Charlotte or something?!

"I think," she began, feeling uncharacteristically and uncomfortably nervous with the reality starting to set in. "That I regret not giving Regan a chance."

Emma's eyes opened widely in wonder and surprise at the truth of those words.

Because – yes. That was exactly it.

She regretted their fallout not *just* because she felt bad about hurting Regan's feelings. But because now that Regan wasn't making any overtures toward her, she felt like she'd made a mistake. Like she'd missed out on something.

There was a reason Sutton loved Regan so fiercely. And Regan had been offering Emma an opportunity this entire time for her to really understand why, but she'd been so determined not to take it.

And now that the olive branch was no longer available and she'd been given a swift kick in the ass out of her stubbornness, Emma *missed* it.

She bit her lip to hold back the groan. Oh, *god*, Regan was right. They were the female, real-life incarnates of Tom and Jerry. Emma, like Tom, was listless and unhappy without Jerry as a constant presence.

"All right, then," Sutton murmured. There was satisfaction in her voice, and her previous irritation at Emma was now completely – thankfully – gone.

Emma couldn't help but feel like Sutton had gotten Emma to admit something she'd already anticipated.

"Now that we've gotten somewhere, what I can tell you is this – Regan might appear to you to be shallow or superfluous. But she is actually really great at reading people. And if she believes that you're just spewing words at her and she doesn't think you're being sincere in trying to apologize, she's not going to really accept it."

Emma was already slowly nodding in acceptance before Sutton had finished speaking. She supposed that was what Regan had said the other night – not that she didn't want an apology, but that she didn't want an empty one.

"All right," she quietly mused. "Thanks for the chat. And – I'm going to fix it," she asserted.

If there was one thing Emma was great at, it was completing an assigned task. And this was now at the top of her list.

She had to be genuine. She had to *try*.

Emma refused to let nerves get the better of her, so she stood her ground in the living room as she heard Regan open the front door.

Though, the idea of slipping the note she'd written to accompany this apology under Regan's door felt more and more appealing as the oncoming embarrassment started to set in with Regan's footsteps coming closer.

She steeled herself, jumping into action as soon as Regan walked into the living room so that she couldn't back out.

"I know you don't want to hear an empty apology, so... I'm not giving you one," she started. She closed her eyes, gripping with everything she had to her resolve to do what she'd planned on.

She lifted Mr. Cuddles in front of her, clearing her throat as she dipped her voice a few octaves and spoke through him. "*This* is what Mr. Cuddles voice sounds like. And Emma wants you to know that she really is sorry."

Cheeks burning, she quickly lowered the bear, though still found comfort in stroking her fingers through his fur, as she continued in her normal voice, "I'm sorry not only for what I said the other day but also... because you were right. My issues with you are largely because of my own perception, and I've never really given you the benefit of the doubt."

Swallowing hard, she looked down at her own hands, rubbing her thumb over Mr. Cuddles' ear. "The truth is that I haven't *tried* with anyone in a while. I haven't wanted to."

This bear that she was clutching was proof of that. How very little had she tried with her own mother?

"Letting people in is really hard for me," she admitted, her voice falling hoarse. "There have been a lot of times in my life when I *do* let someone in and try with them, and it never goes well."

Kimberly, again, popped into her thoughts. Along with a handful of the kids she'd gone to school with, then Felicity... she shook her head – yeah, she was most definitely not sharing those parts with Regan.

Swallowing thickly, she looked back up, meeting Regan's wide, surprised stare with her own. "I've never had a roommate that wanted to spend time with me the way you do," Emma admitted softly, her stomach twisting with the truth of the words. "I've never really met *anyone* that seems to want to get to know me the way you do."

She'd meant to say that part jokingly, but it came out leaving her feeling unexpectedly vulnerable.

Trying to push through that feeling as quickly as possible, she added, "And I think I've dug my heels in even harder with you *because* I don't understand why you feel that way, especially when all I've done is push you away. So, it makes me feel... uncomfortable. And a little..."

"Prickly," Regan supplied encouragingly.

Emma narrowed her eyes as she corrected, "Guarded."

And when Regan brightly grinned, Emma didn't feel the immediate urge to glare. Which was new.

Maybe this whole *facing the truth* thing had some merit.

"And, I guess..." She felt she had to admit it because this was the moment of truth. "We kind of are Thom and Geri."

The grin on Regan's face grew to a nearly blinding wattage, and Emma didn't quite understand the relief she felt in seeing it.

"I guess I've never known when to quit," Regan admitted, her voice soft. There was no showing of bravado as her smile dimmed slightly. "I honestly think that *because* you seemed so resistant to me, I put in even more time and energy trying to get you to like me. Which, is crazy." She breathed out a quiet, self-deprecating laugh. "And I'm sure that roots back into my own... stuff." She gestured vaguely with her hand before letting it fall to her side.

Emma's eyebrows lifted in unexpected interest. That felt like a different side of Regan that she'd never seen before.

Feeling bolstered by it, she pushed herself to finish her peace offering. "To show you that I'm making a good faith effort and not just giving you lip service to try to get you to move on from the other day, I'm offering you a full day hang out."

It did scare her a bit to say those words. Mostly because she still thought Regan was a wild card, and Emma didn't like unpredictability.

But, she had to admit that seeing the way Regan's dark eyes widened with surprised delight made her breathe a little easier as she pushed through that feeling.

"Nothing crazy," she was quick to warn. "I'm not taking a road trip with you. We will not be leaving the city." She'd heard Sutton's cautionary tales of Regan getting them lost far too many times. "And I'm not joining any clubs or downloading any apps."

Again, she'd been in the same social circle as Regan for too long and had heard of far too many stories to be truly comfortable letting Regan run rampant with no parameters for their full-day hang out. She may feel contrite and she wanted to make things right with Regan, but she still had her limits.

"Deal!" Regan pounced on the offer, reaching out her hand.

Emma studied the offered hand skeptically as wariness rose inside of her. "A part of me feels like I'm making a deal with the devil, but…"

She slid her hand into Regan's, startlingly aware of how soft and comfortably warm Regan's palm was against her own.

"Please," Regan scoffed. "You flatter me; I'm merely a humble servant to Lucifer." She tightened her grip on Emma's hand, and her strength was surprising. "I have to tell you: I'd already forgiven you after you spoke through Mr. Cuddles. But I appreciate everything else you shared with it."

Emma groaned loudly, feeling that sense of embarrassment return, which only made Regan laugh. And she'd admit, if only to herself, that she was relieved by the sound.

Still, she tightened her grip back and arched an eyebrow at Regan. "We never speak of the Mr. Cuddles thing to anyone else."

"It's between you, me, and the bear. Scout's honor."

eight

REGAN STARED down at her phone, debating how to answer.

It didn't come as a shock to her that Sutton was questioning her silence in the last week. After all, Regan was typically in contact with her best friend every day, in some form or other.

But after the debacle with Emma, she'd felt strangely reluctant to talk to Sutton, even about topics unrelated to Emma. This situation, which had only been compounded by her conversation with Charlotte, put a spotlight on how much Regan truly depended on Sutton. How much she'd *always* relied on her best friend to be her anchor.

And Sutton's current absence highlighted the reality that Sutton couldn't always be there to make everything feel normal and okay. Even when she returned from Rome – which wouldn't happen for almost half a year – she was now in a relationship. Like, a serious relationship. One that Regan sensed would only continue to get more serious as time passed.

While Regan knew she would always fill a role in Sutton's life, the position she'd held for nearly twenty years as Sutton's Most Important Person was a title that Charlotte had snuck in and claimed for herself in the last year.

So –

REGAN – 9:19 AM

> Everything's hunky dory on my side of the Atlantic

SUTTON, THE ONE AND ONLY – 9:19 AM

> You sure? It took you a while to answer my message

REGAN – 9:19 AM

> It was 2 minutes...........

SUTTON, THE ONE AND ONLY – 9:20 AM

> And 2 minutes for you to answer a text you'd read right away is a long time...

Damn Sutton and how well she knew Regan!

Also, damn this feeling in her gut that she had whenever she felt like she was being dishonest with Sutton. But what she'd said to Charlotte the other day was the truth.

For once in her life, Regan needed to stand on her own two feet.

Besides, she *wasn't* lying to Sutton. Not really.

Everything was – tentatively – hunky dory between her and Emma.

Today would be the true qualifier of that, and –

"Are we baking cupcakes together for our hang out?" Emma's voice came from over Regan's shoulder.

"Oh my *god!*" Regan jumped in surprise, fumbling with her phone before it fell from her grasp.

She and Emma watched as it clattered face-down onto the floor.

Regan's heart was still racing in her chest as Emma quickly bent to retrieve her phone. She examined the screen as she handed it over to Regan, her pouty lips pulled into a considering frown. "It looks like it's all in one piece still. Sorry, though; I didn't think I'd scare you."

Regan gratefully took her phone back, giving it a cursory glance as she placed it on the counter behind her. "Yeah, I mean, I don't know why you might possibly scare the shit out of someone when you come creeping up behind them like a ninja."

Emma huffed out a laugh, crossing her arms over her chest in a move that made her breasts seem like they were about to pop out of the thin tank top that she'd slept in. Regan's eyes lingered for a few seconds.

"If *I* were the only one to make that statement, I'd believe it was sarcasm in a not-so-nice way. But since it was you, I'm assuming you're being humorous," Emma mused slowly, studying Regan's face.

Regan lifted her gaze to meet Emma's, an easy smile sliding over her face. "You assume correctly."

Emma's eyebrows furrowed, before she shook her head. "You know, a part of me was *really* hoping that I could poke even a small hole in your theory that my attitude is the reason our relationship has never..."

"Blossomed," Regan supplied, leaning back against the counter as she angled her head up at Emma. She was undeniably curious as to where Emma was going with this.

Emma grimaced. "I mean, that makes it sound like we're pre-pubescent, but – yes." She shrugged. "But the truth is that if you snuck up on me like this and made me drop my phone, I'd have flipped out. So. I guess that's a big point in the Regan Gallagher column."

Regan felt her smile grow even wider at Emma's admission, entirely too pleased with it. Even more so because Emma didn't even sound like she was begrudging the truth. She sounded almost... amazed by it.

"It's a good outlook," Emma murmured, studying Regan's face carefully. Like she was really trying to *see* her. Maybe even for the first time.

Regan's first instinct was to preen into the compliment, to ham it up, but she faltered. Instead, her cheeks felt a little warm at the observation, and she shrugged. "It's really not that big of a deal."

"It's nice," Emma countered firmly.

"You really *are* stubborn."

"And the sky is blue."

The laugh that escaped Regan was swift, and she rolled into it, especially when Emma cracked a small, genuine smile back at her.

After another few seconds, Emma lifted a questioning eyebrow. "So – cupcakes?" She nodded at the ingredients, mixing bowls, and pans Regan had neatly laid out on the counter before Sutton's text had distracted her.

"Uh, well. I didn't *plan* for us to bake together, no." She hedged, clearing her throat as she rocked from one foot to the other as if she could hide the slew of ingredients behind her back.

"An interesting choice, then," Emma drawled.

"I didn't think you were going to be awake so early," Regan countered truthfully.

In fairness, Emma *was* still in her pajamas. A gray threadbare tank top with a pair of tiny black shorts – honestly, Regan knew they were pajamas because there was *no way* Emma would dare brave the New York City streets in shorts that barely covered her ass; she'd detest the attention it would garner her. Her silky hair was still piled on top of her head the way Regan had noticed Emma often did before she slept – if she hadn't fallen asleep while working, that was.

"You told me when we went our separate ways last night that you were opting for our hangout day today," Emma deadpanned. "Correct me if I'm wrong, but I assumed you'd intended for it to be an all-day affair."

"I'm intending for us to use this as a bridge into a true friendship, actually, and that means accepting you as you are. Which for you – I've gleaned through my *amazing* powers of deduction – means sleeping as late as humanly possible on days you don't have work." She offered Emma a proud, hopeful grin. "I was thinking I'd bake these myself, and by the time they were done, you'd be waking up."

That thoughtful, studious expression returned to Emma's face again. As soon as Regan felt her stomach tingle with it, she pressed her hand there. Strange.

"Uh," she valiantly pushed through the feeling. "Yeah, so... you know. If you want to go back to bed for a while, you totally can."

She believed so wholly that Emma would take her up on that offer that it legitimately shocked her when Emma shook her head. "No, it's fine. I mean, I offered you the whole day, and even though I may be stubborn and have a penchant to believe the glass is half empty, I'm a woman of my word. Besides, I'm already up. Getting out of bed means I won the battle."

A surprised, nervous titter escaped Regan's lips. "Okay, then. We can... bake... together..." She slid her gaze toward the counter, trying to figure out how to sort through her unexpected anxiety.

Apparently, Emma noticed. "I honestly assumed you'd be thrilled by the offer. You may soon come to see that my company isn't everything you've been dreaming about, but baking together feels like exactly the sort of thing you've suggested we do for weeks now." There was a raw curiosity reflected in her gaze that Regan hadn't ever had directed at her before.

And *of course*, it was regarding this. The one thing in the world that Regan did by and for herself.

"Ha, yeah." Regan dragged a hand through her hair and looked between the ingredients neatly arranged on the counter and Emma, before admitting, "Only, not really?"

Emma's dubious stare silently asked what the hell she was talking about.

Regan clasped her hands together behind her back, feeling uncharacteristically sheepish. "I don't bake with other people," she informed Emma, feeling a little silly.

More than a little silly, actually.

Those blue eyes blinked back at her as if unable to process what she was saying. Which was reflected by Emma's skeptical expression. "I've heard you banging around in here tons of times. And I've seen you bring containers of baked goods out of here."

"Exactly; I bake when you're asleep, and yeah, I love when people try my finished products," she tried to explain. "I mean – I don't know. It's stupid, but... baking has always just been for me. The process of it. It's stupid," she repeated, shaking her head at herself.

Because it *did* sound stupid when she said it aloud. After all, she did love it when people ate the food she made; she enjoyed sharing it. But the idea of sharing the *process* felt... nerve-wracking.

Emma's eyebrows furrowed together, critically. "I don't think it's stupid."

Regan's fingers tightened where she had them clasped together. "You don't?"

"I mean, we all have the things we like to do just for ourselves. And if anyone understands the desire for privacy, it's me." Emma flashed a sharp grin. "If you want to do this by yourself, that's fine–"

"Wait." Regan jumped forward as Emma started to take a step back, reaching out to grab at her wrist. "Stop. Let's do it together."

Even though it made her nervous, she pushed through it. Because – really, why *did* it make her nervous? She could pull herself together for this. For this bonding activity that Emma was finally willing to give her.

Letting Emma walk away from this opportunity felt like a complete and total waste. She'd wanted Emma to spend time with her for over a month, and now that Emma seemed to be genuinely willing to give her a chance, she wasn't going to pass it up. She wasn't an idiot.

With that, she nodded, willing herself to get over that weird hiccup of hesitation. "It's fine. It's cool. It's going to be fun."

Emma's eyebrows lifted higher on her forehead with every word she spoke, revealing her doubt. "Are you trying to convince yourself or me?"

Regan considered it for a second before she shrugged. "Both?"

"You know we can still hang out today even without the cupcakes. I understand boundaries, and if this is one for you–"

Shaking her head, Regan vehemently dismissed the idea. "No, it's fine." If Emma was willing to challenge her perceptions, Regan could, too. She wasn't in the business of being a hypocrite in any way. "It's actually a good thing, probably. Personal growth and all that."

Emma rolled her eyes but was smiling as she did so. "Riiight."

It *was* a good thing, Regan reaffirmed to herself, remembering she was still holding onto Emma's wrist. She gently released her. "So, how much do you know about baking?"

"I don't," Emma answered promptly.

"Now is not the time to be glib, Emma. I need to know how in-depth you're going to need my instructions to be while we work."

"Being glib isn't really my thing." Which, fair point. "I'm telling you that I've never done any baking unless you count buying pre-made cookie dough and popping it into the oven."

Horrified, Regan shuddered. "That is a tragedy. If I needed an extra push to get me to a place where I was ready to bake with someone – which I didn't... mostly – there it is. Let's get to it."

She reached out to where she hung her aprons, flinging one in Emma's direction, before grabbing one for herself. And when the thought struck her, she gleefully spun around as she pulled the apron over her head. "You know what this means? You have to listen to, like, everything I say! What a way to start our bonding time."

Emma nailed her with a look as she tugged her own apron over her head. "There's still time for me to go back to bed."

But she was tying the apron behind her back as she spoke, so Regan laughed.

Okay... maybe this could be fun.

By the time the cupcakes were in the oven, Regan's anxiety around baking with someone else had entirely dissipated.

It was made easy, really, because Emma's genuine naivety throughout the entire process was so damn entertaining. Once they'd really gotten into it, Regan had been so caught up in their conversation to be concerned about feeling self-conscious.

"Here, use this for the dry ingredients," she'd instructed, handing Emma the sifter as Regan moved to pre-heat the oven.

Emma had dubiously looked down at it. "What... is this?" She flexed her hand on the handle, rotating the sifters.

Regan gasped, whirling around to face her again. "Emma – wait, what's your middle name?"

"Not necessary information," Emma clipped, turning back to the counter to grab her coffee.

"We will work on that." She held herself back from pressing the matter – this was a beginner day for them. Regan didn't want to test the limits too much on day one! "Emma Bordeaux," she started again, "*That* is a sifter. You have to spoon the dry ingredients into the measuring cups, then you sift them into the bowl."

Emma arched a doubtful look at her. "Now I know you're messing with me. That's why we have the measuring cups; you scoop them and dump them in the bowl. I know how that works."

A baffled laugh escaped Regan as she held up her hands. "Why would I be messing with you? That's *not* how this works! Scout's honor." She sidled up to Emma, pressing against her side, gesturing at the ingredients. "You don't want them to be... heavy," she decided on the word. "If you just scoop, it won't be accurate. We're going for light and fluffy, here, not thick and dense."

Even though Emma still clearly thought Regan was fucking with her, she reached for the spoon. "I guess – for today – you're in charge."

Regan bumped her hip against Emma's. "You're damn right!"

Emma shot her a look, and everything in Regan went on high alert... before Emma shook her head and bumped Regan's hip right back.

The most exciting moment had been when she'd heard Emma, surprise in her tone, say, "You know, this actually looks pretty good."

Regan turned from where she'd been checking on the cupcakes in the oven... only to solidly bump right into Emma.

Eyes widening, she'd watched as the raspberry simple syrup they'd made – well, Regan had made, while Emma had poured the cupcake batter into the tins – slosh over the side of the jar it was in... all over Emma's right hand. Completely covering the opal ring she always wore.

She flicked her gaze between the syrup dripping over Emma's hand, to Emma's face, the easy rhythm they'd found in the last hour quickly replaced by anxiety. She'd ruined this tentative truce in true Regan fashion – by accident – and now Emma would respond in typical Emma fashion – incredibly irritated.

Quickly, she reached out and took Emma's sticky jar and set it on the counter. "Sorry! I'm sorry. I didn't realize you'd lifted the jar or that we were standing so close. I'll wash the ring," she offered, gesturing for Emma to take it off. "Really, I'll be careful. I'll watch a YouTube video on how to do it properly."

Her stomach knotted as she watched Emma close her eyes and take a deep breath.

Waiting.

Until Emma shook her head, those blue eyes opening again as she breathed out slowly and evenly.

"It's... fine," Emma murmured. As soon as she said the words, she nodded with them, doubling down. "Seriously, it's fine. Because," she arched her eyebrow down at Regan, "I know you didn't mean it."

Regan quickly shook her head. "I seriously, truly didn't." She brought up her hand, making an *x* over her chest. "Cross my heart and hope to die." She ended by diligently stepping out of Emma's way, giving her a large, hopeful smile. One was entirely genuine as relief washed through her.

Emma hadn't flipped out! Or stormed to her room! Progress!

She hadn't known just how nice it would feel for Emma not to assume the worst about her.

As Emma grimaced and tugged her ring off, she shot Regan an amused look. "I don't think I've heard anyone over the age of, like, ten say that. But somehow, I feel like you really mean it."

Regan positively beamed.

After Emma had washed her hands, she started on the ring. Carefully cleaning it without submerging it in water.

Curious, Regan walked up to her, pressing herself against Emma's back so she could look over her shoulder. "It's a really pretty ring. It's not, like, damaged, right?"

Emma glanced at her. Rather than tell Regan to back off, though, she slowly shifted her attention to the ring. "No, it's fine. I mean, it's not *amazing*, but it's definitely not damaged."

Regan relaxed, thoughtlessly propping her chin on Emma's shoulder so she could watch the thoughtful movements Emma made to rid the ring of the syrup. "Good. It's the only piece of jewelry you wear basically every day, so... I would've felt really bad. I mean, I would have replaced it! But, still."

She could feel the deep breath Emma took as her back pressed solidly into Regan's front as she continued to methodically clean the ring. "You couldn't have replaced it, actually. My grandfather had it made for my gram for their tenth anniversary."

Regan angled her head to look at Emma, eyes wide and excited.

Emma?! Sharing information with her?! *Voluntarily*?!

"But I know you would have offered."

Regan returned her look to the ring, smiling softly down at it.

126

"That's so sweet. And your grandmother gave you the ring? Because you two are close, right? Because that's what set off our argument – her believing we're together."

Emma paused after she swiped the damp cloth over her ring, slowly turning her head to look at Regan.

Who only realized at that moment just *how* close that made them, as she was still resting her chin on Emma's shoulder. She felt Emma's warm breath hit her cheek, shivering with it as their eyes met, both widening at the proximity.

Swallowing hard, Regan slowly pulled back, leaning against the counter behind her. "Um... yeah. Sorry. Personal space is something other people like, usually."

"Yes," Emma said shortly. But she didn't look annoyed; Regan was very familiar with Emma's annoyed face.

Not wanting to give Emma a moment to delve into her thoughts and get into an annoyed headspace, she waved her on. "Anyway – the ring. Your grandmother."

Emma cleared her throat, nodding at the ring in her hand. "Yes. She gave me the ring, and we are close. She gave it to me on my sixteenth birthday because it had always been my favorite."

Eager to learn more, Regan hitched herself up to sit on the counter, facing Emma. "That's really nice. Are you not as close to your grandfather?"

"No," Emma said after a beat, a softness in her voice that Regan knew she'd never heard. "He died the year before I was born, so... no."

Before Regan could delve into more questions – she certainly had them – Emma shook her head. "That's enough about me."

Unsurprised by the change in Emma's tone, Regan accepted it. No pushing, she cautioned herself again. She fluttered her eyelashes as she asked, "Does that mean we're going to make this about *me*?"

"I thought that was obvious," Emma deadpanned. "So, you don't even bake with Sutton? I feel like you two do everything together."

Regan's joking smile dimmed because *oh*. Emma was asking her something serious, whether she knew it or not.

Gamely, though, she shrugged and answered honestly. "I mean, we *have* baked together, back when her mom taught us the basics." The memory of those afternoons in the Spencer home with Katherine standing between them at the kitchen island, softly but firmly giving them direction, made a warmth slide through Regan's veins. "And obviously, we live together, so we've baked together, or she's been home when I've baked sometimes. Sure."

Emma's sharp gaze stayed on her, intently, though. Regan squirmed with it, gripping the counter tightly where her fingers curled over the edge. "But?" Emma prompted.

"But we don't when it's – this." She gestured to the oven, where their cupcakes were nearly done.

"What, exactly, is *this*?"

"Oh, you know. New things. Some stuff for the café." She shrugged, acting like it was nonchalant when it actually felt anything but. In reality, it felt very personal. "The recipes I create by myself."

"I didn't realize you did any baking for the café." Emma's mouth fell open as she seemed to connect the dots for something. "I *knew* I'd seen those cookies – the ones you baked a few weeks ago? With the pretzels and the cranberries? At Topped Off!"

Undeniably pleased, she beamed. "Yeah, those are my own creation. They're pretty popular."

"Because they're delicious," Emma easily complimented, still staring at Regan in wonder. "I have to stop myself from getting one whenever I notice they're on offer."

Even more pleased, Regan's smile grew. "Why? You should always grab one."

"You bake them, then? At the café?" Emma asked, staring at Regan curiously.

It was by far the most interest Emma had ever expressed in Regan, and it made her sit up straighter.

"No, not always. I created the recipe but shared it with everyone who bakes there. I don't really work in the back," she explained, feeling compelled to hold Emma's intense stare. "I, uh, make the schedules for the bakers, but I only hands-on manage the front of the café. Sometimes, though, when no kitchen staff are there yet or when they've left, I just..." She shrugged. "Have fun."

It felt so *strange* talking to Emma about this, about her process.

Even at the café, with the people who knew about Regan's baking, their attention and positive comments never felt so... personal? They praised Regan's desserts but never asked for details.

"I can't believe Sutton hasn't told me about this. It feels like something she'd love to talk about."

Regan rolled her lips, tapping her fingers against the counter as unease flowed through her. Finally, she confessed, "Honestly? Sutton doesn't really know how much I do this."

Emma's stare was the picture of confusion. "Seriously, am I in the *Twilight Zone* right now? *What*?"

Stomach working into knots, Regan quickly shook her head. "I mean, I'm not *hiding* it from her; she knows I bake in my free time. It's just – it's only been since last fall that I started branching out. Making my own recipes, that sort of thing."

Emma leaned back against the wall opposite Regan, looking skeptical. "Yeah, that still sounds weird to me, that Sutton wouldn't know about this. That you keep your *baking* a secret from her."

Refusing the urge to pick at her fingernails – a childhood habit she'd long kicked – she denied, "It's not a secret," and she only felt somewhat defensive. "I just – I only started playing around with recipes and doing my own thing last year when Sutton started dating Charlotte."

Emma slowly shook her head. "It's still not clicking for me."

Exasperation welled up inside of her, dragging out the words she'd never spoken aloud. "Because before that, Sutton and I used to hang out, like *all* of the time. We watched our shows together – which was *great*, because watching reality TV by myself just isn't much fun. In fairness, watching it with Sutton sometimes wasn't the most fun, either, because she's too nice to make bitchy or judgy commentary about people, but still. And we'd chat about life stuff, work, school, and – and, I mean, we still did after she met Charlotte. But it wasn't the same," she confessed, feeling that awful, restless, lonely feeling that she tried to stave off when she started thinking about *this*.

"On my nights off, when Sutton and I would normally hang out, she was with Charlotte more than half the time. And they'd spend the night at Charlotte's place. And I'm *glad* she has Charlotte," she added quickly, not wanting Emma to get the wrong idea. Because it was true.

She wanted her best friend to find happiness; she wanted Sutton to love and be loved, and Charlotte was really shaping up.

Only... she deflated, sighing to herself. "I guess I just never thought about how much would change for me when Sutton wasn't around all the time. Suddenly, I had nothing to do during all of these nights and weekends that I used to hang out with Sutton. So, I started baking more. Branching out from the normal, basic recipes I've used in the past and just... started doing what felt right. Having fun with it."

There had been a lot of trial and error in the first couple of months. Some flavor combinations hadn't worked the way Regan thought they would, or adjustments she didn't correctly account for.

But she'd found that the more she baked her own creations, the more she'd enjoyed it. Even if the apartment was empty and her relationship with Sutton – the most solid thing in her life – was changing so rapidly, baking made their apartment feel... full. Warm. Like a home.

She didn't know what she'd find when she lifted her gaze to Emma's after that full-on word vomit. But she was met with something thoughtful. Softer than she'd expected.

It was a look she found far more comforting than she'd imagined because she felt like Emma *understood* her in this moment.

She paused, heart beating quickly, wondering what exactly Emma might say. Hoping more now than at any point earlier in the day that this wouldn't be the moment Emma turned grumpy or dismissive.

"Well, if you want to spend our night of bonding watching reality television, I'll do it with you. And I promise you that I'm certain I *will* have bitchy and judgy commentary," Emma offered.

Both shocked by the offer and delighted with it, Regan's mouth fell open. "*Really?*"

"You don't think I can come through with colorful commentary?"

She laughed, shaking her head. "No, on *that* end, I think you will do really well. I just mean – I didn't expect the offer, is all."

She really hadn't anticipated that Emma would listen – really listen – to her long ramble and focus on the heart of it. That Regan missed having someone, especially the person she lived with, to do day-to-day things with, like watch TV. That she'd felt that way even before Sutton had left. And she certainly hadn't expected Emma to make the offer.

"Well, it *is* bonding day."

"True. Though, I'd initially planned for us to do karaoke together for our bonding evening." She didn't miss the way Emma blanched. "But that is a great substitute."

"Good, because karaoke is *not* my thing."

Regan's mouth fell open in mock surprise. "You don't say!"

It was half the reason she even wanted to do it with Emma. The first half was because Regan really enjoyed karaoke–the camaraderie feeling, putting on a show. The second part was because she really wondered what Emma would be like when pushed a little bit out of her comfort zone. Or even if she'd allow herself to be pushed out of her comfort zone.

"I'll get you to my favorite karaoke night at some point," Regan asserted.

Emma *pfft*'d. "You sound really sure of yourself about that." She pointed to herself. "Stubborn, remember?"

Regan pointed to herself. "Doesn't know when to stop, remember?"

"Looks like we have a real *what happens when an unstoppable force meets an unmovable object* situation on our hands," Emma mused.

"The force wears the object down," Regan answered easily. "It's called erosion."

As the timer on the oven started to go off, Emma turned away from her and reached for an oven mitt. As she did, she quietly asked, "What in the world did I get myself into?"

But her tone was amused, no trace of irritation in sight.

Which delighted Regan down to her very bones. Because Emma clearly didn't realize that she was a lot more movable than she'd thought.

And Regan would be quite happy to help her find out.

nine

REGAN FREAKING GALLAGHER – 2:33 PM

[image]

REGAN FREAKING GALLAGHER – 2:33 PM

had the most genuinely delightful tourists come in today. Guess where they're from (no, really, you will never guess)

EMMA GLANCED down at her phone surreptitiously as possible as she sat next to Allegra in the backseat of her boss's town car. And then choked on her laughter when she saw the picture Regan had sent to her. A family of six, all with identical mullets, wearing neon-colored *I <3 NY* t-shirts. Regan had blocked out their faces with emojis, but if anything, it added to the amusing quality of the photo.

Quickly, she darkened her phone screen, doing her very best to smother any sounds of amusement as she shot a look toward Allegra.

Her attempt to hide that she'd clearly looked at something amusing on her phone was futile, as her boss had already turned her sharp gaze from where it had been focused on her tablet to stare at Emma.

"Are the follow-up emails from our meeting all that entertaining?" Allegra drawled, winging an eyebrow up at her in question.

Emma slowly shook her head, feeling her cheeks burn. Honestly, she'd love to blame Regan for sending that picture to her, but the reality was that it was on Emma for looking at it.

Growth.

"No. Sorry. That was... personal. But I've already sent all of the follow-up emails and forwarded the notes to Renee," she quickly added, needing Allegra to know that despite Emma's foot-in-mouth syndrome, she hadn't been bagging off on her responsibilities.

Allegra *hmm*'d under her breath before she waved her hand in Emma's direction. "Then, by all means, use the rest of the drive back to the office for personal correspondence."

Emma's eyebrows shot up in obvious surprise.

"You've been by my side in nonstop meetings since eight-thirty this morning; I'm counting this as your lunch break." Allegra turned her attention back to her tablet.

Willing herself not to snort in laughter again, Emma took a deep breath and unlocked her phone.

EMMA – 2:35 PM

> And... you HAD to send me that in the middle of the work day...

REGAN FREAKING GALLAGHER – 2:35 PM

> Emma, I would have sent you that at three in the morning if need be. If you were on death's door, even

Emma pursed her lips, fighting off another snort of laughter at Regan's ridiculousness.

REGAN FREAKING GALLAGHER – 2:36 PM

> But the main reason I needed to text you is because I need to know – chicken or steak?

Emma couldn't help her first, cautious, instinct.

EMMA – 2:36 PM

> For what?

133

REGAN FREAKING GALLAGHER – 2:36 PM

For a surprise!

Without allowing herself to dive too deep into the question, Emma answered.

EMMA – 2:37 PM

Chicken

REGAN FREAKING GALLAGHER – 2:37 PM

Amazing! I'll see you later

Won't bother you at work again (today) unless I come across another undeniable must-see'

Wait – seriously, guess where they're from!!

EMMA – 2:38PM

Ummmm Idaho

REGAN FREAKING GALLAGHER – 2:38 PM

NEW JERSEY!!!! LIKE WTF!!! Lmao

Emma shook her head, finding that she was annoyingly amused. She shouldn't be surprised, she knew, because Regan *was* amusing. Emma had known that for the past couple of years. It had just been an easy personality trait to overlook because she hadn't wanted to get sucked in.

It had been a few days since their bonding time over the weekend – Emma hated referring to it like that, but there was simply no other word for it. They'd *bonded*. First over the cupcakes, and then over watching that damn reality show Regan had put on that Emma was forced to admit she'd gotten sucked into – and she really did feel like they'd started to turn a corner.

Regan had been trying with Emma for a while, and it was now up to her to reciprocate that effort.

Emma was finding that it was startlingly and disconcertingly easy to do so.

So, she'd been doing little things. Like answering Regan's texts when she had a break. She'd ignored them before because... she didn't even really know – to prove a point, maybe? That they didn't have to be friends even if they were roommates?

Regan's messages were often dramatic or hyperbolic, for sure. But now that Emma wasn't dismissing Regan's attempts at communication, she found that Regan's texts – under the theatrics – fell into two categories: either it was something unfailingly amusing, much like the text she'd just received, or it was something thoughtful.

Like asking Emma what her favorite brand of tissues were because they were out, and she was going to run to the store on her way home. Or if Emma needed any menstrual products because Regan had – somewhere along the way – clocked that they were synced up, and she was grabbing herself tampons.

It was... nice. Emma had to admit it.

As if summoned by her thoughts, her phone buzzed again.

SUTTON SPENCER – 2:40 PM

So – how's it going? Regan told me you two baked together??

Emma shook her head slightly, noting that the car was turning onto the block *Olly* was located on.

EMMA – 2:40 PM

It's good. Unsurprisingly, Sutton, you may have been right.

Emma wasn't surprised to find Regan in the kitchen when she got home after work. After the question Regan had asked her, she also wasn't surprised to find that Regan had made them chicken for dinner.

She *was* surprised as she came to a slow stop in the doorway to the kitchen to see the extent to which Regan had gone to.

A whole roasted chicken was on the counter, fresh out of the oven, accompanied by mashed potatoes, stuffing, brussels sprouts, rolls, and gravy.

She blinked, trying to take it in. "Am I missing something? It *is* July, right?"

Regan turned, her mouth falling open in faux shock. "Emma, what are you talking about?! It's November! This is our Thanksgiving spread!"

"You know, if I hadn't just walked from the subway to our apartment in cloying heat, I *might* be tempted to believe you," she dryly shot back.

Regan's expression easily melted into a smile, and she shrugged. "Yeah, well, I had to try."

Emma tentatively took a few steps into the kitchen, lured by the incredible smell. "Just to be clear – I'm *not* missing some sort of major holiday, right?"

"As far as I know, the only major holiday in July is the Fourth, and we don't celebrate with roasted chicken," Regan returned.

"Right," she cautiously agreed. "So, the meal is for?"

Regan's large, expressive eyes stared into Emma's, the playful hint falling away from them as she answered, "I told you before: I really do like to cook. I just hate cooking for one. So… I figured this could be a do-over?" There was a hopeful edge in her tone, something so earnest that it grabbed onto something inside of Emma. "I know I totally fucked up the last time I did this for us. But this is one hundred percent nut-free."

Regan reached up and quickly drew a little *x* over her heart.

Emma slowly blew out a breath, eyebrows lifted on her forehead as she looked around the kitchen. Taking in the food before looking at Regan herself. Her dark hair was tousled, half-up and half-down, and her cheeks were slightly pink from having been cooking for likely the last few hours.

She then dropped her gaze down to the table. Where Regan had set them plates and silverware, as well as… pieces of paper?

"What is this?" She asked, walking over to the table so she could grab it.

Regan jumped forward to answer, obviously excited. "Oh! I totally forgot I put those out already. It's a little *get-to-know-you* game. I figured we could play over dinner. You know, since we're becoming friends and all."

Both papers were identical – one for Emma, one for Regan – with lists written in Regan's neat scrawl.

Birthday, favorite/least holiday, color, TV show/movie, day of the week, animal...

... Emma scanned her gaze over the paper quickly before lifting it to look at Regan skeptically.

"Over dinner, I figured we could both fill these out and then we could guess the other person's answer!" Regan explained as if it were obvious that this was going to be a guessing game.

Emma scoffed out a laugh because this was so *Regan*. Even if she hadn't anticipated that they'd be playing 20 Questions over dinner, she wasn't surprised.

She took a deep breath, finding that more than anything, she felt... amused.

"Sure," she agreed after several moments.

After all, she imagined that *this* – dinner together, little getting-to-know-you games – was exactly the kind of thing Regan had envisioned for them when Emma had moved in. It seemed fair.

Regan pumped her fist in an absurdly adorable celebration.

"I already know your birthday, though," Emma stated unthinkingly as she reviewed the list again.

Regan's little happy dance paused as she tilted her head up at Emma in obvious surprise. "You do?"

"May seventeenth," Emma informed her, almost slightly insulted. "Regan, we've been in the same small friend circle for over two years; I know your birthday."

"Well, I didn't want to assume. We can cross that one off because I know yours, too."

Emma bit the inside of her cheek, debating if she should say the thought that popped into her mind. But because they were *trying*, she forced the words out. "I got you a birthday gift."

All of Regan's movements stopped as she spun quickly around to look at Emma, baffled. "No, you didn't."

At the memory, Emma's stomach twisted uncomfortably. "Uh... yeah. I did."

Regan shook her head, her eyebrows furrowing in thought. "No, you *didn't*. I would have remembered because it was only a few days after you moved in. And we barely spoke that day."

Ugh, yeah, Emma did not enjoy this feeling in the pit of her stomach at the reminder. "Yeah, well, at the time, you'd just broken my gram's hummingbird figurines, and I wasn't feeling particularly..."

"Celebratory," Regan supplied kindly.

"Right," Emma latched onto it. "So, I didn't give it to you. And I'm sorry. But I'll grab it for you after dinner."

"What is it?" Regan asked, walking a few steps closer to Emma as if she were magnetized toward her.

It was disconcerting how close Regan came to her. Emma drew in a sharp breath, wondering if Regan had any concept of personal space. Because she only stopped inches before their chests brushed together.

But those dark eyes were so wide, so curious, affixed to Emma's, and... she really *didn't* think Regan had any conscious thought to how close they were standing.

Emma wondered if Regan even knew she did this if she was aware of her lack of personal space. It had *always* been something Emma had noted about Regan, even before they'd made peace. The way Regan never moved out of her way or the casual touching she engaged in. But ever since last weekend, it seemed to be more intense. Like when they sat on the couch together to watch tv, Regan always took the seat immediately to Emma's side, so their legs and arms brushed.

"Um." Emma cleared her throat, her cheeks flushing as she stepped a few inches back. "It's just a blanket. I was there when you and Sutton debated who got to keep that Helene Pierce sherpa throw blanket, and Sutton ultimately ended up bringing it to Rome, so..."

Emma honestly hadn't thought much about buying the blanket for Regan. She'd been at the store later that day, buying a few necessities for her move, and had seen the exact blanket Regan and Sutton had debated about on the shelf. Even if she hadn't had any desire to befriend Regan, she felt it would be a little shitty to move in with her two days before Regan's birthday and then totally ignore the occasion.

Which... had ended up being exactly what Emma had done.

"The Helene Pierce blanket?!" Regan gasped, reaching out to grasp Emma's wrist. A wide smile played on her ridiculously full lips as she bounced onto her tiptoes. "Seriously?"

"It's just a blanket," Emma muttered, embarrassment filtering through her. "Don't make it a big deal."

Regan's gaze stayed solidly on Emma's eyes wide and alarmingly soft. "You got me a birthday present."

That feeling in the pit of Emma's stomach fluttered again, and she deliberately stepped away from Regan in the direction of the food. "*Anyway*, let's eat before you make it weird."

"Too late!"

ten

"NOT TO BE TOO GRAPHIC, but I could feel my own asshole puckering just from being able to see the look on Allegra's face when she was dressing down Henry earlier," Brynn commented as the elevator doors shut behind them to bring them to the lobby.

Dubiously, Emma shot a look at her coworker. "*That* was you not being too graphic?"

Brynn didn't blink. "Did you feel differently?"

Emma, admittedly, did not. Brynn had done her job and scoured through Henry's articles for the last several months, making notes on them and landing them on Allegra's desk last week.

She hadn't been pleased with the findings; Henry had heard all about it today. He was on very, very thin ice at *Olly*, and now everyone knew it. At least Emma, Brynn, and Henry all did.

"There's always an upside to a staff writer getting fired, though," Brynn stated brightly as they stepped off the elevator together, walking toward the exit. "It means that Allegra will be farming out for replacement pieces in the meantime before hiring a new one. Opportunity."

Emma's ears perked up at that, and doubt followed quickly on its heels as she dug through her bag for her sunglasses. Even though it was nearly six in the evening, it was still the dead of summer and would be several more hours before the blaring sun went down. "Do you really think we'd have a chance for that?"

Her skepticism was clear in her tone, but she stood by it. Emma was just starting to really find her feet here as an assistant – as of today, it had been the first whole week without her putting her foot in her fucking mouth in front of Allegra. She wasn't even sure she had the right to dream about having an *opportunity* to write right now.

But she couldn't deny that there was a sense of excitement trilling inside of her at the very idea. Because while being an assistant to Allegra Pantone was a big fucking deal, a job she was lucky to have, Emma had never dreamed of being an assistant; she dreamed of being a writer.

"I don't know for sure," Brynn answered. "But I *do* know that the lead assistant before I was here was Abigail Talle, so..."

Emma did a double-take. "Like, the staff writer in the food section, Abigail Talle?"

"The very one. All I'm saying is that Henry's ass getting fired in the near future *could* be a potential boon for one of us." Brynn smartly finished as they walked through the revolving glass doors and onto the sidewalk.

Now that July had rolled in, they were in the thick of the summer humidity, which Emma had never been a fan of. But she supposed she had something to be grateful for – the disgusting heat wave that had attacked for most of June had finally abated. Now, they were living in *normal* city swamp temperatures.

Before she could say her goodbyes to Brynn, she heard her own name being called from behind her. "Emma! Perfect timing."

Baffled, she spun around to spot Regan quickly approaching. As always, an exuberantly large smile split her wide, plush lips and revealed the picture-perfect dentistry Emma was sure Regan's wealthy parents had paid for.

Granted, it paid off. She wasn't sure she'd ever seen a more beautiful smile than Regan's, nor had she ever met someone who wore it more. It had certainly been on display around their apartment near-constantly in the last two weeks.

Emma lifted a finger to slide her sunglasses slightly down the bridge of her nose to peer at Regan over the top. "Regan? What are you doing here? At my work?"

"*Regan?*" Brynn echoed her name, amusement dripping from her tone.

Emma had somehow forgotten Brynn was still there amidst her confusion in the last thirty seconds. She turned back to look at her just as Regan reached them, standing right against Emma, their bare arms touching.

"You must be Brynn," Regan assessed, still with that large grin. She offered her hand, which Brynn took and shook it firmly.

Emma was staring in confusion at Regan because she didn't recall telling Regan much about her job. Sure, she'd mentioned work here and there and had definitely brought up Brynn's name in passing, but it wasn't like she'd regaled Regan with tales about her. Then again, she'd found that she'd been continuously surprised by how observant Regan truly was.

She turned her attention back to Brynn, absolutely not trusting the mischievous look in her eyes. "Ah... *roommate* drama has all been worked out, then?"

"Yes," Regan answered, leaning into Emma's side. Even though it was over eighty degrees, Regan seemed to take no issue standing right against Emma's body heat.

"We're doing better than ever," Regan informed Brynn, bringing Emma back to reality.

The reality of Brynn staring between the two of them – the smug expression on her face telling Emma that she continued not to believe they were literally just roommates.

The sincerity with which Regan said those words – that they were doing *better than ever* – didn't help the case. Nor did their proximity to each other, especially given Regan's attire.

Wearing denim cutoffs that just barely covered the bottom curve of her butt and a red crop top, Regan's outfit *was* appropriate for the weather.

It also appropriately showed off the fact that Regan was undeniably attractive.

It was less appropriate for the way Regan miscalculated physical boundaries. Emma had started to get used to it in the privacy of their apartment in the last two weeks – at times, to even find some strange enjoyment from it. But with Brynn staring at them like this? And *in public*?

Emma deliberately side-stepped, putting a couple of inches between them as she slid her sunglasses pointedly back up. "I'll see you tomorrow."

"Can't wait," Brynn sing-songed back. "Nice to meet you, Regan."

"You, too!" Regan called after her, immediately turning her attention to Emma and staring up at her expectantly.

Emma matched her stare. "I'm still waiting for the answer?"

"What answer?"

"About what you're doing here?" She repeated her question from minutes ago, exasperated.

This was the sort of thing that may have annoyed her about Regan before. That she would do something like randomly show up at Emma's office unprompted, acting obtuse and dodgy about the reason why.

But it was far more difficult to get annoyed when Regan did things like leave the dishes in the sink after she'd been up baking last Thursday night, when she'd left Emma a homemade chocolate croissant for breakfast and a little note promising to clean everything up before Emma returned from work. And, true to the note, Emma had returned to a spotless home that evening.

The note also had a little elephant doodled on it – Regan had learned that was Emma's favorite animal, via their questionnaire, whereas Emma had learned that Regan's was a *shark*. So, so strange – which Emma had found disarmingly sweet. For some reason, she'd kept that little note. Maybe it was because Emma couldn't remember the last time someone had some something like that, something so simple as a doodle on a note, but also so... thoughtful and personal.

They'd even found a bathroom rhythm that was surprisingly seamless. Even when they'd both had to get ready in the morning, Emma found that communicating very simply and concisely with Regan really did go a long way.

Sure, Regan still did silly little teasing things – like when Emma went to grab her toothbrush from the holder and found that it was missing, as Regan gave her big, too-innocent doe eyes... but before Emma could get truly riled up, Regan offered her toothbrush that she'd held in her free hand, already prepared with their toothpaste. "I knew you'd be coming in sooner rather than later," Regan had easily commented around her own toothbrush in her mouth. She'd proceeded to list off the precise order in which Emma got ready every morning.

"Ahh, right! I realized that my shift ended, like, a half hour before you said you were likely going to be coming home tonight. And then I thought, well, thirty minutes is basically the amount of time it would probably take to meet you here. Obviously," she tacked on, gesturing around them as if to prove her point.

"Obviously," Emma indulged.

"*So*, I thought – well, it would be kind of fun to see where you work! Plus, since we're both out at the same time and we're down the street from one of my favorite diners, I figured we could grab dinner together?" There was a clear, hopeful edge in her voice, reflected in how Regan was biting her lip as she looked up at her, awaiting her response.

It seemed that the literal seconds it took Emma to process put Regan on-edge, as she rambled on, "I know we haven't, you know, debuted our friendship anywhere beyond the apartment yet. And our home hangouts have been great, don't get me wrong," she rushed to say. "But... meeting you out and about because we have similar schedules is what friends would do."

"Not in my experience," Emma stated, but she wasn't trying to be difficult.

Honestly, she had always held her friends an arm's length away. Even Sutton, to a degree.

But, as she eyed Regan, she was forced to admit that keeping Regan at a distance wasn't really a possibility. Regan was essentially a puppy; Emma had been slow to learn that. Now that she *had*, though, it was almost impossible for her to do anything to make Regan give her those big, sad eyes.

And, she found that as she stared at Regan's absurdly optimistic expression, she really had no desire to say no, anyway. Regan was right: their home hangouts had been very enjoyable. It... it was nice to come home to someone who wanted to talk to Emma about her day and in turn, share their stories. They'd started to settle into a rhythm now, and Emma liked a settled rhythm.

"All right," she acquiesced. "Where's the diner?"

It really *was* only a few blocks away, which Emma was grateful for as they stepped inside the blissful air conditioning. The slightly dingy sign outside proclaimed a 24-hour breakfast, which Regan had assured her was the best she'd ever had.

"Regan! Hi, honey!" A woman who appeared to be in her sixties, shouted on sight from where she was leaning against the wall next to the door to the kitchen. "Sit anywhere you like; I'll be over in a minute!"

"Thanks, Patty!"

Emma stared back and forth at the interaction before following Regan to a booth on the far side of the restaurant. "You really *are* a regular here."

"Yeah, I worked here for the first three months that I was in New York," Regan informed her as she gestured for Emma to slide into the seat.

Surprised by that information, Emma opened her mouth to question it. *That* hadn't been on their get-to-know-you questionnaire!

However, she quickly lost track of that question as Regan slid into the same side of the booth she was sitting in.

Slowly, Emma made a point of looking at Regan, before sliding her gaze to the empty side of the booth across from them, then back. "You know people *normally* sit on the opposite side, unless we're expecting other people?"

"I figured you knew by now I'm not normal," Regan cheekily retorted, her dark eyes twinkling up at Emma as she slid a laminated menu at her.

"You make a very good point," Emma conceded.

Still, though. It felt *weird*. The sort of thing that would have made Emma double-take when she'd gone out with Felicity, as her ex would have undoubtedly commented some snarky remark about couples being so clingy.

But, she reasoned with herself as she felt her cheeks heat, she and Regan *weren't* a couple.

Besides, given the chill of the air conditioning, having the solid, warm press of Regan's thigh against her own was kind of nice. It left Emma feeling very pleasantly warm.

"I like it better this way," Regan said, her voice taking on a quieter, more thoughtful tone. "When the dinner rush hits – which will be any minute now – it's going to get way louder. This way, we can hear each other so much more easily."

She was so earnest in her defense of sitting on the same side that Emma's argument against it again folded. Was it so wrong that Regan wanted to be close enough for them to actually converse without shouting? Besides, Regan very clearly felt no embarrassment at anyone possibly giving them a second look, so... why should Emma?

"I'll move to the other side if you want me to," Regan offered.

Emma found herself shaking her head. "You're lucky you smell nice," she muttered, looking down at the menu.

Her tone was sardonic, but the comment was true. Regan used a peppermint shampoo and conditioner that always left her hair smelling minty and fresh, and whatever perfume or products she used complimented it perfectly. When Regan ignored normal societal personal boundary rules, it made Emma feel like she was taking a breath of fresh air.

Emma found it enjoyable and far more appealing than something floral or cloying. She'd gotten very used to it, even before the last two weeks of bonding.

"Why, thank you!" Regan fluttered her eyelashes exaggeratedly at her. "Might be the sweetest thing you've ever said to me."

"Regan! How the heck are you? It's been a couple of months," Patty's loud voice boomed as she neared them, staring down with a broad grin.

"I'm good! Been busy. Sutton's in Rome; this is Emma, my new roommate," Regan tilted her head in Emma's direction as if she could possibly be introducing anyone else.

The bells above the entrance jingled, and Patty looked up, grimacing. "Ah, shit. I can't stay and catch up, but I'll throw your order in before the kitchen gets crazy. What'll you have?"

"I'll have my usual," Regan answered without having spent a second looking at the menu. Emma supposed this made sense, given that she'd worked here. "Pancakes." Regan turned to inform her. "With a side of bacon and home fries. Literally the best pancakes in the city."

Emma was sold. "I'll just take the same, then."

"Making it easy for me, I like you already." Patty nodded at her approvingly.

She'd take it because getting the approval from waiters was one of Emma's favorite things.

Regan's eyes widened as she reached out to put her hand over Patty's before she could walk away. "Wait – there's no nuts of any kind that go into the pancakes, right? Not even in the flour? Emma's allergic. Let Johnny know that he has to be careful."

There was a demanding urgency in her tone that Emma had never heard from Regan. And with it came a deep, warm appreciation.

"Will do, sweets." Patty nodded diligently before walking away.

Regan turned back to face her, sliding a hand through her hair. Before she froze, her eyebrows high on her forehead as she looked questioningly at Emma.

"What?" Emma asked, as Regan's expression made her feel alarmed. "What is it?"

"Um... nothing," Regan hedged, sliding her fingertips along the metal edge of the table. "You were smiling at me, is all. You don't normally just *do* that unless I say something amusing."

Emma hadn't even realized she'd been grinning at Regan, but she supposed it wasn't a surprise. She felt herself flush from having it pointed out. "I just – people don't normally do that." She gestured at where Patty had stood moments ago. "Make a point of my allergy; I usually do it for myself."

"Most people probably haven't hospitalized you, either," Regan allowed, a guilty expression creeping up on her face.

"True." Emma allowed. "But still."

Unbidden, she thought about how the only other time she'd had to go to the hospital for her allergy in her adult life had been when she'd been dating Felicity. One of the desserts in the "nut-free" zone on the table clearly hadn't been truthful, and instead of spending the remainder of the evening at Felicity's Friendsgiving, she'd been in the ER. Her ex had looked conflicted but ultimately hadn't joined her because she'd been hosting the party at her apartment, and Emma hadn't held that against her.

But she'd been lonely and felt like shit in the hospital by herself.

Something told her that even if Regan hadn't been the one responsible for hospitalizing her, she would have done exactly what she'd done that night – spend the entire time by Emma's side.

And she supposed that was the benefit of having Regan in your corner. After all, she'd seen the ferocity with which Regan had defended Sutton over the years. Emma guessed it was extended to most people Regan cared about.

Which, wildly, seemed to include her.

Emma cleared her throat, and Regan immediately turned to look at her. "So, I've kind of noticed that you bring up the night you sent me to the hospital... a lot."

Every time they had dinner together – which had been three more times after the roasted chicken of last week – Regan made a point to clarify that there were no nuts, always saying it with a stricken expression.

Regan nodded, that same expression creeping up on her face. "Yeah. I mean, I think about it a lot." Her big, dark eyes searched Emma's, imploringly. "It was terrifying to experience. And if it was that bad for me, I know it was way worse for you."

Emma rolled her lips, almost feeling *exasperated* by how damn genuine Regan was. "I want you to let it go. Seriously."

Regan's forehead crinkled as her eyebrows lifted in surprise. "Really?"

She found herself nodding slowly, reconciling that she did *really* feel that way. "I know it was an accident. Yes, you should have read the roommate contract. But... it's okay, Regan. I'm totally fine, and I can clearly see it's a mistake you will never make again – or let anyone else make." She gestured in Patty's direction.

Regan eagerly nodded, her hand falling to Emma's, squeezing intently. Her touch was warm and soft. "*Never*," she swore. "I'll eat every nut in the world before I let it get to you. That includes byproducts."

The sincerity with which she said those ludicrous words made Emma chuckle. As she did, she studied Regan closely.

There really *were* a lot of sides to her. Positives Emma wouldn't allow herself to have seen in her own stubbornness.

And now that she'd opened her eyes, she was curious.

Curious about these aspects of Regan that she really didn't know. Even though Regan was the first person to claim she was an open book, even with that silly little questionnaire, Emma had a lot of gaps in her knowledge.

Which brought her back to, "You worked here? I always thought you started at Topped Off as soon as you moved to the city?"

"I basically did. I moved seven years ago this last May, and started at Topped Off in August. Been there ever since," Regan explained, running her eyes slowly over the restaurant. A small smile played on her lips by the time she returned her gaze to Emma. "I discovered that I wasn't quite the *best* waitress."

Easily recalling their first encounter, Emma dryly stated, "You don't say."

But, again, she felt no malice. Didn't feel the pull of that embedded grudge. She just... wanted to know more.

Regan laughed her full-bodied chuckle. "Yeah. There was a lot of carnage; it was my first-ever job. I got relegated to making the coffee by the end of my second week, and I realized that I was really good at it. So, going to Topped Off made a lot more sense."

Seemed simple enough. Emma accepted the explanation with a nod. Still, her curiosity wasn't sated, and she continued to stare at Regan, trying to make sense of the knowledge she'd accumulated over the years. "I *still* don't understand why you moved here. As a native, I've seen it all. People from small towns looking for a big change. People hustling to make it big in some industry or other. But... all you said when I asked you before was because Sutton lived here?"

Really, Regan *was* such an oddity in that sense. And Emma wanted to understand it. To understand *her*.

Regan nodded, looking at Emma as quizzically. "Yes? We've already talked about this."

Emma couldn't help the incredulous frown that tugged at her

mouth. "I just... you moved to one of the most expensive cities in the world with no plans because – your best friend lived here?"

She didn't mean to sound judgmental. Really, she didn't. But Emma's logic-driven brain simply couldn't compute that answer, though. Not when Regan had her life set up for her back in Massachusetts. She'd known Regan had attended Brandeis University for a year, that she could have finished her education without a single student loan, to have a degree to fall back on as a security blanket at the very least.

Regan was frowning back at her. "Yes," she doubled down, firmly. "That's exactly what I did."

Emma bit the inside of her cheek to hold back any thoughts she had that could possibly come out that weren't very positive. Literally, she bit down and averted her gaze from Regan's to stare at the table and mind her own business.

The sigh Regan let out was full of obvious frustration, though, as she dropped her hand down to the table and tapped her fingertips against it. "Just say it."

Emma cleared her throat as she shot Regan a look. "Say what?"

Regan's stare alone demanded Emma cut through the bullshit. "Whatever you're obviously thinking but not saying. Just say it so you aren't stewing on it."

"I shouldn't," Emma disagreed. "Because I'm *trying*, remember?"

"You putting in effort to our friendship doesn't mean you don't have opinions; I'm fully aware you have them. And we won't ever get anywhere if we aren't being ourselves." Regan squared her shoulders as she turned in the booth to look at Emma fully. "So, I will tell you again: just say it."

"You *really* are as persistent as I am stubborn," Emma muttered as she turned sideways to face Regan, as well. If Regan could take criticism head-on, Emma could deliver it the same way. "Look, I'm sorry, but that's something I've always found really frustrating about you. If you want the spirit of honesty between us as *friends*, then... there it is."

The way Regan's eyebrows furrowed made her confusion clear.

Emma elaborated, "The fact that you *could* have had that path in life! College completely paid for, a bright future that you don't have to beg, borrow, and steal anything to achieve. I don't hold it against Sutton that doors were opened for her in life because she was born into a wealthy family, because I can respect that she understands how privileged she is, and she's using it to work toward her own dreams."

She shook her head slightly, staring at Regan, feeling just as baffled as she'd been a minute ago. Feeling echoes of frustration she'd had with Regan for years.

"Do you even understand how lucky you are? To have gone to the school system you grew up in, to have the doors opened to you that you did?" She searched Regan's gaze, really *wanting* to know; this wasn't rhetorical to Emma.

"Do you know how hard I've had to work to get to where I am? How many jobs I've had to work to slog my way through college, to pay the tuition I owed even after maxing out all of my student loans? Do you think I wanted to graduate and start my career only a few months shy of turning thirty? A career in which I'm currently spending my days sifting through applications for the Alton Writing Fellowship, and every single one is a giant reminder that I earned one of those Fellowship spots myself – and then couldn't go. Because I couldn't afford it."

The words burst from her, from a place so far down, Emma hadn't expected it to bubble up to the surface. She blinked in surprise, embarrassment quickly on its heels to tie knots in her stomach.

And Regan's crystal clear gaze – which had gone from confused to defensive to curious and had now settled on sympathetic – held hers, refusing to let go. "I never knew you got into the Alton program thing."

Emma shrugged, the movement jerky as she reached up a fidgeting hand and swiped her hair behind her ear. "Yeah, it was before I met you. Er, before I met Sutton," she quickly corrected, feeling her cheeks burn under Regan's watchful gaze.

What she wasn't going to say to Regan was that Emma didn't discuss the brief moment in time that she'd been accepted into the Alton Fellowship with anyone. She'd been utterly elated when she'd gotten accepted, had wanted to shout it from the rooftops. She'd already been gripping her phone so she could call her grandmother and tell her the news...

But then she'd finished going through the envelope and realized that while she had a spot in the program, she hadn't received any grant money.

Meaning that to partake in the four-month-long California-based fellowship, Emma would have to somehow find the money to get herself across the country, find a new place to live, and try to find a job that would allow her to work around the fellowship hours. All while living away from the only supports she had, in the forms of her gram and her girlfriend.

And the fact that she'd factored how much she'd miss Felicity and their stable relationship, only for Felicity to turn around and unceremoniously dump Emma, had been a retroactive slap in the face, on top of it all.

She cleared her throat. "Anyway, I wasn't trying to be an asshole to you about the decisions you make in your own life. Because – it *is* your life. I just... it's... hard to see someone have access to so many opportunities, like you have, when I would have *killed* to have half of that access."

She still felt embarrassed, saying it aloud. Because saying it aloud brought Emma back viscerally to the memories of when she was the only kid in her middle school class who was there on scholarship. Being poor and feeling ashamed of being poor. Then, on top of that, feeling ashamed of being ashamed, because she knew how fucking hard her grandmother worked to provide for her.

Emma couldn't even remember the last time she'd talked about any of these feelings, the last time those core memories had felt so present in her mind. And she couldn't understand *why the hell* she'd just laid out so much about herself to Regan in a diner booth.

Regan's hand landed softly on Emma's again, soft and warm, and when she squeezed Emma's wrist, Emma forced herself to look up at Regan.

Much like in middle school, she'd put on a brave, defiant expression, even if it didn't match her feelings.

But Regan's expression didn't match the middle school bullies, not at all. It was sweet and filled with an understanding Emma hadn't anticipated. "I really appreciate you telling me all of that."

Emma arched a doubtful eyebrow at her. "Really?"

Regan was *glad* Emma had spilled her deep-seated, bitter feelings on Regan's privilege?

Still, Regan's guileless face didn't lie. "Yeah, because I feel like I actually get it, now. Why you've always been so *grr* towards me. And..." Regan's white teeth dug into her lip as she dropped her gaze for the first time. "I understand why you feel that way. It makes sense."

"It does." Emma knew she wasn't adding anything helpful to the conversation, but she couldn't help it.

She'd expected Regan to jump right back at her, defending her own life choices. It would probably have been what Emma would have done if the roles had been reversed.

Regan took a deep breath, her shoulders lifting with it, before she slowly blew it out, then turned back to Emma. There was a lightness in her eyes again as she said, "Yup, it does. And now that it's been voiced aloud, I feel like we can *finally* move beyond it, right?"

Emma didn't immediately agree. She took a second to think it over but ultimately nodded. "I guess so. I mean, we kind of already are." She paused as the reality of the words hit her.

Regan's insanely enchanting, exuberant smile returned as she squeezed Emma's wrist twice, letting go of it just as Patty returned with their food.

Emma had to admit after taking a bite – they *were* pretty damn good. And judging by the knowing grin Regan had on her face as Emma chewed, she knew exactly what she was thinking.

Emma rolled her eyes in response, before she gasped at how Regan was haphazardly scraping her knife through the stack of pancakes on her own plate. "Oh my god, has anyone ever taught you how to hold a knife?"

"Ha-ha," Regan mimicked a laugh before gesturing at Emma's own plate. "Has anyone ever told you that this isn't a math class, and you don't have to cut your pancakes into equally sized pieces?"

Emma brought her hand up, protectively cupping it around the side of her plate. Where she had, indeed, methodically, neatly cubed her pancakes a minute ago. "You're literally *sawing* at them."

Regan made a dramatic point of using her knife like a saw, then, and

Emma couldn't help but laugh, even as the image of the mangled pancakes looked like the result of an angry toddler.

"So," Regan said, pointedly changing the subject. "Why did you want to get into publishing?"

Emma rolled her lips like she had to think about the answer, even though she didn't.

But she looked back at Regan, at her shameless mushy pancake mess and wide, genuinely curious eyes. At how she had a smudge of maple syrup right at the edge of her full lips.

And she realized – that was it.

Something about Regan's blatantly open, honest approach to life may be loud and chaotic, but it was always honest and accepting.

Emma spoke before she even realized what she was doing. "It was because of magazines," she admitted with a self-deprecating shrug. "I was *obsessed* with magazines when I was little. My grandma would bring me to the store, and I would wander away from her as soon as we walked in, grabbing a handful of whatever the latest ones were, and then sequester myself away in a quiet aisle, trying to read as many articles as I could before we had to leave. She'd let me buy one, so I'd always pick the thickest one – whatever it was – to take home."

A small smile played on her lips at the memory. Even though they hadn't had much money to spare, and her gram considered magazines a frivolous expense, she'd always gotten Emma one.

"God, I loved reading celebrity gossip in the glossy papers at the supermarket," Regan agreed, exhaling a dreamy, exaggerated sigh. She cut her gaze to Emma's. "But I didn't read all of the articles in them; I was more of a picture-speaks-a-thousand-words girl."

"Unsurprising," Emma deadpanned, amused.

It felt – good? Sharing this with Regan. God, that was weird. But, Regan was weird – in a good way, Emma was coming to see. So, she supposed it made sense.

"And?" Regan prompted.

Emma sent her a questioning look as she took a bite from a piece of bacon.

Regan used her fork to gesture at Emma. "When did you know you wanted to be a part of their world? Like, I loved reading magazines, but I never thought I wanted to write in them."

"Almost immediately." Emma scoffed out a laugh at her young self. "I'd write articles for my grandmother constantly."

Regan's interest was apparent as she set her elbow on the table, resting her chin on her fist and looking at Emma with her full attention. "Do you still write? I mean – I know that's the goal, right? But, like, your days at work aren't filled with writing."

Emma's chewing slowed that creeping self-consciousness returning. "Uh, not... really." She hedged after she swallowed.

"Ohhhh," Regan sang out, eyebrows lifting as she leaned in even closer to Emma. "*Not really* also means *yes, a little.*"

Regan stared at her unwaveringly. Emma stared back, that squirmy nervous feeling in her stomach.

"Fine," she gave in after a few seconds. "I don't *really* write. Like, I'm not writing books or articles or anything. I..." She licked her lips before admitting, "I have a bookstagram. Where I write reviews of the novels I read."

Regan reeled back, her face filled with shock and delight. "Emma!"

She narrowed her eyes. "Why is that so crazy?" She demanded, even though she admittedly had just been reluctant to confess to it. "I love to read, and I have a lot of opinions."

"Yeah, *that* part isn't shocking." Regan laughed. "What's shocking is that – I follow you on all of your socials. And you hardly ever post on them! It's hard to believe you care enough about any social media to keep up with it."

"Well, I wasn't doing it for a following or whatever," she muttered, shrugging. "Look, I started it when I was in undergrad when I didn't have any time to write anything other than essays. Writing out my thoughts on books was just a fun idea."

Regan was already sliding out her phone. "Emma, you don't have to convince me you aren't here for the clout." She looked at Emma over her phone. "Now, what's your name? How do I find you?"

Cheeks burning, Emma pointedly turned away from Regan. "Yeah, that is *not* happening."

Mouth falling open in offense, Regan demanded, "Why! You'll let strangers follow you, but not your literal roommate-slash-friend?!"

"Yes."

"That's crazy."

"Isn't bonding supposed to be a two-way street?" Emma asked, turning the tables on Regan before they could dig in any deeper.

Honestly, Regan was the only person in her real life who knew about Emma's book reviewing social media life; Emma felt like that was plenty of sharing on her end.

With obvious reluctance, Regan set down her phone. "Indeed it is. What do you want to know about me?"

Of course, Regan offered herself to Emma without hesitation.

However, instead of finding that annoying, Emma found it... admirable.

Even though Regan was freely inviting Emma to ask anything, Emma found that she didn't know what exactly to ask. There was so much she didn't know, and she didn't know where to even start.

"Tell me something other people don't know," she challenged, mostly because *she'd* just spent the entire dinner so far telling Regan things that she never talked about with anyone else. Leveling the playing field would be nice.

Regan's lips twisted in thought as she pondered Emma's comment.

"I like to draw maps."

The sheer randomness of that statement made Emma choke on her water. Coughing, she blinked at Regan. "*What?*"

But the grin on Regan's face wasn't joking or teasing. If anything, it was a little sheepish. "Maps. I like to draw them."

Emma frowned. "Like... of New York? The subway? The country?"

"Of made-up countries," Regan corrected, staring at Emma incredulously. "The *subway*?"

Emma mirrored her expression. "How are *made-up countries* less wild than the subway?"

"Who do you know that draws subway maps?"

"I don't know anyone that draws maps at all," Emma countered, then paused as she slid her gaze to Regan. "Well, I didn't *think* I did, anyway. How did you get into the world of fictional cartography?"

Regan chuckled. "Fictional cartography. I like that. Um, it wasn't *planned*. Much like baking – I started hanging out more with some of the people at the café last fall, and I tagged along with Dustin to one of his D&D games, just to see what it was like."

Unexpectedly fascinated, Emma nodded along. "And you got into it?"

"No," Regan's response was so flat it stole a harsh, ugly laugh from Emma's throat. "Turns out I'm not super into the gameplay. But I *did* love the world-building stuff! So I spent the couple of hours there drawing up a map for them." She shrugged, toying with the end of her napkin. "They seemed to really like it, and so did I. So now I draw them maps for every new campaign, and they've passed my name along to some of the other people they know. You'd be surprised at the size of the fantasy roleplaying community interested in having a map made for them."

"I'd love to see these maps." Really, she was utterly fascinated.

"And I'd love to see your bookstagram," Regan countered with a devilish grin.

Nearly two hours later, they walked down the hall toward their apartment, and Emma barely even noticed how Regan leaned into her side as she laughed. Cackled was actually more apt, as Regan defensively was telling her about an unfortunate road trip she'd taken with Sutton back in high school.

All right, Emma still noticed how Regan leaned into her. But it felt... nice. It felt like camaraderie.

"And *then*, by the time we got back to the car – it had been *towed*!" Regan said the word as if the very existence of a tow truck was offensive to her. "So, you see, even though the trip was my idea, the fact that we were stranded in the middle of Nowhere, Maine really resulted from freak accident after freak accident!"

"That's *not* the way I heard it from Sutton." Emma was unable to stop chuckling at the outrage in Regan's tone.

"And that's because Sutton was traumatized by the series of events, and that's fine and all, but it did mess with her ability to recount the tale correctly," Regan countered.

Before Emma could respond, she felt her phone buzzing in her pocket and pulled it out. It was a little late for either her grandmother or Allegra to be contacting her, but –

Emma honestly hadn't realized what a genuinely good mood she'd been in until that moment when the laughter died on her lips and her stomach churned as she read Kimberly's name on her screen.

Regan immediately noticed the change in her body language, pausing a few feet away from their door as she glanced down at Emma's phone. "Everything okay?"

"It's fine," Emma claimed, and it mostly wasn't a lie.

She hesitated with her thumb over the red decline option, unable to bring herself to actually turn the call down.

She'd dodged Kimberly's attempts to reach out for the last week even more doggedly than she'd been doing before. And it had nothing to do with Regan or her mom's belief that they were together.

For some reason, the return of Mr. Cuddles to her life and the insistent image of her mom's desperately earnest expression as she'd offered the bear to Emma had made this need to avoid her become even more intense. Even more vital.

And yet, conversely and bafflingly, it also made Emma feel terribly about her avoidance. The watchful eyes of Mr. Cuddles sitting on her bookshelf made her think about the times her mom would puppet the bear and sing ridiculous songs until Emma laughed so hard she could barely breathe.

That feeling took over as she flicked her gaze to Regan. "I think I need to take this."

Regan watched her carefully, nodding. "Sure. Whatever you need to do."

Emma took a deep breath, held it for a few moments, trying to quell the nerves in her stomach... then answered.

Before she could say a word, her mom spoke. "Emma? Did I catch you on the first try?!"

Despite Regan starting to meander forward, tugging out her keys to unlock their door, Emma knew that she could still hear everything Kimberly said, given the decibel her mom talked at.

Still, she supposed she would give it to Regan – she was fiddling with her keys and making it appear *somewhat* like she wasn't absolutely riveted by what was playing out on the call.

"Yeah. Seems like you did," Emma replied, feeling the way she often did with her mom – painfully awkward. She wished she knew some other way to be; she had when she'd been younger, but over time, that had shifted. Leaving... this.

"I won't keep you long – unless you want to chat?" Kimberly asked but then continued on without waiting for an answer. "It's just been over two weeks since I saw you, and I didn't want to let too much time pass before we confirmed those dinner plans! So, like I said, I won't keep you; I just wanted to know when you and Regan will be available. Maybe sometime this weekend? I could even do tomorrow, if you're free?"

Regan immediately zipped her gaze up to stare at Emma as soon as she'd heard her name. So much for pretending like she wasn't eavesdropping.

Emma froze where she stood, her stomach twisting at the reminder. Right. Her mom – *and* her gram – still believed she was in a relationship with Regan.

And Emma had been so focused on everything else playing out with Regan – their argument, then subsequent friendship – that she hadn't exactly had the time or energy to think of what the hell she was going to say to her family about it.

The stupidest, most ridiculous lie, honestly. And the stupidest, most ridiculous thing was it still seemed easier to let her mom believe than tell her the truth.

Emma slowly started speaking, shaking her head at that thought, "Uh. You know. About that. Regan and I – we actually aren't..." She heaved a sigh, her stress mounting as she dragged her hand through her hair and blinked at the ceiling.

Should she tell her mom she and Regan broke up? Was the truth – that she'd lied in order to find another excuse to put off spending time with Kimberly – even a viable option? It felt too cruel at this point.

Especially since Kimberly had seen them with her own eyes, keeping up the charade.

"We aren't available tomorrow, unfortunately, because I have work," Regan answered, her voice coming from right next to Emma.

She snapped her eyes open, looking down at Regan, who was pushing up onto her tiptoes to get her mouth closer to Emma's phone.

The result was their shoulders pressing tightly together, as she breathed in Regan's fresh scent.

"But maybe Saturday?" Regan suggested, sliding her gaze to Emma's, eyebrows lifted in question, waiting for her to give her agreement.

She could feel every warm breath Regan exhaled, washing over her jaw, as their eyes were only inches apart, and it – it was jarring. She'd never stood so close to Regan in her life, close enough to see that there were little flecks of amber starbursting around her pupils.

Her stomach fluttered for an entirely different reason, and Emma found her breath catching in her throat, before she remembered abruptly *why* Regan was standing so close, staring at her like this.

She'd never been so relieved to have reality crash back down on her, and she found herself nodding, "Uh... I guess Saturday works for me, too."

Okay, so, they were doing this, still. Both because it made Emma's life easier in the immediacy in dealing with her mother, and because it allowed her the freedom to pull back, away from being so startlingly close to Regan.

Kimberly's answering squeal of excitement was *piercing*. "Saturday is perfect! I'll see you both then!"

The silence in the hallway was deafening when Kimberly hung up.

She was still trying to process it when Regan tentatively spoke, "That was, kind of, my act-first, think-later mentality. It seemed like you were in a pickle, still, so I'm sor–"

"You didn't have to do that," Emma cut in, not needing or wanting to hear Regan's apology.

Sure, maybe Regan had jumped into her crazy lie. But Emma was the one who had made this situation unnecessarily complicated by avoiding telling the truth in the first place.

"This weird lie is what got us into that... predicament," Emma said, because it was the truth. She'd spiraled and accidentally insulted Regan because her grandmother had found out about the lie. "So, I'm not holding you to it or anything; it's not why I'm doing this," she gestured between them.

Crazily, it was the truth.

"I know. But if it makes your life a little easier right now with your complicated-mom-stuff, why wouldn't I do it? I already told you that I love a little scheme. This is what friends are for. Besides, I really don't have any plans Saturday night."

Regan said the words so simply, so easily, as she unlocked their apartment door.

It was as if she wasn't doing Emma a giant favor, as if she wasn't going along with this lie, helping Emma out, and giving up her own weekend night off to do so.

And Emma stared at Regan, feeling like she finally – *finally* – understood. Like everything really was clicking into place.

She'd wondered for years why Sutton was such a staunch friend to Regan, even when Regan did crazy things like message women on her behalf on dating apps or got them lost on road trips. Why Sutton wasn't bothered by Regan's eccentricities or lack of ambition.

But *this* was why.

Because Regan did things like show up to take her friends out to dinner, listened to every story with intent, and remembered every detail. Because she was willing to throw her own lot in with someone she cared about and ride out the storm together.

She felt like she'd put in the final puzzle piece.

And she didn't realize how intently she'd been staring at Regan until Regan turned to face her and asked, "Do I have something on my face?" She was already reaching up and brushing the back of her hand over her cheek before Emma answered.

Emma flushed, shaking her head intently as she dropped her gaze. "No. You're good."

But *Emma* wasn't – she was getting pulled into Regan's crazy orbit! If she weren't careful, the next thing she knew, *she'd* be the one getting traumatized on impromptu weekend road trips!

"It's EditorialEmma," she said, deliberately averting her stare as she shut the door behind her.

"What is?"

"My book-reviewing name," she explained, breathing through the weird feeling in the pit of her stomach at being *vulnerable*. But Regan was doing her a favor, and Emma liked to replay favors to make sure everything was even.

Regan's face absolutely lit up at the information, and her obvious excitement helped quell Emma's embarrassment. "You just saved me so much time I'd already mentally set aside for tonight to find your secret social medias!"

Oh no. It really *was* happening. She should have found Regan's determination to find Emma's private accounts annoying, an invasion of privacy.

Instead, she found it... was this *endearment*?

It was, she realized, as she watched Regan do a little excited dance as she walked down the hallway.

God help her.

eleven

REGAN PAUSED where she stood in her bedroom, frowning at her sister's text. She opened her calendar app to double-check her suspicions, feeling triumphant as her suspicions were confirmed.

She'd taken calendar notifications a little more seriously since last month. Keeping an orderly schedule was obviously incredibly important to Emma, and Regan – in her determination to be a better roommate and... dare she say, friend? – was adhering to that.

And Regan would have to admit that checking in with her calendar and keeping track of things on there had been making her more far more organized and less frenzied.

It's not on there. That's why I'm texting you,
Regan. To let you know that you should
make a note of it in your calendar.

Regan stared down at her sister's text for a few seconds – since when did Audrey throw together a last-minute bridal party event? But... whatever. She responded with a thumbs-up, added it to her calendar, and tossed her phone onto her bed.

Right now, that was unimportant.

Emma's family was the focal point of the evening. She took a deep breath, shaking off Audrey's weirdness as she looked in her full-length mirror.

She ruffled her hair a bit, the dark strands falling in their natural waves down to her shoulders. She wore minimal makeup, but she figured that was a good decision. Even though Regan hadn't ever gotten to the stage of a relationship where *meeting the family* was a thing, she wasn't an idiot. She was aiming for the sweet spot – looking good but not looking like she was trying too hard.

With her hands on her hips, she turned to look at the outfit options she had laid out on her bed.

The thing Regan desperately needed to concern herself about not fucking up was this. Because things with Emma had been going *so* well lately. Like, really well.

Like – Emma actually *smiled* at her, all cute and sleepy, when they were in the kitchen to get coffee at the same time in the morning.

Like – Emma was even getting into watching *The One* with her. Not only did she not get annoyed when Regan paused the episode to make her commentary about each of the candidates, but Emma liked to do that, too.

"*Now, that guy definitely poses with a fish on dating apps,*" Emma scoffed derisively about a contestant the night before.

Regan had giggled, settling down deeper into the cushion next to her as she gestured to the other guy on screen. "*And he takes all of his pictures from an angle beneath his chin.*"

Like – she'd literally *shared* her secret book-reviewing social media page with Regan!

Regan couldn't – wouldn't – blow this newfound friendship tonight by not making a good impression at family dinner. It meant a lot to her.

With that thought in mind, Regan strutted to her bedroom door and tossed it open. "Emma! Can you come here? I need you."

She stared intently at Emma's adjacent bedroom door, itching to walk over and open it herself.

She *didn't*, though, because Emma wasn't Sutton, and she wouldn't like that. Even with all of their progress.

Thankfully, a few seconds later, Emma stepped out. "Is everything okay?" She asked, looking down at her phone, her thumbs moving over the screen.

The question on Regan's lips died, falling back down her throat as Emma stood in front of her in high-waisted black shorts with a baby blue button-up tucked into them. But the buttons weren't all done up just yet.

No, the top... five? Six? Were still undone, and her breasts were being showcased in the seriously *incredible* white bra she wore.

Regan didn't know what it was about Emma's breasts that she found so fascinating. She really didn't. But it was an undeniable fact by now, something she'd simply had to come to accept.

Maybe it was because the sight brought Regan back to the first time they'd met at the café, when Regan had ripped her shirt open, and Emma's prodigious chest had been there, right in front of her face. Maybe it was because her breasts were so much bigger than Regan's own – or Sutton's or... *any* woman's that Regan had ever seen in real life.

They were mesmerizing.

"All right, I ordered the Uber," Emma commented as she tapped her phone again, finally lowering it. "What did you–"

Emma abruptly cut herself off, mirroring Regan's wide-eyed stare. Those blue eyes traced down Regan's body, then back up before Emma promptly dropped her gaze pointedly to the floor.

"Regan! Why did you call me out here? You're naked!"

Shaking herself out of her stupor, Regan glanced down at herself to double-check before she defended, "I am not."

She wasn't; she was wearing one of her favorite lingerie sets. A lacy purple pair that showcased her breasts as best as possible. However, as she looked at Emma's, she felt very humbled.

Amused, she took a closer look at Emma. "Are you *blushing*?"

"Well, you called me out here so that I could apparently look at you in your underwear," Emma scolded, her tone scalding. "Which – you know we need to leave in like five minutes, right?"

"I know, that's why I called for you. Come," she ordered, waving Emma to follow her into her room.

Emma sighed before several seconds passed... and finally, she followed into Regan's room.

She still was pointedly avoiding looking at Regan, though, she noted with no small amount of amusement. Instead, Emma was intently peering around at her bedroom.

"I thought you'd be way more chill about seeing a woman in her underwear, given that you're bisexual and all. I've literally met your ex-girlfriend," she pointed out, poking Emma lightly in the arm. She frowned as the thought hit her. "Wait, are you asexual?"

Emma aimed a frown in her general direction. "No, I'm not. But," she tipped her head back, sighing at the ceiling. "On an average day, I don't see women... especially like you... walking around like this."

It was Regan's turn to frown – *women like her*?

"Women like me?" She echoed.

Yes, the blush on Emma's cheeks most definitely deepened as she steadfastly avoided looking at Regan. "Mhmm."

"Who are *women like me*?" She pressed, taking a step closer to Emma. "Women you've lived with? Baristas? Your friends? Your ex-nemeses? Your–"

"Women who look like they've stepped out of a lingerie ad, literally *wearing* that lingerie," Emma explained, her voice tight as she frowned down at the clothing options on the bed.

Whatever other goading words Regan was going to say fell back down her throat as she felt herself flush, butterflies erupting in her stomach. Again, she gave a cursory glance down at her own body, before looking back at Emma. "You think I look like I could have stepped out of a lingerie ad?"

Emma finally looked at her, exasperated. "Are you fishing for compliments?"

Equally exasperated, Regan tossed her hands up into the air. "No! That was the last thing I expected you to say."

"Regan, look at yourself," Emma retorted, her forehead crinkling in what looked like genuine confusion. "You look... good."

Regan *did* look back down at herself. Even though she was never shy around her own nudity, she felt – well, she felt different in this moment, as her stomach squirmed pleasantly. "I guess I'm just used to standing next to Sutton," she murmured without thinking too much about it.

But the first time they'd gone to buy bras and underwear by themselves as teenagers was a memory Regan could easily recall. Sutton had emerged from her fitting room, far more self-conscious than Regan, but utterly statuesque.

"You're *both* thin and very... traditionally attractive," Emma said quietly, still clearly baffled, even as she was still blushing.

Regan rolled her lips. "I mean, I know that. But – look. Spending my entire life standing next to Sutton, who's tall and has all her muscle tone and flame-red hair... people notice Sutton first. Even I do," she added with a self-deprecating laugh.

Saying that aloud made her stomach churn unpleasantly, especially when Emma stared at her as if she was trying to read Regan's mind.

"Anyway," Regan cleared her throat uncomfortably – wow, did her texts with her sister really did get into her head so easily or something? "I *am* ready – except for the outfit." She made a sweeping gesture at her bed, where her top contenders were laid out.

Emma slowly dropped her gaze from Regan's face, and Regan wasn't sure she'd ever be so pleased that Emma was ingrained to never pry. She stared at the clothing on the bed, her expression scrunching up adorably. "Regan, you're the one doing me a favor. Wear whatever you want."

But Regan shook her head. "No way! We're doing this as a ruse for your family, and I won't half-ass it. If I'm going to full-ass it, I need your input on what will impress the most."

Grandly, she gestured to the clothing closest to the head of the bed. "We have option number one: the dark blue sundress with the flowers on it."

"It doesn't really feel like *you*," Emma commented, staring down at the dress with a skeptical look.

Regan studied Emma's profile, surprise sliding through her. "That's because it's not; this is Sutton's dress. I think it reads: *yes, I'm dating your daughter, but I'm a very sweet girl. Don't worry, I don't do unspeakable things to her at night.*"

The color rose high on Emma's cheeks at that before she vehemently shook her head. "Not that dress."

Regan pulled her lips to the side, nodding in agreement. "All right; so we aren't going for a politician's daughter."

"No, and we aren't going for option number three, either," Emma vetoed as she eyed the mint green cocktail dress. "It looks like we're going to a five-star restaurant instead of my mom's house in the New Jersey suburbs. Unless that's what you want to wear, of course."

Regan shook her head. "No, I just wanted to have every option available. Granted, the one meeting I had with your mom didn't really make it seem like she'd be super... fancy."

She thought about the woman who had shown up on her doorstep with the short skirt and animal print blouse. Yeah, okay, that dress would definitely be overkill.

"The one in the middle is good; it looks like you," Emma commented, looking at the winning pick.

It was one of Regan's summer usuals – denim shorts and a band tee – and she found a sweet warmth moving through her at Emma's comment. Emma's comment clearly hadn't even been intended to be a compliment, but Regan felt like it was one.

Moving quickly – they *were* on a deadline – she tugged on the outfit. "Thanks."

Finally, Emma looked at her. "For helping you pick out clothing?"

Breathing out a slightly embarrassed laugh, Regan shook her head. "For wanting me to be... me."

The blush on Emma's cheeks deepened as she cleared her throat.

"It's not a big deal. In terms of what you're doing for me, it's miniscule."

It wasn't to Regan, but she wouldn't push it.

"Uh, anyway. The car is outside." Emma held up her phone, where the app informed them that their driver was waiting.

"In that case, you might want to button up your own shirt," Regan commented, letting her eyes drift down to her cleavage once more. "Unless you planned on wearing it that way to your mom's house."

Emma's gaze darted down to her top before she cursed under her breath. She shot Regan a dark look as she quickly brought her hands up to do up enough buttons to cover up her bra. "I got distracted from dressing myself to help *someone else*."

Regan merely shot her an unbothered grin. "I wasn't complaining."

Emma had already turned on her heel. "Let's go before the driver leaves."

∿

AUDREY L. GALLAGHER – 5:20 PM

> You KNOW I hate when you do that thumbs-up response. Can you acknowledge my message like an adult? Are you coming to brunch?

Regan stared dismally down at her phone in her lap as their Uber set off through their neighborhood toward Englewood.

REGAN – 5:21 PM

> Yep.

And because Regan hated when her sister talked to her like she was a misbehaving pet instead of a person, she reacted to Audrey's text with another thumbs up before turning off text notifications and sliding her phone under her thigh as she stared out the car window.

It felt... weird texting with Audrey this much. Twice in the last month – even if the messages were Audrey not being particularly nice to her – was discomforting. It went against the distance they'd both put between them, and she didn't like it.

"Are you still okay about doing this?" Emma asked, her voice quiet and intent.

Regan turned to look at Emma in confusion. "Yeah? Why? Because I'm being quiet for once?"

She'd intended for the words to be joking, but she winced as soon as she said them aloud.

All right, so maybe Audrey's text – and the subsequent weird feelings – had made her a little... sharp.

"Sorry," she sighed, folding her arms around her waist, not offering any further explanation.

Not only did she not want to get into talking about her sister *at all*, but she was also still treading lightly on certain topics with Emma. The last thing she wanted when she was trying to completely win Emma over was to let her know that Regan's own family totally agreed with every negative belief Emma had ever held about her.

Emma's eyebrows furrowed as she watched Regan closely before she shook her head. "Honestly, it's fine. I've said way worse to you," she added, tilting her lips in a teasing smile.

It made Regan chuckle, breaking through her weird mood. "True. I take my apology back because I believe in a level playing field."

Now, Emma laughed, but she still watched Regan closely. Disarmingly closely. "I was asking because you're the one who told me you love partaking in a little scheme, so I figured you'd be more excited right now. In the last two days, you've texted me four times about *our relationship details*. And that's not even counting how you spent last night making a batch of cookies because you didn't want to show up empty-handed tonight."

Regan tilted her head in acknowledgment. "True and fair points."

"Listen, if you aren't up to this, it's not too late. We can go back home, and I can tell Kimberly that you aren't feeling well," Emma offered.

The eagerness in her voice snagged Regan's attention, and she shifted to face Emma in the back of the car. "Why do I get the feeling that you'd like that you'd like to do that more than I would?"

Emma's generous lips drew together tightly, and she turned away from Regan's gaze to look out the window.

Her own family issues completely pushed aside, Regan couldn't help the question that escaped her. "Can I ask – what *is* the story here? Between you and your mom?"

She knew that Emma didn't want to talk about it; Emma was the way she was because she valued her privacy so deeply. Regan had accepted that about her – finally – given everything that had happened since they'd moved in together.

But, *god*, she was so fucking curious. Since the morning Kimberly had shown up on their doorstep weeks ago, she'd been ravenous for the truth.

"I'm not asking because of, like, wanting to gossip or *anything* like that," she swore. "This stays between you and me – all of it. Even if you don't tell me the whole story."

She really hoped Emma could hear her sincerity because it was all true.

Regan had taken some of what Emma had said to heart. She *did* like to gossip – not out of malice, but because she loved a good story, and she loved regaling them to others. But she understood that Emma didn't like people knowing her personal business, and she could honor that.

She had been honoring that.

"You don't have to tell me if you don't want to. I get it; family stuff can be complicated." With the texts from Audrey sitting on her phone, Regan really, *really* understood the truth of that statement. "But I want you to know, especially before we see your family, that I haven't said anything about this to anyone. Not even to Sutton."

And she'd really, *really* wanted to tell Sutton; she told Sutton just about everything. And Sutton had been texting very regularly, pointedly asking how everything was going with Emma, so it had taken Regan more than a little restraint to hold back.

As Emma slid her gaze from the passing cityscape to Regan, she fully expected to not get an answer.

"You're right – I don't *have* to tell you," Emma allowed, several seconds later, seeming as if she'd come to terms with some internal debate. "But you are going out of your way to help me out, which you've been doing since the second you've been thrown into this mess.

You didn't have to do any of this, but here you are." She used her hand to gesture at Regan, up and down.

Regan found herself sitting at attention, eager anticipation working through her. She was so, *so* wanting to know, she was practically vibrating with excitement.

Emma's dark eyebrows drew together as she took a deep breath. "My mom had me when she was fifteen," she began, and Regan's eyebrows shot up in surprise – not where she'd expected the story to start.

Then again, as she pictured Kimberly, she could easily connect the image with this information.

"My grandpa – her dad – had died the year before that, and she... obviously, didn't handle it that well." Emma shrugged. "So, she was *not* ready for me, in any way."

Regan nodded. "Sure. What teenager could be?"

"Exactly. So, we lived with my gram, and Gram... well, she did everything for me. She's amazing," Emma informed Regan so seriously, and with such warmth in her voice Regan couldn't help but smile.

"Makes sense why you're more worried about what she thinks about me than what your mom thinks, then," she commented without any bite. Regardless of that being the starting point of their argument, Regan understood the root of it now, at least.

Emma's face was full of consternation as she hummed softly, clearly thinking over what to say next.

Regan almost told her that she didn't have to say anything more, now that she understood the fundamental aspects. But like hell was she going to stop Emma from sharing with her, not when she was so ready to soak up every drop of information.

"Kimberly... was unreliable, I guess, is the best way to say it. She'd dropped out of high school and lived with us, on and off. And when she was there, it was – it could be great," Emma whispered, and Regan wasn't sure if Emma even realized it.

"Like when she took you for bagels at the deli," Regan slipped in quietly, thinking about Kimberly clutching those bagels like a lifeline.

Emma blinked several times as if coming back to reality in the back of the car. "Right. Anyway. If she wasn't with Gram and me, she was staying with some guy. Kimberly always had a... sketchy dating life. But when I was thirteen, she met Ted. And I don't know what it was about him or if she was just finally *ready*, but – she grew up. They got married when I was fourteen, and he got offered a job in Miami soon after that."

She gave these details perfunctorily, as if she'd decided that she'd given enough emotion into the story.

Regan was completely invested as she found herself scooting closer to Emma. "You didn't go with her," she filled in expectantly.

Emma snorted with laughter. "Uh, no." Still, the look on her face grew pensive as she quietly said, "She asked me if I would, if I'd even consider it. *A lot.* But I didn't want to; I couldn't imagine living away from my gram, and I'd already started high school. So, she went with Ted. Then she had my sisters."

Regan blinked, shaking her head as she held up a hand to hit pause. "Wait – there are going to be sisters there tonight?" Had she known this? She didn't think so.

Confused amusement etched into Emma's expression. "Yes. Eva's twelve, and Everly's... eight? Yeah, eight."

"Are they fun?" Regan asked.

"I don't really know," Emma admitted after a few beats. "I'm not close to them. Obviously."

Contrite, Regan nodded. "Obviously."

Emma shrugged, exhaling deeply. "I've only ever met them a couple of times, whenever my mom brought them up here for visits. But they all moved up here in March. And Kimberly's been... intent... on trying to bond ever since." Emma turned to stare intently out the window once more as she murmured, "And you saw about how well that went when she came to the apartment."

Regan had a million more questions. She wanted to know *every-thing*, and questions nearly spilled past her lips.

But, as she looked closely at Emma, the anxiety she was feeling was clear as day. And Regan found that the questions she would normally ask fell right back down her throat.

She didn't need verbal confirmation to tell her what she could see with her own eyes.

They arrived only minutes later, and they both came to a halting stop on the sidewalk as soon as the Uber drove away behind them.

Regan gave a low whistle as she stared up at the house before them. The home itself was sprawling, with a large, well-maintained front lawn and a long stone walkway in front of them, leading up to the front door.

"So... I didn't expect a McMansion to be our final destination," she finally said, turning to look at Emma as she gestured up at the house.

Emma's expression was grim as she made no move to conquer the walkway up to the front door. "Yeah. Me, neither."

The emotion in her words made Regan wince as she dragged her gaze back to the house. "I'd expected something... different."

Maybe she'd been relying too heavily on stereotypes based on how Kimberly dressed and how much makeup she'd worn. Which, no judgment on Regan's part! But Regan had grown up in a neighborhood very similar to this one, and none of her neighbors styled themselves the way Kimberly had.

Also, there'd been that whole thing about how Emma hadn't been able to afford the Alton Writing Fellowship, so she'd made some assumptions about money...

Which this home did not align with.

Emma sighed, capturing Regan's attention once more. She watched as Emma swallowed heavily... and still made no attempt to move closer to the house.

"You know, we haven't even knocked yet," Regan lowered her voice conspiratorially. "We don't have to."

Finally, Emma's stare tore away from the house to blink down at Regan in confusion. "What?"

She wiggled her eyebrows as she whispered, "We can go. Call another Uber. Go get a pizza. Hang out at home. I'll let you pick the entertainment tonight, even though I'm terrified of what you might choose."

Last weekend, when Regan had extended Emma the option of picking what they'd watch for the first time since starting their hang-outs, Emma had simply shrugged and informed Regan that she didn't watch many shows or movies. When Regan pressed, baffled, Emma had informed her that she'd been so busy between school and work in the last few years, she hadn't kept up with anything current, and she hadn't wanted to pay for any subscriptions.

Terrifying, really.

Emma rolled her eyes, scoffing out a laugh as she pushed Regan's shoulder with her own.

And that reaction – so normal, a little bit of color returning to Emma's cheeks – gave Regan a rush of relief.

"No. It's fine. We're here. We're finally here. Now, we just go in and... it won't be so bad, probably," Emma muttered as she returned her attention to the imposing Stepford-like home in front of them.

"It won't be," Regan assured her. "I'll be here with you the whole time, running general interference. I'll be the best buffer you've ever seen. When we go in there, we're a team," she promised. She didn't hesitate as she offered Emma her hand. "Thom and Geri?"

Emma laughed, staring at Regan for a few seconds as she slid her fingers firmly and warmly between Regan's. "Thom and Geri."

twelve

Weird.

It was the only word Emma could properly think of to describe this evening.

So, so *weird*.

From the literal moment that Kimberly pulled the front door open when she and Regan were halfway up the winding walkway.

Her mom was dressed in a satin cocktail dress, and she waved at them exuberantly as she wore the widest smile. "Look at you two!"

"I thought you said my cocktail dress wasn't appropriate tonight?" Regan whispered to her, laughter in her voice, as she squeezed Emma's hand.

And it was that hand squeeze – warm, firm, coaxing – that kept Emma going. One foot in front of the other into the belly of the beast, so-to-speak.

"Oh, my Emma Bo Bemma," Kimberly murmured. She hugged Emma as soon as she and Regan were on the porch, her arms bracketing Emma tightly. And she felt the way she always did when her mom hugged her – comforted yet deeply uncertain at the same time. A very disconcerting feeling.

She pulled back from their hug.

"Look at you!" Kimberly reached out and ran her fingers lightly over the collar of Emma's shirt, then over the cotton fabric of the shoulders. "So sharp."

"I thought the same thing," Regan cut in from beside her, immediately snagging her mom's attention.

"And Regan, just as cute as the last time I saw you." Kimberly blessedly released Emma entirely and moved to pull Regan against her.

And Regan shot her a wink over her mom's shoulder, which, bafflingly, loosened the knots in Emma's stomach.

Regan let Kimberly hug her for entirely too long to be normal, and Emma's stomach churned again, wondering... was this how long her mom wished she could have hugged her for? Only she knew Emma wouldn't have liked it?

"Mom, you have to, like, let her breathe." A voice commented from a few feet back.

Kimberly laughed as she pulled away from Regan, and all three of them looked toward the doorway.

And there they were.

Eva, Everly, and Ted, completing the perfect family that fit into this perfect home.

Emma wished she could disappear into the manicured hedges.

Kimberly clasped her hands as she stood in the gap between Emma-and-Regan and everyone else. "Regan, these are Emma's sisters. Eva." She pointed at the frowning preteen – at *Emma's sister* – that had made the snarky comment, then at the younger, grinning girl. "And Everly."

It always took Emma aback, seeing both Eva and Everly. Seeing these girls that looked like her – at least a little. Emma got her height and her build from her unknown father's side of the family, but she shared the same features as these girls. It never failed to serve as a jarring feeling.

"And this is Ted, my husband," she finished, taking a few steps toward the doorway before she paused and looked unsure if she should continue closing the distance to stand with her actual family or stand in the middle.

"Everyone, this is Regan, Emma's *partner*," she stressed the word, throwing a proudly beaming smile in Emma's direction.

And she found herself smiling back, even though the movement felt awkward.

She never knew how to do this. How to greet her... family? These girls shared half of her DNA. When Emma looked at their little faces, she saw herself. And yet, she didn't know what to do with that fact. She didn't know what they thought when they saw her, either. She couldn't imagine they loved her; they barely knew her.

"Uh, hey, everyone. It's nice to see you again." Emma offered a wave.

Was that stupid? She felt stupid. And she felt annoyed at feeling stupid.

Regan stepped in closer to her, their sides brushing firmly together as she smiled that bright, brilliant, breathtaking smile. And it wasn't awkward or stilted looking at all, as she easily greeted, "Oh my *god*, you all look so much like Emma!" She looked back at Emma briefly before leaning in toward the doorway. "The crazy blue eyes, those cheekbones. That's amazing." She paused, tilting her head toward Ted. "Except for you; you don't have the striking family features. But I think it's a good thing that you don't resemble your wife!"

She laughed, then, and Emma wondered if making a joke about... incest? Should be normal or funny when first meeting someone, but for some Regan-reason, it worked. She found her own smile melting into one that felt natural as Ted – serious, quiet Ted – laughed as well.

"You guys took forever to walk up here," Eva cut in, not laughing or smiling.

Instead, she arched a blonde eyebrow up at Emma. Eva was different from the last time Emma had seen her – naturally older, as it had been... two years? Yeah, almost two years since Kimberly had brought the girls on a visit up to New York. The last time she'd seen her sisters, Eva had been ten and curious, asking Emma a million questions about her life. Emma answered as readily and honestly as she could, figuring that the best way to handle the conversation was to act the way she would if Eva were a kid she was babysitting, which had been her main gig throughout high school and into undergrad.

But she seemed more serious right now, more direct. Direct enough for Emma to know that she was no longer the same curious kid she could talk to as a babysitter.

"What, were you watching us?" Regan asked teasingly.

"Yeah, mom's been staring out the window for like an hour!" Everly added, giggling.

Emma could easily imagine her mother pacing. Likely wondering if Emma was even going to come or if she'd get a text that excused her and Regan's absence at the last minute. She knew, as she scanned her gaze over everyone else's expressions – well, everyone over that age of ten – that they all knew that to be true, too.

Kimberly's lips twitched into a forced smile, but before she could speak, Regan was already chatting, "Well, this house is absolutely gorgeous." She used the hand not holding onto Emma's to gesticulate dramatically around them. "Honestly, *I* needed Emma – Miss Punctual over here – to allow me to take a minute and marvel at it. The front gardens are really incredible; do you upkeep them, Kimberly?"

"She does," Ted asserted. Well, as much as Ted ever asserted in his heartily soft-spoken voice.

Her mom flushed as she waved her hand in front of her. "It's not a big deal. The last owners left very detailed instructions on maintaining the grounds when we moved."

"Trust me, it's a big deal," Regan doubled down with a serious nod.

"Do you garden?" Kimberly appeared as though having a shared interest with Regan was a dream come true.

Regan made a *pfft* sound. "Not really. I mean, you saw our apartment; we don't really have a yard."

Emma frowned and shook her head as she looked at Regan. "No, wait. You *do* have a ton of plants."

There were a handful of plants artfully arranged in the living room, near the bay windows, that were always lush and thriving. On top of that, Emma had seen earlier tonight that Regan's room held several more plants.

There were a variety – a couple of hanging ones, a large potted standing plant, one on her desk – but they were all plush and green and had made Regan's room look so... fresh. Alive. Inviting.

She'd never been in there before Regan called for her earlier, insisting she needed help choosing an outfit. After all, she granted

Regan the same privacy she'd like to be afforded. She'd imagined that Regan's room would be a little chaotic, much like the woman herself.

But she'd been pleasantly surprised.

No, it wasn't as organized as Emma's own space was. But it fit her large bed, desk, dresser, and plants with some extra space to spare. It was bigger than Emma's room was, which she'd found surprising – because that meant that between Regan and Sutton, Regan had the larger room – but it felt cozy. There were a litany of knick-knacks, which she'd expected from Regan, but from what she'd taken note of, it wasn't insanity incarnate.

Granted, she hadn't studied anything too closely.

Not when Regan had stood only feet away from her in that lingerie. Looking absolutely, ridiculously sexy.

It didn't shock her that Regan was so forward, so unassuming about herself. It *shouldn't* have shocked her that Regan would summon her while looking like... well, like an underwear model, not an ounce of shame in her body.

And, honestly, Regan had nothing to be ashamed of.

Emma *knew* that Regan Gallagher was beautiful; she had eyes. Emma even knew that she was attracted to Regan; she wasn't delusional.

But it was one thing to know those things to be true, and another entirely to be faced with the most attractive woman she knew, who happened to be her roommate, who also just so happened to be worming her way right through all of Emma's tried-and-true armor, wearing basically nothing.

She could feel herself blush as Regan smiled up at her. Even though she was doing exactly as she'd promised and acting as a world-class buffer, the look in her eyes was nothing short of genuine.

"I do love my plants," Regan confirmed, tilting her head slightly up at Emma before she turned her attention back to Kimberly.

Emma was able to take a real, deep breath again as alarm bells – ones that had nothing to do with Kimberly or her sisters – rang in the back of her mind.

"But it's not the same thing as keeping up this kind of yard."

"I think keeping your plants thriving when you live in an apartment in the city is even more impressive," Kimberly readily disagreed.

"I think you said that dinner was supposed to be ready in ten minutes, fifteen minutes ago," Eva cut in, obviously bored by the conversation about greenery.

Kimberly's eyes widened. "You're right, honey!" She clapped her hands together. "Let's head in. I'll give you a tour before we settle at the table."

Emma let out her first easy breath since they'd arrived once her mom's back was turned to them.

"Anything you need me to change? I can be adaptable," Regan whispered, dark eyes staring into her own.

Looking down at Regan, Emma took comfort in the sincere look she wore, and she was already shaking her head before she realized it. "No. Please, keep doing what you're doing."

She was certain she was going to need it.

Yes. Weird was the most fitting word.

Getting a tour of the three-thousand square foot home her mom now lived in with her husband and two children was weird. Weird being told that there was a guest room upstairs that Kimberly would just *love* for Emma and Regan to stay in sometime.

It was weird to be on the receiving end of so many dirty looks and snarky remarks from Eva.

It was weird to be seated across from Everly, who bounced in her chair and looked at Emma like she was a celebrity.

She supposed the only thing that wasn't weird was Ted. As his mostly silent presence was the same as she'd remembered since meeting him as a teenager.

And it was the weirdest thing was that the biggest comfort she had was having Regan by her side.

Never in a million fucking years would she have thought that Regan Gallagher would be her savior, especially not when it came to Kimberly, but... she was living in proof of it.

Regan kept up conversation with Kimberly, asking about the food she'd cooked, about what it was like living in Miami. She talked about dance trends and a popular children's show – something Emma had never even heard of – with Everly. She'd easily and brightly responded to every remark that Eva made.

Even as Eva had stared at them from across the table as they'd sat down and remarked, "You're *still* holding hands? It's been, like, forever." Her gaze had fallen defiantly to Emma. "What's that about?"

Emma had felt simultaneously like she wanted to laugh at the idea of a twelve-year-old trying to shame her and embarrassed at the fact that she *was* holding Regan's hand like a lifeline.

Rather than let go, though, as they pulled out their chairs with their free hands, Regan had made a point to flex her fingers around Emma's. The touch was firm and grounding, and Emma found herself holding tighter.

She'd never been a big hand-holder, not even when she'd been with Felicity, but the constant reminder that she wasn't alone tonight felt... it felt remarkably, insanely *good*.

"I just love to hold her hand," Regan had commented back, humming contentedly as she stroked her thumb over Emma's hand.

Emma felt herself shiver at it, the touch feeling like some sort of casual intimacy that she *shouldn't* have with Regan. But, at this moment, she did. And it was the least uncomfortable occurrence happening to her.

"Sometimes, holding someone's hand can feel so nice. Like second nature. It might be something you enjoy with your future partner," Regan had said, her voice so warm.

And it hadn't mattered to Emma that Regan's words were technically a lie. They'd felt true enough in the moment.

Regan even drew *Ted* out of his shell as she asked him about his job as a senior accountant at the firm he worked at. "I don't know much about numbers, but I *do* know that I once had to take a basic accounting class as part of the managerial program at the café, and it taught me that no matter where I end up in life – it won't be in finance."

Emma smiled at Regan's dramatic expression as she moved the food around her plate.

"You said you're a barista, right?" Kimberly leaned in with interest from where she sat at the head of the table. "Where, exactly, is that?"

"Topped Off. It's right near the NYU campus where most of Emma's classes were," Regan answered, tossing her a large, deliberately cheesy smile. "It's how we met."

"Ohhh, a meet cute?" The excitement in Kimberly's voice was palpable.

"Absolutely," Regan confirmed, heartily.

Emma couldn't stop herself from scoffing. "I don't know about that."

"I do," Regan defended, narrowing her eyes at Emma.

Emma held her ground. "A meet-cute is something *charming*."

"It's a memorable, exciting first interaction," Regan argued, turning to face everyone else, who were staring with undeniably rapt attention. "I *accidentally* spilled coffee all over Emma's shirt–"

"Which she then proceeded to literally tear off of me," Emma cut in dryly, garnering laughter from around the table.

Being the cause of the laughter in that light moment made her feel strangely... proud, and she found herself sitting up straighter in her chair.

"Not all the way off," Regan attempted to reason. "I just had to open it to ensure she didn't get burned!"

"Liquid burns are no joke," Ted added with a firm nod.

Emma couldn't help the incredulous laugh that left her throat. "Oh my god!"

Regan's grin was sheer triumph as she tossed a look at Emma. "Thank you, Ted. I agree."

Emma stared back, a ridiculous smile working onto her face at Regan's self-righteous expression. A smile she could not get rid of, even as she explained herself, "There were dozens of people there, watching this happen."

"*But*, I promptly took her back to the break room and gave her my favorite sweatshirt to change into." Regan *tsk*ed at her, eyes gleaming with laughter. "You always forget that part."

"It *is* a very comfy sweatshirt," Emma admitted with a defeated sigh. That much, she would give Regan.

She didn't realize what exactly she'd said to make the sweet playfulness drop from Regan's expression, shifting to something that looked curious.

And she didn't have much time to think about it before Kimberly let out an *aww*. "That is a meet-cute! You don't really ever hear about people meeting in person like that too much these days."

"Um... yeah," Regan quietly agreed, still looking intently at Emma.

So intently, it made her stomach clench, not with nerves but with an... awareness.

Finally, Regan shook her head and looked back at Kimberly. "It's so true; not in the day and age of dating apps."

Eva cleared her throat. "Can I start clearing plates? I'm done... and it looks like Emma is, too."

Emma's attention – and everyone else's – went to her own plate. Where she'd been pushing around the same carrot in the beef stew Kimberly had made for a while.

"Did you not like it?" Kimberly asked. "I know it's summer, so this is a bit out of season, but I thought – well, I remembered that you always loved Gram's beef stew, and this is her recipe."

There it was again, that hopeful edge in her tone.

Emma had always loved her gram's beef stew, and Regan's effusive compliments toward Kimberly when they'd first sat down were true; it was delicious. At least, the few bites Emma had managed to take of it.

But she felt so uncomfortable, her stomach so tight, she hadn't been able to eat much at all.

"No, it's good. I'm just, um, I'm not super hungry tonight, I guess," she muttered.

"Maybe for dessert, then?" Kimberly asked, ever optimistic, as she looked between Emma and Regan. "I know it's a Saturday night, and you two probably have some other plans, but–"

"But every Saturday, we have dessert during family movie night," Everly eagerly interrupted, grinning widely. "It's *my* turn to pick the movie!"

"If you're able to stay?" Kimberly finished, focusing on Emma, her eyes bright.

Emma's stomach churned again, and she placed her fork down in her bowl, steadfastly avoiding her mom's gaze. "I actually need to use the bathroom. Excuse me."

She stood and blindly made her way from the dining room to the full bathroom down the hall, unable to take a breath until she had the door shut behind her.

God, why was this so *hard*?

She sat down on the lip of the bathtub, dropping her head into her hands.

She shouldn't be surprised, right? Because this feeling had been exactly what she'd been trying to outrun by avoiding Kimberly for the last few months.

Even if she wasn't surprised, though, it was suffocating. It made her face feel too hot, and her chest feel too tight, and Emma squeezed her eyes closed against the sensations.

Panic arced through her when the door to the bathroom opened, and she snapped her head up. "Occupied. A little privacy, please."

If she couldn't get privacy in the bathroom, where could she?!

"Emma, if I have to try to find another bathroom in this house, I might get lost!" Regan whisper-shouted dramatically as she shut the door behind her. "Besides, next time you need privacy, you should make sure you hit the lock." As if to demonstrate, Regan did, indeed, lock the door.

Emma tried to summon some frustration. Really, she did.

But when she was faced with Regan and her gentle smile, Emma's guard was nowhere to be found. With Regan, she found herself... defenseless. She didn't need to be guarded from Regan. Not anymore – maybe not ever, she'd been learning – and definitely not here.

In this house, Regan was her biggest ally. And she had taken up that mantle as if Emma were paying her handsomely.

"I'll leave you alone." Regan's voice was surprisingly soft and soothing – a tone Emma had never heard from her before. "You've just been gone for almost ten minutes, and I... well, I got a little worried. I'm *still* a little worried, honestly."

Emma inhaled sharply. It had been ten minutes?!

She swallowed thickly, shaking her head. "I'm fine."

Across the bathroom, Regan leaned against the door, shooting her a disbelieving look. "Wow. I kind of thought you'd be a better liar than that."

Again, she wished she could summon up the energy to glare at Regan for the gently teasing tone.

"I'll be fine," she amended, her cheeks still feeling too warm.

"I'm sure you will be," Regan readily agreed. "But, as your *girlfriend*," she added with a cheeky smile. One that – insanely – made the tightness in Emma's chest relax a little. "I think it's my job to make sure you're okay right now."

Emma closed her eyes again.

"I turned down family movie night, even though Everly seems quite distraught that we won't be here to watch the latest Pixar release. I cited that I promised to take you to the bookstore before they close so you can enjoy a relaxing Sunday tomorrow with a new read."

Emma felt Regan sit on the lip of the tub too-close next to her, her solid warmth feeling like an anchor.

"It's a good lie," she whispered, still keeping her eyes closed. "If you *were* my girlfriend, that would be a perfect way to end a bad night." She frowned, considering, "Or a good night. Any night, really."

Regan scoffed. "I know. I've seen the bookshelves in your room. You know those things are digitized now, right?" As she spoke, she dropped her hand to Emma's forearm, stroking up and down.

The shockingly calming sensation of Regan's touch, mixed with Emma's visceral internal reaction to that comment, had her opening her eyes. "A digital book doesn't come close to capturing the magic of physical one. You will *never* convince me."

"Hey, I'm not the person raking in money from e-readers." Regan held up her free hand defensively.

Emma merely sighed, leaning sideways against the cool tiled wall.

"Look, Emma. I know things – as you told me – are complicated here. And I'm not going to tell you that you should be grateful Kimberly wants to spend time with you or whatever because... your feelings, whatever they may be, are valid. But you're usually so straightforward. At least, you are with me," Regan added, a grin flashing over her face as she stroked her thumb over Emma's wrist.

"Because talking to you is a lot easier than talking to Kimberly,"

Emma retorted. At least, she'd meant to. But her words came out a lot softer than she'd intended.

What alternate universe had she found herself in, she wondered, as she stared at the woman next to her. Surely, something had to have torn in the fabric of time and space in the last few weeks, meaning she was *here* in her *mom's house*, taking comfort from *Regan*.

Regan's smile grew impossibly brighter. "I just think that maybe you can try to talk to her with half of the brutal honesty you've used with me? Things might get resolved – one way or the other – a lot... neater. Without you needing to hide in the bathroom like you're skipping third-period chemistry."

She *wanted* to tell Regan that her advice was a lot easier said than done.

But a much bigger part of her wanted to take Regan's advice. Wanted to lean into it. She desperately wanted to move beyond this limbo she was in with her mother. The one she had been in for months, maybe even years, though it had been much easier to avoid, before.

"All right." Regan sighed, slowly sliding her hand from Emma's arm. "I'll get back to it; a fake girlfriend's work is never done."

Her put-upon tone pulled a hoarse laugh from the back of Emma's throat.

Regan paused with her hand on the doorknob as she looked back at Emma. "You got this, Thom."

She stared at the spot Regan had been standing in for several long moments before clearing her throat and dragging her hands through her hair. If nothing else, Regan had already bought them a ticket out of there, and Emma held onto that as she let herself out of the bathroom.

As she quietly pulled the door closed behind her, her eyes latched onto the photos that lined the wall of the hallway.

She'd glimpsed them during her tour but hadn't looked too closely.

There were, perhaps, too many photos for it to look truly balanced or artistic or whatever interior designers aimed for. But all of them reflected the happy, grinning faces of the family that lived in this house.

The family that had movie nights together every Saturday. The family that had bickered, playfully, over how big of a pool was big enough to have in their new house after leaving Miami.

There were photos of her mom and Ted together, a whole smattering of Eva and Everly – individually and together. Birthday photos, school pictures, family photoshoots. So many pictures of her mom with her sisters, living their quintessential childhoods. Not in any way reflective of the childhood she'd experienced with their mother, nor had she been a part of it when this new family had been built.

Yeah, there was that sickening feeling again.

Everything inside of Emma froze as her eyes landed on a photo of herself. On... a few photos of her, actually, she realized as she looked closer.

The biggest, most prominent Emma photo was from her senior yearbook. Hair done up, posing as directed by the school photographer, a muted smile on her lips.

There she was at her eighth birthday, where Kimberly had surprised her by not only showing up but also lugging a box of beginner chapter books – Emma had been elated by both things.

There she was at her seventh-grade science fair. Kimberly had – again – shocked her by showing up. By twelve, Emma had learned not to expect her mom to make it to school events. And when she did, she knew her mom would show up – the only parent from Emma's grade that was still in her twenties – wearing bright, flashy clothing cut inappropriately short. Kimberly beamed in the photo, her arm slung over Emma's shoulders. At twelve, she'd been hitting her growth spurt, so she and Kimberly had been nearly the same height. She was smiling, but adult Emma could see the embarrassed, hurt strain starting to form underneath.

There was the selfie Emma had taken with her gram when she'd been accepted into NYU. At the very least, that one made her lips curl into the ghost of a smile. Gram's grin in the picture was as big as Emma's.

And then her smile froze in place. There she and Kimberly were, in the hospital after Kimberly had given birth to her. Emma couldn't recognize herself in the photo – to her untrained eye, she, Eva, and Everly all looked exactly the same in these freshly born pictures. But she knew this one was her because Kimberly was just *so* young compared to the other two.

She looked like... like a kid. Which she had been.

Emma had no idea when Kimberly had gotten all of these photos from Gram, but – obviously – she had, at some point over the years.

"Emma," Kimberly's voice startled her as she stood a few feet away, pausing at the other end of the hall. "I," she flicked her eyes to the photos Emma had clearly been staring at. "I, um, see that you've found the family photo wall."

"Yeah." Emma clasped her hands together, feeling distinctly like she'd been caught doing something wrong. "Sorry."

Kimberly nearly tripped over herself as she jumped forward. "No! No, please don't be sorry. It's okay – it's better than okay! You should look."

But Emma didn't want to look anymore. She wanted, more than anything, to leave. In fact, she wanted – startlingly – very badly for Regan to return to her side, for her to swoop in and save this conversation.

She didn't know how to hide her discomfort, and she knew Kimberly could feel it; it was oppressively strong. She hoped, futilely, that her mom would just let it go. That she would let Emma leave without another word.

Emma had never been that lucky.

"I know Regan said you two have plans. And it's really sweet of her to take you to the bookstore; you've always loved a new book." A wide, soft grin slid over Kimberly's face as she gestured without looking at the picture of her bringing Emma books for her birthday. "But – maybe you can stay for dessert? Just a little while longer? You don't have to stay for family movie night."

Not only could she hear her mother's hopeful tone, she could *feel* it, and it cut like a knife.

Unable to stop herself, she looked again at the slew of pictures on the wall. At the family that had family movie night every weekend.

"Sorry, but we can't stay," Emma's voice was rough as the words escaped her.

Because she wasn't a part of this family. Not in *that* way. It was a truth that stung when she was confronted by it so blatantly, but it was a truth nonetheless.

"I know you don't want to be here," Kimberly's voice was tight with sadness, disappointment, and a whole host of emotions that Emma didn't want to try to decipher.

Not when the shock of her mom's words was still rushing through her. She opened her mouth, unsure of what to say. Even though she knew she hadn't hidden her feelings – Regan was right; she'd never lied well – she'd never expected Kimberly to call her out on it.

Kimberly waved any possible comment away, her lips tugging into a small, unhappy smile. "You don't need to say anything; it's very clear. And I hate pushing you so much, I really do. Every time I call or text, it feels awful because I know you don't want to answer. But I can't stop," her mom confessed, taking in a trembling breath.

Emma's stomach tightened into the biggest, tightest knot of the night. It made her feel sick, but also made her feel like she wanted to cry. And she hated it, she hated every second that was crawling by.

"I just – I *love you* so much, Emma Bo Bemma. I know it might be hard for you to believe. But I do. I know you hate it when I call you that name, too, and I can't help it. Because I miss the days when I'd come to see you, and your little face would just light up. When you were so excited to see me, and you wanted me around." Her voice went reedy, "When you loved me, too. And I regret everything from back then. Every time I flaked out. Every time I didn't call. Every time I left."

Emma's throat was so tight with every word her mom spoke, she couldn't have possibly responded even if she wanted to. It was so tight, she struggled to simply *breathe* through it.

"I know our relationship is the way it is entirely because of me. But that's why I haven't been able to give up trying to get you over here for the last few months. I've had this hope that if you just... if you came here, if I could have you here with your sisters, as a *family*, it would feel right." There was a desperation in her words, which burrowed deep into Emma's chest. "Because it feels so right, to me."

"I thought – I *hoped* – that maybe it would feel right for you, too. Being here." She took a deep, shaking breath and lifted her wide, sad eyes to Emma's. "But I can see that it doesn't," she conceded, bowing her head with the words. As if just *saying* that she was going to give up pained her.

"I understand why you hate me, Emma." The tears brimming in her mom's eyes – the same blue as her own – spilled over in thick trails down her cheeks. "I wasn't a good mom to you, not even close to the mother you deserved. And I don't want you to resent me even more, so I... I'll back off."

Kimberly sniffled, reaching up to press her hand over her mouth, and Emma felt like her chest had been cracked open. It could no longer contain the tightness, the pain. The pain that she wished felt hollow, but it didn't; it would be easier if this pain were hollow.

It was so achingly full.

"I don't hate you," she managed to push out, trying her best to blink back her own tears. The backs of her eyes burned with them.

"You – you don't?" Kimberly asked, an undeniable hope in her voice as she searched Emma's face.

God, Emma *wished* she did. She couldn't say that. She couldn't summon that kind of cruelty. But this would be so much simpler if she hated Kimberly.

"I don't know how to feel around you," she confessed the truth in a whisper, dropping her gaze away from her mom's. It felt like it was far too much to handle. "Because I do... love you." The words nearly stuck in her throat, feeling so *heavy*. Saying them felt clunky and awkward, but also not wrong.

What Kimberly had said minutes ago was true – throughout her childhood, Emma had been utterly thrilled every time her mom returned home. Every time she'd taken Emma out for bagels, every time she'd surprised her by simply *being there*. But it got harder as the years went on. Then, the wall was built, solid and nearly impenetrable, when her mom moved to Florida and started her family anew.

She hastily reached up to swipe her hand over her eyes, trying to take a deep, stabilizing breath.

Emma did *not* want to break down here, surrounded by family photos in this hallway.

It took effort to clear her throat, trying to rid some of the tightness there, as she blinked her eyes open. "You – you don't need to stop texting or calling. But... maybe less? Just – I need to be able to breathe."

Kimberly's eyes were wide, and she nodded along as if soaking in every word Emma said. "I can do that."

"And please stop calling me during the workday."

"Yes, absolutely. I'll stop," she promised, breathing a watery laugh.

As Emma took a deep breath, she realized that she didn't feel like she was drowning. She could do this; she could try with Kimberly.

After all, *trying* with Regan had been working wonders. Maybe it could work here, too.

~

The last thing Emma had expected to come from her night was *actually* browsing through the bookshelves at On the Same Page, the bookshop a block away from their apartment.

Regan had called for their Uber, which had dropped them off here twenty minutes ago.

Even though she was mentally and physically *exhausted* from the emotions that had wrung her dry tonight, being here, surrounded by the stacks of one of her favorite bookshops, gave her an immediate sense of calm. A soothing balm over the jagged edges inside of her that had been exposed tonight.

But right now, she was in her happy place. She'd combed through the general fiction section and had taken ten books from her TBR list, settling in one of the comfortable, worn chairs to decide which ones she was going to purchase.

Regan had disappeared when they'd walked through the doors, but Emma figured she would hear a commotion somewhere in the store and find her eventually.

As if summoned by Emma's thoughts, Regan appeared next to her.

"There you are!" In her hand was one of the little white paper bags from the small café at the back of the store.

Emma placed her hand over her small stack of books. "You know, I didn't *actually* expect you to take me to the bookstore tonight."

Regan shrugged as she walked closer, wedging herself between the little round display of books and the chair, so that she could perch on the arm. "I know. But you said that this is the best way for you to end a bad night, so I figured... why not?"

The rush of appreciation that she felt for the woman taking up far too much of her personal space was alarming. But after the emotional toll of the night, Emma didn't have it in her to fight it.

"You don't have to buy my books, though," she commented, leaning her head back and tilting it up to look at Regan properly.

Who was already looking down at her.

It was annoying, honestly, that Regan's jaw looked so good from this angle; no one was supposed to look good from an angle under their chin.

Emma figured it had something to do with that radiant grin.

"Emma, what kind of girlfriend would I be if I didn't buy your books?" Regan's gaze dropped to the books in question, her eyes widening. "Wow. I leave you alone to go to the café, and you amassed half an aisle."

Before Emma could respond, Regan smiled suddenly, as if just remembering something, as she lifted the bag.

"Right! The bakery." She opened the bag, reaching into it and emerging with a double-chocolate cookie and a triumphant grin. "Here you go!"

Emma hadn't even realized how hungry she actually was until she was presented with the treat. Still, she hesitated before taking it. "I can wait until we get home to have something else."

Regan frowned, first at the cookie, then at her. "I thought it looked good."

"It does," she agreed.

Regan pushed it toward her, again, insistently. "Between the enormous stack of books in your lap and then the walk back, it will be at least another half hour or so before we're home. Take the cookie."

Emma pursed her lips as she reached out for the dessert, giving into her body's demands. "It's a dangerous thing, living with you," she grumbled. "The desserts you're always baking. The stuff you like to bring home from the café. This cookie." She held it up, waving it in front of Regan's face as if she needed the reminder.

Playfully, Regan leaned forward and took a bite. Her dark eyes

193

grinned down at Emma as she flicked her tongue out and licked a wayward crumb from her bottom lip.

Emma diverted her gaze. Yes, it had been a *long* night.

"Emma, you hardly ate anything at dinner. Like, you ate *nothing* tonight. Besides, you have a great body. A little dessert is fine."

She glanced up at Regan dubiously. "You know, we're not at my mom's house anymore. You don't have to keep up the compliments and the adoring girlfriend thing."

Regan's eyebrows knitted together as she turned even more inward on the arm of the chair. Her thigh settled firmly against Emma's side as she asked, "What's that supposed to mean?"

Emma stared at her, feeling the burning sensation in her cheeks returning. "The comment about my body," she muttered.

But Regan didn't back down. "No, I got that; I still don't understand what you mean."

"Regan," she grit out, exasperated.

"Emma," Regan mirrored her tone.

It pushed her enough to gesture down at herself. "I *mean* that I'm not... fun-sized like you are. Obviously."

"And?" Regan immediately asked, her stare intent. Demanding.

Emma squirmed where she sat. "You've seen me without my shirt on multiple times," she reminded her, frustrated with how embarrassed she felt. "Not by my choice, I might add."

"Uh, yeah? I think that actually makes me a wonderfully qualified source."

Emma groaned, dropping her head back against the chair, leaving her eye level with Regan's chest. Which she immediately looked away from, staring straight up at the ceiling.

She didn't hate her body; she'd come a long way from the issues she'd had with herself in school. She'd towered over most of her classmates when she'd hit her growth spurt, pushing her to nearly her full height. Her breasts had grown insanely fast, as well as her butt, hips, and thighs, and her skin still had the stretch marks to prove it.

"Regan, come on. I'm five-ten and not a waif, like Sutton is. We both know that."

Still, Regan stared down at her, confusion clear. "Yeah, I obviously know you aren't a *waif*." She then frowned and muttered, "What a strange word choice."

Before Emma could interject, Regan's gaze returned to her. And not her face, either.

No, Regan's intent stare started at her thighs. "I really like your body, though. Why do you think I'm being disingenuous?"

Emma really *wanted* to make an easy quip back. But she found herself incapable of doing so, as Regan's eyes slowly took her in, moving up her body as if studying...

"Art," Regan's voice was so low. Low enough, Emma wasn't certain she was supposed to overhear her. "You look like all of those classic sculptures of women in a museum. Like a piece of art."

Emma's breath caught in her throat as the pit of her stomach tingled at the compliment. At what – insanely – might have been the most beautiful sentiment anyone had ever expressed about her.

And it felt – it felt damningly uncomfortable. But not in the same way she'd been uncomfortable at Kimberly's. This was far more... aware. It made her shiver, an unexpected heat sparking alive inside of her.

Emma minutely shook her head, denying its very existence.

"You have an incredible figure," Regan continued in that quiet, thoughtful, slightly raspy tone. "Which you have to know; most of your outfits highlight the perfect curve of your waist."

When those dark eyes fell to her chest, she shivered. Then cursed herself for it before she silently cursed Regan. Why was she *looking* at her like that?!

It was – it was wildly inappropriate.

And it was very, very wrong for a straight woman to stare at another woman like this, a voice said in the back of Emma's mind.

Before she thought... well, this was *Regan*. So.

"And your breasts are out of this world. Just – so impressive. They look soft," Regan finally said, staring –

Emma followed her gaze, feeling her own breathing grow more erratic at the way she was being watched as she realized that from Regan's vantage point, she had a clear shot...

"Are you staring down my shirt?"

She felt flustered, both baffled and heated. Emma tried to tell herself the heat was from frustration, but –

"Oh my god!" Regan shouted out as her solid presence disappeared from Emma's side.

She watched, wide-eyed, as Regan pitched herself off the side of the chair, knocking into the small display of books behind her. All of the books joined Regan on her descent to crash onto the floor.

Emma jumped up in alarm, sending her own potential book purchases falling down.

If she were any other customer, she'd be annoyed by the chaos. But, as it was, she could only be grateful for this moment cutting through whatever insane, dangerous place her mind had started to go to.

"Are you okay?" She asked, genuine concern starting to set in when Regan didn't immediately pop up.

Instead, she stared dazedly up at Emma, blinking several times, her mouth agape but not saying anything.

"Did you hit your head?" She pressed, leaning down next to Regan as her worry grew.

Regan looked at her, eyes moving over her face slowly before she slowly shook her head. "I'm fine. I'm – I'm totally good."

Emma offered her a hand, which Regan stared at with wide eyes for several long moments. Long enough that anxiety started to set in; was it now going to be her turn to escort Regan to the hospital? Finally, thankfully, she reached out and slid her palm against Emma's, letting herself be hauled up.

When Regan was on her feet – looking shell-shocked – Emma peered down at her, scanning for injuries. Regan seemed fine, though. Just... wide-eyed, staring back at Emma.

Yes.

Weird was the appropriate word for the evening, indeed.

thirteen

REGAN DIDN'T CONSIDER herself the type to suffer in silence.

Regan also didn't know if she was suffering.

Because, frankly, Regan had no fucking clue what the hell was going on in her own mind. In her own *body*, which was a first for her.

All she knew for certain was that last night, she'd been acting super, duper normally – as a friend! – and complimenting Emma's body. That was the kind of thing Regan did for her friends all the time!

She couldn't even count the number of occurrences over the years in which Sutton had been fretting over something in the mirror, and she'd swooped in to dissuade any and all self-conscious notions from her best friend's mind. She'd done the same for other friends over the years; just the other day, Beth had been lamenting about how she'd spotted a gray hair, and Regan had hyped her up: tons of women wore their naturally gray hair and were totally fucking gorgeous! Aging was normal! Why was it sexy when men started to gray at their temples, but not women?!

Hell, Regan did that for customers. For the random woman she shared an elevator with at the gynecologist – *hey, your legs look great in that dress*!

Regan merely viewed that as her job as a woman. Who else would be there to hype one another up, sincerely and genuinely, without expecting anything in return, if not for other women?!

She'd believed she'd been doing that with Emma at the bookstore.

Yeah, she understood that Emma was implying that she wasn't as attractive as someone who was *waif-like*. But she honestly hadn't understood why Emma would think that.

Fine, Emma wasn't, like, super thin – big deal.

Regan had never been captivated by another woman's physique the way she was by Emma's. She was voluptuous and curvy, and her clothing clung to her in a ridiculously hot way, and Regan intended to say that.

Hype woman!

Only... she hadn't been able to get the words out. Not in any normal sort of way.

Because, as she'd stared at Emma's body, she hadn't just felt the need to hype Emma up. She'd felt – she'd *felt*.

Her heart had skipped a beat, and she felt a heat start to simmer low in her stomach. That tingling awareness had started buzzing through her body, and she hadn't truly recognized it for what it was until she'd realized she *was* feeling attraction. While staring down Emma's shirt, like a perv.

And that insistent, heart-pounding feeling hadn't faded as soon as it arrived.

It had remained throughout their walk back home as they'd gone down the hallway to their respective bedrooms. When Regan realized her eyes had fallen to Emma's butt as she'd walked in front of her –

How often did that happen?! She didn't even know! Was it brand new?

– she was grateful, for once, that Emma proclaimed to be too tired to do anything other than fall into bed with one of her new books as soon as they'd returned home.

Regan had her own thoughts to ponder.

Like, how did she know if she was attracted to women?

The thought had kept her up for most of the night. It had her pacing back and forth in her room this morning.

Google was surprisingly unhelpful; Regan had taken all sorts of quizzes before about whether she was a lesbian! Obviously, they hadn't gotten her anywhere so far.

She clutched her phone tightly, staring down at Sutton's contact info. She'd very nearly hit that call button, oh, only about a hundred times in the last ten hours.

How was she supposed to get through this situation without Sutton's input?!

Finally, she hit the call icon.

Doubt seeped in, though, by the very first ring.

How could she call Sutton and get her honest thoughts when Regan couldn't tell her the truth? Because Sutton didn't know that Emma was attracted to women, and Regan couldn't – wouldn't – break Emma's confidence, even if she didn't understand her need to be so cloak and dagger.

Another ring.

And Regan knew herself; she knew there was no way she could even begin to assess this situation with Sutton and omit any details. Even if she tried to, Sutton would know she wasn't telling the truth.

"Damn you, Sutton Spencer, and your truth-seeking eyes," she muttered, canceling the call.

She startled as her phone started buzzing in her hand.

Incoming call – Sutton, The One and Only.

Regan bared her teeth down at her phone, indecision warring, before she picked it up. She couldn't start screening Sutton's calls; she was already in the midst of a personal crisis! If she had sent Sutton to voicemail, she wouldn't know who she was anymore.

"Hiiii," she sang out brightly.

There was a beat of quiet before Sutton questioningly spoke. "Hey. Is everything okay?"

"Ha. Ha. Yeah. Why wouldn't it be?" Regan asked, feeling pretty good about herself for turning the question back on Sutton.

"Um, because you just called me but then hung up before I could answer? Was it a butt-dial?"

Right. "Yes. Yes, my ginger sunflower, it *was* a butt-dial. Just me and my silly ass, literally."

Sutton hummed, the sound full of disbelief. "And everything is okay with Emma?"

Regan's eyes widened as she pulled the phone away from her ear and stared at it, baffled; did her best friend develop some sort of ESP?! "I – what did you hear? What's on your mind?"

"Nothing...? All you've said in the last week or so is that you two are *peachy keen*." Sutton's tone was full of suspicion as she quoted the exact phrase Regan had texted her regarding the state of her and Emma's relationship.

Friendship, that was. Friend relationship.

"Because it is! It's peachy keen." Which, actually, wasn't even a lie.

"Uh huh," Sutton shortly hummed. The skepticism was so loud that it rang in Regan's ears. "So, what did you do last night? You didn't answer my texts."

Seriously, *had* Sutton developed some sort of brain link with her?!

Because Sutton was still being kept in the dark regarding the "dating" situation with Emma's family so, naturally, Regan wasn't able to tell her what her Saturday night plans were.

"Yeah. Sorry about that. Nothing to worry about; I just turned my notifications off for the night because Audrey was being Audrey." Which – again – was the truth.

"Aw, I'm so sorry," Sutton's disbelief immediately melted into sheer sympathy. "Was she rude to you?"

"Is the sky blue?" Regan joked.

"I feel so awful saying this, but I really can't stand her." The muted anger in Sutton's voice made Regan feel supported, as always. After all, if anyone understood her and had her back with her family, it was Sutton. Granted, Regan's sour feelings about Audrey yesterday had long faded by now.

"You and me, both. But it's fine. I'm all right."

Which was true. Because the realization that she might be attracted to Emma had overshadowed Audrey's texts. Like, by a lot. By a *whole* lot.

"I feel so bad that I won't be there with all of her wedding stuff happening. I want you to call me if you need me, even though I'm in a different time zone. Okay?"

Comforted by how genuine she knew Sutton was in that, she found herself smiling. "I will. Even if it's two in the morning your time and you're having phone sex with Charlo–"

Regan cut herself off with a gasp, her eyes widening as the idea struck her.

Sutton groaned. "I already told you; we are *not* discussing my phone sex life with Charlotte."

"Yes. Yes, shame on me for bringing it up. I should hang up and think about what I've done. That's what I'm going to do. Love you, starfish, kick ass!"

Sutton barely managed a confused goodbye before Regan hung up. Quickly, her anticipation mounting, she scrolled through her contacts until she came to the right person.

She needed help. And it so happened that she knew a lesbian guru.

REGAN – 8:08 AM

Heyyyy what are you up to today?

Given that your hot gf is out of the country, I figured you might be available

Esp for the best friend of your hot gf who is in need of some serious counseling rn

SAPPHIC counseling!

STUNNING CHARLOTTE THOMPSON – 8:14 AM

You know, I distinctly recall when I gave you my number in March that it was for emergencies.

REGAN – 8:15 AM

First and foremost, I am experiencing an emergency

Second and secondmost, if my memory serves, I was there for you on the worst night of your life and then played an integral part in you winning back the love of your life...

I feel like that kind of warrants us being text pals on occasion

STUNNING CHARLOTTE THOMPSON – 8:19 AM

Fine. You have my attention.

But I would like to stress that this number is private.

REGAN – 8:20 AM

What do you think I'm gonna do, write your # in sharpie in a bathroom stall and write: call for a good time?

In fairness, Regan *had* that thought – and other similar ones – when Charlotte had broken Sutton's heart six months ago. But she'd never do that to Charlotte, *now*.

STUNNING CHARLOTTE THOMPSON – 8:27 AM

I think it's better if I refrain from answering that.

Regan was usually totally thrilled to engage in a little texting banter with a friend. Or whatever Charlotte was to her.

But right now, she felt so antsy. Just the very thought that Emma was sleeping across the hall and could get up at any moment – granted, Emma didn't normally rise so early, but you never know! – made her feel like she was ready to climb out of her skin.

REGAN – 8:27 AM

Charlotte, are you available today?

Regan had never been inside Charlotte's apartment before.

It had the startlingly similar feeling of running into a teacher outside of school. Like she was getting a glimpse at the private life of someone she had no business seeing.

Only, this was her best friend's girlfriend, which meant Regan – in her opinion – had the right.

There was a lack of personal items on display, though Regan supposed that didn't shock her.

She paused when she got to the only framed photo in the living room that wasn't professional artwork, and she grinned down at it. A picture of Sutton laughing, which looked very familiar. In fact... Regan bent down to get a better look at it.

"If you're satisfied poking around in my personal business," Charlotte drawled from where she sat at her kitchen island, watching Regan roam around her home. "Maybe we could discuss why you were contacting me before nine in the morning on a weekend, proclaiming to have an emergency?"

Regan sent her an impish smile over her shoulder, pointing at the picture beside her. "I took this, you know. And I put it up on Sapphic-Spark. Safe to say I made a good choice, huh?"

Charlotte sipped on her coffee, giving Regan a measured look over the rim of her mug. After she swallowed, she hummed. "Yes. You very obviously made a good choice, though I'm not sure it would be possible to pick a bad picture of Sutton."

Oh, there it was. Beneath whatever exterior Charlotte put on when Sutton wasn't around, even talking about her made the corniness jump right out. Regan loved it.

"You fucking sap."

Charlotte didn't verbally disagree. Instead, she nailed Regan with one of her serious stares and asked, "Am I mistaken, or did you state that you needed *sapphic counseling*? What in the world do you mean by that?"

Oh, right.

Immediately, the reminder of her current sapphic dilemma – dilEMMA – rushed back to the forefront of her mind, bringing with it the jangling of her nerves.

She could feel her face heat, not from embarrassment but simply from the image of Emma that popped into her mind's eye.

"How do you know if you're attracted to women? Like, how do *I* know if *I'm* attracted to women?"

Charlotte's eyebrows both lifted in obvious surprise. Normally, surprising Charlotte would have made Regan feel pretty good, but right now, her own conundrum was all she could focus on.

"Is this hypothetical or...?"

Regan shook her head. "Totally not hypothetical."

Charlotte pursed her lips, delicately clearing her throat, as she set down her coffee mug. "I *do* feel the need to ask before we go any further: this has nothing to do with Sutton or me?"

Regan reeled back with a disgusted grimace. "Ew! No!"

"*Ew?*"

"Sutton is like my sister! Only *closer*, because Sutton and I actually like one another. And you're..." She stared critically at Charlotte, some revulsion fading as she took a few steps closer.

She kept her eyes trained on Charlotte's face, carefully studying her.

Charlotte Thompson *was* incredibly attractive; Regan had known that since she'd first seen her profile on SapphicSpark. She had big, doe eyes that had a knowing gleam to them, a small, straight nose, and full lips. Her skin was flawless, as was her long, wavy brown hair.

Humming to herself, Regan ran her gaze down Charlotte's body appraisingly. Yeah, her body looked great, too.

But Regan didn't *feel* anything. None of the urges and desires that had swiftly entered her mind last night when she'd been looking at Emma.

Stumped, Regan crossed her arms over her waist, sighing to herself.

"Should I pretend that you *didn't* just blatantly check me out?" Charlotte asked incredulously.

Regan met her incredulous level. "Only to check and see if I was attracted to you!"

"That is generally why someone checks out another person, yes."

"Well, I'm not. So, don't go letting your ego get any more inflated."

Charlotte closed her eyes, reaching up to pinch the bridge of her nose. "Regan. Please, I truly beg of you, will you explain yourself? If you want advice, I need context."

She could literally feel the words bubbling up in her throat, the desire to spill the beans and try to find more insight into whatever was going on inside her overwhelming.

"Okay, so I've been spending a lot of time with this woman lately. That I know from the café," she rushed to add on because it technically was the truth – that *was* how she'd first met Emma – but also because she felt it would help throw Charlotte off from connecting any dots to the fact that she was, in fact, referencing Emma. "And when we were hanging out, I was complimenting her. You know, the way I do. Like, with Sutton – in a *friendly* way," she emphasized, lest Charlotte ask any other ridiculous questions.

"Yes, I have heard the many interesting complimentary choices," Charlotte confirmed, motioning for Regan to continue with a regal wave of her hand. "Very sweet, but very fascinating at times."

Regan could accept that.

"I was going to just... just be honest with her. Trying to make her feel a little confidence boost because I *do* think that she is really attractive."

As she spoke, she replayed the moment with Emma in her mind. The intention she'd had, the way she'd looked at Emma with platonic intentions, but her thoughts had then been... intercepted. By something very not platonic.

"But I felt – I felt – it didn't feel how I feel when I compliment Sutton. Or when I just checked you out."

"And... what *did* you feel?" Charlotte pressed coaxingly.

Regan swallowed thickly. "I felt like I didn't just want to compliment her thighs or her boobs, but I wanted to touch them. Like, I didn't want her to just think I was *saying* these words for the sake of saying them. I felt like," she licked her lips, "Like she had no business feeling bad about herself in any way because she looked *sexy*. And I didn't just think, objectively, she was sexy. I *felt* like she was."

Even saying those words made her feel dazed all over again.

"That certainly sounds very telling," Charlotte commented after several beats.

Regan stared. "That's all you have to say?"

Charlotte matched her stare easily. "What else would you like me to tell you?"

Tossing her arms in the air, Regan resumed her pacing from this morning. "I don't know! You're the expert here. You're the one who was essentially tutoring Sutton in the art of dating." She frowned. "Then again, you didn't do that great of a job, given that she never went on any dates with anyone else."

"She went speed dating," Charlotte corrected, her voice dipping to a jealous mutter.

"You know what I mean." Besides, Regan had signed Sutton up for that, so it didn't even really count.

"Regan, the difference between my interactions with Sutton in the beginning, other than the obvious–"

"That you desperately wanted to make passionate love to her."

Charlotte's nose wrinkled up in disdain. "I was going to say that I was interested in her."

"To-may-to, to-mah-to."

Charlotte took to ignoring her, then. "As I was saying, the difference is that when Sutton wanted my advice, she knew for a fact that she was attracted to women. What *you're* asking my advice on is a far more difficult subject."

Confused, Regan slowly paused her pacing. "Why?"

Charlotte stared critically at her for several moments, and Regan nearly squirmed. She had to hand it to Charlotte; she had an incredibly direct stare. One that made Regan feel *seen* from the inside out. What a skill to have.

"Because – there simply is no one size fits all here," Charlotte explained before taking another sip from her mug. She seemed too calm right now, especially given the storm Regan was feeling inside.

She waited several more seconds to see what other sage wisdom Charlotte would offer, only to be met with quiet.

"That's all you have to say?!"

This time, Charlotte let out a quietly amused chuckle. "There *is* no real answer, Regan. I can't tell you if you're attracted to women or not. Or even if you're attracted to *this* woman or not."

Regan stared at her dismally. "Charlotte, please. You want to be a leader of our country. I need more leadership right now. Win my vote."

Charlotte seemed to take her statement seriously. Seemingly as a challenge. She focused that intense stare on Regan, tilting her head slightly as she asked, "Fine. Why are *you* doubting this? My intuition about you is that you typically follow your feelings without fear. Why is this different?"

Huh. Okay, that was a good starting point. Regan's eyebrows

furrowed in thought as she slowly resumed her strides back and forth across Charlotte's living room.

"I think... I think it's because – shouldn't I *know*, by now? Shouldn't I have figured it out?" She demanded from both of them and the universe. "If I'm queer, shouldn't I *know*? I was with Sutton every step of the way through her sapphic self-discovery. I did all of the research for her on different queer dating apps–"

"Appreciated," Charlotte interjected.

"You're welcome," she answered easily, continuing without missing a beat. "But none of it made me feel like I was missing a piece of myself. Shouldn't I have felt some sort of... stirring, too?" She challenged, her hands falling to her hips as she faced Charlotte. "Shouldn't I have felt my awakening, then?"

"It's not some sort of sixth-sense tingling," Charlotte's amusement was clear in her tone, even if her small smirk was reserved. "And just because you witnessed Sutton going through something doesn't mean you'd have felt the same way."

Regan wondered if, in some way, maybe watching Sutton go through her self-discovery journey had made Regan totally dismiss the idea for herself. She'd been fully focused on working with Sutton through her newly realized bisexuality and becoming the number one best friend ally. She hadn't contemplated her own sexuality at all. Not really.

"When did *you* know that you were into women?" She asked, shaking her head.

"Middle school," Charlotte answered unthinkingly.

"Exactly!"

"I'm also not attracted to men in the slightest, so that may have facilitated my discovery. If *you* are attracted to men, it makes sense that it might have taken you longer. That's a very normal thing," Charlotte informed her, her voice softening. Enough that Regan *did* feel comforted. "Sexuality is fluid; it's a scale. You are – bafflingly – attracted to men. Maybe your sexuality scale is ninety percent men, ten percent women, or an even smaller percentage. It's not one-size-fits-all. Some women don't even realize they are full-fledged lesbians until they're decades older than you are."

Regan felt like some of the wind was taken out of her sails, abruptly feeling very aware that she'd gotten very little sleep all night.

"That's not exactly the information I'd hoped to hear, but I guess it makes sense. Guess I'm luckier than the women that don't figure their shit out until they're even older than I am."

"What I *can* say," Charlotte aimed a look at her. "Is that – even if you've never experienced this kind of attraction before, it doesn't mean it's invalid. Sometimes that's how it is. Maybe you really haven't been attracted to women before. Maybe there's something about this person. Maybe it *was* just something you felt in the moment and isn't going to be replicated. None of those potential avenues are wrong."

Regan ultimately collapsed onto Charlotte's couch, blowing out a long-suffering breath. "What would you do, then? What do I do now?" That was really what Regan needed a guiding light for, she supposed. What was the appropriate next step? "That's something you can help with, right?"

Charlotte softly sighed, slowly standing from the island and coming to join her on the sofa. "First, you continue to hang out with this friend. See if you feel those same... stirrings again. If you do, then you'll have your answer."

Regan blew out a breath, slumping down on the couch even more as she stared blankly ahead. "God, this sapphic shit is exhausting."

She felt better going home than when she'd left in the morning, at the very least.

After all, Regan felt her emotions very strongly. Maybe last night had been a strange one-off. It could happen, according to her conversation with Charlotte. And she had no reason to doubt Charlotte, who was a veritable lesbian lothario. Pre-Sutton, of course.

Regan took a deep breath as she entered the apartment, feeling nervous anticipation weigh heavily in the pit of her stomach.

Honestly, she didn't even *know* what she wanted to be the outcome here.

Everything would probably be way simpler, clearer, and better if she didn't have any attraction to Emma, she decided as she toed her shoes off.

And that was probably the reality she should expect, she reasoned with herself. Why should she believe that the way she viewed Emma was fundamentally altered? It was *probably* a fluke, a weird one-time response.

Walking down the hall into the kitchen, she came to a stumbling stop.

Emma sat at their table, wearing a black tank top as she pressed one of Regan's small gel ice packs – she'd found them online, all in bright colors with little slogans on them – against the bare skin of her neck.

Her hair was thrown up in a bun on the top of her head, and she wore a pair of wide-framed glasses, and... fine, yeah. Okay, so she was attractive. That was true. But –

Regan's throat ran dry as Emma slowly slid the ice pack down her neck, and she choked on the sharp inhale she'd just taken.

Because there it was.

That same feeling from last night. This insanely strong urge to replace Emma's own hand with her own as that ice pack slid over her warm, soft skin.

Emma lifted her gaze away from her computer as Regan choked on nothing. "Are you all right?"

Regan wheezed. "I'm fine! Fine, I am. Why do you ask?"

Attention completely off of her work, Emma sat up straight in the chair, eyeing Regan closely. "Because you're standing in the doorway, staring at me, sounding like you can't breathe?" She offered, drawing out the words slowly. "On top of that, last night you took an intense fall to the ground, and – based on how you've been acting ever since – I'm still not convinced you didn't whack your head."

"Oh. Right. That makes sense, then, why you'd be concerned." She paused for only a second, unable to take her gaze off Emma. "You *are* concerned, right? About me."

Emma's blue eyes – Regan really was constantly amazed by her eyes. Seriously, so crystal clear. Stunningly so – narrowed in suspicion. "No, I'm asking about your well-being because I couldn't care less if you keeled over."

A titter of laughter escaped her as she felt her cheeks heat. "Funny. Funny woman."

Regan forced herself to walk past Emma so she could brace her hands on the porcelain edge of the sink. She *was* attracted to Emma. She was *attracted to Emma*. A woman she'd known for two years. Her roommate. Her new-found friend.

What did it mean? What happened now? Her mind buzzed with questions, and Regan felt like her veins had been lit up by a sparkler.

"Where were you? I saw that you didn't have work on the calendar," Emma commented.

Regan could feel Emma's eyes on her back, and she couldn't help but wonder what Emma saw when she looked at *her*.

Emma had said that she'd looked good in her underwear. But – as Regan well-knew – that didn't denote feeling attraction.

"I was hanging out with Charlotte," she pushed herself to answer. Did she sound normal?

"Sutton's Charlotte?" Emma clarified, sounding surprised.

"The one and only. Why? Did you miss me?" She couldn't help but ask, meaning to tease, not feel like she was invested in the answer.

But... she hoped Emma missed her. At the very least, she liked that Emma had thought about Regan when she'd been gone. Because she thought about Emma when *she* wasn't home.

"Desperately," Emma dryly responded. "I just didn't realize you two were friends. Like, hang out without Sutton there to buffer kind of friends."

Regan shrugged. "It's a relatively new development."

There were a lot of those going around in Regan's life.

Speaking of Charlotte, Regan pulled her phone out of her pocket.

REGAN – 2:34 PM

Mayday, captain, mayday!

The attraction is REAL and verified

Looks like I'm in the club

Regan spun around, finding that she *needed* to face Emma. To be able to look at her, to take her in. To try to make sense of this attraction or brush it off or...

Or immediately dip her gaze to Emma's chest.

"Have you always worn such low-cut tops?" She demanded to know. She could see the cups of her bra, and... yeah. Wow.

Emma really did favor those pretty bras, like the red one she'd been wearing in the kitchen last month when she hadn't expected Regan to be home early from work.

Regan's mind conjured that image in perfect clarity as if playing on a tape.

Oh, *wow*.

Had she been attracted to Emma, even then?! Was that why she could picture every time she'd seen Emma in any state of undress so easily? That was definitely not normal; she couldn't summon an image of any of her other friends in specific bathing suits or similar attire for the life of her.

"What?" Emma spun around in her chair, draping her arm over the back to stare at Regan above the frames of her glasses. "Did you seriously just ask what I think you asked?"

Regan forced herself to stop staring at Emma's chest like a perv, which honestly wasn't that difficult. Because she found that exciting, buzzy *zing* continued thrumming through her when she was also looking at Emma's face.

Had she always found glasses to be so attractive? That was something she was going to need to look into.

"Do you always wear glasses?" She asked.

"Yes – I mean, kind of," Emma corrected, still frowning concernedly at Regan. "I've had them since I was little, but I normally wear my contacts." She rolled her lips before softly confessing, "Last night was... emotional for me."

"Better to give your eyes a break after you cry," Regan surmised, feeling her emotions pitch out of heat and into sympathy.

Emma's cheeks turned pink as she cleared her throat and turned back to her laptop. "Ah, yeah. Ergo, the glasses."

"They look really good. You should wear them more." She couldn't hold the comment in. Really, she couldn't.

Emma spun back around quickly, eyeing her closely as the color on her cheeks deepened. "The compliments – enough with them. Seriously. And *what* did you say about my shirts? What, would you prefer me to change into something else?"

"No!" Regan all but shouted as she jumped forward, as if propelled by an invisible force.

She found herself standing in the middle of the kitchen, dropping her hands listlessly to fall on her thighs as she stared at Emma.

Who stared at Regan with nothing short of alarmed confusion.

"That is to say, no. You should wear what you feel comfortable in. Always. But especially here, at home. Of course."

"Of course," Emma repeated skeptically.

Regan hadn't even registered that she was still clutching her phone until it vibrated in her hand.

> STUNNING CHARLOTTE THOMPSON – 2:37 PM
>
> Congratulations. I will personally send you a toaster.

> REGAN – 2:37 PM
>
> Charlotte, this is no time to talk about random kitchen equipment!
>
> This is a MAYDAY
>
> What do I DO now!!!

> BTW we really need to talk about your text response times. Like what if there's a national emergency – and you take 5+ minutes to see it?!

"Uh, so," Emma started, easily regaining her full attention.

Regan licked her lips as she stared at the way Emma drew her own bottom lip between her teeth. She'd always admired how full Emma's mouth was.

She supposed now she understood why.

"I talked to my gram earlier today. She heard all about our dinner from Kimberly, and she, ah, she really wants to meet you now." Emma blew out a deep breath, as if she'd been preparing herself for this. "Is there any time next weekend that you're free?"

Regan could only stare for several beats as her heart rate doubled. Amidst this whole realizing she was attracted to Emma aspect of her life, she'd forgotten that she was also Emma's *fake girlfriend*. Oh, wow.

Real attraction for a fake girlfriend. Not on her bingo card!

"It's fine if you're not." Emma frowned as she tapped her fingers lightly against the edge of the table, looking uncomfortable. "And, really, it's fine if you don't want to do it again. You going out of your way to meet Kimberly for dinner was enough. I can–"

"No!" She asserted again, far too loudly, as she took another step forward. She was only a foot away from Emma now. "I mean, no. I'd love to meet your grandmother; I told you that before. I'm free all next weekend. Just tell me when, and I'll be there."

She grimaced, the day's excitement dimming slightly as she remembered Audrey's weird brunch. "Except for Saturday, late morning and early afternoon. But any time other than that, I'm yours."

The smile that bloomed on Emma's face was tentative, sweet, and far more than enough to shake Regan out of any stressful Audrey thoughts. "Thank you *so* much. Really. How's Friday? I checked your work schedule – off by one? You're doing the morning shift?"

Regan nodded; honestly, she didn't have her work schedule memorized that far in advance, but she believed that Emma and her love of schedules properly checked their calendar, so...

"Allegra is taking that afternoon off; she's going to the Hamptons for the weekend. I'll be home around lunch. So, we can plan to leave here by three?"

"That sounds great. Consider it booked."

And it really did sound great.

She was eager – *really* eager – to meet Emma's grandmother. She'd felt that way before she'd become aware of this tingling attraction.

Now, she felt even more excitement around meeting the woman who'd shaped Emma so completely!

STUNNING CHARLOTTE THOMPSON – 2:41 PM

> Are you likening your sexual awakening to a national emergency?

REGAN – 2:41 PM

It is for the sovereign nation of Regan C. Gallagher

STUNNING CHARLOTTE THOMPSON – 2:42 PM

Shockingly, I am unfamiliar with that country. I should clearly brush up on my world geography.

REGAN – 2:42 PM

Yes. But FIRST – WHAT HAPPENS NOW

She was shocked and elated when she saw that Charlotte was writing back to her already.

STUNNING CHARLOTTE THOMPSON – 2:43 PM

What happens when you're attracted to anyone? I assume you've had romantic encounters before?

Apologies. I do forget that figuring out women for the first time can be... scarier.

First, you need to decide if you want more. If not, then your quandary ends there. If you do, then you'll need to discover if they want more.

Did Regan want more? She stared at Emma, who was also texting. Presumably her grandmother, to solidify their Friday plans.

Wanting more with Emma would make things infinitely more difficult.

They were forming a real friendship. Something that made Regan feel *good*. Made her feel seen. Made her feel heard, funny, and useful.

They were roommates. Something blowing up could make living together incredibly awkward and uncomfortable. That had the potential to be very, very bad.

And yet...

REGAN – 2:44 PM

And, if I did decide I want more... what do I do next?

STUNNING CHARLOTTE THOMPSON – 2:45 PM

You'll need to figure out if she feels the same attraction. Subtle looks and touches can usually do the trick. Figure out what she's looking for, what she likes. It can all be very casual.

REGAN – 2:45 PM

aye aye cap'n. Appreciated. Seriously

She slipped her phone into her back pocket as she slipped that tidbit of information into the back of her mind.

Because she didn't know what to do about this attraction. And she really didn't know how Emma would respond to it.

Probably not well, Regan could admit to herself. Which *should* have dampened the electrified draw she was feeling the longer she stayed in the same vicinity as Emma, breathing in the subtle scent of her shampoo.

Should, being the keyword.

And yet, she found herself staring intently at Emma, her thoughts racing...

Did Emma have any sort of attraction to her as well? Did that matter? What –

She snapped back to the moment as Emma pointedly cleared her throat. Regan startled, bumping her hip into the counter, sucking in a breath through gritted teeth at the pain. Damn, between her fall last night and now this, her attraction to Emma was resulting in so many bruises.

"Are you *sure* you're doing okay?" Emma asked, an urgency in her tone that Regan wasn't sure she'd heard before.

Regan blinked her eyes open, glancing down at Emma's wide-eyed stare. God, she really *did* look concerned for her. And knowing that felt... nice.

"Totally fine," Regan lied as she gingerly rubbed a hand over her hip.

Physically, she'd be fine. Emotionally and mentally – that remained to be seen.

Emma's doubt was etched into her face as she frowned at Regan.

"Why don't we ignore my question, and instead, you go and relax? It seems like you need it."

"Question? What question?"

"When you were spacing out a minute ago, I asked if you wanted to go through the applications with me." Emma gestured at the table, where her laptop, notebook, and an array of papers were spread out in orderly piles. "I have to finish reviewing the portfolios for the Alton Fellowship by Tuesday. Right now, I have them narrowed down to the top two hundred, but Allegra only wants to personally review our top fifty. We move on to interviews in the next couple of weeks. I came up with a system – a rubric – that I think will help decisively make some cuts, and I thought I'd run it by you to get your thoughts."

Regan told herself she should leave; that was the logical decision. She should return to her own room and give Emma time and space to work. She should take some time and space to work through everything herself. Emma was right; she could definitely use some relaxation.

She *should* go to her room and get her shit together. She shouldn't come out of her room until she was positive that she could act like a normal, functional human being around Emma. Until she was reasonably positive that she could think – *yeah, sure, I'm attracted to my roommate and experiencing some sort of sexual awakening because of her, but hey, that's fine!*

That would probably be the soundest choice she could make.

"I'd love to," she said, quickly pulling out the chair next to Emma's and sitting down.

The thing was, Regan didn't always make the soundest decisions.

Besides, she'd only just realized she was attracted to Emma, to a woman. What was the harm in letting herself revel in it?

fourteen

EMMA WAS *FAIRLY* convinced that Regan had, in fact, sustained a head injury at the bookstore last Saturday.

What kind of head injury, exactly? She wasn't sure, but that wasn't really her expertise as a non-medical professional.

All she knew for sure was that literally every time she'd seen Regan for the last five days *something* was... off. Again, Emma would be hard-pressed to say exactly what it was, but there was always something.

Sunday, it had simply been the staring. Regan had sat with her and discussed her work project for a couple of hours. Which had, honestly, been even more helpful than Emma had imagined it would be. How frequently she'd turned to catch Regan just... staring at her had been weird, though.

Monday, there'd been what Emma had started thinking of as the coffee incident. In which she'd left her cup of coffee in the kitchen, so she'd run back into the kitchen while in her bra and underwear to grab it. Only to bump into Regan – not literally – who had promptly spilled her *own* coffee down herself.

Tuesday, Regan had tripped over her own feet, landing face-first against the living room floor when she'd been on her way to join Emma to watch TV. Luckily, her face had hit the plush area rug, but *Jesus*.

Emma had been stretching and hadn't actually seen what had made Regan fall.

Wednesday, they'd barely seen one another due to their work schedules, as Regan had to close. Still, though, she'd been a little weird when Emma texted her to ask if she'd remembered to bring something for dinner or needed anything.

Last night, Emma had entered the bathroom while Regan had been showering; she'd just needed to grab her moisturizer and assumed she'd be able to slip in and out before Regan would even notice. After all, Regan was singing – loudly and heartily – along with the music playing on her phone.

But Regan *had* noticed. She'd paused her admittedly decent singing that Emma had finally gotten used to – and might, just the littlest bit, have started to enjoy – cutting abruptly off as Emma opened the medicine cabinet.

Emma had frozen in place as Regan asked, "... Emma?"

"Who else?" She'd returned playfully, in a manner she'd only realized was very *Regan* after the fact.

"An axe murderer, serial killer, abductor... New York's full of weirdos."

Emma had let out a laugh. "I'm living with one of them."

Regan hadn't laughed back, as Emma had expected. Instead, she'd hummed before she'd wrapped her fingers around the cloth of the shower curtain. Long, slim fingers, and Emma should have turned around and left the bathroom right then and there. She really should have. Because she was staring far too intently at Regan's hand, as the laughter in her throat completely died away. Why was Regan holding the shower curtain like that? Like she was about to open it?

And why wasn't Emma leaving? Or asking Regan what the hell she was doing?

She *should* have been doing either or both of those things. Instead, she'd inhaled sharply and stared, those brief seconds seeming to drag on entirely too long.

That breath had held, stuck in her lungs, as Regan had slowly tugged the shower curtain, and Emma could barely breathe – the air was far too steamy. Too thick. Too much, and Emma's heartbeat quickened.

Before Regan poked her head out, the curtain stopped moving.

Her dark hair was slicked back, and she stared at Emma, dark eyes wide and curious, as droplets of water slid down the soft skin of her cheeks. One made a home right at the edge of her full lips, and Emma's eyes zeroed in on it as Regan spoke.

"I'm in the shower," Regan had said, studying Emma carefully.

"I know that," she found herself saying, though she couldn't summon a scoff for the life of her.

Regan rolled her bottom lip between her teeth, that droplet disappearing with it. "I'm – I'm naked in here."

What Emma had *wanted* to do – what she did in the aftermath – was roll her eyes as hard as she could and say something like, *"Right, I hadn't realized that even though you were showering that you were also naked in there, thanks for enlightening me,"* or even, *"No, really?!"* because – obviously!

People showered naked! Obviously!

Regan hadn't said that the way she'd normally say something like that. She hadn't laughed and flicked water at Emma or worked in any theatrics.

And Emma... Emma had realized, in that very moment, that amidst the very in-depth pro/con list she'd made before agreeing to move in with Regan, she'd left off one aspect. An aspect that, right at that second, was something crucial. Something that Emma, as a very thorough person, should have thought about – that Regan was one of the most attractive people Emma had ever met in real life.

A few months ago, she'd have called herself ridiculous for factoring that into her Regan Roommate Pro/Con. But, as she breathed in the headily heavy air, staring at Regan, who was naked in the shower only a foot away, she thought – *I should have factored that in.*

As a pro or a con? A snarky voice – the voice that occasionally liked to pop up and remind Emma that she hadn't dated in two years – had asked in the back of her mind.

Definitely a con, she'd been able to realize as she finally regained her mental faculties and dragged her gaze away.

She'd cleared her throat and finally opened the medicine cabinet. "I just needed my moisturizer," she muttered, shaking her head. "I didn't think you'd mind, given your proclivity for ignoring boundaries and all."

"So... you weren't trying to join me in here?" Regan had asked, and Emma didn't understand her tone.

She didn't understand it because it didn't sound like jovial teasing.

But she refused to let herself look at Regan again as she exited the bathroom without an answer to the *ridiculous* question.

All right, Emma would admit to being partially responsible for the weirdness of the shower incident last night. But she maintained that Regan was at the root of it.

As they were on the subway heading to Astoria to see her gram, the staring thing was happening again. Emma could see it out of the corner of her eye, the way Regan had turned in her seat to look at her.

Luckily – or not, depending on how she looked at the situation – Emma didn't have the time or energy to dedicate to Regan's possibly head-wound-related strangeness of the previous week.

Not with how tightly wound her nerves were about the impending clashing of her worlds.

Regan was going to meet her gram. Gram was going to meet Regan, who she believed was Emma's girlfriend. Her serious, live-in girlfriend.

A meeting that would happen in less than twenty minutes, as their stop was rapidly approaching, and Primrose Grove was only a five-minute walk from the subway station.

"So, speaking of the episode of *The One* that we watched last night," Regan started in a completely random non sequitur, "I've been meaning to ask you about something you said."

Emma turned to look at her ludicrously. "*When* were we talking about that?"

Regan grinned, guilelessly. "Guess I was just thinking about it." She barreled on, "So, anyway, you said something I thought was interesting – you said that you thought Samantha should potentially keep Chelsea around as a contestant even though they haven't necessarily connected as deeply as Samantha's connected with several of the other contestants still there."

Even though Emma was still unsure how they'd gotten onto this topic, she was willing to take any distraction she could take. "Right," she slowly said, switching gears in her mind to focus on the show.

Honestly, it made Emma feel a little embarrassed. She'd doggedly avoided watching any reality television for literal decades, looking at it with no small amount of disdain. And now, she was several seasons deep into watching a reality dating show with Regan and *enjoying* it.

But she couldn't deny that she was. "All I was saying is that I think that Chelsea is worth Samantha keeping around for a little while longer because she's the person Samantha is most attracted to. They haven't had that much time one-on-one to explore it, so... I don't know; it feels like a little bit of a waste to send her home so soon when she feels such a physical connection."

"Hmm," Regan hummed softly, watching Emma closely. Closely enough that it made her stomach start to squirm. "So, is that how your past relationships started, then? Because you were really attracted to them?"

Emma thought she might have whiplash by the end of this conversation. "I thought we were talking about *The One*? When did it become about me?"

However, Regan's gaze was unwavering as she dropped a hand on Emma's thigh. "I'm distracting you. It's a distraction technique."

She did her best to stop herself from shivering at the touch. Which didn't work, so she switched to hoping Regan didn't notice and wouldn't comment on it.

This was a part of her strange behavior, though!

All of the touching in the last few days. While Regan was always very tactile, Emma felt like it had somehow shifted this past week. Post-head injury. Rather than Regan landing a hand on her knee as they would sit and talk, she touched Emma's thigh. Rather than bump shoulders together with a joke, she seemed to... cuddle in?

Granted, it wasn't all that different from how she'd been in the weeks before. So, maybe Regan was just being *Regan*, and maybe it was Emma who was different.

Maybe her mind was catching up with the fact that her body was so damn attracted to Regan.

"So?" Regan prompted her as she stroked her thumb along the inside of her thigh.

Emma inhaled sharply, disguising it as a cough.

If Emma didn't know any better, she'd have to believe Regan was doing this to her on purpose! Was Regan teasing her?

She stared back at Regan, wondering...

"Uh – no," she answered, trying to get herself back on track. Well, back on track with this weird avenue of conversation, anyway.

"What was it, then? That drew you to people, if not attraction?" Regan asked, leaning in as her eyebrows furrowed slightly. It was a look of utter concentration.

Emma felt her cheeks flush as she thought about Felicity. About the naïve way she'd viewed her in the beginning. "I mean, there *was* attraction," she hedged. "It was just about other stuff, too."

Regan leaned in even closer, only inches away, as she clearly waited for Emma to elaborate.

Which she did, sighing. "She was my TA, my sophomore year. I thought she was so... so smart. Passionate. I really respected her."

"Respect, the ultimate panty-dropper," Regan murmured.

Emma continued to stare because Regan *wasn't* teasing. At least she wasn't speaking in one of her joking tones. It was... thoughtful.

And the longer Regan stared at her like that, the more Emma's face heated.

"Well, what about you?" She turned the question on Regan, needing the focus to be off of her.

"Me? What about me?"

"Your past relationships, how did they start?" As soon as the question left her lips, she found that she was utterly riveted by the answer. Because, shockingly, she knew next to nothing about Regan's dating life.

How had *that* happened?

Regan shrugged. "I haven't really had relationships."

Emma could only stare in disbelief. "Come on."

"I'm serious," Regan insisted.

"That's not... that doesn't make sense." This time, she turned to study Regan closely, trying to reconcile that information. And trying not to think too hard about the fact that not too long ago, Emma would have probably said something like *can't imagine why not.*

But, as she stared at Regan, she really *couldn't* imagine why not.

"Why doesn't it make sense?" Regan asked, staring at Emma with just as much confusion as Emma was feeling.

"I–" Damn, she really should have let that *be*, feeling the embarrassment sweep through her. "Just that, you know. You're straightforward, you're fun, you're... pleasing to the eye."

Regan's eyebrows lifted, a smile playing at her mouth. "Oh? Pleasing to the eye?"

Rather than push and needle her, Regan leaned back with a little smirk on her face. A very attractive little smirk, something Emma had never seen.

Emma huffed out a breath, leaning back into her own seat and staring forward as she waited for the blush on her cheeks to fade.

She could feel Regan shrug against her. "There've been some guys that I've had *things* with. Relationship-lite. But I don't know. Dating in the age of apps... sucks. For most of us that aren't Sutton, anyway. It's all non-answers and half-assed conversations."

Emma slowly nodded. "Is a real relationship even something you want?"

There really was so much she didn't know about Regan. And now that she'd thought about all of the romantic relationship aspects, she found that she really wanted to know.

She turned to face Regan again, watching as she nodded. "Yeah. I do." She dug her perfect teeth into her lip as she looked up at Emma, eyes glinting and bright. "So, for my first official role as *girlfriend* – how am I doing?"

Emma swallowed hard, holding Regan's gaze with her own. Finding it difficult to look away.

She was incredibly grateful as the subway came to a stop, giving her something else to focus on as she stood up. "Well, this is us."

As Emma led them out of the subway station and down the sidewalk, those nerves that Regan had successfully distracted her from returned.

As if on cue, Regan commented, "All right. I can literally *see* the anxiety rolling off of you in waves."

"I know that this isn't the same thing as meeting Kimberly, but Emma, it's going to be completely fine." Regan reached out and squeezed Emma's hand before rubbing her thumb over the back of it.

Much like last weekend at her mother's house, Emma – crazily – felt it was so soothing. Rather than say anything else, Regan silently stared down at their hands.

Emma swiftly tugged at their interlocked hands to pull Regan away from where she was about to walk right into a telephone pole.

"Are you *sure* you're okay?" She asked for at least the tenth time this week.

Regan snapped her eyes back up to Emma's. "Fine – me? Fine. Anyway, your grandmother met *Felicity*, right?" Regan said her ex's name with an inflection that Emma couldn't quite decipher, having never heard it from her before.

Weird.

"Yes. Several times." The reminder wasn't making her feel much better, especially as she could so clearly recall the uncomfortable quiet that would fall between Gram and Felicity, neither seeming able to nor interested in coming up with conversation topics.

"And Felicity was... well-educated, organized, responsible, and ambitious," Regan recited, listing the adjectives off. "I'll just *pretend* to be those things, only better. So you won't catch any flack from being with me."

The guilt that dug into Emma at Regan's words – at Emma's own words being parroted back at her – was startling. Quite literally, it made her stumble over her steps at how strongly she felt it slam into her. This time, it wasn't even guilt at kicking a puppy; it was real shame. About hurting *Regan*. "I shouldn't have said that before. And definitely not the way it came out."

Regan shrugged. "We've moved on. I'm not saying it to throw it in your face."

Emma used their still entwined hands to pull Regan to a gentle stop, feeling an urgency for Regan to *hear* her. "I know you aren't; that's not the point. The point is – you don't need to pretend to be anything, okay? You're smart, loyal, funny, and kind, and this will probably go better because you *aren't* like Felicity." The raw honesty escaped her, propelled by that heavy feeling in her stomach. By the need to make Regan know that she meant it. "Felicity would never do what you're doing for me."

And as embarrassing as that truth was for Emma to admit, it was the truth.

"Well, why would you have needed your real girlfriend to pretend to be your girlfriend?" Regan asked, and the smile on her lips looked like something she'd wear while joking around, but her voice was hoarse.

And Emma didn't laugh. "What I mean is that she wouldn't have gone along with some silly scheme, even if it would have meant the world to me. She wouldn't have sacrificed so much of her own time just to do something to help me out of an emotional bind. She, honestly, would have been very judgmental around the fact that I found myself in this situation in the first place just because I was afraid to face my own mother."

Emma looked at Regan earnestly. Very much needing her to see that Emma didn't have the same stubborn beliefs about her, anymore. "So, I mean it. *Don't* dwell on anything I said in the past, please. Because if you're *you*, it'll probably go a lot better."

Even though she'd said her comments with the sole intention of making Regan feel better, she realized as she finished speaking that it had made her feel better at the same time.

Because... yeah, Regan *wasn't* Felicity.

And maybe they weren't really in a relationship, but she couldn't imagine that Regan would fall into awkward and uncomfortable silences with her gram, unable to find anything to talk about; Regan could talk to anyone. She couldn't imagine that Gram would think Regan was pretentious and rude because it was simply true.

The grin on Regan's face was more an additional sunbeam than anything else, and Emma's cheeks heated at being the recipient of it.

"Anyway." Emma cleared her throat. "We're almost there, so we should..."

Regan fell into step next to her jauntily. Nearly skipping, as she agreed, "Don't want to be late!"

Regan only let go of Emma's hand as they entered Primrose Grove, so she could sign in at the front desk.

"This place looks really nice," Regan whispered, leaning her entire body into Emma's.

Ostensibly so that her voice didn't carry, but Emma swallowed thickly at the proximity just the same.

"I didn't expect this when I imagined your grandmother in a nursing home."

"It's not a nursing home," Emma corrected, steel in her tone, after finishing their sign-in. She shuddered about how much her gram would *detest* if Regan said she lived in a nursing home. "It's an assisted living facility – and the assistance depends on what the resident needs. A ton of people live here who don't need any daily assistance, like my gram."

As she was wont to do, Regan accepted Emma's information with an easy nod. "Ah. So, it's just like a place for older people to hang together. Like a fancy, elderly dorm."

Emma's mouth pulled into a laughing smile; honestly – shockingly – she really did like the way Regan saw the world sometimes.

Regan beamed back at her, obviously pleased with herself, before her gaze landed on something over Emma's shoulder. She pointed eagerly. "Ohhhh, there's a buffet dinner and bingo tonight! That should be fun."

Emma turned to follow where she was pointing, and she ended up staring at the large calendar on the lobby wall, which was lined with events that Primrose Grove was putting on. Indeed, in bright, colorful letters, there was a notice for a buffet/bingo night, inviting all residents to come and join in.

"We probably won't be going," she informed her regretfully. And the regret ran deep – first because she desperately wished her gram would try to be more involved. Second, because the excited gleam in Regan's eyes dimmed a little.

"Your grandmother's not much of a joiner?"

"It's not – she *is*. I mean, she could be. If she was more comfortable, she would be. She's always been very..." How could Emma explain the intricacies of her gram? Especially so that an extrovert like Regan would understand. "Reserved. Shy, even."

Emma wondered why no one ever talked about that; she never heard about what happened to older people who grew from shy, reserved youths into shy, reserved elderly.

"She led a fairly regimented life, surrounded by the same people for decades, before she had to move here earlier this year because she had a heart attack. A second heart attack," she amended, her stomach twisting as she so easily recalled the phone call she'd received from their old neighbor, delivering the news.

"Before, she always participated in events in her community, where she was comfortable. She worked at Rettol Academy–"

"Oh, so *that's* why you went there," Regan cut in, nodding as this information dawned on her.

Emma snapped her mouth shut as she eyed Regan in confusion. "I mean – yes. But how did you know that?" Emma didn't often discuss her pre-college days; it wasn't all that interesting.

"Your mom had a picture at her house from your senior year," Regan informed her.

Which – *duh*. Emma had spotted the picture, too. And she wasn't surprised anymore that Regan was so observant.

Still, the knowledge that Regan seemed to see *everything* about her made Emma's stomach flutter, and she quickly pushed past it.

"So – yeah. She worked under the headmaster for over forty years, living in the same apartment complex. It was easy for her to take part in community nights and get-togethers. But... it's been different here," she finished quietly.

The sympathy on Regan's face made Emma feel very seen. Even before Regan surmised, "And you're worried about her."

Emma automatically wanted to deny that – no, she wasn't worried about her grandmother. Her gram was strong and independent, and she raised Emma all on her own. But... she found that she didn't want to lie to Regan. That it felt impossible, on the receiving end of that imploring gaze.

"Yeah. I am," she admitted, softly. "But don't bring that up to her. Please."

She knew how much Gram would hate being spoken of like that, especially to someone she didn't know.

"Sure. Clearly, you get your need for privacy somewhere, and it obviously wasn't from Kimberly."

The scoff that burst from Emma's lips at that was loud. Loud enough to garner several looks from residents walking by, prompting Emma to turn it into a cough, clearing her throat. "We should head to her room."

"Lead the way." Regan gestured for Emma to lead. And – strangely – she stayed a pace behind for the walk all the way down the hall. Which was *fine*, technically, but she swore she could feel Regan's eyes on her, and it made Emma feel a tingle at the back of her neck.

When she peered over her shoulder at Regan, trying not to look as suspicious as she felt, Regan's gaze snapped up to meet hers, and she had a smile that looked... too innocent? Was that a thing?

She stopped in front of her gram's suite, and Regan drew up next to her. As if she'd walked with her the whole time.

Before she could give Regan any last-minute instructions – what, exactly, Emma wasn't sure – or even knock, the door opened.

Gram stood before them, with her long, white hair pulled back into her signature bun, a look she'd worn almost daily for Emma's entire life, in her straight-legged jeans and light blue button-down. She'd worn the same outfit in slightly different color variations on every single non-workday for... ever.

As always, seeing her brought Emma a rush of comfort. Even now, with the nerves still swimming through her.

"Gram! Were you waiting by the door?" She joked, bending down and pecking her grandmother on the soft, thin skin of her cheek, as she always did.

"Only when I realized you were two minutes later than you'd said to expect you," Gram returned, patting Emma's shoulder.

"Emma does have the pathological need to always be early," Regan chimed in with a ridiculously warm, indulgent smile as she looked up at Emma.

She felt her stomach flutter because... *wow*, seriously, Regan was so good at this.

When Gram slightly raised her eyebrows at her – undoubtedly expecting Emma to use the manners Gram had taught her – she blushed, jumping into action. "Gram, this is Regan Gallagher. My girlfriend."

Okay, that rolled off of her tongue easier than she'd expected. Especially to her grandmother, someone she never lied to.

Grateful for it, she turned to Regan and gestured at her gram, who stood barely five feet tall with her head coming up to Emma's chin. "And Regan, this is my gram. Sheryl Bordeaux."

"You can call me Sherry," her gram insisted, aiming a small, crooked smile at Regan.

Emma could read her grandmother like a book, and she knew that her gram was wondering the best way to greet Regan. A handshake? A warm pat on the back or shoulder, as she tended to do with Emma? A simple wave? Introductions had never been her grandmother's strong suit.

It seemed any worry was superfluous, though, as Regan decided for them both. She went right in for a hug, the move fluid and natural. Emma could read the surprise on her gram's face before she wrapped her arms around Regan's waist, patting her softly on the back.

Even when Regan pulled back, she lightly cupped her gram's elbows, smiling that enchantingly sunny smile. "You can just call me Regan."

Gram chuckled, nodding as she did so. "That sounds good; easy to remember, at the very least."

"I guess you're right," Regan agreed, removing her hands from her gram only to slide one arm through Gram's, linking elbows. "And I would really love a tour of your place if you don't mind. I'm not sure if Emma's told you, but I have a bit of a nosy nature."

Was Emma crazy, or was Regan... charming? Like, truly, genuinely *charming*? With that slightly self-deprecating, slightly unashamed grin and the candid way she announced her nosiness?

"A tour of this old place? If that's what you want..." Gram trailed off, looking at Emma briefly with an undecipherable glance before turning her attention back to Regan. "Emma *didn't* tell me about your curious nature, though."

She trailed her grandma and Regan through the suite. Which wasn't

229

large, but it was enough for her gram's preferred belongings and favorite furniture.

"This is mostly, well, *it*." Gram concluded as they circled back into the kitchenette a minute later.

"It's so great to see where Emma disappears to for hours every weekend," Regan stated with such verve that it was impossible to think she wasn't telling the truth.

"Well, it's not much," her gram muttered, in a tone that dug into Emma's heart every time she heard it. A tone that reflected how deeply Gram missed the apartment she'd called home for nearly forty years, the one she'd moved into after marrying Emma's grandfather.

Regan wheeled around, staring at Gram like she was crazy. "Shut up; this place is fucking amazing. I didn't even know that there were places like this that existed before I knew you lived here!"

Emma held in a chortle, knowing Regan's knowledge had only been expanded ten minutes ago.

"Seriously, I love the idea of living in this kind of micro-community. Is there an age cap? Isn't it ageist to keep me out of living here?" If the comments came from anyone *other* than Regan, Emma would have thought it was corny. She would have rolled her eyes because the words alone sounded like a ridiculous suck-up.

But Regan didn't sound ridiculous or corny. She sounded so eager and earnest that it made both Emma and her gram laugh.

"You can feel free to take my place if you want." Gram offered, "I'll move into your apartment with Emma."

Immediately, Regan vehemently shook her head. "Uh... sorry. I have to rescind the comment. I'm not ready to give up living with Emma; I just got her."

In a fluid move, she slid out of her linked arm with Gram and returned to Emma's side. True to Regan fashion, she stood close enough for their bodies to brush as she reached down to lace her fingers through Emma's.

Emma's cheeks heated again, and she instinctively flexed her fingers around Regan's as she thought once more: Regan was *so* good at this.

Her gram seemed satisfied with that response as she gave a small nod.

"Why don't we sit?" She gestured at her small kitchen table. "We can get to know one another a bit more."

"Actually, before we go that," Regan jumped in before anyone moved. "I was hoping I could get a tour of the whole place? If you wouldn't mind? Like I said, I'm really nosy."

The winning smile on her face could have melted a solid block of ice. It was clearly enough to melt through her gram's resistance to leaving the security of her suite as Gram slowly nodded, "Sure; it would be good to get some more walking in today."

"Great!" Regan squeezed Emma's hand, sending her a wink as Gram walked past them toward the door.

Emma's breath caught in her throat, her own smile freezing in place. What was *that* about?

She didn't have time to ponder it, as Regan tugged her along out into the main hallway.

"So, Sherry, I'm dying for you to tell me more about yourself," Regan stated, her voice so encouraging, as they started walking.

Emma disengaged so that the three of them didn't take up the entire hallway, walking a couple of steps back.

Her grandmother sent Regan a surprised look, eyebrows furrowed.

"I mean, Emma has already told me about you – you gave her those beautiful hummingbirds and her favorite opal ring, which was a gift from your husband. That you worked at Rettol Academy. I know you raised Emma like a boss." She turned that quick smile up at Emma, so brief but so *full*. "But I feel like I don't know enough about *you*, you know? What do you like to do?"

There was a small flush on her gram's cheeks at having Regan's direct and persistent attention on her. But Emma didn't intervene because she believed her gram looked... pleased.

"Well, uh. Hmm," Gram hummed thoughtfully before she shrugged. "I've always liked knitting. When Emma was little, I made her the cutest hat; she wore it every winter until it started to unravel."

Regan aimed another look at her over her gram's head, eyes glinting. And Emma couldn't do anything other than *smile*.

"I enjoy a fun game–"

"Oh, what kind?"

Sherry chuckled at Regan's eagerness. "Cards, mostly. It's always fun to try my hand at most card games."

Emma scoffed loudly. "Oh, *you suppose*? Don't listen to her; she's a shark, and she will take you for literally everything you have."

Her gram sent her a look over her shoulder. "Emma must really like you, being so willing to tell you about my secrets like that."

Emma's heart skipped a beat as she ducked her head, rolling her lips so she couldn't disagree. Why *would* she disagree, anyway?! She wanted her gram to think she was crazy about Regan.

"I'd love to play against you sometime," Regan offered, bringing her gram's attention back to her.

"Don't say I didn't warn you," she muttered.

"Why don't you tell me more about *you*?" Gram urged Regan.

It was only here, at this moment, that Emma finally recognized that look in her gram's eyes. The measuring one, waiting to see which way the scale tipped in terms of Regan. Was she good enough for Emma? Was she the right one?

Emma's stomach clenched again, and she made herself blow out a breath. It didn't matter that this wasn't real. Because Gram thought it was.

So, it *did* matter to her, what her gram thought of Regan. She wanted, she realized in this moment, very badly for Gram to approve of Regan. Because *she* did.

Not to date, she mentally backpedaled. Given that Regan was straight. Yes, total straight-woman vibes all of the time. Most of the time, anyway. When she wasn't being... odd.

"What do you want to know?"

"Anything, really. Emma hasn't told me all that much," her gram tossed Emma another look, making Emma's stomach sink.

Was this the moment? Did her gram doubt this... this sham? Was she onto Emma lying to her?

"I don't mean offense," Gram added, turning her attention back to Regan. She looked contrite.

But Regan waved her off, chuckling. "That sounds right; Emma isn't much for sharing unless you make her."

Gram laughed. Emma furrowed her eyebrows, "Hey!"

Because – she'd shared! She'd shared *a lot* with Regan in the last few weeks. She'd told her about Kimberly, Gram, her book reviewing account, stories about her job, Felicity, her love of magazines, the Alton Fellowship, her feelings on their TV shows, and her insecurities.

Startled by her own thoughts, Emma nearly stumbled over her feet. She had shared a lot with Regan, and she hadn't even noticed how much.

"You're exactly right," Gram confirmed, much to Emma's chagrin. "I guess I hadn't realized I was supposed to be asking." Her voice took on that thoughtful quality as she tilted her head to the side and studied Regan's profile.

It was the same look she wore when she was trying to puzzle out which was the best decision in a card game, and Emma couldn't, for the life of her, figure out what she was thinking about Regan.

"Then again, you *do* look familiar," Gram murmured.

Emma stumbled over her own two feet, catching herself on the handrail that lined the hallway. The cold bolt of fear struck through her.

Oh. Oh *no*.

Regan shrugged, entirely unaware of Emma's distress. "I get that a lot." She brought her free hand up, tapping at her chin. "I'm from Newton – just outside of Boston. Born and raised there. Well, actually, I lived in Springfield – western Mass. – until I was seven. Then, we moved to Newton. I went to college for a year in Massachusetts, but... it wasn't for me. So, I moved here because my best friend lived here."

Emma was just as interested in Regan's life story as her grandmother.

"Sutton," her gram mused. Which made sense, as Emma had told her several stories that involved Sutton over the last couple of years. Usually quick mentions of weekend plans or tales about their adventures being teaching assistants.

Regan's smile flashed over her face. "Yes! Exactly. Um, in the last year, I've really come to find that I enjoy baking."

"She's really good at it," Emma added, remembering how vulnerable Regan had been when she'd shared that with Emma.

The pleased flush that slid over Regan's face made her feel satisfied.

Her gram's eyes lit up. "A baker! How would you feel about making a cake? Everly's birthday is next Sunday, and the woman Kimberly hired for the cake and all of the desserts literally just canceled this morning – something about a family emergency, and she has to fly to Iowa? I was on the phone with her before you arrived, and she's a mess wondering how to fill the gap on such short notice."

Right. At the world's most awkward family dinner, her mom had mentioned that Everly was having a pool party next weekend. An invite had been offered to Emma and Regan, but she hadn't really responded.

"Oh," Regan's lips formed a perfect circle, and she looked thrown off for the first time since they'd arrived. "I've never really been responsible for *an event* before."

Gram shook her head. "Kimberly won't mind; in fact, she'll probably want to hire you even more because of it."

Regan's wide, dark eyes slid to meet Emma's, her uncertainty clear.

"It's all right if you don't want to," her gram said assuredly. "And it is very last minute."

"No, it's... I mean, it is. It's not that I don't want to do it, I just..." Regan blinked down at her gram before looking at Emma once more. Searching. Asking.

"If you want to do it, you should do it," Emma said, trying to breathe through the knot in her stomach before it could really form.

"Does that mean you're coming?" Gram asked, turning to face her as well. There was an excited light in her eyes that needled right into Emma.

It combined with how she could hear Kimberly saying *I know you hate me* and how Everly had stared at Emma like she'd hung the moon at dinner. The way she'd told her mom that she would try, and how she'd meant it.

"Yeah," she whispered before clearing her throat and speaking louder. "Yes, I'm going to the party."

The party seemed like a good way to start *trying*, after all. Her mom and sisters would be preoccupied with other activities, other people. Emma would have time to simply exist there, trying to find her footing.

Regan's gaze – which saw more than Emma wanted to allow – stayed on her for several more seconds. She only looked away when Emma nodded at her, feeling as sure as she could about it.

"In that case, yeah, I'll totally do the desserts."

"That is *amazing*. I'll give you Kimberly's number later." Gram positively beamed as they turned the corner at the end of the hallway.

The hallway that had the large rec room off to the right side, where the people were starting to settle in at tables for the buffet/bingo affair.

"You know what, Sherry? I, too, love games!" Regan announced, coming to a stop as she admired the setup in front of them. "And it seems we've stumbled right into one. What do you say?"

She turned to face Gram with such a hopeful look that saying *no* really would have felt – again – like kicking a puppy.

Her grandmother paused, looking apprehensively around the room. "Well. I don't know... it doesn't seem there's a lot of seats left..."

"Right there!" Regan pointed to a table with three open spots to their left. Two others were taken by two of the women Emma regularly saw hanging out in the common areas.

Without hesitation, Regan walked over to the table. "Hey, are these seats taken?"

"Who's asking?" One of the women asked, while her friend crowed with laughter and pushed her arm.

"Don't listen to her, honey, they're free."

"Awesome! And I'm asking – I'm Regan, by the way."

"You're a little young to live here," the first woman surmised as her friend rolled her eyes.

"You're right, but I'm trying to get the hang of it early. Oh, and my girlfriend – Emma – her gram lives here." She gestured to where Emma and her grandmother stood several feet back. "Sherry Bordeaux, you know her? She's competitive as all hell – so I hear – though, so that should be your biggest concern."

"We've seen her around," the second woman – the cackler – said, offering Emma and her gram a wave. "I'm Bea, and this grumpy old broad is Phoebe. Come on over!"

Emma led her gram to the table, who gave a tentative smile to the women. "Ah... nice to meet you."

"Nice to see you finally come out of your cave," Phoebe responded, laughing lightheartedly.

Her gram breathed out a chuckle.

"*Shush*," Bea hit her friend's shoulder. "It can take a while to adjust; we get it. My biggest piece of advice to you, Sherry, is at buffet night? You should get in line early."

Gram offered a small smile. "Thank you, I'll do that."

"Early meaning *now*, by the way," Phoebe cut in, nudging Bea with her elbow as she nodded to the buffet set up. "Come on, I can't be stuck behind Gary again."

They hustled to the buffet line as Emma, Regan, and her gram watched.

Regan grinned broadly. "I like them! They seem nice. And I always appreciate a good tip about beating a line." She ran her gaze over the rest of the room, landing on the beverage station on the other side of the room. "Ohhh, let's grab drinks first. I'll go – what would you like?"

Gram's eyebrows drew together before lifting high on her forehead, looking like some sort of realization. "Right! I finally remember..." She ran her eyes over Regan's face again, her smile knowing. "It all makes sense."

The fear from minutes ago struck all over again, and Emma's eyes widened with it. No. No, no.

Regan's confusion was palpable as she threw a look at Emma. Who shook her head back. *No.*

"You're the barista," Gram asserted, her tone imbued with understanding.

Those terror erupted in nervous butterflies. "Yeah, she's a barista." Emma tried to head off where she knew this was going.

But, unsurprisingly, her gram wouldn't be dissuaded. Not when she looked like everything had finally come together for her as she stared at Regan, her smile growing.

"I'll be honest with you, Regan. I was very confused by this whole... situation. By Emma not ever mentioning your relationship to me, before. Emma's a good girl; she's got a level head."

"Thanks, Gram," she interjected, hoping that she could derail anything coming next. "Why doesn't Regan go get those drinks?"

Regan, this time, was the one who ignored her. She wore a small, understanding grin. "I know; Emma has been really private about our relationship."

"Even so." Her gram shook her head. "I realize, now, that it wasn't out of the blue." She turned to look at Emma, a look that was both excited and understanding reflecting in her gaze. "I wish you'd *told me* that your little crush on the barista had becoming something more."

Emma squeezed her eyes shut, feeling her face heat so quickly and strongly that she was sure smoke must have been exiting her ears. Those butterflies in her stomach morphed into something more akin to frogs.

Maybe, she hoped – stupidly and desperately – that Regan wouldn't push it. Maybe Regan would do the least Regan thing in the world, and –

"Crush?" Regan echoed, sounding utterly mystified.

Emma tried to hold in a groan.

"That's why you looked so familiar when you walked in earlier. I couldn't quite put my finger on it." Her gram looked between Emma and Regan. "The summer before Emma started her TA job, she'd finally showed me around campus, her favorite spots. And we went into your coffee shop... Tipped On?"

"Topped Off," Regan corrected, looking like she was a kid on Christmas morning.

Emma wanted to bury her face in her hands. Actually, she wanted to bury her entire body in the ground.

"Right, Topped Off. And she pointed you out."

"She pointed me out," Regan echoed, the amazement dripping from her tone.

"Like I said, it all makes more sense for me now," Gram finished with an accepting nod.

Well, Emma was glad her grandmother was finding peace, and at the same time, she was simultaneously making Emma regret her life.

"Regan, why don't you go get those drinks?" Emma suggested abruptly. "Why don't I help you?"

Yes. She needed to separate Regan from her grandmother before this got even more out of hand. That was priority number one, and what she focused on as she put her hand on Regan's lower back to make her start walking away.

She needed to use a little more *oomph* than she'd expected because Regan seemed to be glued to the spot.

"You had a *crush* on me?" Regan wasted no time in asking, staring up at Emma in wonder.

Emma's heart fluttered as her stomach clenched and her legs felt a little weak, and she remembered vividly how she'd felt in freshman year when she'd gotten paired to work on her science project with Christy Logan, the prettiest girl at their school.

"No," she quickly denied, vehemently shaking her head. She tossed a look over her shoulder at her grandmother, who had finally taken her seat at their table and was looking over her bingo card.

"You're calling your grandmother a liar, then?"

"No!" She denied, again, pressing her palms to her cheeks and wishing they would return to a regular body temperature. "I – it wasn't a real *crush*," she hissed, staring Regan down. "It was... I just..." How did she possibly explain this and get out of this situation without making a fool out of herself?! "I was going through a shitty time because Felicity had broken up with me, and I'd started going to Topped Off, and I thought you were cute. That's *all*."

Really, that *was* it. Basically.

Regan gasped, her mouth falling open with a smile of shocked delight. "You thought I was cute?!"

Emma squeezed her eyes closed, cursing her gram for the first time in her life. "Like that's news."

"It is to me! And I would like to know more. Everything, actually."

"There's nothing more to tell! I obviously think you're attractive, Regan. I've told you that before. Like when we were going to Kimberly's, and you were wearing..." She trailed off, swallowing thickly. As she often did when the scantily-clad image of Regan appeared in her mind's eye.

Which happened disturbingly frequently.

It wasn't Emma's *fault*, not really! Not when she was living with Regan and had constant reminders all of the damn time about how much her body betrayed her and responded to Regan.

"You thinking that I'm not bad looking and you being attracted to me are two very different things," Regan corrected, shaking her head slowly. As if she just couldn't get over what she'd heard.

There was a gleam in her eyes that Emma didn't understand, didn't trust.

"It's *not a big deal*," she grit out, pouring her gram a glass of water. Unfortunately, in this moment, she was having trouble convincing herself of how *not a big deal* this was.

But it *wasn't* a big deal; people had meaningless, irrational, silly "crushes" on random people in their daily routines all of the time. People you see on the subway on your work commute, the person that lives down the hall from you that you exchange a smile with but don't ever really talk.

Baristas, with bright smiles who always remember your order.

Then, those crushes fade. Because you realize the person on the subway has gross politics. Or the neighbor moves away.

Or because the barista spills coffee down your shirt and proceeds to pop up in your life to constantly remind you that you two *don't* work as a duo in the real world.

"Big enough deal for you to tell your grandmother about it," Regan's response was cheeky and downright jaunty. In fact, Emma felt as though Regan might start floating away with her glee.

God, of course, Regan was having a field day with this.

"I – it was because she was worried about my getting over Felicity. So, I told her that I knew I was starting to move on... because I was attracted to you. That's it." She haltingly explained.

Still, the smile didn't leave Regan's face. In fact, she was grinning so widely, so brightly, Emma wondered if it would ever fade.

"It was before you spilled the coffee on me and ripped my shirt open, so I didn't really know you," she added for good measure.

Regan shrugged both of her shoulders, clearly unbothered by the fact.

Somehow, Regan's excitement in learning about Emma's attraction – she would *not* call it a crush – calmed Emma a little. At the very least, Regan was never awkward or uncomfortable and would never hold it against Emma. If anything, she seemed... thrilled.

"I'm going back to the table now." She needed a second away from Regan's insanely beautiful, too-excited smile. Damn her grandmother!

"I'll get us a place in the buffet line, sweetheart!" Regan called after her.

Emma took a deep breath at how her stomach clenched in that not-entirely-unpleasant way.

Finally able to take a deep, butterfly-free breath, she walked back to the table and placed the glass down in front of her gram. "Here you go. I'll, uh, I'll join Regan in the line in a second to grab us dinner in a second."

She couldn't help but toss a glance toward Regan, who continued to absolutely *beam*. Even as she animatedly spoke to the woman next to her in line, she was grinning around her words.

All because of a so-called *crush* that Emma didn't even have anymore! Even if you could call it a crush in the first place... which *she* wouldn't have.

"I admit, honey, I was a little concerned. When I'd heard about this relationship. Worried that maybe you'd rushed into something or... I don't know. But I really like Regan," Gram said, placing her hand over Emma's and giving her a warm squeeze.

"I really like her, too." Only after she spoke was she struck by how sincerely she meant that.

She couldn't stop herself from looking over at Regan once more. This time, Regan was already staring at her. Still smiling.

Emma could only blink back at her, her heart beating a little harder in her chest as if buzzed to life by the exuberance of that grin. Weird.

Still, she stared. Regan was funny, unguarded, and observant... mostly, she was a joy to exist in the same sphere with, and Emma really liked her. She liked her enough that it was unsettling when she really thought about it.

"I'd hope so." Gram chuckled, pulling her out of her own thoughts.

Emma pulled her gaze away from Regan, managing out a chuckle. "Right."

fifteen

"REALLY, I'm just *so* grateful, Regan. You have no idea," Kimberly effused for at least the tenth time on their phone call. "I have no idea what I would have done otherwise. And Everly is ecstatic that you're going to be the one making the cake! And that you and Emma are coming to the party!"

Regan was slightly out of breath as she responded, "I'm excited, too! I just – I need you to know, again, that I don't have any professional experience with this–"

"You'll be amazing. Really, without you, my daughter would be having a ninth birthday without a cake, and we'd be hosting a horde of elementary schoolers at a party without any desserts! And all of the sample pictures you sent me last night looked delicious."

Kimberly wasn't shy about her praise, and Regan found herself soaking it in, even as she ran down the street, dodging in and out of people as she finally approached the Fox and Hyde Hotel doors.

"Sorry to cut this a little short, Kimberly, but I really have to go. Text me, though!"

"Okay! I'll see you and Emma next weekend!"

Regan simultaneously disconnected the call and slowed her pace as she walked through the doors into the blessedly air-conditioned lobby.

She hadn't known what she'd been getting into yesterday when she'd agreed to make the desserts for Everly's birthday party with only a week of notice. All she'd known was that it *did* sound like a fun challenge and, mostly, she'd found that she didn't want to say no to Sherry.

She wanted Emma's grandmother to like her. To approve of her.

And she'd wanted Emma to feel proud about being with her, even if it wasn't real. To Emma's family, Regan was Emma's girlfriend. And Regan had realized yesterday just how seriously she'd taken that title on.

It made her feel good about herself to be able to jump in and help Emma's family in a crisis. It made her feel like these people – those who loved Emma and wanted the best for her – could think that Regan *was* that person.

It made her feel even better to know that Emma might think so, too. That she would think that Regan was dependable. Even if her baking wasn't a serious career, it was a skill Regan possessed, something she brought to the table that people could be impressed by.

And she wanted, she'd realized, for Emma to be impressed.

REGAN – 11:01 AM

> Off the phone with your mom. Apparently, Everly has a deep enjoyment of unicorns? First time making a unicorn cake, but I'm going to give it my all. Think I can manage it?

That was the other thing – she didn't *need* to text that bit of information to Emma. Emma didn't necessarily need to know it, but Regan wanted to tell her. She wanted to open a line of communication with Emma, like, all of the time.

EMMA – 11:02 AM

> Somehow, it really speaks of the perfect Regan vibe to me

Regan grinned at her phone, her stomach sparking with a pleased warmth at Emma's reply. And though she was *itching* to answer immediately, she realized she was only a few feet away from her sister.

Who was watching her expectantly.

Disappointed that her texting with Emma would have to be cut off for now, Regan reluctantly tucked her phone into her back pocket. It was all right, she reasoned with herself, because she would be able to see Emma at home, later.

Slowly, she approached the table. Only to pause as she went to pull out the chair opposite Audrey as she realized, "Um... why are there only two chairs at this table?" She pointed at Audrey, then to her own chair, then circled her index finger to gesture at the small table that was clearly only appointed for a pair.

"Because it's only you and I having brunch...?" Audrey responded as if *Regan* were being ridiculously obtuse.

"What do you mean, it's only you and I for brunch?" Regan asked, unable to connect whatever dots she was being presented with in a way that made sense.

"Exactly what I said." Audrey leaned back in her chair, folding her arms over her lap as she flicked her eyes down at the chair Regan was still clutching the back of. "Are you going to sit down or not?"

"I don't know." Regan glimpsed down at her empty chair as well, wondering if there was some joke being played on her. A whoopie cushion? No, Audrey would rather die than sit through that in a public place. A scorpion? No, there was no way Audrey could have made it stay still for so long. Besides, her sister's barbs were always more mental than physical.

Audrey sighed, a frown tugging at her mouth. "If you're going to be so ridiculous, then we can just go home and forget about this; you're already late, anyway."

"I'm not *trying* to be ridiculous!" Regan shot back before she plunked herself down in the chair. "And it's only by two freaking minutes."

She was giving up texting with Emma – being home with Emma! – for this. Whatever *this* was.

"I just don't understand–" She broke off, the dawning hitting her mid-sentence. "Oh. Is this you telling me that you don't want me to be in your wedding party anymore? You're doing it one-on-one instead of in front of your group of friends, but in a public place, so I can't make a scene?"

"I'm not sure I believe you wouldn't make a scene, first of all. Secondly, *no*. Why are you acting like two sisters having brunch together is the strangest thing to happen in your life?"

Regan stared at her sister, wondering if that was rhetorical. But when Audrey lifted an eyebrow at her, she realized she was actually waiting for an answer. "Because... it is?"

Before Audrey could respond, Regan shook her head. "We've *never* gone out to brunch together! Or any meal, for that matter. No breakfast, lunch, or dinner. Happy hour drinks. Not once in our adult lives, even though you've worked in the city I've lived in for four years, have you asked me to brunch. So, yeah, it's weird."

"You've never asked me, either," Audrey shot back, pursing her lips.

Regan felt like she was losing her actual freaking mind here!

"Look, I know I'm only in your wedding party at all because it would have looked bad, like we aren't some picture-perfect family, and Mom and Dad would have murdered you otherwise." She'd known it since she'd received the formal bridesmaid invitation at the beginning of the year. First, upon receipt, she'd been very confused before she'd put it all together. "You don't need to keep inviting me to these brunches or whatever. It's not like I'm going to tell on you or something."

Hell, even if Regan would tattle on Audrey to their parents, it's not like their parents had ever sided with Regan on anything.

She could see the way the muscle in Audrey's jaw tightened, and she fully expected the tell-off she was about to receive.

Only for Audrey to release a slow breath as she muttered, "Mom and Dad didn't *make* me ask you to be in my wedding."

Regan let out a disbelieving scoff. "Yeah, *right*." That ugly feeling reared its head inside her, and she lifted her hand to pick lightly at the pristine tablecloth. "You've never actually wanted me around, Audrey. Not only is it stupid to pretend otherwise when it's just the two of us, but I don't want you to."

"You've never wanted to *be* around, Regan," Audrey's voice was low and tight. "Not me, anyway."

Regan whipped her gaze up to meet the burning look in her sister's. "What the hell are you talking about? You *know* how Mom and Dad treat me. You *know* they think I'm a total fuck-up." Regan knew her sister knew that because her parents had never been shy about saying it. Maybe not in those exact words, but Regan's earliest memories with her parents were of being scolded, reprimanded, lectured. For everything she did. "Even my ADHD is my own fault; I should have the internal fortitude to overcome such *issues* on my own, and shame on me for not being strong enough."

Actual words her parents had said to her more than once.

"I've never said that to you, have I?" Audrey challenged as she tilted her jaw up superiorly.

Regan was already opening her mouth to argue that fact as she sifted through as many memories as she could summon, and...

"Fine," she deflated slightly. "But you sat right there behind them, how many times? And you never stuck up for me. Not *once*."

Maybe she couldn't recall Audrey verbally supporting their parents in their assessment of Regan, but she could easily picture the way Audrey would physically align herself with them. Glaring at Regan from behind their parents, as she received her dressing down. It was a very distinct line.

"What did you want me to say?" Audrey hissed. "Every time you were unhappy, you ran right off to be with *Sutton* and the *Spencers*."

Sutton and the Spencers would be a great band name, Regan errantly thought, but didn't have the wherewithal to even joke about it. Not while her sister's eyes glittered with so much pure resentment, it slammed into Regan with a startling intensity.

"You were ensconced into their *actual* picture-perfect family, getting your hair braided by Katherine and going on family vacations with them. Parading around like you were one of their own fucking children." The unfettered emotion in Audrey's voice was something Regan had *never* heard before. Her sister's eyes glinted in anger, hurt, frustration, and... well, other emotions that Regan didn't know her sister well enough to name.

"I didn't have that; I had to stay at home with our parents, who took every single ounce of pressure that they couldn't put on you and added it to my back. Regan got a C in math, so Audrey better have an A+. Regan dropped out of college, so Audrey better be getting her Ivy League MBA after she graduates summa cum laude." She swigged viciously from her mimosa. "If we can't brag about Regan because she's a single barista, then we need to be able to brag *doubly* about Audrey – climbing the ladder at her company, getting married to the right person."

Regan could only stare, slightly shaking her head against everything she heard. She wanted to argue with her. She wanted to disagree, to tell Audrey that wasn't how this had all gone down.

But the thing was, even if that had been a side of their parents Regan hadn't personally experienced – given that they'd given up on her long before they'd gotten to that point – she knew very well that this was who they *were*.

And... it didn't feel good. She'd wondered, when she'd been younger and had felt so fucking terrible for being such a disappointment to her family, how good it would feel to be able to take Perfect Audrey down a peg.

Only, right now, as her sister's eyes filled with tears, Regan felt awful.

Like her entire worldview was turning on its head. She stared down at the immaculately set up table for several long seconds, trying to figure out how, exactly, she could reconcile this. How she could understand this – this shifted world order.

"I'm sorry," she found herself saying, eyebrows knitting together as she looked at Audrey.

And for the first time in literally forever, she felt like someone was staring back at her that she could potentially understand.

"I'm sorry that was your experience with them. I'm not okay with you taking it out on me," she was quick to add because *years* of their shitty relationship couldn't be undone by Regan understanding Audrey's perspective. But... it was a start, maybe. "I wish you'd said something about it before."

"You were too busy with *Sutton*," Audrey muttered into her glass before taking another swig.

"Why do you have to say her name like that?" Regan demanded, not even able to summon the anger she typically felt. She just – she just wanted to understand, now.

"Because you were always so busy being *her* sister, you never cared about being mine!" The words burst from Audrey's mouth and seemed to startle them both.

At the very least, Regan knew *she* was startled. Baffled and shocked, she could only stare across the table for several long seconds before she found her ability to speak, "You didn't even *want* me to be your sister. When I became friends with Sutton, you used to talk about how you were thrilled that I wasn't following you around anymore."

Because that had been exactly what she'd done when they were little. Before their dad started working for Sutton's, they'd gone to a private school. Though Regan had transferred in the second grade, she hadn't had any friends there. *Any* friends. She'd been known as the weird girl since day one of kindergarten. Her only comfort at school was in her older sister, and Regan had followed her around like a lost puppy.

Audrey had hated it, complaining loudly and often about being unable to get rid of her.

"I was *nine*, of course I complained about you being my shadow! But I–" She broke off, staring at Regan with big, sad eyes, the heated fight in her fading. "I missed you when I didn't have you anymore. And I never got you back. You were barely ever home once you had Sutton in your life, and you were miserable the entire time you had to be in our house."

Regan nearly shot back *can you blame me*? But the words didn't leave her throat. Because she saw, very clearly, that Audrey did understand. That maybe, despite Audrey being the perfect golden child, it hadn't been a label she'd worn in victory but in necessity.

"You know that time Dad's ties ended up being slashed up?" Regan asked, the memory popping up unbidden. "Like, all of them."

Audrey's expression was a picture-perfect blend of confusion and intrigue. Regan felt hesitant to get personal in any way... but she *wanted* to say this to her sister. She found, at this moment, she needed to say it.

Audrey slowly nodded. "Of course, he lost his mind. And no one could ever figure out where that stray cat had come from."

"That was me," she confessed. "I wanted to perform in the sixth-grade talent show as a magician, and I couldn't master that trick, where you pull all of the ties out of your sleeves. So, I got it in my head that if I cut them up, I could pull them out seamlessly. You know, if they were thinner and flimsier."

"Sure…" Audrey agreed, clearly placating her, but Regan would take it. She blinked several times. "But, Regan, there *was* a cat in the house."

"Well, obviously, the tie trick didn't work. And I panicked when I realized how badly his ties were messed up and that I was going to get in so much trouble. So, I snuck out after bedtime and brought the cat in–"

Audrey was shaking her head, ludicrous laughter spilling out of her mouth. "Where did you even find the cat? It had one eye."

"His name was Blackbeard, thank you very much. And he was mine; he lived in the shed in the back of the yard. Dad never got around to tearing down the one on the edge of the property after he got the new one built."

Her sister's laughter grew louder before she slapped a hand over her mouth to quiet down when she seemed to realize it. "So *that's* why you took it upon yourself to catch the cat. You know, I always thought it was weird that you took such a personal offense to Dad's tie collection being ruined."

Audrey studied her for a few moments, her eyebrows knitting together. "I think… it might be nice to get to know you."

Regan found herself studying her sister back. "I think that could be arranged."

Regan got home two hours later, collapsing onto the couch with a loud exhale as she dropped her forearm over her eyes, utterly exhausted.

Utterly exhausted, she still had to go into Topped Off for the night shift, given that two of her typical weekend staff were on vacation.

What a truly crazy, batshit brunch. What a worldview-altering morning. What –

"Hey," Emma's voice broke into her thoughts. "I didn't realize you were home."

Regan slid her arm away from her face to look up at Emma, who stood a few feet away from the couch in the kitchen doorway with an apple in her hand.

At the very sight of her, Regan felt something inside of her spark to life, and she didn't even realize she was smiling until she felt herself doing it. "Hey, yourself. I just got here."

Emma frowned as she studied where Regan was laying in repose. "Are you all right?"

Yeah, there it was. This swooping, pleasant feeling inside of her stomach that Emma not only cared if Regan was okay but she noticed – so easily – that something was off.

"I'm fine. I think." She was honestly going to need to take stock of everything with Audrey later. When she was alone. Which was what she always did, when it came to her family issues. After she had some time to think and settle with her feelings, she would download to Sutton.

It was the way she'd operated for a very long time.

Only, as she stared up at Emma, she found that the words were begging her to vocalize them. She found that she *wanted* to share what happened this morning – that she wanted to share it with Emma, in particular.

She wanted Emma to know. To know *her*. The things that made her who she was.

The realization was startling, especially because Regan hadn't ever discussed her issues with her family with someone who wasn't Sutton in... ever. Even in her sorta-kinda-relationships with the guys she'd dated, this was an unexplored topic. She hadn't wanted to divulge, and they'd never asked.

Trying to comb through how she felt about this turn of events, she slowly pushed herself to sit up.

"I, um, I had brunch with my sister, and it went really... unexpectedly." That seemed like the most fitting word.

"You have a sister?" Emma asked.

Regan laughed, ridiculously charmed by the baffled look on Emma's face, her eyebrows lifted so high on her forehead in consternation.

"I do. Audrey. Two years older than I am. Getting married soon. I'm one of her bridesmaids," she elaborated.

As she talked, Emma's mouth fell open in obvious bewilderment.

"How do I not know any of this?" Emma's voice was demanding. But not at Regan, she realized, as Emma drew a hand through her hair.

249

Emma was clearly directing her ire inward. "I mean, we've known each other for years. We live together. And we've actively been hanging out for weeks now." Emma's lips pulled into a deep frown as those crystal-clear eyes slid back to Regan's. "I feel like I should know this about you by now."

Regan waved her hand. "It's not a big deal."

Emma scoffed. "It feels like one," she asserted, her voice so soft but so intent that it melted something inside Regan. Something soft and fluttery. "Also, you've literally met my whole family and know my entire life story. So, it seems crazy that I wouldn't know your basic family facts. Like that your sister exists and lives here in the city."

One side of Regan's mouth quirked into a small grin. "Let's just say: you're not the only one with a complicated relationship with your family."

"Regan, come on." Emma's insistence started blooming into this feeling inside of Regan. Something sweet, making her heart skip a beat.

"It's true," she insisted, unsure why Emma was so insistent that it wasn't.

It seemed as though Emma was able to read Regan's confusion as she gestured helplessly toward her. "I just... you seem so secure in yourself. In your place in the world. You come off as someone who had a very secure upbringing."

Regan chuckled darkly, both tickled by the idea and how absolutely incorrect it was. "Couldn't be more wrong, actually." She drew in a deep breath, her stomach fluttering with unexpected nerves. The nerves born from this desire to tell Emma more. "You know how you found it so strange that I moved here to be with Sutton?"

She could so easily recall how Emma stared at Regan like she was *crazy* for that.

Apparently, so could Emma. "Of course. You aren't the only one that remembers things about the other."

To Regan's delight, Emma walked closer to sit on the couch with her. Quickly, Regan pulled her legs up from where they'd been sprawled over the cushions. She sat cross-legged, facing Emma, who mirrored her.

As they sat facing one another on their couch, Regan was able to inhale Emma's subtle but enticing scent... and totally lost her train of thought. All she could really think about at that moment was how much she enjoyed it. This closeness. They shared the same physical space when watching a television show or eating dinner together, but this felt very different where they were each other's point of focus.

She liked it.

"Is there more?" Emma asked several beats later, hesitantly. "I mean, you don't *have* to share."

Right. Regan blinked, realizing she'd forgotten why Emma was sitting so close to her, staring intently into her eyes.

"No, I want to tell you." God, it was *so weird* because she really did.

She fiddled with the edges of the throw blanket over the back of the couch, trying to figure out how to explain herself to Emma. Explaining her family and her life in a way she hoped made sense.

"Growing up, Audrey and I couldn't have been more... different." She settled on, smiling mirthlessly at how very true that was. "She was the golden child, and I was the fuck up."

Flicking her gaze to Emma, Regan's nerves momentarily spiked. They were in a good place, the two of them. A really, really good place, the best place. A place Regan was finding herself increasingly addicted to spending time in.

But as she so vividly recalled Emma's feelings about her prior to this good place they were in, she realized – she was a little worried that Emma knowing what her family thought of her might remind Emma that she'd once felt the same thing. Not too long ago, either.

Regan didn't know what that would do to these emerging *feelings* she had for Emma, but she knew that the very thought of Emma thinking poorly of her made her stomach clench tight enough to make her feel sick.

There was no trace of judgment on Emma's face, though. No look that said, *ah, yeah, I totally get why your family thought you were a loser.* There was curiosity there. A quiet sympathy, even.

It bolstered her to keep going. To think... maybe Emma really would *get* her.

"You thought I was crazy to move here because you see Sutton as my best friend. And she *is*, but... for most of my life, she's also been my *family*." Regan searched Emma's gaze with her own, hoping she could see how strongly Regan meant that. "After high school, when she came to New York, I stayed back and went to Brandeis. Because it was what my parents wanted, and... there was still a part of me that wanted them to think I wasn't a total waste of space. A little piece of me that wanted them to see that – I wasn't their screw-up kid. That I could be successful, or something. I don't really know."

She shrugged, clearing her throat as she looked back at the blanket. Even though she didn't feel that way anymore – at least, not so acutely and much more infrequently – she remembered very vividly what it had been like. Just wanting to do *one thing* right in the eyes of her parents.

"And that's the normal thing, right? You finish high school, and you go to college. You say goodbye to seeing your best friend all of the time because they are on a different path in life. It seems like everyone else can do it. Go to school, slog through a degree even if you don't love it. Accept that the closeness you share with your high school best friend isn't going to be forever. But..."

She dug her teeth into her lip, her insides churning as she could so clearly recall how that year had felt, even if it had been eight years ago now.

"It sucked." She summarized, simply. "It sucked so, so much. And not just in an *I miss my friend* way. But in a..."

She paused, the words catching in her throat as she lifted her eyes to Emma's, who was watching her with such a close, intent focus.

Suddenly sheepish, Regan dropped her hands to her knees, gripping them tightly. "You're going to think it's stupid."

"Okay, maybe, but when has that ever stopped you before?" Emma teased, but her voice was gently coaxing.

A nervous titter escaped her. "True."

The difference was that Regan rarely got in her own head, worried that she would sound silly. In fact, she was all too willing to fall on her sword and play the fool – play into what people so often thought of her – in order to direct a situation to an easy resolve.

Only she didn't *want* that with Emma. She didn't want Emma to think of her as silly or as a fool in any way. She wanted – badly – to keep the respect she'd started earning in Emma's eyes.

But she only wanted it if Emma really meant it.

So, she continued. "I missed Sutton in a way that – everything felt wrong. Like, there was one person in my entire life that didn't think that I was too much or... or not enough, or both at the same time." She rolled her lips, eyebrows furrowing as that unpleasant feeling burrowed into her stomach. "My parents feel that way about me. And I always thought my sister did, too. It wasn't even something I inferred, you know? Like, it was the truth."

She slid a look toward Emma. "That's why I felt kind of sensitive to you thinking the same way." Her voice fell quiet, that last part leaving her lips unexpectedly. She bit her cheek because she *hadn't* meant to say that part.

Quickly, she shook her head and pushed on. "Not a big deal. Anyway... I did have other friends back home. People I could hang out with sometimes, or whatever. But it wasn't the same thing. Like I wasn't *home* with them." Regan shrugged heavily, dropping her hands into her lap, away from the blanket. "I was going to a college I didn't even deserve to go to – my grades weren't that great," she admitted, scoffing out a laugh. "Your irritation at the idea of me and my familial privilege was definitely right about that."

"And my undiagnosed ADHD was a total bitch. All the while, I was pursuing a major that I didn't understand and didn't want to follow – my parents were paying for me to get a business degree. *Something useful*," she parroted their choice phrase. "And I was surrounded by people that didn't understand me. Because that is what you're *supposed* to do after high school."

Regan straightened her spine, taking a deep breath. "I didn't follow Sutton here just because living with my best friend in New York would be super fucking awesome." She gave an amused look to Emma. "Following your best friend here is *weird* and not what you're supposed to do; I get that."

Emma didn't mirror her amusement. Instead, she looked at Regan with wide, insightful, sharp eyes, looking undeniably guilty.

But Regan didn't want Emma to feel guilty about her past judgments, and she really didn't.

She dropped her hand down to rest over Emma's, subconsciously stroking her thumb over it, wanting to soothe it away. "I followed

Sutton here because I hated every second of my life back home. I was lonely and miserable, and I felt stupid all of the time. Even though I was living with my family, I'd never felt more alone in my entire life."

"So, even though it wasn't what my parents approved of – like, they really did not – I decided that I had to do what would make *me* happy. Since when had I ever made my family happy or proud, anyway?" A self-deprecating smile playing on her lips, only a hint of an old bitterness burning the back of her throat.

But that had been her big turning point. The moment that she'd really decided for herself what her life was going to be.

"This is my life, not theirs. And I'm going to live it for me. So... yeah. I'm managing a coffee shop and don't have glamorous plans or huge ambitions. But I like my life." She nodded as she spoke, affirming her own words. Feeling them settle inside of her in the right place.

"You don't have to prove that to me," Emma spoke for the first time in what felt like forever, her voice firm, as she searched Regan's gaze with her own. "I know we had a rocky couple of years." Her lips pulled into a smile, quick and sharp and captivating. "But things are different now. The way I see you is different now," she softly amended.

Regan's smile froze on her face as her heart skipped a beat. Skipped *several* beats, actually. Was this what swooning felt like?

She'd been having that thought with increasing frequency when it came to Emma. Yesterday, when Emma stopped on the way to her gram and told Regan, so sincerely, that she thought Regan was funny, loyal, kind, and smart, her knees went weak. And then, when Emma's gram had told Regan that Emma had a crush on her...

Even now, the memory of it stole Regan's breath, making butterflies erupt in her stomach.

"What happened with your sister today?" Emma questioned, tilting her head to the side. "If it's okay to ask."

"Um." Regan shook her head, trying – very, very hard – not to get too swept up in those thoughts. After all, Emma had denied having a *crush*; only insisting that she'd found Regan attractive. Still.

Finally, she re-focused her attention on their actual conversation. "It's definitely okay to ask."

Especially because Emma wouldn't have asked if she hadn't invested in Regan. Miss Privacy Please would *never* ask... if she didn't really want to know.

And an electric thrill shot through her at the fact that Emma wanted to know more about her.

"It was just – it was weird," she mused. "My sister lives in Stamford with her fiancé. And we *don't* have a relationship, not really. Which is why you've never heard me talk much about her. But... I don't know." She dropped her gaze down to where she realized her hand was still on Emma's.

Transfixed, she watched her fingers softly stroke the back of Emma's hand. Then watched in fascination as the hair on Emma's arms stood up.

"I, uh, I just... I've always thought one certain way about my sister. Thought she was very similar to my parents. But it turns out that I might be wrong. She invited me to brunch today just because she wanted to talk. Just us, together." Regan could still hear her own shock in her voice.

"Did brunch go well?" Emma asked hesitantly. Those crystal-clear eyes stayed trained on Regan's face, watching for any sign of upset Regan might express.

"It did." Yeah, she was still shocked. "I think so, anyway. I think maybe we're both kind of learning about each other."

"I'm not surprised that your sister might be starting to see you in a different light," Emma asserted, her tone so confident. "You have a lot of surprising sides to you."

Oh, no.

Oh, yes.

Regan didn't know which one to think of properly; all she knew was that she could feel the same feeling as yesterday. The one where Emma said something and made Regan feel so swept up.

"And I'm glad that your brunch sounded like it went well; if you were feeling down, I was about to offer to sing karaoke with you," Emma informed her, the slightest, cutest smile quirking at her lips.

The mirroring smile that had been sliding onto Regan's lips froze. Completely froze in place as she stared wide-eyed at Emma. "*Really*? Can I take it back? It went terribly. Horribly. Awfully."

Emma scoffed out a laugh. "Yes, *really*. There were going to be stipulations, of course. It was only going to be karaoke here at home, first of all. I'm not going anywhere in public and singing."

"Secondly?" Regan pressed eagerly.

God, she felt – enamored? Was this what that feeling was?

This feeling of her stomach swooping low, making her feel impossibly light, at the sight of Emma's adorable smile. At the fact that Emma was going to offer to sing karaoke with her to cheer her up, something Emma would never typically choose to do?

"Technically, there's no different second reason; it was a doubledown on the first rule."

Regan's heart pounded in her chest so hard she could hear it in her ears. The butterflies in her stomach demanded to be *felt*, growing by the second.

"It may come as a surprise to you, but I know my way around a 3G song," Emma's tone was both haughty and playful as she tossed her hair over her shoulder.

"I love 3G," Regan breathed, almost lightheaded with this headiness. "How did you know that?"

Emma's eyebrows knitted together incredulously. "Regan, you sing *all of the time* around here. It's not difficult to pick up on your favorite artists."

Emma was hardly done speaking when Regan found herself pushing forward, drawn in as if magnetized.

She used the hold she still had on Emma's hand to balance herself, squeezing it as she brushed her lips against Emma's.

Regan had never kissed another woman before. It hadn't ever been something she'd really thought much about. But, *god*, maybe she should have.

She sighed against Emma's lips; they were so unbelievably soft. So full. So plush against Regan's own, she gently slid her mouth against Emma's, letting herself revel in that feeling.

Her own slight movements made heat spark through her body. A heat that cranked up when she felt Emma move her lips against hers, opening on a sharp, gasping inhale.

Oh, yes. She absolutely should have been doing this before now,

Regan dimly registered, rocking forward more firmly, wanting – needing – to get closer. To be able to feel Emma's body – this body that had taken hold in Regan's mind as the root of so many fantasies lately – against her own in any way.

She felt Emma's hand land on her shoulder as she pressed her lips to Emma's again, deliberately slotting Emma's bottom lip between her own.

She'd had so many thoughts about this mouth in the last few weeks. So, so many. Whenever Emma laughed, pursed her lips, or bit down in thought, Regan wondered.

And now, right in this moment, she knew. Now, she knew, and she would never un-know this sensation. She knew that in her very bones.

Emma breathed a shaky exhale against her lips, her firm hand on Regan's shoulder flexing. Taking a fistful of Regan's shirt, the grip pulling Regan inches closer.

Inches that Regan was happy to give. She'd be happy to give up all of the space; in fact, she'd be ecstatic to crawl right there into Emma's lap. To press herself into Emma, to immerse herself in her.

Before she could do it, though, the hand Emma had on her shoulder stopped pulling her in.

Rather, it pushed her back.

Regan moved with the motion, her lips breaking away from Emma's. As soon as the contact was broken, she could hear the disappointed whimper that escaped the back of her throat.

For just a second, she stayed in that in-between space, keeping her eyes closed as her lips tingled and her blood thrummed through her veins. She'd kissed Emma. She'd kissed Emma, and she'd really, really liked it.

A pleasant warmth followed quickly on the heels of that heated desire, her lips curling into a small smile.

"What was *that*?" Emma breathed. The hand she had still clutching Regan's shirt tightened even more against Regan's shoulder.

Finally, she opened her eyes to look at Emma. Who was staring at her with wide-eyed surprise, her lips pink and moist and – *wow*. Yes, Regan had become aware of her attraction to Emma, but when her mouth looked like that, all plump and freshly kissed *by her,* she felt herself throb.

"It was a kiss," she whispered back, heart still pounding in her chest.

"I *know* it was a kiss," Emma hissed, shaking her head vehemently. "But – but *why?*"

Regan could say that she didn't know what possessed her to do it, but it would be a lie.

She did it because this attraction she felt for Emma refused to let up intensity; if anything, Regan felt like its hold on her only got stronger.

She did it because Emma was attracted to her, too.

She did it because it felt *good* being Emma's girlfriend. Even if it wasn't totally real, it felt good.

She did it because she'd wanted to share herself with Emma, and Emma had wanted to listen.

She did it because Emma would sing 3G with her to make her feel better after a hard day.

And, mostly, she did it because she wanted to. She really wanted to.

She still wanted to. Right now, all over again. In fact, as she traced her tongue over her own bottom lip and tasted the remnants of Emma's chapstick, she wanted to do it again very, very badly.

Slowly, she slid her gaze back up Emma's face to meet her eyes, a sheepish smile playing on her lips. "Um... so here's the thing–"

Abruptly, Emma released her grip on Regan's shirt, as if only realizing in that moment that she'd been holding onto her. She quickly pushed herself up from the couch, her movements awkward and stilted, as if she couldn't quite catch her bearings.

"Actually, I don't want to know," she quickly said, holding up her hand. A hand that was shaking, Regan noticed.

"I don't want to know anything. I don't want you to say anything. I don't want to talk about it. This never happened."

Emma raised her hands and scrubbed them over her face, looking dazed. Well, more aptly, looking like she wished she could wipe that dazed feeling away.

"Emma–" she tried to start again, moving to stand up herself.

She was stopped as Emma reached out and lightly pushed her back down. "No. You – you stay. Right there."

Regan slowly settled back onto the couch, tilting her head up at Emma, amusement mixing with confusion. "How long do I have to stay here?"

"Until I leave," Emma countered firmly. "I'm leaving."

Deflating – it was jarring, this intense come-down after such a ground-shaking kiss – Regan dropped her hands listlessly to the couch cushions next to her. "Where are you going?"

"I'm going... to see my gram. That's where I'm going. And when I come home – things are going to be normal," Emma insisted, slowly backing away from Regan. As if she was worried that Regan would pounce on her or something.

In fairness, Regan could admit that she'd felt very close to pouncing on Emma only minutes ago.

"Emma–" She tried again, feeling the desperate need to at least try to explain herself.

She realized she had no idea what possible explanation she could offer that would make Emma feel better. Which kind of made having a conversation moot.

"*Normal*," Emma repeated darkly before she turned on her heel and hurriedly walked away. She walked out of the living room, down the hall, pausing for only a few seconds – presumably grabbing her keys and wallet from the entryway table, and a pair of sandals from the shoe rack – before the front door opened and closed.

Regan fell back against the couch, staring up at the ceiling. "Idiot," she whispered derisively at herself. "What is *wrong* with you?"

She'd finally – finally – found this footing with Emma. And then, in a moment of action-first thoughts-later, she'd ruined it. Typical Regan.

God, she really hoped she hadn't ruined *everything*, hoped all of this progress they'd made as friends and roommates wasn't completely flushed down the drain over one simple kiss.

One simple kiss...

She reached her hand up, lightly brushing her fingertips over her lips. One simple kiss that had totally rocked her world. One simple kiss that left Regan aching for more. One simple kiss that left her feeling far more than any other kiss she'd ever experienced.

Oh, boy.

sixteen

EMMA'S HAND was still trembling slightly as she determinedly shut the apartment door behind her.

She only got a few steps away, though, before the steam that had been fueling her started to dissipate. Whatever post-kiss fueled energy that had sparked through her – or maybe it was energy sparked *from* that kiss? – zapped out of her, leaving her standing in the hallway a few feet away from the elevator.

But she couldn't force her feet to move any farther.

No, she felt like she was stuck here, in this spot, as her mind and body reeled from what had just happened.

Regan had *kissed* her.

There had been no mistaking it, no way to brush it off as some sort of insane accident. Emma's mind had already tried that in the last five minutes. But no. Regan had gripped Emma's hand, taken a deep breath, and closed the gap between them on the couch. There was intent.

Her hand still tingled where Regan had held it, a physical reminder for Emma. As if she needed it when she could still very much feel the phantom sensation of Regan's lips on hers. Those plush lips that had caught Emma's attention so many times before – she didn't need to harbor a crush on Regan to think that her mouth was incredibly sexy – had just been against Emma's own.

Unthinkingly, she lifted her hand to her chest, where her heart was still beating too fast to be normal. Her heart rate had gone through the roof when Regan's mouth had met hers, and it still hadn't slowed completely down. Much like the fluttering sensation in her stomach hadn't quite stopped.

It wasn't a feeling Emma was familiar with. Had this happened with Felicity? With the few other people she'd kissed before? *Probably*, she told herself, even though she couldn't quite recall it. Which, she decided, made sense. Of course, her memories of past kisses were a little hazy right now, in the immediate aftermath of what was absolutely the most shocking kiss of her life.

But now that she had some space and wasn't surrounded by Regan's scent, now that Regan wasn't looking at her with big, dark eyes, and Emma couldn't get tripped up by the way Regan's lips looked all freshly kissed – slightly bruised, entirely too appealing – Emma was able to grasp onto some clarity.

Only, *clarity* wasn't quite so clear.

Because she just... she couldn't understand. She didn't understand.

As she stood in the hallway, staring at the elevators but unable to bring herself to continue walking toward them, Emma tried desperately to make sense of what transpired.

She'd walked into the living room, not expecting to see Regan home. She'd gone out this morning while Emma had been in the shower, and Emma... well, she'd been a little disappointed. Because Regan's schedule informed Emma that Regan wasn't going to the café until this evening.

She'd been hoping they'd be able to finish the season of *The One* they'd been bingeing, honestly. But she'd known the minute she opened the bathroom door that Regan wasn't home; the apartment had been dead silent.

Which – was totally fine, Emma had reasoned with herself. Because she had a ton of stuff she could do. She could answer work emails, read, and work on her latest book review. All valuable uses of her time.

And yet, she'd felt an undeniable zap of excitement when she'd seen

Regan lying on the couch after having quietly returned home. Wow, Emma couldn't believe that it had only been thirty minutes ago; it felt like a lifetime.

Her excitement had dwindled when she'd gotten a good look at Regan. When she'd been able to see the look in Regan's eyes. And she'd realized that she'd missed Regan's usual verve, that glint of life that made Regan feel so full of vitality.

Then, Regan shared her vulnerabilities with Emma and told Emma the parts of her life that she didn't share with many people. Regan hadn't explicitly said as much, but Emma could tell.

She'd opened up to Emma, and Emma... she'd felt close to Regan. For the first time, she felt like she truly understood who Regan was, and why.

Yes, they'd become closer. Yes, she cared about Regan. But hearing Regan tell her about her past made something click into place inside of her.

She'd felt this need to be there for Regan. To support her. And not because Regan had supported her for the last month through all of Emma's family issues, but – because she *cared*. More than she'd expected to, honestly. Because she'd hated seeing that sad, dejected look in Regan's big, dark eyes, and it had twisted Emma up inside.

To the point that she'd been very seriously going to offer to sing karaoke! Emma did *not* sing in front of other people. Not sober, anyway.

For some reason Emma couldn't wrap her mind around, that was the moment had Regan had kissed her.

Like, what?!

Latching onto that confusion, using it to energize her and to help her push through post-kiss haziness, Emma turned sharply on her heel and marched back toward their apartment.

No, she wasn't going to get caught up in the kiss or how it seemed to have left a lasting imprint on her mouth. No, she wasn't going to ruminate on how her blood seemed to race hotter through her veins.

Because *that* wasn't what was important here, Emma wouldn't let it be.

She tossed the door closed behind her, storming down the short hallway until she stood right back in the living room. "What the hell was that?"

Emma was only slightly surprised by the fact that Regan was still sitting exactly where Emma had left her on the couch a few minutes ago. Regan was typically so full of life and movement, she didn't sit still for long.

Regan snapped her gaze to Emma, her dark eyes wide and startled. "What are you doing here?"

"I live here," Emma reminded her, hands falling to her hips as she stared Regan down. "I live here, which means that I can't do what I would normally do when someone kisses me completely out of the blue."

"What would you normally do?" Regan cocked her head, sounding entirely too interested in something totally irrelevant.

"I don't know! Because it's never happened before." She'd probably need to take some time to figure out her thoughts. To read into her feelings. To feel whether the kiss felt warranted, whether she'd liked it or not. If she'd want to do it again. But – "And that doesn't matter. Because the *point*, Regan, the point is that no matter what, I can't do that with you. Because *I live here*," she gestured around their apartment.

Taking a deep breath, she tried to center herself. She tried very, very valiantly not to dip her gaze down to Regan's mouth. The mouth that had been on hers only minutes ago causing all of these unexpected, overwhelming feelings coursing through her.

Clamping her hands down on her hips, she repeated her question again. This time, calmer. "Why did you kiss me?"

She *needed* to know; Emma needed to make sense of this so that she could dismiss it.

Regan blinked up at her. "I thought you didn't want to know?"

Emma could hardly remember saying those words. She'd been too caught up in her thoughts, in the way she could barely catch her breath and how Regan had been looking at her.

"Well, I realized that I need to know. Okay? Just... I don't get it," she confessed, feeling on the edge of desperation.

"Uh... so what answer will make you freak out the least?" Regan asked, sounding like she was teasing, but there was a tone of seriousness underneath.

Emma's lips uncontrollably tugged up into the briefest of grins before she smothered it. This was *not* the time for laughter. "The truth."

After all, she reasoned, this could be something... simple. Emma had no idea what kind of misunderstanding, but it could be a misunderstanding nonetheless.

"The truth," Regan quietly echoed, biting her plush bottom lip. "Well, okay. The truth," she murmured again, interlocking her long, nimble fingers and wrapping her arms around her legs.

Emma couldn't help but be amused, staring at Regan as she waited for a response.

Finally, Regan seemed to come to some sort of peace with herself as she turned her attention – direct and intent – toward Emma. She couldn't make sense of the look in them. Heated but hesitant?

"The truth is, Emma, that I kissed you because I find you really attractive."

It made no sense for her to feel totally fucking shocked, Emma knew, because Regan had literally just kissed her. But she *was*. Surprise rushed through her, and she shook her head. "Wait – what? You *what*?"

Regan nodded, with no hesitation this time. "I'm attracted to you."

Emma's cheeks flashed with heat as her heart started to thrum in her chest. "Since when? How do you know? I thought you were – you aren't into women?"

She meant to assert that as a fact, a statement, but it came out far more uncertain. Understandably, in her opinion.

While Emma felt struck, frozen, and rooted in place at this revelation, saying the words seemed to bring Regan back to life.

She nodded quickly, snapping her fingers in Emma's direction. "See, that's what I thought, too! But it turns out I kind of am?" She slowly arched her eyebrows, a self-deprecating smile working over her face. "I realized it a few weeks ago after dinner with Kimberly. You know, when I fell off the chair?"

Emma nodded, but it felt surreal. Everything felt surreal.

"It's because I realized I was checking you out. Like *really* checking you out," Regan's tone dipped into an octave Emma had never heard from her. Something edging on raspy, and it made her shiver.

Between the tone and how Regan looked at her, Emma's stomach clenched in wanting an answer.

No.

"I think I've probably been attracted to you longer than I realized," Regan continued, entirely unashamed. As she spoke, she pushed herself up from the couch, seeming filled with too much energy to stay seated anymore.

Emma subconsciously took a step backward.

"I just – *god*, you have amazing breasts. I remember thinking that the first time we met. So, maybe that was a moment, but I didn't realize it. I don't know." Regan shrugged, looking at Emma, so full of wonder. "All I *do* know is that ever since I realized I can't stop thinking about it. About you. Like that."

"Is that all?" She asked faintly. But she thought that was justified when Regan was standing in front of her, talking about how much she loved Emma's breasts!

Regan just stood there across the room, seeming totally normal. Sure, her cheeks were flushed, and her gaze was a little too intently focused on Emma, but she didn't seem like her reality was about to crack wide open and spill out at the edges.

"I think about your breasts and your thighs and your lips all of the time."

Emma's mouth fell open with a sharp inhale. She didn't even realize she was sliding her hands, one to rest over her stomach to quell the strange butterflies there, the other moving up to card through her hair and press down against her skull, as if she could physically stop her thoughts from racing.

What was Regan *doing* to her?

"Which isn't abnormal for me lately. But then, just a little while ago," Regan gestured behind her toward the couch. As if Emma could misunderstand what she was referencing. "You were just – you were so sweet to me. And I... I felt good telling you everything about my family. And you looked at me like you really got it. Got *me*."

Regan blew out a deep sigh, turning her gaze back on Emma's, as she expectantly said, "So – that's why."

Emma could only blink back in confusion. Why... what?

"Why I kissed you," Regan elaborated, taking a tentative step closer to Emma.

Had she spoken aloud, or was Regan really able to read her that well by now?

For some reason, *that* thought snapped Emma out of this surreal haze and sharply back into reality.

"Emma?" Regan softly voiced her name, taking another step forward when Emma didn't respond.

"Stop," she cautioned, holding her hand up between them. The last thing she needed was to feel engulfed by Regan's scent right now. "Just – hold on."

Regan froze where she stood.

The hand Emma still had clasped to her head slowly moved until she was rubbing at her forehead. Trying to organize her thoughts, sort out everything whirling inside her.

The only thing she knew for sure was, "Regan, we *can't* do that again."

Regan's eyebrows knit together, her lips pursing in a cute little pout.

And, despite *everything*, Emma couldn't help the exasperated laugh that escaped her lips. "Are you really surprised by me saying that?" Emma gestured to herself. "What about me suggests to you that I would really love for my world to be thrown into chaos?"

She realized her mistake too late, as Regan's eyes followed Emma's gesture, looking her up and down with that – that *glint*. Emma's throat ran dry.

Which, no. Not happening.

Coughing, Emma pointedly drew Regan's gaze back to her own. Regan, unsurprisingly, smiled at her with zero concern at having been caught blatantly checking her out.

"Okay, being attracted to women is – it's great. I'm happy for you." Was she?!

"So far, it's just *woman*," Regan corrected.

Emma felt that heat spark through her again, even as she took another step back. This time, that step put her back right against the brick wall of the living room. "Uh. Okay. That's – be that as it may," oh, *god*, she had to clear her throat a second time! "We really can't kiss again. I'm sure you've been attracted to a ton of men before and not kissed them."

Finally, Emma felt like she had her thoughts in order enough to make a salient point!

Regan hummed before nodding. "Yes. You're right."

"Great. So, that's what this is. It's not like you're in love with me or anything, so–" Emma's eyes widened as soon as she spoke the words, and her stomach didn't flutter this time; it tightened into knots.

The very idea of romantic love hadn't crossed Emma's mind in any sort of *real* way since Felicity had broken up with her over two years ago, and the last thing she'd ever expected was for it to be Regan Gallagher that made that thought surface.

Relief pounded through her when Regan let out a hearty laugh. "No, I'm not in love with you," she conceded, her voice falling to a softer, sweeter tone. "For a second, I considered joking about it. But the look on your face makes me think you'd pass out if I did."

Emma slid her palm down her face. "Yeah, I might have."

Still leaning back against the wall, Emma felt herself truly breathing for the first time in what felt like forever, even if it had only been the past hour.

"More than anything, Regan, I like what we are. I like what we've figured out here in the last month. I like that we've *finally* reached this place in our relationship. Where we can trust each other and actually talk to each other. Where we like each other – er, spending time together," she quickly corrected, feeling herself blush.

Still, she maintained eye contact with Regan, wanting her to see how much Emma meant this.

"We're both roommates and friends, and doing anything to jeopardize that isn't in the cards," she stated firmly. And she felt good about it. "We kissed because you're attracted to me, and I'm the first woman you're experiencing attraction to. It doesn't have to become this big *thing*, and I don't want it to. I want to watch *The One* with you and have dinner together and text you throughout the day without it being weird."

Emma honestly hadn't realized how much she'd come to enjoy those things that had all become regular occurrences for them until this moment. Until the idea that they might go back to not being in a good enough place to do those things struck her and made her stomach twist.

She didn't have many people in her life like Regan; she didn't even know anyone like Regan. Yes, she had a friendship with Sutton and a sort of friendship with Brynn, but Regan – by virtue of both who she was as a person and the situation they'd found themselves in – was... different. Somehow, she was closer to Regan than anyone else who had come into her life in a long time.

Regan held onto Emma's words for several beats before she finally nodded. "Yeah. I mean, I don't want to lose those things, either. If you recall, I was the one that pushed for them in the first place."

An annoyingly attractive cheeky smile slid over Regan's face, and with it, a calming feeling flooded through Emma.

The kiss and all of the big, bright, tumultuous feelings it had alit in Emma fell into the background, allowing her to take a real deep breath for the first time since the kiss had been placed on her lips.

"Great. So... things are fine, then. Between us," she pushed to solidify. Needing to make sure she and Regan were both on the same page about this.

Regan rocked back and forth on her feet. "Yep. Absolutely fine."

Even though things were clearly *fine*, Emma remained where she stood. Her back against the wall, her knees still weak, and her lips tingling from Regan's kiss.

Which had to go away soon, right?

"Well," Regan clapped her hands in front of her, startlingly loud. "Since things are so *fine*, let's do something normal. We only had a few episodes left in season three of *The One*, right? We probably have enough time to finish it before I have to go to work."

Regan dipped her gaze down at her wrist, where she was not wearing a watch.

Emma's lips pulled into a hesitant smile as she skeptically acquiesced, "Yeah, I guess we do."

Turning on her heel, Regan walked back to the couch and dropped to the spot she'd been sitting in earlier. The sight gave Emma pause.

Was this a good idea? Emma could really go for some processing time right now, but if she did that, it would mean she was admitting that she wasn't feeling totally *fine and normal* about this.

Regan looked at her with an innocuous smile as she patted the cushion next to her. "Come on, Emma. I'm not going to jump you. Promise."

"We'll see," Emma muttered, pushing off the wall and walking toward the couch.

The only way this would start to feel normal again was if they made it normal. They were both adults. It was one kiss that hadn't even involved tongue.

Emma let out a breath she hadn't even realized she'd been holding as Regan didn't scooch in closer to her. Yes, Regan often sat close enough to Emma's side that they were touching, and Emma had come to expect it. To enjoy it, even – which was a *startling* realization to have in this moment. But it was true. When they weren't watching TV, Regan still sat that close because she loved to slide her phone screen in Emma's direction whenever she came across an amusing video or meme. To Regan's credit, Emma really did find herself amused by whatever content Regan curated for her.

Right now, though, she was glad Regan was able to read the room – read *Emma* – and maintain some distance.

Regan merely curled up against the arm of the couch and reached for the remote, navigating through the streaming apps before putting on an episode of irritatingly addictive reality television.

Emma took a slow, deep breath and held it for a few seconds... before measuredly letting it out. And with it came some of her tension. There.

As the drama unfolded on the screen, Emma's shoulders relaxed even more. *These* people, going on a reality dating show, had real romantic drama to deal with. Emma just had one kiss with Regan.

She only *just* started to find some semblance of true calm fifteen minutes into the episode – sure, she was hyper-aware of Regan, but that was to be expected right about now – when Regan ruined it.

"You know, it actually feels really good to let that all out," she commented, her tone thoughtful, immediately pulling Emma's entire attention from the TV. "I've been holding onto it so tightly for the last couple of weeks. Literally falling over myself because I didn't know what to do about this attraction. But now, I can just be toootally normal."

Emma's blood rushed through her ears as she stared agape at Regan, who was splayed out over the couch, looking so relaxed. Pensive but relaxed, with one arm curled behind her head, making her shirt ride up over her smooth, pale stomach and her other hand resting on her revealed skin.

Jesus. Emma snapped her eyes closed.

Even so, all she could see with her eyes closed was still – damningly – *Regan.* Her mind replayed the images of Regan falling over herself, and she snapped her eyes open with a gasp as surprise rushed through her. "That was all because you were attracted to me?"

Regan falling over her feet, dumping the coffee over herself... good god!

Emma did not appreciate the feeling that slithered through the pit of her stomach. This feeling of being *pleased.* Flattered. Amazed. It was a resoundingly positive, heated feeling, and she clenched her jaw, doing her best to stifle it.

Regan nudged Emma lightly in the thigh with her socked foot. "Duh."

Dumbfounded, Emma turned blankly back toward the TV and tried to filter that information into the neatly organized sections of her brain.

Only for Regan to throw her for another loop, as she poked Emma with her toe again and asked, "Does it at least feel nice to know? That I'm so attracted to you?"

Why? Why was Regan like this? Just as Emma thought she would move beyond this kiss fiasco as seamlessly as possible, Regan had to do *this.* Had to make Emma think about it, to think about Regan's attraction and – ugh!

She wanted to retort that, *no,* it didn't feel good. In fact, she opened her mouth to tell Regan as much.

Damnably, though, she also couldn't deny that feeling that was still demanding to be felt because that was precisely what it was. It felt terrifyingly, disarmingly good.

Underneath the panic from the kiss and the fear that this would throw Emma's newly settled life into chaos, it made her feel ridiculously satisfied. Not as in *a job well done* kind of satisfaction, but something heady and wanting.

Bad. Bad train of thought.

"It felt great for me, if you can imagine when Gram spilled the beans you were attracted to me," Regan continued, seemingly unbothered by how this afternoon was unraveling.

Still, Emma couldn't help but admire Regan's ability to talk through any potential weirdness, speak her mind, and vocalize her feelings like this.

But, for her own sanity, Emma needed to cut this off at the knees.

She kept her tone as sharp and factual as she could. "Yes, it's nice to know."

Oh, you helped Regan figure out her sexuality, and she's really attracted to you – that's nice to know!

A peel of amused laughter escaped Regan. "It's nice to know," she parroted, poorly mimicking Emma as she unthinkingly tapped on Emma's thigh in some sort of silent rhythm that only Regan could hear.

"I'm sticking with it." Emma cut a look to Regan, entirely unsurprised by the wide, bright smile on her face.

"I would expect nothing less from you."

"No more questions, okay? I don't want to miss Chelsea picking Samantha."

With that, Emma resolutely turned back to face the TV, shaking her head. Bafflingly, Regan's teasing was what made Emma feel any semblance of normal. Which was *so* messed up.

And so irritatingly, charmingly, Regan.

seventeen

"You *have* to come out with us tonight," Beth called to Regan from across the back room at Topped Off.

"Oh, I *have* to?" Regan teased back, reaching for her large purse after she hung her apron up in her locker. She pawed through her bag, making sure that her keys, wallet, and phone were all in sight – there was absolutely nothing worse than leaving work and getting all the way back home, only to realize that she'd left one of her essentials at the café.

Which, unfortunately, had happened to Regan more times than she'd like to admit.

Satisfied that she had everything, she reached in and grabbed her phone. She usually kept it secured in her back pocket during her shifts, as it was always handy to answer messages when a brief lull hit. Or to take a silly picture. Or to leave herself quick reminders about scheduling, or observations about coffee blends or pastries.

Or to text Emma.

Which, admittedly, was what Regan was doing more than anything, these days. And was the main reason she'd made herself leave her phone in her locker after her break a few hours ago.

Regan had never before had a problem ignoring the vibrations against her butt cheek signaling a new text when there was an influx of customers needing attention. She *did* have a work ethic. She also had a love for tips.

She'd found, though, that it was very, very hard for her to ignore when Emma texted her, even when she was facing a line of customers. It was addictive; what was Emma saying, now?! Had Regan made her laugh with her last quippy – if she did say so herself – message?

And she was so, so relieved that Emma hadn't turned away from their friendship or shut Regan out after the Couch Kiss Debacle of last week.

Regan really did consider herself lucky that they were both totally normal, post-kiss. After all, it wasn't like Regan was super familiar with what to do in this situation, either! The only people she'd ever been super attracted to and kissed were guys she was dating or wanting to sleep with, never a friend. Never someone she cared about, beyond a sex/dating sphere.

She could see it going so terribly, horribly wrong in her head. Emma getting the wrong idea – that Regan was, like, uncontrollably, unstoppably in love with her or something – and putting an end to their closeness.

But, nope. Emma seemed to have been able to act like the kiss had never happened. In the last six days, they'd slipped back into this rhythm they'd seemed to have found, and that was *great*.

Really.

Okay, the only thing that maybe wasn't super great was that Regan couldn't slip into normalcy with the ease Emma seemed to be able to.

It really made no sense, right? Because Regan considered herself to be an amazing friend! Being a friend came to her as easily as breathing. After all, she'd spent most of her life with her biggest defining quality being *Sutton's best friend*. Could she be a little exuberant? Perhaps. A little dramatic? Sometimes.

But if there was one thing Regan never, ever doubted about herself – no matter how poorly she did in school or what her parents said – it was that she was a damn good friend.

So, it really made no sense that Regan had to remind herself that she was just Emma's totally platonic *friend* multiple times in the last few days.

It's what she told herself in the aftermath of the kiss, when Emma seemed so freaked out. There was no other word for it – freaked out really summed up the look on Emma's face. While Regan really wished that hadn't been the expression on Emma's face in the minutes after they'd shared the most thrilling first kiss of Regan's life, there was no denying it.

And after she'd listened to Emma's side of everything, Regan came around to Emma's way of thinking... generally. Mostly, she agreed that having an attraction didn't have to mean anything more. They were friends that were attracted to each other. Big deal! She really liked place they were in. She did have fun with Emma and all of her acerbic, dry commentary and the way she got really into reality television even though she'd been so reluctant to watch it in the first place. She didn't want any of that to change, that was all the truth.

So, in that regard, yeah. They could absolutely just be normal friends, still.

Yet, she'd had to remind herself of that fact again only two days later. When she'd texted Emma *I don't know how I'm going to make it through this shift without my head exploding from this migraine. Please come and collect my remains, I want to be sprinkled in the apartment.*

Emma's response in text had been simple – *... like, your ashes or the remains of your literally exploded skull? I'm going to have to check the lease before I comply.*

But when Regan had returned home, Emma had picked them both up dinner from the Italian place that Regan had found weeks ago, recommended by an influencer she followed. She'd sent Emma the post, telling her: *We should go here sometime – it's close to your work I think!*

Emma had then lit candles to keep the living room in low light, informing Regan in a soothing voice, "I get migraines sometimes, too. Just, relax."

Very thoughtful. Very sweet. Enticingly so. She'd sat in the living room with Regan, quietly working on her laptop while Regan had napped.

"Just in case your head really did explode; I figured you could use a witness," Emma had drolly informed Regan when she'd woken up.

Which was very – platonically – sweet. And had made Regan's stomach – platonically – swoop.

She'd reminded herself yet again that she was merely Emma's friend only a couple days later, come Wednesday afternoon.

Because Regan had realized – shit. She was going to be responsible for all of the desserts at a child's birthday party in only days, and she'd never had that kind of responsibility on her shoulders!

So, she'd buckled down and created a vision board for all of her ideas, which had been approved by both Kimberly and Everly. Then, still a little apprehensive, she'd shown the board to Emma.

But Emma had pulled out her phone and showed Regan a picture of cupcakes posted from Topped Off that she'd made earlier this summer, designed to look like upside-down, melting ice cream cones. "Look – these are *incredible*, and you made them. You can do this." She given Regan such a strong reaffirming look, it offered no room for disagreement.

Beth cleared her throat, regaining Regan's attention. "Yes, you have to come out tonight. For a multitude of reasons. First, because Mike actually has a slot in the comedy show, at the dive bar," Beth gleefully informed her.

Regan nearly dropped her purse in surprise. "No fucking way! How?!"

Mike was one of their vendors, who frequently updated them on his comedy dreams. Which was actually hilarious because Mike was one of the least funny people Regan knew.

Beth shrugged. "Bribery, I'm guessing? Either way, he's on at nine, and everyone from the day crew is meeting us there."

Regan slowly tilted her head in thought. All right, that was a fairly convincing argument. On the *other* hand, though, it was Friday night, which meant Emma was going to be much more likely to stay up and hang out later into the night. The sooner Regan got home, the sooner they could hang out, and the more time they could spend together before Emma went to bed.

"Secondly," Beth pointedly cleared her throat. "It's Liz's birthday this weekend. Thirdly, and most importantly, you haven't gone out with us in over a month."

Reeling back, Regan refuted, "That can't be true."

Ever since she'd started at Topped Off, Regan had been the person to spearhead inter-shift staff bonding. She'd covered for people on every shift, much like she did now, and she'd been looking to widen her social circle. Ever since then, she'd made a point to go out with people from work a couple of times a month. Sometimes even more frequently after Sutton had started dating Charlotte.

Beth arched a look at her. "It's very true."

Shaking her head, Regan leaned back against her locker, thinking back...

And she startled when she realized that Beth was *right*.

She hadn't gone out with work friends since before she and Emma had started bonding, which was over a month ago, now.

"Holy shit," she whispered to herself.

How that *that* happened?

Even when Sutton was living with her, Regan had always spent time with her other – more casual – friends. Mostly because Sutton didn't enjoy going out very much, plus she often had paper/grading deadlines and stuck to a strict schedule.

"That's what I'm saying." Beth tossed her hands in the air, baffled. "Every time we've gone out in the last six weeks, everyone's been asking where you are. Why you never hang out anymore. Who you're always texting. And they keep asking *me*, as if I know the answer." She bit her lip, eyeing Regan. "On that note... who *are* you always texting? A new beau?"

Regan blinked widely back at Beth, still at a loss for words as her thoughts were spinning beyond her control. "Uh. No. It's no one." As soon as the words left her mouth, Regan cringed. Her stomach cramped with them, because it felt like a lie. More than that, it felt insulting to Emma, to refer to her as *no one*. "It's just my roommate."

"Ohhhh, Emily."

"Emma," Regan quickly corrected, feeling absurdly slighted that Beth didn't remember.

"Right." Beth accepted with an apologetic wince. "Anyway – are you coming tonight? We should probably head out soon, so we can meet up with everyone and have Liz's celebratory birthday shot before Mike goes on stage."

"Ah..." Regan bit at her cheek, as she looked down at her phone. Her lifeline to Emma.

As if reading her mind – granted, *fine*, her phone was set to light up and remind her of unread notifications every five minutes – her lock screen lit up to reveal a text from the woman in question.

EMMA – 7:07PM

> Just wanted to let you know that I made some soup for dinner. I put some away for you – don't pick anything up on your way home

> Unless you don't want soup. Then you should pick something up for dinner on your way home

Regan's stomach burst to life with those crazy strong butterflies. Emma made her soup for dinner!

She didn't want to go out with everyone from work when Emma was at home with soup. She wanted to curl up on the couch and listen to Emma tell her about the rest of her day. She wanted to watch a movie or a show and listen to the way Emma commented as if she weren't totally invested.

Which was precisely why she hadn't gone out with her work friends in weeks, she realized, gripping her phone tightly.

Because every offer of plans with anyone else felt so... unappealing when it was put up against the idea of going home and hanging out with Emma. Or going out to dinner with Emma. Or *anything* with Emma.

Regan just hadn't noticed what she was doing before now.

Fuck.

That wasn't what purely platonic friends did! They didn't plan as much of their availability around one another as they possibly could, because being around each other felt addictive and fun and just *better* than being around other people.

Regan's heart leapt in her chest. Oh, boy.

So, she did what she'd have done if Sutton was currently living with her – what she'd do with someone that was strictly a friend.

> Hey roomie! I'm totally looking forward to that soup. But I'm going to be home a little late tonight bc I'm going out with some friends from work. See you later and DON'T watch more of our show(s) without me!!!

Humming under her breath in a way that was maybe a liiiittle off-beat, Regan giggled to herself as she scraped her key into the lock.

Only to pout at the keys when the dumb thing didn't actually turn! Why did keys all look so similar, anyway? Who made that design choice?!

"The real question is who allowed other keys to fit in a lock that they don't open. What the hell is that about," she muttered, yanking her key ring away from the door before frowning down at them in her hand.

And *why* did she have so many keys?!

"That's the best question," she affirmed for herself, squinting at them all. "Lit-tle keys, lit-tle keys, which one fits in my door?" She sang her song to the tune of *row, row, row your boat*, before chuckling at herself all over again.

Leaning her forehead against the cool wood, she braced herself against the door and took a little break from the arduous process of finding the right key – a task that occasionally took more than one try when she *hadn't* had anything to drink.

A second later, her balance was completely ruined, as the door opened. With her weight braced against it, the door actually *flew* open, and Regan yelped in alarm.

She flailed her arms as she fell forward, already closing her eyes and bracing for impact...

Only to crash into something much better than the floor. Someone, more aptly. Some*one* much softer and warmer, who smelled so good...

"Emma," she identified, delighted with the new turn of events.

Regan contentedly leaned heavily into Emma, who let out a surprised grunt in her ear as her arms wrapped quickly around Regan's waist to catch her.

"Woah! Jesus. Are you okay?" Emma asked, her warm breath washing over the side of Regan's face, making her shiver.

Regan grinned, nodding against Emma and reveling in the softness of Emma's shirt brushing against her cheek. "Tot-ally good. Yep."

Indeed, she was really, really okay in this moment. This was great!

Emma huffed out a quiet laugh. So quiet that Regan wasn't sure she'd have been able to hear it if she weren't pressed right up against Emma like this.

Which, logically, meant that she *should* spend as much time as possible pressing against Emma. Right? Because Regan wanted to hear all of her little laughs and sighs and sounds.

At least, it was logical to her tipsy mind.

"All right, then, come on." Emma tightened her arms around Regan's waist and took a couple small steps backward, forcing Regan to walk forward to keep up with her and ensure their bodies didn't lose contact. One of Emma's arms disengaged its hold from Regan to swing their apartment door shut. "Is it safe to assume that you had fun with your coworkers?"

Regan inhaled deeply, loving this feeling of being wrapped up in Emma's scent. It made her stomach tingle so pleasantly. "Mmm. It was fine."

"Don't take this the wrong way, but being drunk enough that you aren't standing on your own seems like you had more than a *fine* time. Or less than a fine time, depending."

But – no. That was factually wrong, and Regan needed Emma to know that.

She needed Emma to know that Regan wasn't – she wasn't someone that went out and got so plastered that she couldn't enter her own home. That she wasn't a messy drunk that couldn't stand up by herself.

Even though it went against every fiber of Regan's being in this moment, she pulled away from Emma. Away from her warmth and the comfort and the way her body felt against Regan's, because she needed to prove herself.

"I can stand on my own," she insisted, reluctantly dropping her arms away from Emma so that Emma knew she really didn't need her support. "I just – the keys were hard. I was taking a short break!"

She scowled at the keys in question that were still clutched in her hand, before tossing them to the entry table. Then she dumped her purse on the table, too, feeling significantly lighter after.

"See?" She held her arms up and kicked her feet out in a little dance, making Emma see that she was still in control of her own body. Not a single stumble, thank you very much.

She might not be sober, but she wasn't a total lush. And Regan objected at her very core for Emma to see her that way.

Emma's eyebrows lifted as she slid her gaze down Regan's body in the dim lighting of their hallway. "I do see. Did you wear that to *work*?" The incredulity dripped from Emma's voice.

Confused, Regan looked down at herself to take in her fitted crop top and sort of scandalously low-cut shorts. Ah. She scoffed out a laugh, which came out maybe a little louder than she'd intended. "Ohhhh, no. No, no." She lifted her eyes to meet Emma's. "You see, Emma, at work? I'm in charge; I'm a manager. I can't wear this to work."

"Mhmm, but you *can* go out and drink with the people you manage?" Emma asked, tilting her head.

Regan held up her hand to stop her right there. "*First*, I started our going out traditions way before I ever became a manager. And secondly, Emma Bordeaux, secondly – you see, without me there, who would be the responsible one? Hmm?"

She arched a victorious look at Emma, who was staring back at her dubiously. Mixed with that skepticism, though, was the softest little smile. A smile that made Regan's cheeks feel warm and her heart did that pitter-patter thing.

"And *you're* the responsible one?" Emma asked, teasingly.

It *was* teasing, yes. But it was also so... dare Regan say – affectionate? Because she really, really wanted that.

God, she wanted it so badly. It ached inside of her, how very deeply she wanted Emma to feel as affectionate for Regan as Regan felt for Emma.

She wanted to have a picture of this look on Emma's face right now, this soft look, so that she could look at it whenever she felt down about herself. She wanted to document it, so she could study it when she was sober, wondering if what Regan felt when she looked at Emma was reflected in this look.

Unfortunately, Regan's phone was buried in her purse, and she didn't want to look away from Emma right now.

"Yes, I am the responsible one. If you think *I'm* drunk, you should have seen Liz and Beth and Mike and Dustin and Jackie. I'm the one who got them all in Ubers and sent them home to the right address! Addresses?" Which one was right? Anyway. "Ergo, therefore, my going out with them is also kind of my duty."

Emma slowly nodded, folding her arms over her chest. "Right."

Regan *also* saw – saw that Emma wasn't wearing a bra and that her nipples were hard and poking through her shirt. Damn it! Regan hadn't known that when they'd been pressed together a minute ago! If she'd known, she could have relished the feeling while it had lasted.

She slapped her hand to her forehead. Before she winced – *ouch*, too hard. Still. Bad Regan. Bad, bad Regan.

Platonic friendship meant that she shouldn't be noticing or caring about whether Emma was wearing a bra or not. Or how she felt about that fact.

In all honesty, Regan hadn't meant to get as drunk as she was. She'd intended to go out just long enough to see Mike's set and have a drink for Liz's birthday.

But every time she'd thought about going home, she'd gotten so excited to see Emma. Which, in turn, had driven Regan to *not* go home. It had been a very weird paradox.

Wait – Emma wasn't wearing her bra, and she was wearing her little shorts that she only ever wore to bed.

God, she had amazing thighs. So soft and so thick and Regan felt like they could squeeze her head off, but something about that made her want to clench her own thighs together.

Wait, what had she been thinking before?

Regan shook her head, dragging her gaze back up to Emma's, feeling stricken. "Did I wake you up? Were you in bed? I was trying *really* hard to be quiet!"

After all, it was... Regan squinted in thought. It was definitely almost midnight the last time she'd checked, a while ago.

But Emma shook her head. "No, you didn't wake me up and I wasn't in bed." She reached out and gently nudged Regan to turn around, facing the direction of their kitchen. "Did you have dinner?"

"Um... no." Had she? "Not unless a few chicken wings count."

"The jury rules that they don't. Come on, let's get you some soup." Emma brushed past her, leading her down the short hallway, through the archway into the kitchen.

"They were really good, though," Regan insisted distractedly, her gaze falling to Emma's butt.

Wow. In these shorts, she was so close to seeing Emma's actual butt! The shorts were so *short*, and they were so worn, it seemed like they were threadbare. Was Emma wearing underwear?

A heat she'd been so intent on avoiding all week long crept up. But she couldn't help being attracted to Emma, right? Attraction was beyond her control; people couldn't help who they were attracted to.

When Emma turned to face her with a mug of reheated soup in her hands, Regan blinked up at her in dazed shock. Had she really been caught up in staring at Emma for *minutes*?

Emma tilted her head toward the living room. "Dinner time. Let's go."

Regan trailed Emma, caught between feeling like she would diligently follow Emma anywhere, like a puppy, and worried that Emma felt obliged to take care of her.

Emma set down the soup on the coffee table, followed by a bottle of water that Regan hadn't even noticed her carrying. "There's also some ibuprofen that I took out about an hour ago, when you weren't home yet. I figured you'd probably need it."

"Emma," Regan sighed out her name, and she wondered if it had ever sounded that way when she'd said it before. So... reverent. That's how she felt, anyway. "You don't have to do this, you know. I'm a big girl. I've come home after drinking at the bar with my friends and taken care of myself many times. Never died. Promise."

She held up her hands to prove she wasn't crossing any fingers.

"Obviously you haven't died," Emma dryly responded, before she shrugged and sat down on the couch. "Look, it's not a big deal. Just some food – which I was making for myself – and water."

Regan braced a hand on the couch as she kicked off her shoes, not taking her eyes off of Emma. She *couldn't*; she felt like her stare was magnetized to her. She sat down next to her leaving scant inches between them, as she stared at the side of Emma's face. "I appreciate it, though. I really, really do."

"Sutton didn't wait up for you?" Emma asked, turning ever so slightly to face Regan. "When you went out without her?"

She didn't turn to face her completely, because they were *so close*, but Regan's stomach clenched just the same.

"No," she answered, scoffing out a laugh. "Sutton hardly ever stays up until midnight! Are you kidding?"

She leaned forward to eat a spoonful of the soup, closing her eyes and moaning at the taste. "Emma!" She exclaimed as soon as her mouth wasn't full. "This is amazing!"

"It's chicken noodle soup, let's not get too crazy."

"It's perfect." Regan took a few more mouthfuls, before reaching for the ibuprofen and her water. Only once she'd downed the majority of the water bottle did she turn to fully face Emma.

And realized that not only was Emma in her bedtime clothing, but she also had one of the soft throw blankets she kept on her bed draped over her lap. The only light that illuminated the room was from the small lamp on the table next to the couch, casting Emma in a warm glow, and there was a book placed on the arm of the couch.

Regan liked to think that had she not been drinking, she'd have put all of this together minutes ago.

As it was...

"Were you staying up to wait for me?" She asked, and her heart flip-flopped with the question, as she stared at Emma and waited for the confirmation.

Emma tapped her fingertips against the spine of her book, her plush bottom lip poking out in a subconscious pout. "No. I was reading, like I do every night before bed."

"But you *never* do it in the living room," Regan countered, a breath-less giddiness sliding through her. Emma had waited up for her!

And with that feeling, she maneuvered so that she was firmly against the back cushion of the couch, pressed completely against Emma's side.

She'd been careful not to sit this close in the last week; it was the smart thing to do. Give a *little* breathing room, post-kiss.

But Regan didn't want to do the smart thing right now, and she was just drunk enough to disregard logic. She wanted to be as close to Emma as she could be, as this feeling completely took her over. This soft, sweet, powerful, yearning feeling.

Emma had made a little nest on the couch so that she could wait up for Regan to come home and make sure she was safe and sound. She'd made sure Regan had food and water and ibuprofen.

Emma took in a deep breath as Regan curled up next to her, her eyebrows furrowing. "Well, usually you're home. Tonight was different. So, I did something different."

"Sure," Regan graciously allowed Emma to lie to her. It didn't matter what Emma *said*, Regan knew the truth.

And if she wasn't growing more lethargic by the minute, that truth would be enough to make her do one of her happy dances in the middle of the room. Then again, she wasn't willing to sacrifice this snuggle for anything.

"Look, you're clearly not sober. I could hear you struggling to open the door. You have a really busy day tomorrow, given that you have to make all of the desserts for Everly's birthday party Sunday. And I thought," Emma cut herself off, rolling her lips. "I thought that you'd be home earlier, so when you weren't, it felt... strange."

"You were worried about me." Regan could hear the wonder in her tone, and she leaned right into it. Physically, she leaned even more into Emma.

God she was so *soft*. And she smelled so good. Regan turned her head even more so she could press her nose right against Emma's shoulder.

"I was mildly concerned, if anything," Emma corrected, staring down at Regan as best she could given their closeness.

"You were mildly concerned about me," Regan echoed, her words muffled against the thin fabric of Emma's t-shirt. Letting out a content sigh, she shifted to drop her head against Emma's shoulder to rest. "I'll take it."

She'd take just about anything Emma wanted to give her, she thought, stifling a yawn.

"If you don't want to have any more soup or anything, do you want to go to bed?"

"With you?" Regan breathed the question out as she squirmed closer, close enough to essentially wedge herself in between Emma and the couch.

"*What*?" Emma spluttered the question, her voice higher pitched than it typically was. "I – no. I meant to your bed. By yourself," she quickly added.

Even though Regan didn't lift her head up, she shook it. "Mm, then no. When I'm drunk, I like to snuggle."

"I thought you weren't drunk."

"I'm not *that* drunk," Regan corrected, giggling sleepily. "I'm not that drunk and I'm wide awake, and I want to hang out with you. My platonic friend and roommate. And I assume you're also wide awake, since you weren't waiting up for me or anything."

She could feel Emma's sharp, huffy inhale, and she smiled widely to herself. Gotcha.

"Yeah. I'm awake."

"Great. Why don't we put on a show, then?" Regan suggested, lifting an arm that was already starting to feel heavy with exhaustion, to gesture at the television. "Late night weekend drunken cuddle couch hang outs are a normal rite of passage for any roommate that you're friends with."

She felt the need to tack that on, in case Emma got any big ideas about moving away from her or putting space between them. In this moment, any space between them seemed downright offensive to Regan.

"I thought you said that Sutton didn't wait up for you?" Emma countered, even as she was turning on the TV.

"Don't get smart with me."

"Can't help who I am," Emma spoke through a yawn.

Regan's eyes were closed, but her lips curled into a grin. Not waiting up for her – yeah, right.

Her head felt pleasantly heavy, perched on Emma's perfectly sloped shoulder. Her muscles were absolutely lax as her entire body leaned into Emma's supple curves. And every breath she took filled her lungs with *Emma*.

So enticing. So relaxing. "What a combination."

"What was that?" Emma's voice was barely audible over the episode starting to play on the television.

"Nothing," she breathed. Honestly, she didn't even remember what she'd said. In this moment, Regan's mind was blissfully blank.

～

Regan blinked awake – drowsy and still not sober, judging by the way the room spun a little.

Apparently, she was in the living room, and there was a pop-up on the TV that asked *Are you still watching?* Through the windows, she could see that night sky was still pitch-black.

Slowly, she slid her gaze from across the room to herself.

Regan had fallen asleep on this couch many times before. But she'd never been as comfortable as she was right now.

She wasn't surprised that *she'd* fallen asleep, but she was a little surprised that Emma also had. Rather than both of them sitting up and leaning into each other as they'd been in Regan's last fuzzy memory, they'd both repositioned themselves. Emma was laying on her back, and Regan on her side, wedged snugly and comfortably between Emma and the back of the couch.

Emma's blanket now covered them both, and her arm was slid underneath Regan, pulling her in snug against her side. Not an inch between them.

She traced her gaze over the contours of Emma's face, bathed in the dim light coming from the television. Emma was always so... formidable. Solid and strong and opinionated, with those slashing cheekbones and wary eyes.

In sleep, like this, that softness that she'd slowly been revealing to Regan reflected in her face. She'd never seen Emma look so relaxed.

A voice in the back of Regan's brain told her that she should wake Emma. That they should both go to their own rooms. That they should let this cuddling session be pushed to the same place in their minds that their kiss lived in. A place that it seemed Emma was able to totally forget, but one that Regan had been reliving constantly.

She slid her hand from where it was resting – on the perfect curve of Emma's hip – up, ready to shake Emma's shoulder and do just that.

Yet, Regan couldn't bring herself to do it.

Her hand felt so cold after breaking contact with Emma's body, and Regan just knew that her very being would feel the same way, as soon as this was over. And she wasn't ready for that. Achingly, needily, she was so not ready for this feeling to be over.

"I'm in trouble," she finally admitted as she stared at Emma, listening to the very quiet – nearly nonexistent – snores that escaped her.

She was in deep, deep trouble, and it was high time Regan admitted it to herself.

Because this feeling wasn't merely *attraction*, and it definitely wasn't platonic.

It was much, much more. More than she'd ever felt for anyone before, which was a realization that both thrilled her and terrified her.

Slowly, gently, she laid her head back on Emma's shoulder and closed her eyes. Dealing with this realization in the middle of the night, still tipsy, was not a good idea.

Besides... Regan stroked her hand back down, ever-so-softly over the curve of Emma's waist, feeling both thrilled and calmed by the contact. If this was the only time she'd ever have like this with Emma, then she wasn't going to waste it.

eighteen

"... Emma? Hello? Em?"

Emma snapped her gaze to her gram, who was waving a hand in front of her face, a blush already creeping up her cheeks. "What? What did you say? I'm sorry."

Gram arched a look at her, filled with undeniable amusement. "I said that I'm really proud of you for coming here today. I know it isn't always easy, being around your mother."

"It's... not," she admitted, though her gram already knew. "But today isn't so bad. Granted, we've only been here for thirty minutes."

On the other hand, she'd been at Kimberly's house now for thirty minutes, and her stomach wasn't cramping to the point where she felt sick. In fact, Emma hadn't experienced much anxiety at all – which was highly unusual. And all because her focus was locked on something – someone – else.

Unthinkingly, her gaze slid back across Kimberly's expansive back-yard. The birthday party was in full swing – every table was decorated, along with the streamers and banners and fairy lights. There were unicorn likenesses everywhere, including several giant floats in the pool that Everly and her friends had been jumping on under the watchful eye of a lifeguard that had been hired for the day.

Emma had led her gram to one of the shaded patio tables as soon as they'd arrived. Her focus, however, had been fixed on one particular person located across the yard.

Regan had really come through with the baked goods for the party. She'd made three different flavors of cookies – all customized with sparkles and sprinkles to fit the theme – as well as immaculately decorated unicorn cake pops. The cake itself had been carried in by Ted, and Emma knew from pictures that Regan had sent her yesterday that it looked amazing.

Currently, Regan was chatting animatedly with a small group of parents that had flocked to her as soon as she'd started setting up. Her full lips – unbelievably soft, Emma couldn't fucking forget – were moving a mile a minute, before curving into a smile.

Emma knew she couldn't actually hear Regan's boisterous laugh all the way across the yard with the sounds of all of the kids running around and screaming, but she *swore* she could.

"I'm still so proud of you," Gram's voice cut into her thoughts, making Emma wince.

God, what was *wrong* with her?

Actually, she knew very well what was wrong with her.

"You know, little lady, you don't have to sit with me; I'm not an invalid. You can join your girlfriend." Gram nudged Emma's arm with her elbow, exasperatedly laughing.

"What?" Emma asked yet again, ripping her gaze from Regan once again. "Sorry, um..." She screwed up her face, before managing to latch onto her gram's words. "No, I'm sitting over here because I *want* to sit with you."

Her gram arched an incredulous look at her. "I might be getting old, but my vision is perfectly fine. You're staring at Regan like you want to eat her alive."

Emma could feel the heat burst to life in her cheeks as she immediately shook her head. "No," she denied. "No, that's not–"

Gram reached out, gently patting her hand on Emma's. "It's nothing to be embarrassed about." She tilted her head, studying Emma. "To tell you the truth, I think it's very sweet. I haven't seen you look at someone so intensely in... well, I'm not sure how long."

"Yeah. I... uh, you might be right," she muttered. Because Emma, herself, couldn't even really think of a comparison of what she was doing right now. The reality was that she'd never felt so compelled to simply stare at Felicity, obsessing over her thoughts the way she was right now.

Still, though, Gram's statement wasn't actually *true*. Not really.

The reality was that Emma was staring because Regan was slowly driving Emma crazy, plugging away at every ounce of her sanity and self-control.

First there'd been that kiss. Which Emma had done a good job at filing away; Emma was *great* at compartmentalizing. If the kiss was all there was to this growingly complex dynamic with Regan, Emma could be mostly fine.

Then Regan had to go and add in the fact that she thought about Emma's breasts and thighs and lips *all of the time.*

All right – Emma could be... fine with that, too. Mostly. She could work around it.

Because she thought about how attractive Regan was, often, and she was fine – totally great! – being platonic roommate friends with her. Even though Emma was so attracted to Regan that it was distracting, she hadn't ever had any issues keeping her thoughts PG and keeping her hands to herself.

But when she added in the way she'd woken up yesterday morning, snuggled so closely with Regan on the couch that there was literally *no* space between them... well, that made Emma's stomach flutter. Uncontrollably.

Emma hadn't even remembered falling asleep on Friday night – rather, early Saturday morning. All she'd known was that Regan had stayed out later than any other night since they'd lived together, and Emma really had been worried. But she hadn't wanted to be weirdly clingy and text Regan *when will you be home* or anything like that, because it wasn't any of her business! She wasn't Regan's keeper or her girlfriend or anything else.

They were roommates and friends. Regan had told her she was going out and would be home *later*, which was all the due diligence

Emma should expect. She just hadn't known *later* would mean so much later!

And when Regan had arrived home, she'd been so alarmingly and disarmingly charming. Her cheeks were rosy, and her dark eyes were wide, and her smile was so full, and her giggles were so sweet sounding.

It had been a weak moment for Emma. She'd been concerned about Regan for a couple of hours, and on top of that? She'd missed Regan's company, which had been jarring. When she'd realized that was the first Friday night in nearly two months that she wasn't spending hanging out with Regan, and not only that, but that she *missed* her?! Dear god.

But it was the undeniable truth.

Then, Regan had cuddled up to Emma, fitting against her as if their bodies knew one another far more intimately than they actually did. Emma had been tired and relieved that Regan was home safe, and her body... her body had missed that feeling.

That closeness, that warmth. It was intoxicating. It had been so easy to succumb to it, telling herself it would only be "for a few minutes."

Before Emma had realized it, she'd woken up and it was Saturday morning. Daylight streamed in from the windows, and she'd sighed in sleepy content. Inhaling a deep breath of Regan's minty fresh shampoo as she'd rubbed her nose against the crown of her head, then she'd lightly stroked her hand up and down Regan's back.

Regan's... bare back?

Emma's morning drowsiness had dashed away as her mind fully caught up to her body. Her eyes opened widely, heart thundering in her chest, as she'd stared at Regan. Who was now half on her side and half sprawled over Emma.

Blessedly, Regan was still wearing her clothing from the night before. But her crop top had ridden up to the point that it was essentially just a bra, and Emma's hand was pressed against Regan's spine, moving with every inhale and exhale Regan let out. Every exhale that made Emma shiver, as warm puffs of breath washed against the sensitive skin of her collarbone.

Not only did she become acutely aware of the sweet-cuddling intimacy of the situation, but she'd also been faced with the reality of the unexpected yet undeniable sexual intimacy.

Because Regan's hot breath made her shudder, and her hand was resting against the curve of Emma's waist, her thumb under Emma's shirt, so close to the bottom of Emma's breast – too close. Mere centimeters away. Though it wasn't touching her, the excruciatingly close non-touch almost felt like a tease. Added to both of those things, one of her legs was slid between Emma's, slotted perfectly between her thighs.

Everything combined to remind Emma that she hadn't experienced real intimacy of any kind with another person in over two years.

Emma reached up to rub her fingers at her temples, trying to stave off a headache. The lack of sleep she'd gotten last night – alone and in her own bed, but her thoughts tormented by the night before – in combination with the sunny heat and loud music and squealing children and the way Regan had a little sheen of sweat over her cheeks that somehow looked cute – it was all too much.

"So?" Gram nudged Emma once more. "Go and talk to her! I promise you, I'm just fine sitting here without you for a while. In fact, I think I'll wave Eva over to keep me company."

"No," Emma quickly refused. "No, that's – I'm fine here. She's busy."

Unerringly, Emma's gaze slid back to Regan. Who *was* busy.

Even more parents had amassed around her, and...

And Regan's eyes met hers across the lawn, as she lifted her eyebrows and jerked her head, mouthing *help me!*

Beside her, Gram chuckled. "Oh, I think she'd appreciate you right about now."

Emma couldn't disagree, obviously.

"Um... right. Then, I'll go over there," she murmured to both herself and her grandmother, gearing herself up.

"Yes, you will go over there. I'd like to think that I didn't raise you to throw your girlfriend to the wolves."

"No, you didn't," she agreed, because her grandmother had very much raised her to show up for the people she cared about.

And even if she and Regan weren't under the guise of being in a relationship, the reality was that Regan had slid in some side door

Emma didn't even know existed and had become someone Emma cared about. A lot.

She stood, aiming a look at Gram. "I'll be back. If you need me for anything, just text."

Gram leveled her with a look. "I can walk on my own, Emma. My god, I don't think I've ever hovered over you like this."

"It's incredibly humid today, the UV index is high, and your doctor's orders are to take it easy in the heat," she reminded, citing from her gram's paperwork from her last appointment.

"Fine," her gram relented with an aggrieved sigh. "If necessary, I will call you over."

"Good."

"Now, go rescue your girlfriend." Gram lifted her hand, shooing Emma away.

She obliged, throwing her grandmother one final look over her shoulder. By the time she was only ten feet away, Eva had slid into Emma's chair, talking animatedly with Gram, which Emma supposed was a relief.

At least, it meant she could focus her attention on rescuing Regan from... whatever situation it was she needed help with.

The closer she walked to Regan, the more the pit of her stomach erupted with tiny butterflies. No, she forcefully corrected. She wouldn't classify these are *butterflies*. Maybe just... flies?

She pulled a face, nixing the thought.

The point was, she wasn't nervous around Regan; Regan Gallagher didn't make her nervous.

After all, Emma had been able to act totally normal post-kiss. Sometimes she hadn't always felt completely normal, but she had an iron will. She could act totally normal post-cuddle, as well.

The moment she was in the vicinity, Regan ducked out from the middle of the group of parents surrounding her. "I'd really like to chat more, later, but my gorgeous girlfriend is here, and I really have to talk to her. Enjoy!"

She called her final words over her shoulder as she essentially sprung herself at Emma, hooking her arm through Emma's with a force that nearly spun her off of her feet.

Stumbling for a moment to keep pace despite her height advantage, Emma stared between Regan and the group they were quickly leaving behind in the dust. "Is everything all right? Were they trying to cannibalize you or something?"

"Basically!" Regan hissed, resolutely staring forward, as she led Emma around the corner of the house to the smaller side yard. Finally, she let out a deep sigh of relief. "Where *were* you?! I was drowning there!"

"I was sitting where I'd been the entire time!" Emma defended, even though she couldn't help but laugh at the exaggeratedly distressed expression Regan wore. Because if she didn't make herself find amusement in it, then Regan's big, puppy-dog eyes and pouty mouth would drive her to distraction. "I figured when you wanted to join me, you would."

"I wanted to join you forever ago, as soon as I set up the dessert table. But I was accosted by PTA parents!" Regan whisper-hissed.

"I assumed you were more than capable of handling yourself in any crowd." Emma was being entirely honest; she genuinely had no concerns about Regan talking to anyone, at any time, about anything.

It was something she deeply admired.

"I *can*! But they were never-ending. Just when I thought I'd be able to slip out of the conversation, more of them came to chat. It was like that snake, where you cut off one head and more grow back in its place." Regan unlinked their arms to swing around and face Emma, leaning back against the side of the house. "What's that thing called?"

"A hydra," Emma filled in for her, turning to lean her back against the house as well, standing shoulder-to-shoulder. It seemed... smarter, than facing Regan head-on, for some reason.

Maybe because the little flush over Regan's cheeks, with the heat and the passion in her voice was entirely too appealing to look at.

"I knew you'd know it." Tilting her head up, Regan searched Emma's gaze with her own. "And – thanks. Yes, I can hold my own in conversations with just about anyone. But the whole reason I'm even here is because I'm supposed to be helping *you*!" She leaned in, nudging her arm against Emma's. But she didn't slide back a few inches, after. Instead, she stayed, maintaining the contact.

Emma swallowed hard; maybe this wasn't the smartest idea. Maybe she needed to figure out a way to experience less contact with the most tactile person she'd ever met until she could forget about Friday night.

"The whole reason I'm here is to be your girlfriend, at your side when you need assistance. I saw Kimberly and your sisters come to you a little while ago, and I couldn't extract myself in time!" The earnest expression on Regan's face mixed with the heated intensity in her tone forced all of Emma's conflicted feelings to scatter. Instead, a warmth lodged itself right around her heart; of course, that was what Regan cared about.

She shook her head. "Don't worry about it. Honestly, it was fine. I had Gram there."

Interest sparked into Regan's eyes. "It was seriously-everything-is-actually good kind of fine? Or *ugh*-I-guess-it-*was-fine* kind of fine?"

"The first one," she admitted, and she didn't know who was more surprised.

Regan's hand immediately reached out, grabbing Emma's in excitement. "Really? That's – what happened?"

"Nothing much; she came over to check on me and Gram, make sure we didn't need anything. Then..." Emma rolled her lips, thinking of the slightly uncomfortable dip in the brief conversation. "She told me she was really sorry she never threw me a party. And she offered to keep the pool open for my birthday this year, if I wanted to throw a big pool party."

Her mom's eyes had been wide and hopeful with the offer, which had been the height of Emma's discomfort.

Regan snorted, before she slapped her free hand over her mouth. "Sorry. Not funny, I know. I just can't imagine you wanting your mom to throw you a giant pool party, even if you were on the best of terms. Honestly, it sounds like the opposite of what I'd imagine you want to do for your birthday."

Emma's smile turned sardonic. "You nailed it."

She wasn't even surprised, anymore, how well Regan knew her.

"So, I turned down her offer, and then she went on the hunt for her "good camera" because apparently, she loves to document as much of birthdays as she can. That was it." Emma shrugged.

All-in-all, it had been a fairly painless exchange. Kimberly was pressed for time, and her acknowledgement of their past didn't make Emma feel like she needed to throw up – huge progress.

"That's amazing!" Regan insisted, smiling so brightly up at her as she bounced onto her tiptoes in barely restrained excitement.

Oh, damn, there was that fucking feeling in her stomach again. Emma quickly let go of Regan's hand, hoping it would help diminish that fluttering.

It did, but not by much.

Especially not as they stood so close to one another that Regan's bare arm was pressed into Emma's, and their eyes were locked, and was Regan's breathing coming faster?

Emma coughed. "Yeah, so it went fine. I think the weirdest thing for me now isn't even Kimberly; it's my sisters."

Regan blinked several times, shaking her head slightly. "Right, right, right. Sisters. What happened with them?" Her tone was slightly higher pitched than normal.

"Well, Everly wanted me to agree to join in on some viral dance video thing that she's going to be doing with her friends, before the party ends?" Emma's face screwed up in confusion. "I don't really know, but she was *so* excited when she asked; you'd think I'm a celebrity. And Eva... who even knows. She was just scowling the entire time. And I think she was waiting for me to leave so that she could talk to Gram?"

Regan settled back against the side of the house, staring up at Emma with the gentlest expression. "Do you really not get it?"

Emma could only shrug in response, especially as Regan was looking at her like *that*.

"Everly talks to you like she reveres you because she's so young, and you're her *big sister*. You live in New York and work at a magazine, and she doesn't know you all that well, and Kimberly is clearly super proud of you; that's a big deal to her," Regan explained, her tone exasperated but warm. She leaned in as close as she could possibly be as she continued, "You're cool and smart and funny and pretty."

Emma felt her heart beat a little faster. Regan always had those compliments ready to fall right out of her mouth, and they always sounded so genuine; Emma had never been around someone that effort-lessly made her feel so good about herself.

"And Eva?" She prompted, her voice a little hoarse.

"Hmm? Oh. Eva," Regan muttered, shaking her head softly. "To Eva... well, you're her big sister. You're cool and smart and funny and pretty, and she doesn't know you all that well, and Kimberly is super proud of you," she echoed with laughter in her voice. "Those facts mean different things at different ages; it's complicated. But that's what it's like to have a sister."

"I guess you would know," she murmured, thinking about every-thing Regan had shared about her own sister.

All of the stories about her life that she'd shared, pulling Emma in, making her feel inexorably close to Regan. Before she'd kissed her.

"I would," Regan confirmed, softly.

The sound of a camera shuttering jarred them out of the moment.

At once, Emma snapped her head to face forward, to see Kimberly standing only a few feet away with the camera she'd apparently found.

"Sneaking away for a stolen moment? Ah! I love it!" She exclaimed, smiling at them brightly.

God, what the hell was going *on*? What was Emma doing? And how did she not know if she was more grateful for Kimberly coming along to interrupt... whatever this moment had turned into, or irritated by it?

Grateful, she told herself. She was *grateful* that their moment had come to an end.

"Can I get a picture of you two, together? Being all cute and couple-y?" Kimberly asked, hopefully, as she lifted her camera. "I'd love to have that to put up in the house."

Emma felt clumsy and frozen, which didn't seem to matter as Regan answered, "Sure."

Regan stepped into Emma's side, sliding her arm around Emma's waist and angling herself in.

She had to give Regan all of the credit in the world – she knew how to sell it. How to sell *them*, as if they were really involved. Emma was fairly certain that if it was all up to her, she'd have never fooled anyone about this charade.

But with every touch Regan initiated, it felt so very natural. Maybe

297

she couldn't even give all of the credit to Regan, though. Maybe she needed to give their literal bodies credit, because Regan slotted against her so ridiculously perfectly.

"A little closer; you don't have to pretend modesty for my benefit! I love how in love you are." Kimberly urged, using the hand not holding her camera to wave them even closer.

Regan, ever the dutiful fake-girlfriend, complied.

With Regan's whole body pressed against Emma, she felt her head spin a little. Her arm tightened around Regan's waist, and – when had she even wrapped her arm around Regan's waist?! She didn't remember doing that.

Regan seemed to hesitate briefly, before she popped up onto her tiptoes and pressed her lips to Emma's cheek, mere centimeters from her own mouth. And Emma's breath caught, her skin tingling at the feeling of that full, soft mouth on her again. Lingering, as Kimberly snapped several photos.

Boundaries, Emma thought errantly. They should have established some boundaries, after their kiss last weekend. About what should be allowed going forward.

Because *this* – this shouldn't happen.

"Thank you! I'll send you a copy when I have everything printed; this is so cute," Kimberly gushed. "Oh, Regan, honey – we're going to cut the cake in a minute! I was wondering if you'd like to help? So many people have asked about getting your number."

Emma dropped her arm from Regan's waist, wishing she didn't feel the tingle of the lasting contact so clearly.

"Um – yeah. I'll absolutely help."

As soon as Regan voiced her agreement, Kimberly turned and started toward the main area for the party. "I'll let you finish up over here while I get everything ready."

Emma had no idea what, exactly, she was going to say as soon as her mother was gone. But she knew she had to say *something* before they fell back into a... moment. Especially now, while the imprint of Regan's kiss was still buzzing against her skin.

Only for Regan to beat her to the punch. "I – look, I have to tell you something."

There was an unfamiliar edge of nerves in Regan's voice, as she tilted her head up at Emma. Nerves, but clearly a steely resolve, as well.

Cautiously, Emma nodded. "Okay?"

Regan tangled her fingers together in front of herself, blowing out a deep breath. "At first, being your fake girlfriend was just something fun. Something that I thought could help us bond. Something I could do for you that seemed really simple. But... it's not so simple, now."

Emma could feel her eyebrows lift high on her forehead, surprise sweeping through her. Did Regan not want to do it, anymore? Did she agree that they should have boundaries in place?

Before she could actually ask any of her questions, Regan continued.

"The reality is, Emma, that I like you. In the real girlfriend kind of way. I like you way, way more than just a platonic roommate. That's why I went out and had drinks with my co-workers on Friday, because I realized I've been spending every weekend since you moved in obsessed with spending time with you, in one way or another."

Emma's stomach swooped and her knees felt like jelly, as she fell heavily back against the side of the house once more.

"It's so much more than a simple attraction. I didn't realize it when I kissed you. I'm new to this!" Regan gestured between the two of them. "And Sutton is my biggest sounding board in life, and I haven't talked to her about you or us or this–"

Emma hadn't known she could be even *more* floored than she already was, but somehow, Regan found a way. "You haven't talked to Sutton about any of this?!"

Emma hadn't called Sutton in the past week because she'd been sure that Regan had told Sutton, and she hadn't felt ready to answer any of the questions she was certain Sutton would have.

"No!" Regan looked at Emma as if *Emma* were the person dropping bombs, here. "Because I know you like privacy, and also because I know there's nothing to tell her. Not *really*. Because I know that nothing is going on between us. I know you were super fucking freaked out when I kissed you, and I promise, Emma, I promise – I'm not trying to do that to you, again."

"You're not?" She dimly repeated.

Because Emma *was* freaking out. Her heart was hammering in her chest, and she felt ridiculously – crazily – pleased and flattered and thrilled. And most of all, the alarm sirens were going off deafeningly loud in her head.

"No!" Regan insisted, reaching out to grasp at Emma's, insistently. Her big, dark eyes were wide and imploring and so deep, Emma swore she could fall into them. "I don't want to freak you out; I'm not going to go all crazy-stalker or anything because you don't like me back. It's fine that you don't have feelings for me." She winced. "I mean, it doesn't make me feel *great*, but it's okay."

"Why are you telling me this?" Desperation broke into Emma's tone, and she found that she couldn't pull her hand from Regan's. Instead, she squeezed it. Hard. "Why are you telling me this, at my nine-year-old sister's birthday party?"

Emma couldn't freak out here! She couldn't freak out about the fact that Regan was making the most romantic comments to her that *anyone* had ever made.

"I didn't mean to! I wasn't going to tell you at all! I was going to be an adult and just move past these feelings as much as I could, but then Kimberly came over here. And she wanted us to act cute and couple-y and that's kind of the deal, here, since I'm playing the role of your girlfriend and all." Regan's thumb stroked gently over Emma's knuckles. "I'm absolutely fine, still playing this part. In fact," a self-deprecating, gorgeous smile flashed over Regan's face as she stared up at Emma. "I probably like playing the part too much, now. Which, honestly, is why I have to confess the truth to you."

"Because when I lean into you and kiss your cheek, I get this *rush*. And I really, really like it. But it feels wrong, because you don't know what it's doing to me. It feels kind of like I'm taking advantage, and that is the *last* thing I want to do with you. So, I had to tell you," Regan finished, eyes searching Emma's.

She had no idea what Regan was seeing. Emma had very little idea what *she*, herself, was feeling. Bafflingly, she felt like the biggest anchor she had right now was the hold Regan's hand had on hers.

"Regan?" Kimberly called, before she popped her head around the corner of the house. "I have everything ready for the cake!"

Regan nodded in acknowledgement, keeping her eyes on Emma for several more seconds. "Okay, I'm coming."

"All righty," Kimberly ducked away again.

"So... I'm going to go help cut this crazy unicorn cake I'm responsible for. And I'll let you process. And then we can get back to normal again," Regan stated, as if she'd resolved every problem. As if she hadn't just thrown a major bomb at Emma, and caused a much bigger ripple effect.

She stroked her thumb softly over the back of Emma's hand once more, and they both looked down at the way their fingers were linked.

Somehow, they *really* did fit together so well.

"See, this is what I'm talking about," Regan said, her voice so soft and so... reverent. It was the only word Emma could think of that made sense.

And it made everything inside of Emma that was going haywire at Regan's confession melt to a fucking puddle.

"When I run my thumb over your knuckles and feel your skin under mine, it makes me feel so electric. Like I've never been more alive, and all we're doing is holding hands," she whispered, still staring down at them. "I've never had that feeling, before."

Emma's heart was in her throat at the gentle confession, something big and soft and overwhelming threatening to break free.

Blessedly – or not? – Regan sighed, and slid her hand out of Emma's, shaking her hair back and smiling up at Emma once more. "Anyway. I think it's good that you know, now. God knows I wasn't going to be able to keep this in, and at least this time I was able to tell you with words and not a kiss."

With that, Regan sent her another look, before turning and walking away.

nineteen

"REGAN, this is the best fucking cookie I've ever had in my *life*! I'm going to enter this recipe in the Primrose Grove baking contest," Phoebe announced. "Let's see if Marcia Weatherby and her little chocolate chunks can beat *these*," she huffed.

Bea knocked her shoulder against Phoebe's, rolling her eyes up at Regan from across the counter. "This recipe belongs to Regan; if anyone is going to enter it in the contest, it should be Sherry. Regan's dating *her* granddaughter."

Everyone turned their attention to Sherry, who offered a heavy shrug. "Oh, no. I'm not taking responsibility for any baking competitions. Phoebe, the recipe is yours... especially if it'll help you beat Marcia," she muttered.

Delighted by the assisted living home gossip, Regan beamed. "I'll allow anyone in our quad here to use the recipe, and I'll be so freaking pumped if we win!"

"Regan, you have the right kind of spirit!" Phoebe nodded at her in approval.

Regan grinned back, before the clock on the wall behind Phoebe caught her attention, and her mouth fell open on a gasp. "Oh! It's five!"

"Got a hot date?" Phoebe asked, wiggling her eyebrows.

Bea nudged her, shaking her head... only to then turn her attention to Regan as well. "Bad manners aside – you got a date?"

"Um..." Regan dug her teeth into her bottom lip, unsure of exactly how to answer.

The reality was that she did not have a date, and she knew that.

But the reality was also that she hadn't been able to actually talk to Emma since yesterday afternoon at Everly's birthday party. Since her big confession.

After the cake cutting, Regan had wound up in conversation after conversation with a multitude of parents complimenting her baked goods and asking for her business card. These people believed Regan had business cards!

Even though she'd been flattered and awed that so many people had enjoyed her desserts, she'd desperately wanted to talk to Emma. But she'd made herself linger and chat with the PTA parents, because she was trying to give Emma some time to take in everything Regan had told her. She knew Emma really well, now, and she knew Emma needed to process.

By the time she had some actual breathing room, over an hour had passed and the party had been winding down.

Unfortunately, Sherry hadn't been feeling too well after several hours out in the heat and humidity, and Emma had approached Regan to let her know she was going to bring her gram home.

Regan had stayed for a while longer – mostly because she had to collect some of the fancy food storage containers she'd brought the desserts in, and return them to Topped Off. Once she'd gotten home that evening, though, Emma had texted her to let her know that she was going to stay at her gram's for a while to make sure she was doing okay.

Regan had fallen asleep by the time Emma had gotten home, and – unfortunately for Regan – she'd had to get to Topped Off by six this morning.

She was waiting on tenterhooks to actually see and speak to Emma again. It was making her so... anxious? Exhilarated? Energized? All of the above? That even though Regan had gotten off of her shift four hours ago, she hadn't been able to sit around by herself at home, waiting for Emma.

So, would she say that she had a *hot date*?! Not exactly. She had to talk to a hot woman about the potential ramifications of her feelings declaration.

But, with Emma's grandmother sitting right here, she couldn't really say that.

"Something like that," she settled on. "I want to get home for when Emma is out of work."

There, that was the truth at least.

Bea nodded with excitement. "That could count."

"Depending on what you're doing at home," Phoebe added with an exaggeratedly lascivious wink.

Regan *wished*. God, her body throbbed at how much she wished for that to be the case.

Regan had been through dry spells before, months without sex. Which was fine; she had a vibrator and all. What wasn't fine was that she'd never *lived* with a source of constant temptation, before!

She had to hold in her wistful sigh.

"Ah, I'm going to cut you two off right there. I don't need any more details," Sherry asserted, pushing herself up from the chair she'd been sitting in. "I'll walk you out."

Regan rushed forward, shaking her head. "No, seriously, you don't need to go to any trouble. I know the way... and if I don't, I'm sure I'll run into someone, eventually, to help me."

Sherry cut her a look. "When you're my age, the heat might very well get to you, too. But I'm perfectly fine."

Phoebe scoffed. "Preach."

Regan held up her hands in surrender. "All right. It was really great to hang out with you two again."

"Come back for another bingo night!" Bea encouraged.

"Or the baking contest, so you can see your cookie recipe wipe the floor with Marcia," Phoebe gleefully added.

Laughing, Regan reached out to shake her hand. "Deal."

"Hurry back, Sherry. I'm going to hold you to that offer to teach us Omaha," Bea called.

"And to bitch about Marcia!"

"I'll only be a minute," Sherry affirmed. "Get the cards."

Amused, Regan looked around them to guarantee that they were alone in the hallway they were walking down before she asked, "What's up with Marcia Weatherby?"

Sherry pursed her lips. "Oh, she's always bragging about her grandson, trying to one-up anyone that will listen. She's always got to be the best at everything. Incredibly obnoxious; we're all here in the same place." She shook her head. "I rarely even venture out to join in on group activities, and I've witnessed it a number of times."

"Bitch," Regan muttered, delighted. "This place really *is* like a dorm!"

Sherry laughed, patting Regan's arm as they approached the lobby. "I really appreciate you coming by today. You didn't have to check on me, though; I'm really fine. Just overdid it yesterday."

Regan shrugged as she tugged the strap of her backpack over her shoulder. "I know I didn't have to. I wanted to."

Which was the truth. Not only because Emma had clearly been concerned for her gram, but because Regan really liked Sherry.

"Honestly, it was a good time. I don't really know anyone else who's available for a hangout in the middle of the day on a Monday, so this was great timing for me. Plus, you said yesterday that you'd always wanted to learn how to bake, so it all worked perfectly."

Also the truth.

"And you wanting to bake the cookies in the community kitchen instead of in my suite?" Sherry arched a knowing eyebrow at her.

Guilelessly, Regan shrugged. "I like a bigger kitchen to work in."

"Yes, either that or you have the voice of my Emma in your ear telling you that she's worried about me making friends here."

Holding her hands up, Regan confessed, "All right, that thought crossed my mind. But... I'd say it worked out?" She ventured, hopefully.

Phoebe and Bea had come across them two hours ago, just as they'd started unpacking the ingredients Regan had brought along. They'd paused, recognizing her from bingo, and had seamlessly invited themselves to join in.

Sure, Regan had come here for a multitude of reasons, and aiming to get Sherry more comfortable with her peers was a part of her half-cocked plan. But she'd had a genuinely fun afternoon, and had found that she'd been able to distract herself from the *Emma, Emma, Emma* loop playing in her head. Ironic, since she'd been with Emma's grandmother.

"It did work out," Sherry agreed, a small smile curling at the edges of her mouth. "And... I appreciate it. I appreciate you coming all the way up here to bake with me, too. I–" She cleared her throat, her expression growing more serious. "I'll be honest with you. While Emma worries about me, I also worry about her. Emma is so... closed-off. Perhaps that is pot calling the kettle black, coming from me," she admitted, ruefully. "I know where she gets it from."

"I love how focused and hardworking Emma is; I've always been so proud of that. After her breakup with Felicity, though, it was almost like having any semblance of a personal life wasn't something she was willing to do, again. Even though she didn't want to discuss it with me – and I know, I wasn't the friendliest to Felicity, so that was my fault – I was concerned."

Regan was utterly *riveted*. Because – true to Sherry's word – Emma so rarely discussed her romantic life, at all. Even though she knew some minimal details about Felicity, she wanted to hear everything. She wanted every crumb of knowledge she could possibly get about Emma, wanted to soak it in.

Sherry breathed out a quiet laugh, waving her hand slightly. "I know she'd hate that we're having this discussion, too. So, all I'll say is – I really like you, Regan. I think you're good for Emma. A little louder, more outspoken. You've been supporting her through Kimberly's reappearance in her life – and she's been *letting* you. That says..." Sherry pursed her lips, shaking her head slightly. "That says everything to me. Plus, she never has anything but wonderful things to say about you."

"Really?" Regan found herself asking, her stomach fluttering with the revelation.

She needed to hang out with Sherry more – first, with how she'd told Regan about Emma's past crush on her, and now this?!

"She texts me all of the time about the updates about the shows you watch together and what an amazing cook you are, or the things you say that make her laugh. It's... well, it's really wonderful to see, that's all."

"It's wonderful to hear." As if the full-watt smile on Regan's face didn't reveal that! Her cheeks hurt from how wide this smile was.

Even if Emma didn't reciprocate her feelings, Emma liked her as a person. As a human being. Enough that her gram could see it, and, yeah, Regan wanted *more*. But this? It felt like a pretty big deal to her.

"Anyway, I should get back. Get home safe, and tell Emma I'm absolutely *fine*," Sherry stressed.

Regan saluted her. "Done. Go kick ass at cards."

"Done."

As Sherry turned to go, Regan felt her phone vibrate in her back pocket. Excitement sparked through her as she realized – Emma was officially out of work! This could very well be her!

Quickly, she walked out of the building and hustled toward the subway, as she looked down at her phone.

Only for the excitement inside of her to completely deflate.

EMMA – 5:03PM

> Hey, so I just wanted to let you know that I'm going to grab some dinner with Brynn tonight

Regan halted to a stop, her stomach clenching uncomfortably. Since when did Emma go out for dinner with Brynn?!

REGAN – 5:03PM

> Cool cool cool. So… this has nothing to do with me telling you that I have feelings for you, right??

> Because, if you really think about it, me telling you that I have feelings for you actually doesn't change the fact that I've HAD the feelings for longer than you know

Longer than Regan, herself, even knew!

307

REGAN – 5:04PM

I'm just saying that I don't want to make it weird between us. I told you so that things WOULDN'T get weird, you know?

She watched, more gripped than she was during a reality show finale, as those three little dots appeared.

And then disappeared.

And then appeared again.

EMMA – 5:04PM

No. It has nothing to do with yesterday. I'm just having dinner with Brynn

Regan knew she should let it go. Really, she did. Logically, that was what she should do...

REGAN – 5:05PM

You have to admit the timing is a little weird. Especially since you and I haven't really been able to actually talk since I told you how I'd love to be your girlfriend (real). But if you tell me it's coincidence, then I'll be forced to believe you

Again, with those little dots appearing and then disappearing, appearing, disappearing, appear–

EMMA – 5:06PM

Yes, I will admit that it's strange timing. But... like you said, you were only telling me so that things weren't weird, right? Following your own logic...

Not a single cell in Regan's body believed her, and she heaved a stressed sigh.

REGAN – 5:06PM

All right-i-o. Then, I'll see you at home (sometime)

Seems pretty likely since we both live there,
and we share such a small bathroom

Okay, so *that* seemed normal? Maybe a little teasing tone, if Regan
was interpreting correctly. Maybe she *was* reading into things.

When her phone started buzzing in her hand, her heart leapt in her
chest, making her feel like she was coming back to life. Maybe it was
Emma! Maybe –

"Hey, hi, hello?" She breathed, entirely too excited to sound even
remotely normal.

A few seconds of silence beat by before she was greeted with, "Are
you on anything this particular evening?"

Recognizing the voice, Regan dropped her head back in disappointment. "Charlotte. Hey." A moment later, she perked back up when the
realization dawned on her. "*Charlotte*? Hey?"

"Regan," Charlotte shortly returned, cautiously. "Are you... doing
well?"

Frowning, Regan answered, "Um – well. You know, I've been
better, and been worse. So, I suppose it all evens out."

And that was true.

She was living with Emma, whom she'd befriended, developed feelings for, kissed, and was now uncertain of their status. She saw Emma in
various states of dress and undress. Got to hear her laughter, watch the
way she stared down so intently at her laptop when she was working
that Regan felt like she could *see* the way her mind was moving.

Torturous bliss.

"Weirdest thing that's happened to me all day is that you're calling."
She had no problem admitting that.

Charlotte scoffed. "How is that so odd? We've been communicating
regularly for over a month. You text me multiple times a week and I
always answer. You've even been inside of my home."

"And I'm sure for you that counts for a deeply personal friendship,"
Regan sort-of joked. Not really; she knew enough about Charlotte to
know that she wasn't totally wrong. "But the reality is that *I'm* the one

that's initiated all of our past communications. So, you have to give this to me – you calling me out of the blue? A little strange."

"I'm calling to ask if you'd like to have dinner with me tonight. A dinner party I was supposed to go to was unexpectedly canceled, and I have some free time. If you'd rather not, then–"

Even though Regan stood by what she'd said, and she was still confused as hell, she quickly cut Charlotte off before she could rescind the random offer. "No! Dinner sounds great. Where?"

Especially because Regan's preferred dinner companion was going out to dinner with *Brynn*.

"I'll drop you a pin to the restaurant."

"Be warned – I'm in Astoria, so it'll probably take me a bit to get there."

"And I'm in Midtown traffic, so there's a good chance you'll arrive before me."

～

Regan *did* beat Charlotte to the ritzy Greek place Charlotte had sent her to, but only by a few minutes.

She'd barely gotten settled – still no new texts from Emma. What was that about? – when she spotted Charlotte strutting through to the back of the restaurant to join her at the private table she'd been seated at as soon as she'd dropped Charlotte's name.

She tilted her head, watching Charlotte glide toward her. It was a very specific walk she had, determined and smooth, all in one.

"Why don't I feel any attraction to you?" She demanded to know, as soon as Charlotte reached the table.

Charlotte slowly lifted her sunglasses off of her face, staring down at Regan with exasperation. "Please, not this conversation again."

Regan tapped her palms restlessly against the tabletop. "I just don't get it! I'm into women – confirmed. In a big way. You're super-hot. What's that about?"

Charlotte pursed her lips, gripping the back of her chair as if she wasn't sure she wanted to sit in it or slide it back into the table and leave. "Attraction is an interesting thing. If we were attracted to every person that was stereotypically *super-hot*, we'd have a very boring society, wouldn't we? Besides, it's not just looks that we're drawn to."

Regan knew Charlotte was right, of course.

Maybe that was also what tripped her up about how deeply she was into Emma. Regan had never been that into any man, not even ones she'd been dating. The physical connection had always been there, but she'd never wanted *more* with them. She'd never wanted to make them laugh or hoped they found her smart and interesting or stayed up late at night wondering if they were thinking about her the way she was thinking about them.

She did that with Emma. A lot. Wondering what she was doing or what was on her mind, right across the hall.

"We're not going to have a repeat conversation about attraction," she confirmed, mostly so Charlotte would sit down, already.

When she did, Regan leaned in, intently. "What I *do* still want to know – now that we're already here, no take-backs – is why you called me and invited me to dinner."

Charlotte crossed her arms over her chest and straightened her spine, and – *wow*, she really could look seriously intimidating! Regan wanted to learn how to mimic that. "We're here tonight because I have a girlfriend that is very concerned about her best friend. *Why isn't Regan talkative lately? Do you think Regan's okay? Do you think Regan is upset with me for coming to Rome? Do you think everything really is all right between Regan and Emma?*" She parroted words that clearly belonged to Sutton, with no small amount of dissatisfaction at the situation.

Surprised, Regan's stomach knotted with guilt, and she pressed her hands there, trying to quell it. "Oh, fuck. I was hoping that she was so busy with her internship that she wouldn't have noticed."

"You think Sutton wouldn't notice that something major is going on with you, from even across the ocean?" Charlotte asked, dubiously. "I'm insulted on her behalf."

Regan's mouth fell open in shock. "Here you are, shaming me for not treating Sutton with the highest respect. How the turns have tabled."

Even as she joked, Regan felt *awful*.

"I haven't told her about what you're experiencing, because I don't

311

feel right outing you even if it's to your best friend," Charlotte informed her, imperiously. "But you better believe, Regan Gallagher, that I am not happy. I want this situation resolved as soon as possible. Do you understand?"

Snapping straight to attention, Regan nodded. Even without Charlotte's intimidation, she was more than suitably chastised. "I'll talk to Sutton as soon as possible, I promise. You can take that to the bank."

In fact...

REGAN – 6:11PM

> My beautiful English Rose living in a Roman summer! I'm so proud of you, and I want you to know that even though I've been a little off lately, it has nothing to do with you. I have a ton to tell you, but don't stress – everything really is completely fine with me. Just been reallllll busy

Emotionally, she was the busiest she'd ever been in her life!

Given the time difference, she didn't expect Sutton to answer right away. Yet –

SUTTON, THE ONE AND ONLY – 6:11PM

> Something tells me that this has to do with my chat earlier with Charlotte. Either way, I'm happy and relieved to hear it. I love you and can't wait for the updates

REGAN – 6:12PM

> I love you, too!!! Now, get some beauty rest!

She waggled her phone at Charlotte, who'd been watching her every move. "Already working on it."

Charlotte nodded with obvious approval. "Good."

Their waiter approached with perfect timing. And, after Regan ordered, she stared across the table at Charlotte. Even though she hadn't planned to have this opportunity, it couldn't hurt to have her lesbian guru here, right?

"I love this place–" Charlotte started to say, as their waiter left.

Unfortunately for her, Regan had been counting down the

seconds until she could unleash her words. "Yeah, we totally have to get back to how you discovered this place, later. But right now, I need to know – what would you do if you kissed a woman, and she reciprocated... but then ended the kiss, and said it couldn't ever happen again? Also, let's say you told this woman that you were super attracted to her and that you think about that attraction all of the time, but said it was only platonic? And *then*, imagine some time passed, and you realized that wasn't strictly true. So, imagine that you took back that declaration of platonic feelings and let her know that you have a raging crush on her, so that everything could be above board. How would you proceed?"

Propping her elbow on the table, then her chin in her elbow, Regan stared across at Charlotte expectantly. God, it felt good to actually *say* this to someone!

"Hypothetically," she tacked on.

For several long moments, Charlotte only stared back. Not uttering a single word. Just... staring, her tawny eyes wide.

Finally, she blinked and asked, "Is that all?" Before she took a healthy sip of her wine.

Tapping on her chin with her index finger, Regan slowly shook her head. "Uhhh, no. What if the woman then didn't talk to you for twenty-four hours after that? *But*, you aren't sure if it's because she really was busy at her little sister's birthday party – not the best place for a feelings confession, but it was what I had at the time? – and is genuinely going out to dinner with her coworker for the first time ever... or if it's because she really is avoiding you, because you finally made things weird?"

Charlotte choked on the wine, quickly putting her napkin over her mouth as she coughed and stared over the napkin with watering eyes.

"It's *Emma*?" She finally managed to say, once her choking subsided. "The woman you've been talking to me about all summer is Emma?"

Regan reeled back, her heart starting to hammer in her chest in panic. "What?! I didn't say her name!"

"You said *her little sister's birthday party*, and you posted on your social media yesterday about the cake you made for Emma's sister," Charlotte pointed out, incredulously.

"Well, I didn't think you had enough time or care to be creeping on my socials!" Regan shot back, as her cheeks burned.

God damn it! She'd been so good! So careful!

Charlotte closed her eyes, steeping her fingers to her forehead to take a moment to gather herself. "The woman that you realized you were attracted to – the woman you have *apparently* kissed and confessed having feelings for – is Emma? Your roommate? Sutton's friend? Emma Bordeaux, that Emma?"

"She's my friend, too," Regan defended, weakly. "Now."

Wait – she didn't have to *defend* herself!

"I didn't do anything wrong," she quickly added, bolstering herself up. "It's not wrong to like Emma, that way."

"It's... not," Charlotte cautiously agreed, still looking at Regan as if she'd been dropped into an alternate dimension. "I just didn't anticipate this."

"Me, neither! We're in the same boat, there!"

"Well, you've had time to process this, and I have not."

Fair. But, also, "You barely even know Emma!"

"I know enough. I know she and Sutton are close. I know... wait. Is *that* why you don't want Sutton to know?" Charlotte pieced together, a dawning gleam in her eyes. "Because as far as I knew, Emma wasn't queer. Which means, as far as *Sutton* knows..."

Oh, *damn*. Regan dropped her whole head into her hands, so, so disappointed with herself. "Yes," she whispered, dismally. "That's why I couldn't talk to Sutton, and that's why I haven't been as chatty with her, lately. Because I know that when I talk to Sutton, I'm going to want to tell her all about the way I feel for Emma and how I love the way she smells and the way her lips felt and the night we cuddled and I *can't*, because Emma is so freaking private, that she hasn't come out to Sutton yet!"

Again, though, it felt so insanely great to be able to say it all aloud! Even if she shouldn't be.

"The tangled webs we weave," Charlotte muttered, toying with the bottom of her wine glass with her fingertips, obviously deep in thought.

"I know," she commiserated. "I've really tried to respect Emma in this, and I totally just blew it. I know you don't want to keep secrets from Sutton, but..."

Regan never tried to complicate things, but complications always seemed to find her.

Minutely shaking her head, Charlotte heaved a long sigh. "No. But, as someone who lived with my sexuality under wraps, I promise that I won't take it upon myself to discuss Emma's sexuality, even with Sutton." She drew in a deep breath, her considering and critical gaze dragging up and down Regan's face. "To your credit, I never expected that you would have been able to keep such a big secret like this from Sutton in order to preserve Emma's privacy."

"I should be offended." Regan attempted to glare, but it fell apart in seconds. "But I'm surprised even by myself."

"I think it speaks volumes about how highly you truly regard Emma," Charlotte surmised, sounding utterly fascinated.

Ridiculously, Regan felt her cheeks heat. "I mean... yeah. I guess that's true."

Even though she'd never thought about it like that, Charlotte wasn't wrong.

"Anyway, enough about that." She waved her hand, as if waving the conversation away. "What I need to know is – what do I do, now?"

"You're well aware that I am truly not an expert on relationships," Charlotte pointed out. "Much as it pains me to admit my own gaps in knowledge."

"Eh, you have your moments." After all, it had been Charlotte's idea to sweep Sutton off of her feet at Oliver's wedding. "But, yes, I know. Honestly, you're the best person to talk to right now, because I don't need relationship advice. I need advice on what to do moving forward. Single, and unexpectedly sapphic."

"And... you're positive that Emma doesn't have any feelings for you, as well?" Charlotte asked.

Regan's heart skipped at the very thought. Slowly, though, she shook her head, as the reality quickly dampened that hypothetical excitement. "She doesn't. Shouldn't come as a surprise."

She really, really had been trying not to dwell on that. Because if Regan let herself dive too far into the fact that the only person she'd ever felt so much for didn't feel the same way in return... well, it didn't feel good, that was for sure.

In fact, it made her stomach cramp, and the back of her throat feel a little tight.

Instead, she'd been really, really trying to focus on the future, and the actual possibilities it could hold for her.

Charlotte scoffed. "Your entire experience this summer comes as quite the surprise. Emma seems to have let you in to a degree to which she hasn't even let Sutton in, after years of friendship. You've kissed. You've met all of her family – you quite literally made her sister a birthday cake. Something has shifted enough that you've *apparently* cuddled through the night – don't think I missed that – and you felt comfortable enough to confess your feelings to her. I think it's a fair question to ask if she reciprocates these feelings."

When Regan heard it stated back to her like *that*, it made her want to reconsider her own certainty. To look over all of their interactions with a fine-toothed comb.

Quickly, though, she dismissed those thoughts.

The faster she could figure out how to move on from this, how to make it so that her body didn't tingle every time she and Emma touched, how to get to a place where she wasn't giddy at the prospect of spending time with Emma, the faster life could feel normal, again. The faster she could feel comfortable in her own home, again. The faster she and Emma could dive into building an actually platonic relationship.

Also, the faster Regan could *not* get her heart crushed by continuously having to remind herself that Emma didn't feel this way about her.

"No, she doesn't. We're just... friends." Regan nodded in finality with the word. "We're friends, and I'm happy with that."

And she *was*!

"I just need to figure out the best way to view Emma as *only* a friend, so that we can all just – move on. So, what would you do?" She asked again, trying to push away Emma from her thoughts and focus on Charlotte and only Charlotte.

Charlotte continued to stare at her, lightly drumming her fingertips on the table. Finally, she answered, "Prior to Sutton, as I know you know, I'd never dealt with having *feelings* for someone. When I was stressed – or, I imagine, if I'd been in your shoes and wanted to further explore my sexuality – I'd try to find someone on a dating app to have a bit of... exploratory fun with."

Leaning back, Regan took in those words with shock. A sapphic dating app honestly hadn't even occurred to her.

"If I were you, I'd likely create a profile on SapphicSpark. But, that's just me."

Could that even *work*? Was trying to explore this with a different woman the possible answer?

Like, maybe Regan had never experienced an emotional attraction to a man, but... but maybe if there was another woman out there that caught her eye – maybe she could start there?

Cautiously, she eyed Charlotte. "Maybe you *are* a good guide..."

twenty

"No, no." Brynn waved away Emma when she attempted to put her credit card down to pay for their dinner bill. "This is on me."

Narrowing her eyes, Emma didn't give in so easily. "Come on. We can at least split it."

Brynn slid her card into the holder and closed the book on it with a *snap*. "Nope. I got it. Because my number got called today, Emma, and I am passing on some of my good fortune."

At that, Emma acquiesced. "The entertainment department isn't going to know what hit it."

A triumphant grin played on Brynn's mouth. "Thank you very much. I'll miss you, though, and your very serious attitude, and the way you pretend not to text your *roommate* throughout the day."

Emma's stomach clenched, and she quickly reached for her martini glass. As it was, there was only a sip left, but it was worth it to throw back and *not* think about Regan. "Well, you still have a few weeks left with me."

"Then you'll have to be in charge of showing Allegra's new assistant around," Brynn continued, blessedly not mentioning her *roommate* again. "But if they get too annoying, you can always come and visit me in entertainment. Only a couple floors away."

"You're too kind," Emma dryly replied, shaking her head.

Brynn had gotten the good news from Allegra at the end of the workday. Because she was going to be utilizing Emma during the final round of Alton Fellowship interviews for the next couple of weeks, Brynn's promotion wouldn't officially happen for a little while, but it was in motion.

It was a double-edged sword, watching Brynn level up and get moved to a different department, with far more writing in her future. Emma was happy for her, really. Plus, it was living, breathing proof that if Emma put in her time and performed to her best ability, it would pay off. Eventually. But *damn* if it didn't make Emma burn inside for that eventually to become a reality.

"Thanks, by the way," Brynn commented, taking Emma out of her thoughts. "For coming to celebrate with me after work."

Emma stared across the small table at her, her eyebrows knitting in confusion. "You literally got promoted today." Rolling her lips, she debated whether or not she should say her next thought, but – what the hell. "And I really do consider you somewhat of a friend."

Brynn stared back at her, an absurd laugh bubbling up. "Really? *Somewhat* of a friend?"

Embarrassed, Emma shrugged. "Well, a work friend. Look, I don't make friends super easily. So, *somewhat of a friend* in such a short time, coming from me, is actually an accomplishment."

Damningly, she could see Regan so clearly in her mind's eye. See Regan losing her shit and absolutely cackling at Emma, even as she was positive Regan would also be, well, proud of Emma.

Even more damningly, that felt good.

Sobering, Brynn nodded. "Yeah, that doesn't shock me. I mean, I invited you out to come grab drinks or dinner after work, like, three times in May after you started, and you never said yes. Hence, my surprise and appreciation that you joined me tonight, regardless of the promotion."

Tapping her fingers lightly against her thighs, Emma thought over Brynn's words. "I guess it's also been brought to my attention this summer that I don't always give people a chance. And... I don't neces- sarily like that."

The revelation was occurring to her as she was speaking it aloud, surprising her along with Brynn.

But it was true.

Emma didn't know at what point she'd decided to close herself off from most new people and experiences, approaching everything and everyone with critical caution; it wasn't even something she'd done consciously.

If the last couple of months had proven anything to her, though, it was that she really could be surprised by people, if she was willing to give just a little bit. Kimberly, who'd taken to texting Emma in very reasonable doses, to the point that she didn't even feel stressed by seeing her mom's name appear on her phone.

But... mostly Regan.

I like you, in the real girlfriend kind of way, Regan's confession from yesterday played in her mind. Just like it had in bits and pieces all day long.

Squeezing her eyes closed, Emma effectively stopped her mind from summoning any of Regan's other notable lines. Nope, no, she wasn't going to do it. She wasn't going to let herself hear it again, to let those words tie her up in giddily-stressed conflicted knots.

This wasn't about Regan's attraction to her or Regan's – Regan's *feelings* for her; what she was saying to Brynn was simply about Regan, herself.

It was about the fact that Emma had done her best to write Regan off as a person, when in reality, Regan had turned out to be someone Emma deeply enjoyed spending time with. It was about the fact that Emma had relied for far too long on a default setting to find Regan frustrating, rather than allow herself to see any of the good parts in her.

It was about the fact that Regan had so much... depth. So much going on inside of her very active mind, that she felt so deeply, that she observed everything around her, and Emma would have never been able to experience any of it, if she'd stayed so insistent on closing her out.

Dear god, Emma needed to stop letting Regan derail her thoughts.

She refocused on Brynn, who was studying her with an arched eyebrow. "Huh. And this newfound sense of growth wouldn't have anything to do with the *roommate-not-girlfriend* situation, right?"

Emma felt her cheeks flame, and instinctively, she wanted to shut down in self-defense. But, she took a deep breath and pushed through it. "I don't really think that's relevant to what I'm saying. Which is, really, just me reiterating to you that I'd like us to be... friends."

Brynn signed the receipt their waiter had just dropped off with a flourish. "I, too, would like that." She slipped her credit card back into her purse. "I also wouldn't mind getting more updates about the Regan situation, but I can wait until we're more than *somewhat* friends for that."

The craziest thing, really, was that Emma wanted to confess it all to Brynn, as they gathered their items and stood.

Mostly because... well, Emma felt like she was going *crazy* with this new development in her life, and she couldn't talk to anyone about it. Sutton felt off-limits for obvious reasons –

– like, *Regan* hadn't even talked to Sutton about all of this?! Regan Gallagher, the woman that told her best friend everything, the woman that loved to gossip, the woman that simply loved to *share*, hadn't talked to Sutton about the very major life experiences she was having? Out of respect for Emma?

It was craziness. It was unexpected. It was... it was so, so, achingly thoughtful and sweet and it made Emma's heart flutter every damn time she thought about it.

Her gram was off-limits, because *obviously*, she was under the impression that Emma and Regan were already together.

Regan – because somehow, someway, *Regan* had become a top contender on Emma's list of people to confide in about her life?! – was clearly, unquestionably not the person to try to sort out her thoughts with.

So, even though she very much hadn't intended on to, she found herself asking, "Have you ever been just so – bowled over by someone that you don't even know what to do with them? What to think about them, how to act with them?"

Brynn stumbled to a stop, snapping her head around to stare at Emma with wide eyes. "I didn't think you were actually going to *tell* me?"

Embarrassed – this was why she didn't like to discuss anything personal. Because people's reactions got... weird, and, in turn, made Emma feel so freaking self-conscious – she gritted her teeth and nudged Brynn forward to keep walking rather than draw attention where they still stood in the middle of the restaurant.

"I didn't know I was going to," she muttered, making sure to keep her voice low so that none of the people at nearby tables who were now watching them with interest could hear anything.

Emma didn't feel like she knew anything, anymore. She'd barely found her center after that kiss last week, and now, following yesterday's confession, she had no idea where center even was, anymore.

As soon as they exited the restaurant and were out in the open evening air, Brynn turned around to face Emma, clearly brimming with anticipation. "All right – hit me. I've been dying for you to actually delve into something personal since we started working together."

Again, that reason alone made Emma want to *not*, like a turtle sliding back into its shell.

But... no. She needed this. She needed to voice it aloud, to another human being. Or she might very well explode.

"To set the record straight for you – Regan and I really are *just room-mates*," she stressed, to make that point very clear. "There hasn't been... romantic drama or whatever you think has been going on all summer."

Brynn scoffed, crossing her arms. "So, what you're all wrapped up in knots over right now is...?"

Reluctantly, Emma admitted, "Slightly romantic drama. We've... there's been..." God, she regretted this already, and she reached up to rub intently at her temple. "A single kiss. And a single night of cuddling. And a – a confession of feelings. *Hers*," she quickly clarified, and her stomach twisted and turned at the memory yet again.

Brynn's eagerness was written all over her face. "Please, I am begging you to continue."

But this was where Emma got tripped up. This was where the external facts stopped coming into play, and where Emma's internal feelings came into play. Where all of her conflict was. Where she found herself so... tongue-tied.

She'd never been so relieved about her phone starting to ring in her *life* as she was in this moment.

Regan? She wondered, and then immediately wondered how she'd feel about that.

To her disappointed relief, though, it was Gram's name on the screen.

"Actually, I need to answer this," she held her phone up as evidence to get her out of this conundrum.

Brynn tossed her arms in the air. "You're really going to leave me on this cliffhanger?"

Hesitating before she answered the call, she shook her head and forced *logic* to return. "It's not a cliffhanger; it's just... normal life that got a little complicated. Slightly longer story made short – we're still just roommates."

As her phone continued to ring, she thought of how poorly her gram had felt yesterday, and she flashed another look toward Brynn. "I'm sorry for cutting this long goodbye a little short, but I do need to answer this call. Thank you, again, for dinner, and congrats, again, on the promotion."

Brynn stared widely at her, before chuckling disbelievingly. "You owe me a real resolution to this tale. But, thanks and you're welcome, and I'll see you tomorrow."

Emma waved, solidifying the farewell, as soon as she answered the call, "Hey, Gram. How are you feeling?"

"I'm perfectly fine. Really, Em, I spent a little too much time in the heat – that was all. I'm back to normal today," Gram assured her.

Emma started walking in the direction of her apartment. The restaurant Brynn had wanted to try was, luckily, far closer to Emma's home than it was to work. Only a few blocks away, actually.

She frowned in consideration, before she hesitantly determined that her Gram's tone sounded genuine. "Okay, good. I still think you should tell Doctor Visentine at your appointment next week, though."

Gram loftily sighed. "Yes, I will."

In the brief lull of conversation, Emma heard sound in the background. Eyebrows furrowed in confusion, she tried to focus... but it didn't sound like the television. "Are you having a party over there or something?" She asked, jokingly.

Only, her gram's voice wasn't joking when she answered, "No, it's not a party. Just Phoebe and Bea, the women we played bingo with."

Emma nearly tripped over her feet in utter shock. "What?"

"When we played bingo a few weeks ago–" Gram started.

"No, I remember them," Emma interjected. "I just don't understand what's going on right now. Is it... bingo night again?" She tried to guess.

"Ah, no. We're all in my suite; I really tried to teach them how to play some games out in the common area, but... the card table makes all the difference," Gram informed Emma, as if Emma didn't know how seriously her gram took cards, and the significance of the table.

That wasn't what surprised her, though.

"I – that's really great, Gram." Emma tried to contain her excitement at the prospect of her grandmother making friends, because she knew Gram would fucking *hate* to feel infantilized.

"Yeah," her gram's terse agreement confirmed that sentiment. She cleared her throat. "We're about to start a game of bridge, but I just needed for you to ask Regan if it was all right if I give her information out to someone here? Her cookies have been an absolute hit, and one of the women that works the front desk wanted to know if she'd be interested in baking something for her husband's retirement party next month. I tried to get a hold of her, first, but she wasn't answering. And you know how I don't trust texting important information."

Narrowing her eyes, Emma tried to think over the details of bringing her gram back to Primrose Grove yesterday. "Sure, I can pass the question on." Unable to help herself, Emma pressed, "I just – I don't remember packing any of Regan's desserts with us to take home yesterday?"

In Emma's memory, Regan's desserts had been completely decimated by the end of the party.

"Oh, not *those* cookies," Gram dismissed. "The ones we baked today, here. With Phoebe and Bea."

"We're the ones that told Sherry here to give one to Cindy at the check-in desk!" Emma heard another voice shout in the background. "I know that woman has a giant sweet tooth, and she doesn't shut up about her husband's impending retirement!"

"The cookies... that you baked *today*," Emma stressed, as her mind tried desperately to process this information. "With Phoebe and Bea. And Regan."

"Yes, Emma," Gram confirmed, as if Emma was being obtuse. "And you can let Regan know that she doesn't need to do any of your bidding or running interference again. Not that I don't appreciate it," she added, warmth entering her tone. "But it worked. So, you can officially stop worrying about my being lonely."

"I can officially stop worrying," Emma dimly echoed, but she wasn't sure her brain and her mouth were connected, right now.

Because... what in the world was *going on*?

"I have to go, but please pass the question on. I wouldn't make it such a big deal, but apparently Cindy would like to talk to Regan as early as tomorrow, if possible."

"Right, sure. Love you."

"Love you, too," Gram returned, before hanging up the phone. So that she could return to her evening of being *social*.

Regan had gone to visit her gram today, apparently. She'd taken the time and effort to go to Astoria to bake cookies with Emma's grandmother, while – apparently – being the conduit for Gram to make friends with other residents.

Gram assumed this was Regan doing Emma's bidding, but Emma knew better. She knew very well that she hadn't asked Regan to do any such thing; Regan had already gone above and beyond doing so much for Emma regarding her family, already.

So above and beyond, in fact, Regan now had *feelings* for Emma. How was that for taking her job seriously?

Emma's mind was spinning, and her emotions felt so all over the place right now, that all she could do as she unlocked the door to the apartment was desperately hope Regan either wasn't home or was already in her own bedroom for the night.

Because she couldn't handle seeing and talking to Regan, right now. She couldn't handle it, because Emma couldn't handle her own feelings. She didn't even know what these feelings were.

Or... more aptly, they terrified her.

She cautiously walked into their apartment, shutting and locking the door behind her.

Slowly, she walked into the living room and didn't even realize she was holding her breath... until she walked in to see that Regan wasn't sitting there, waiting for her. That Regan wasn't in the living room or the kitchen. She wasn't waiting for Emma to come home, pouncing on her –

Emma shook her head sharply at the imagery that word invoked.

Emma had expected that Regan would be waiting on tenterhooks for Emma to return home. Wanting to talk about Regan's confession yesterday, maybe. Or maybe wanting to move past it, and excitedly telling Emma to get ready to dive into a new season of *The One*. Or wanting to tell Emma all about her day – about how she'd apparently spent part of that day with her gram.

Yet... nothing.

Regan wasn't waiting for her, with that boundless energy and addictive smile.

Which was the best-case scenario, Emma forcefully reminded herself. This was *precisely* what she'd hoped for – some space from Regan so she could figure out how to deal with everything. How to deal with this major change in her reality.

Unfortunately, that reminder didn't do anything to combat the disappointment she felt.

She had been stressing all day about how she would come home to Regan this evening and have no idea how to handle it. No idea how to handle Regan wearing her tiny little shorts and have her dark hair all tousled and tossed in a ponytail to get it out of her way while she cooked. No idea how to handle the excitement that Regan never tried to disguise as soon as Emma entered the room.

And now that she didn't have those things, she was upset about it.

"Jesus christ," Emma swore at herself, because she was so utterly fucked. Her carefully ordered life was starting to crumble around her, and she had no idea how to pause it.

With a deep breath, she walked down the hall toward her room. A night without Regan being home was great, she tried to convince herself. She could take a long, relaxing bath. She could finish reading the book she'd started on Friday... when she'd been waiting for Regan to come home...

But, where *was* Regan? It wasn't like she'd texted Emma to let her know she was going to be out late, so –

"Oh my *god*."

Emma froze with her hand on the doorknob to her bedroom, as she heard those muffled words come from Regan's room.

Swiftly, she turned around to face Regan's closed door. Regan *was* home, then. And was... in her room? This early? It wasn't even eight o'clock. What –

A long, throaty moan reached Emma's ears, followed by the very distinct sound of panting breaths.

"Yes, fuck," she heard next, and that was most definitely Regan's voice.

The realization of what was happening in Regan's room had Emma's heart start to race, her blood rushing in her ears, and she quickly turned to go into her room, only to bang her head right into the door, as she'd forgotten that she hadn't already opened it.

Emma couldn't even feel the dull ache on her forehead, as she stood, numb, in the middle of her bedroom.

There was no denying the fact that Regan was in her room right across the hall, having sex right now. The moans were undeniable, the vocalizations growing louder and more frequent by the fucking second, and Emma could hear *every single moment*, even with her door closed!

As quickly as she'd entered, Emma turned and literally ran back down the hallway and into the kitchen, where she hadn't been able to hear anything.

She braced her hands on the sink, trying to take deep breaths, and sort through the barrage of feelings swamping her.

The voice – that had *definitely* been Regan. It had been distinctly her voice, even if Emma had never heard her sound like that, before. So... wanton and raspy and needy and –

She swallowed hard, shaking her head and trying to stop the arousal that shot through her. Regan had sounded fucking hot, though, and there was no denying that, and Emma kept hearing it.

Yes, fuck. Yes, fuck. Yes, fuck.

The only thing that worked to stop this feeling from taking over was the fact that Regan was in there, having sex with someone else. Maybe a woman? If Emma had to judge based on those moans that she'd kept hearing in her room.

What the hell was that about?

Just yesterday, Regan was holding Emma's hand, professing to have such serious feelings for her, telling Emma that she was the only person that had ever made her feel this way, and today she was – she was in *their* apartment, having sex with someone?!

Emma needed to get out of here.

Yes, that was the only thing that made sense.

Her wallet and phone were... somewhere. In her room, maybe? Emma didn't remember dropping them on her dresser in their usual spot, but she didn't have them in her pockets, so she must have done so.

No way in hell was she going back down that hall, though, so –

She turned, ready to flee the apartment with only her keys...

Only to come face-to-face with Regan.

Who seemed to notice her at the same time, coming to an abrupt halt as she walked into the kitchen. "Emma!"

Her voice was high and still slightly out of breath, and everything inside of Emma was at war deciding if she was more turned on by that fact or upset by it.

Regan's cheeks were flushed – *glowing*, even, and Emma's stomach turned – and her hair was messy with obvious bedhead. She stood in front of Emma in only a black sports bra and a tiny pair of cotton shorts, something she'd very obviously just thrown on.

"Hmm," was all she could manage in return, with her heart in her throat.

God, what was *wrong* with her?

Regan could do whatever she wanted; she could have sex with anyone she wanted, especially in her own home, in her own room. It was none of Emma's business.

And still, it didn't stop her from *feeling* like it was, and Emma hated this. She hated it, desperately.

"I... ha," Regan chuckled, and it was the most uncomfortable Emma had ever seen her. "I, uh, didn't realize you were home, yet."

"Just got here," she replied, shortly. She felt breathless, herself.

"Great!" Regan nodded with the word, eyes brightening. "Good. Great. That's good. I was just coming to get a glass of water."

"I bet," Emma murmured, because after those throaty moans, she could only imagine that Regan was parched.

She very deliberately side-stepped away from the sink as Regan approached. She could not – *could. Not.* – touch Regan right now. Couldn't handle Regan sidling up to her all casual and brushing her bare, warm – probably still slightly sweaty – skin against any part of Emma's body.

Regan seemed to feel the same way, which rang another alarm bell in Emma's mind. She walked with hesitation over to the cabinet with the glasses, pushing up on her tiptoes, and Emma stared at Regan's bare back, and she – she *wanted*.

She knew how soft Regan's skin was, now. She'd felt it, right under her hands, when they'd woken up together only two and a half days ago. She'd always found Regan ridiculously, irritatingly attractive, and now it was so much *more*.

The sheerly physical aspect was more intense, now, because she lived with her. Because she saw Regan every day, touched her every day, was touched *by* her. They'd kissed and snuggled, and she smelled Regan's shampoo in the shower, permeating through her entire fucking being. There was no escape!

Even beyond that, though, this was so much more than the physical, now. Emma could contain a physical reaction; she could manage that. But Regan was... she was smart and funny and chaotic and she tried so hard and Emma liked it. She liked *her*, so fucking much.

"I'm just, you know, going to go back to my room. Long day," Regan murmured softly, her cheeks pink as she glanced at Emma, before glancing away as she started to close the cabinet.

"Right," she replied, annoyed at herself by how short she sounded. Yet, she couldn't help it.

And Regan was *blushing*? Going back to her room, seemingly for the night, so early? Was she embarrassed about having someone in her room? Did it make her feel as weird as Emma felt right now?

329

When Regan turned toward the sink holding only one glass, Emma couldn't help but ask, "You don't need another one?"

Ugh, she squeezed her eyes closed, irritation flashing through her. At both herself, and Regan, and she felt *crazy*!

Regan paused, slowly turning back to face Emma. "What are you talking about? And why are you being like this?"

"Why are *you* being like this?" She countered, feeling childish and petty, but the words were out before she could stop them.

Regan stared at her, incredulously. "*Huh*?"

Emma gestured at Regan, feeling the words bubble up in her throat. "You're blushing and avoiding looking at me, and I *heard* you when I came home. Obviously, you have someone in your room, and you feel... embarrassed, or whatever. And – that's fine. Because you thought I wasn't going to be home tonight. But... but..."

But *what*? Emma couldn't think rationally right now, for the first time in her entire adult life.

All she could think about were the sounds Regan had made, and how aroused Emma had been by it, and the fact that it ate her up inside, knowing that they'd been made for someone else.

Regan's mouth fell open in obvious surprise. "You think that I was having sex, just now? With someone else? *That's* why you're being all grumbly with me right now?"

Emma crossed her arms, as if the action could help contain all of these messy feelings inside of her. "Well – fine. Yeah. So what? Just *yesterday*, you told me you have serious feelings for me."

"And you didn't say it back!" Regan shot back, gesturing widely at Emma with palpable desperation. "You're the one that said we can't kiss again, that *this* – you and me – isn't happening."

Emma felt the truth of that burn through her, heating her face in an embarrassed blush.

"You can't hold it against me if I date or sleep with other people, after you turned me down, Emma," Regan sharply informed her, and there was a hoarseness in her tone. Something hurt that Emma could hear, and with it, Emma deflated, feeling the prickling feeling of causing Regan any pain digging right into her. "I might be able to keep going on as normal as possible with you, but I *do* have feelings, and I'm trying to process through them the same as you are."

Still embarrassed and still not knowing what to fucking do with herself, Emma dropped her head into both of her hands. "I know. I know, Regan, and I'm *sorry*."

She was; truly, deeply sorry. Sorry about everything; she didn't even know, anymore.

"If you care that I'm having sex with someone else, all you have to do is tell me. If I shouldn't be on dating apps anymore, then all you have to do is say it." Regan's tone was searching, pulling at something inside of Emma. Threatening to make her unravel.

Emma shook her head, though, forcing herself to lift her face up and actually look at Regan. "I don't have the right to say that, I just–"

She hadn't realized Regan had walked closer to her. Hadn't realized that Regan was only inches away, still only wearing the bare minimum stiches of clothing required to not be completely naked, while her body was still flushed and, dear god, Emma's hands *shook* with want.

"I'm *telling* you that you have the right to say it," Regan's voice dipped so low, it skittered down Emma's spine and landed squarely between her legs. Reminding her that the wetness she'd felt from hearing Regan hadn't gone away. "If you tell me that you have feelings for me, too, then you have the right."

Emma's lips trembled open, and she couldn't find any words that she was able to say aloud. Not while her heart was beating so hard in her chest and this heat wound through her, so demanding.

While everything inside of her screamed to tell Regan that *yes*, she had feelings for her – intense, strong feelings – but it was so complicated, and –

"God damn it, Emma, I'm going to break my word to you, and I'm sorry, but I just can't..." Regan murmured, her dark eyes – so intense – flicking from Emma's mouth to her eyes, then back again.

And Emma's mind went blissfully blank as Regan surged onto her tiptoes and wrapped her arm around Emma's neck to tug her down. She didn't have to tug hard, though, because Emma was so willing.

Regan's body surged against hers, and Emma couldn't fight against it, anymore. She wrapped her arms around Regan's waist, her hands tingling at the contact with Regan's smooth, bare skin, groaning low into her mouth as she returned the kiss, matching Regan's intensity.

Somewhere, dimly in the back of her mind, she was well aware that there was no going back from this.

And, as Regan's tongue flicked over her bottom lip, she couldn't bring herself to care at all.

twenty-one

THIS WAS SO MUCH BETTER than their first kiss.

Regan hadn't thought anything would have been able to top that one, but this one did. By leaps and bounds.

For so many reasons.

Because they were standing, and their entire bodies were pressed against each other. Regan strained up, aching to be as close as possible. They *were* as close as possible, and it didn't feel like enough. She felt the buttons on Emma's shirt – the blouse she'd worn to work – press into her stomach so closely, she knew they would leave an imprint, and it still wasn't enough.

She slid her tongue along Emma's, every nerve ending in her body feeling like it was fucking singing. Because she could taste Emma, really taste her this time. She could feel the way Emma's tongue toyed with her own, and *god*, Emma was a good fucking kisser.

She hadn't really been able to definitively know that, from their first kiss. It had been so short, so simple. But she knew, now.

And it only served to raise the already scorching levels of heat surging through Regan's body.

She carded the fingers of her free hand through Emma's hair, reveling in how soft it was. How it was long enough to grab such a good fistful of – which she did – and Emma groaned sharply into her mouth.

Emma's fingers scratched down Regan's back, and her entire body shuddered at the sensation. She moaned with it, rolling her hips intently against Emma's.

It didn't matter that she'd just had an orgasm, apparently. No, if anything, Regan just felt primed and ready for more.

She wanted to climb Emma Bordeaux like a fucking tree.

As that thought hit her, she lifted her other hand to wrap around Emma's back –

Only to realize far too late that she'd still been holding the glass she'd taken out to have some water. The glass that now, due to Regan's eagerness, slipped from her fingers and fell to the hardwood of the kitchen floor behind Emma.

The shattering sound broke them apart.

Regan tugged her head back, panting for breath as she stared, wide-eyed, up at Emma. "I'm sorry," she apologized immediately, concern cutting through the needy, aching want inside of her.

She fell from her tiptoes back to stand on her heels, body still pressed entirely against Emma's. "Don't step backward. Just – you stay right there, and I'll clean it up. And then we can get right back to this."

Finally, Emma seemed to come back to reality. Regan could see it happening, see the dawning of what they'd just done as it hit Emma.

Who shook her head as she closed her eyes and flexed her fingers against Regan's bare hips.

She shivered at the touch, a sigh escaping her.

At the sound, Emma dropped her hands away. "No, you're the one not wearing anything, including shoes."

Emma leaned back enough to rake her eyes down Regan's body as if confirming for herself that was the truth.

Shivering again, Regan felt her nipples harden at the look, and her breathing felt labored all over again, and she loved it. She wanted Emma to look at her like that. With obvious desire in those electric blue eyes.

Again, Emma clamped her eyes closed. As if shutting Regan out – literally – was the only way to not get distracted by her, and *that* was a thrilling realization.

"Yeah. So. You should just go back to your–" Emma gasped once more, eyes flying open as she took a step back from Regan. The shoes she was still wearing crunched over the glass. "Your *room*, where you were just having sex. Fuck, I can't believe I just kissed you after you were... with someone else."

Her hand flew up to her mouth, covering up her kiss-swollen lips. Much to Regan's disappointment.

Feeling the same bafflement from the beginning of this interaction all over again, Regan tossed her hands in the air. "Why are you so freaking certain that I was having sex with another person?"

"Because I heard it!" Emma hissed back, her cheeks flushing.

"No, you didn't."

"Yes, I did."

"You heard *me*," Regan shot back, unsure if she should be amused or incredulous or mortified, or a combination of all three.

At once, all of Emma's movements stilled, as she stared wide-eyed at Regan. Slowly, she shook her head. "No. I heard... more than you."

Fine, in this moment, amusement won out, and Regan breathed an exasperated laugh, repeating, "Why are you so sure?"

"Because! I heard *you*, and I have no doubt about that." Emma's cheeks turned a dark pink as she spoke. "But there were more... moans."

Regan could only stare, that amusement giving away – a bit – into embarrassment. "That was me."

Emma blinked at her, expression morphing from indignant to mystified. "All of it?"

"Well, I was having sex with myself, so... yeah. All of it," she confirmed, and – wow, yeah. She didn't know how to feel, right now.

Still exhilarated from their kiss and still turned on, because – apparently – the leg-shaking orgasm she'd gotten from her vibrator wasn't anything when compared to kissing Emma like that. But she'd never felt so... sheepish, before, about her sex life.

She'd never been scrutinized so closely, as she was now, as Emma's stare seemed to look right through her.

"That was all *you*," Emma rasped, sounding breathless.

Wordlessly, Regan nodded. Even if she *was* embarrassed, it was too late to do anything about it. "I didn't think you were going to be home," she defended, before she remembered, "Also, I don't need to defend myself; I can masturbate in my own room!"

"I know that," Emma shot back, still sounding like she'd run a marathon. "But I've never heard you, before! What, have you not masturbated all summer?"

"I have a very healthy sex life with myself, thank you very much," Regan smartly confirmed, entirely unashamed about that fact. "At least three or four times a week. More, actually, in the last few weeks." She couldn't help it; she dropped her gaze to roam over Emma's body.

As it was, undeniably, the star in many of her fantasies as of late.

Emma seemed to know very well what she was getting at, as her breath hitched in her throat, and Regan could see how she shuddered.

"I'm just usually a lot quieter, because I'm a good roommate. Normally, when I know you're home, I just do it while laying on my stomach and bite my pillow, so–"

An aching, deep groan rumbled from Emma, as she held her hand up to cut Regan off. "Oh my *god*, Regan, you can't be telling me this stuff. Please."

Finding that none of her prior embarrassment was lingering, Regan shrugged up at Emma, unashamed. In fact, based on Emma's reaction, she felt empowered by it; she wanted to tell her more. To see if Emma would make any more of those hot little sounds. "Why not? Do you not like it?" She challenged. She moved to step toward Emma, only to be stopped as Emma's hands shot out quickly, landing on her shoulders.

"Stop! The glass." Worry etched into Emma's tone, as she glanced down at the floor, carefully walking Regan back a step. "Be careful, please." Emma turned away, walking to the other end of the kitchen, to grab the broom. "Just, let me take care of this."

Absurdly touched, Regan stayed still and watched Emma work. She held her tongue for several more minutes, until Emma had swept, vacuumed, and then ran a damp paper towel over the floor for good measure.

When Emma was all done, Regan smiled up at her. "Thank you. Sorry, again, for dropping the glass. I just got so caught up in kissing you that I didn't even register it was still in my hand."

Guilelessly, she shrugged.

Immediately, Emma dropped her head back. "Regan, we can't–"

"If you don't want this, then why did it clearly bother you so much when you thought I had someone else in my room?" Regan challenged, feeling re-invigorated by the thought. This time, she did take a step forward, closer to Emma. She felt compelled to do it, drawn to stand so close to her, wanting to be as near as possible.

"If you don't have feelings for me, then why does it matter to you if I was having sex with someone else? I know you were upset about it, Emma, so please do us both a favor and don't deny it," there was an edge of begging in her voice, and she couldn't control it.

Because she felt pretty damn desperate, right now. Desperate to know the truth. Desperate for Emma to tell Regan that she wasn't delusional; that Emma not only felt this insane attraction but felt *more*, just like she did. That it wasn't limited to only Regan.

"Fine, Regan, I was upset. Are you happy?" Emma snapped back, the same desperation in her voice that Regan felt pulsing through her. "I was upset at the idea that you had someone in your room. The idea of you having sex with someone else in our apartment makes me feel *crazy*, sick to my fucking stomach. Okay?"

"Okay!" Regan accepted, elated by the fact. She felt so... light. Like she could drift away with how happy this made her. "Great!"

"It's *not*," Emma denied, tossing her hands in the air as she looked at Regan like she'd grown a second head.

"Why?" She challenged, because she just didn't understand. If Emma felt half as much for Regan as she did for Emma, then it was *amazing* to know it was reciprocated! "I've tried so, so hard to respect your privacy when it comes to your feelings, I really have. I haven't pressed you to talk to me about them, and I had no plans to. But *please*, Emma, if you want me to understand, I need you to lay all of your cards on the table for me. Just like I've done for you."

Because, otherwise, Regan would never be able to wrap her mind around this. She wasn't sure she'd understand, even after.

Emma stared at Regan, that expression of desire and attraction so clearly on display, even as it was marred with obvious internal conflict.

"I would never ask you to do something that I wouldn't be willing to do, myself," Regan continued, unable to stop the words from falling out of her mouth. "I'll never ask you to bare your soul to me without baring mine, first," she promised, her voice hoarse with how much she really, truly *meant* it. "I know it's not as easy for you as it is for me. I know you like privacy, and I know you're scared to let people in, and–"

"If you were, somehow, a stranger to me, this would all be different," Emma broke in, her voice so soft, but so easily commanding Regan's full attention.

Confusion slid through her, and she tilted her head up at Emma with uncertainty.

"If you were a stranger I happened to meet three months ago at the café, then this would all be different," Emma elaborated, shaking her head. "A stranger that makes me laugh the way you make me laugh, that makes me feel so comfortable like you do. A stranger that has gone through these ups and downs with my family and stood by my side the entire time, a stranger that goes out of her way to visit my gram and *bake* with her. A stranger that took it upon herself to try to help my gram make friends?"

The look in Emma's eyes was so intense, it stole Regan's breath right from her lungs.

"A stranger that happens to be so cute when you smile at videos of animals on the internet, that it makes my heart flutter. A stranger with a mouth that makes me think such inappropriate thoughts, whose smile is like sunshine. A stranger who is not only the most attractive person I know, but who looks at me like *I'm* the most attractive person *you* know?" Emma pressed her hand to her own chest as she spoke, like she still couldn't believe what she was saying was true.

Regan fell back into the counter, her knees feeling so weak as Emma spoke. The emotion in her voice was so strong, so compelling, and Regan's head spun with it.

"If you were a stranger, I would be on my *knees*, begging you to give me a chance. That's how I feel, Regan." Emma finished, searching Regan's gaze with her own, her chest heaving with every breath she took. Like laying that all out for Regan had taken so much out of her, and Regan – knowing Emma – knew that it probably had.

"You don't have to beg me," she breathed, her entire body buzzing with energy. "You don't need to be on your knees–"

She cut herself off, choking on the word as the image of Emma on her knees in front of her – something new for Regan's fantasies, but something very, very welcome – took over her mind.

Shaking herself out of it, she focused on what was important. What was right in front of her. The fact that Emma liked her back?! *That* much!

"I'm right here. No begging required. I've already *told* you that I like you."

"But you aren't a stranger," Emma shot back, dropping her head back with a groan that sounded literally pained. "You're Regan. We share an apartment – an apartment that we could never truly avoid one another in. We share a best friend – a best friend that is undeniably closer to you than to me, and I don't want to risk Sutton's friendship. And I... I really like you, Regan. As a person. As a friend. As the only person in my life that isn't my grandmother that sees *me*, that knows my entire history. It's so much more complicated because you *aren't* a stranger."

Regan stared at Emma, wanting more than anything to reach out to her. To touch her, not in a romantic or sexual kind of way, but just to – to comfort that struggle evident in her face, to ease the tightness in her shoulders.

"Well, what do you want to do?" She asked, plainly. Because it was the only thing she could think of doing, now. "You know where I stand. I *do* think you're the most attractive person I know. I do want to touch you every time we're together, just to feel close to you. I love to look at you. To spend time with you. But..." She rolled her lips, shrugging heavily. "I can try to push past it, like I said. I mean, knowing that you have feelings for me back is going to make it infinitely more difficult. And if you meet someone and bring them home to our apartment, I might need to, like, rip out their hair or something."

Emma laughed, which then turned into a whine. "I hate that I find you so funny," she admitted, before she sighed.

A visceral satisfaction worked through Regan at that. "Well, I love that you do. Furthermore, we can work out a masturbation schedule. I'll let you know every time I'm going to really let loose, and–"

"Oh my god, please, don't," Emma cut her off, aiming a serious look at her.

"I don't know what else to do, then." Slowly, carefully – as if she were approaching a wild animal – she walked forward. And she took it as an amazing, wonderful sign that Emma didn't step back. "I get it; it's complicated. We live together. We share Sutton. We're friends."

She came to stand right in front of Emma, only inches away, and she stared up at her. Breathing the same air, feeling Emma's body warmth, and Regan shivered at the proximity. "Just one date. Give me the chance to take you on *one* date, and if it goes badly or we get the impression that things won't work out for us in any way, then – that's it. We're three and a half months into our living arrangement, so we're halfway through. If the date doesn't go well, then, that's that. We know that we really can't push this, and we will go back to normal."

Regan had no idea that this plea to take Emma on a date had been going to leave her mouth; she'd never even let herself think about that as an option with Emma before.

But now that the idea occurred to her, she wanted it so, so badly. It sparked something to life inside of her, something sweeping and romantic, something she'd never really felt before.

It seemed that was par for the course with Emma, didn't it?

Emma's eyes were wide and beseeching, but Regan didn't know what she wanted from her. Wildly, she thought that she wanted to give Emma anything she could possibly ask for. She just hoped that what Emma asked for was her.

Regan held her breath, unable to breathe normally with the anxiety and anticipation coursing through her as she waited for Emma's response.

It was going to be a no. Logically, she knew it. She knew that Emma didn't like to take chances, didn't like change, and –

"Okay," Emma agreed, her voice so soft. "We can go on one date. To see how it goes."

Regan's mouth fell open as the shock took her over, quickly replaced by elation. She squealed with it, hopping onto her tiptoes and throwing her arms around Emma's neck, unable to help herself. She couldn't contain this! Just earlier tonight, she'd been so convinced this would never be a possibility, that she'd downloaded SapphicSpark! And now...

"I can't wait. I'm going to sweep you off your freaking feet," she swore, her heart pounding in her chest, and she could feel Emma's pounding as well, as Emma's arms tentatively wrapped around her waist, too.

"I'm wondering if I should be a little scared," Emma whispered into her ear.

She shivered at the feeling of Emma's warm breath, chuckling at the exhilaration coursing through her. "Maybe you should be."

Maybe they both should be.

Emma squeezed her hips again, and they both froze.

Abruptly, Emma dropped her hold and leaned back from Regan, breaking their embrace. She took a small step backward. "I think you should maybe put something else on."

Her cheeks flushed, excited pleasure rushing through her as she deliberately tapped her finger against her lips, as she hummed, "Hmm? You think?"

Emma's eyes immediately flashed to watch her, which was precisely what Regan hoped would happen.

Delighted by it, she slid her fingertips down over her chin, gliding down the side of her neck, over her collarbone... Emma's eyes still followed the movement, and Regan wasn't sure she'd ever felt more alive.

Especially as she slowly dragged her own touch down the center of her chest, into the middle of her bra, hooking into the soft fabric. Her own stomach dipped, heat spiraling through her all over again, because she swore she could *feel* Emma's stare, adding a weight to her touch.

Emma wheeled away, a low moan in her throat. "I told you how attracted I am to you and that I have feelings for you less than ten minutes ago, and you're already doing this to me?"

"I'm incorrigible," Regan readily agreed. The full realization of this evening dawned on her all over again, and that awed feeling swept through her as she grinned up at Emma. "And you like it."

"Against my better judgment and all of my willpower... yes. I do," Emma conceded, biting her lip as she tossed another glance at Regan. Only briefly, as she turned away again. "Seriously, though. Nothing is happening before that date, and I *need* you to put some clothing on."

"For you? Anything," she teased, only… not.

As she did a little happy dance down the hall to her room, she could feel it well up inside of her. How very much she needed this date to go well, because she didn't think she could come back from this. The high she was on was already so intense, Regan already knew the come down would be brutal.

She had to plan the best date of Emma's fucking life.

twenty-two

It was irritatingly, disturbingly difficult to focus on work when Emma had a date with Regan in approximately... one hour. Maybe less? Maybe more? She'd be home in less than an hour, but she didn't know what Regan's timeline looked like for when they needed to leave, for wherever it was that they were going.

Emma didn't really know, because Regan was being extremely tight-lipped about it. Which was, in turn, extremely un-Regan-like.

She paused packing up her bag for the day, turning her attention down to her phone.

EMMA – 5:51PM

You really won't tell me where we're going tonight? You know that I don't like surprises, right?

REGAN FREAKING GALLAGHER – 5:52PM

I have known you for years, have lived with you for months, and have come to deeply care about you (neuroses and all)... so, yes, I know this

> But I can't tell you where we're going tonight. It might be a surprise, but I SWEAR it's a good one, you're going to love it (fact), and it's super casual, so you don't need to worry about what to wear or the vibe or anything like that
>
> And it's NOT karaoke, before you ask :)))

Emma couldn't help the scoffing laugh, shaking her head and feeling stupidly endeared. Because she *had* been about to ask. Well, she'd been about to insist that they don't do karaoke, but same difference, really.

"Ahhh, young love," Brynn sighed from across their shared office space.

The grin immediately fell from Emma's lips as she felt the heat rush to her cheeks. "Do you have nothing better to do than watch me text?"

Brynn stared back, winging up an eyebrow. "Obviously. We're packing up, done for the day. What else do I have to do with my time?"

Emma couldn't really refute that and, quite frankly, she couldn't even summon up annoyance at feeling like she was under a microscope right now.

Mostly because her stomach was too preoccupied with this buzzing excitement and anxiety about her impending date.

> EMMA – 5:53PM
>
> Well, you said you wanted me to tell you when I'm leaving work for the day, and I am.
>
> REGAN FREAKING GALLAGHER – 5:53PM
>
> Perfect timing! couldn't have been better even if you knew our plans for the evening already
>
> I'm excited to see you

Oh, and there it was. That feeling swooping so low in her stomach, before erupting and moving somewhere up in her chest.

She held her breath for just a second, before she gave into the feeling.

I'm excited to see you, too.

After all, they were going on a date tonight. They were actually *doing this*, despite all of the logic that screamed at Emma that this was a bad idea. That this had the potential to be disastrous, for exactly the reasons she'd already told Regan.

But that logic hadn't done Emma much good in the last few months, in terms of being able to keep her from developing these feelings for Regan, had it?

"You know I've been dying for the last two days, right? For you to tell me more about you and Regan?" Brynn asked, as Emma tucked her phone into her pocket and slung her bag over her shoulder to head out for the day.

As nervous as she truly was for tonight, she was also ready for it. She wanted to know what Regan had planned for them, what had gotten Regan so excited last night, as she'd proudly informed Emma, "*I know exactly what we're doing on our date. Tomorrow night, book it in.*"

Tightening her grip on the strap of her bag, she rolled her lips tightly... before expelling a deep breath. "We're going on a date tonight. That's the update."

As Brynn fell into step next to her, she reached out and slapped her hand at Emma's arm. "Shut up! That's – wow. That's a way bigger update than I expected after you were so *there's no romantic drama* the other night."

"There have been a few developments," she offered in vague explanation, because it really was the only explanation she had.

She definitely wasn't going to tell Brynn about walking in on Regan masturbating and how she'd never heard someone sound so uninhibited, so fucking sexy, that it drove her to the brink of insanity. Drove her right to the brink of confessing every little feeling for Regan that she'd tried to push down and ignore this summer.

But how could she have held it in? How could she have, when Regan had lit up Emma's every nerve ending with that kiss, and then talked about touching herself, and then begged – so earnestly, so genuinely – for Emma to bare her soul?

Especially when Regan had been utterly correct. She'd never asked Emma to share anything that Regan herself hadn't already shared, freely and openly, just because she wanted Emma to know.

Yeah, she wasn't going to discuss that with Brynn, either.

Apparently, she didn't need to. They shared an elevator to the lobby and Brynn merely shook her head, a thoughtful expression on her face, before she finally turned to look up at Emma. "You know, you have *really* surprised me. When you started in May and you were all-business, no gossip, didn't ever want to share about your personal life, I really thought I was in for a real bummer summer. But now, look at us. Somewhat friends, and you're telling me about your date with your hot roommate." She bumped her shoulder lightly into Emma's. "Not half-bad."

Emma found herself smiling even as she rolled her eyes. "Not half-bad," she agreed.

As they walked out of the building, Brynn let out a low whistle. "I'm having some déjà vu."

Confused, Emma looked at Brynn, then followed where Brynn's gaze had landed.

She shouldn't be surprised, and yet, she was. Because there Regan stood, about ten feet away from the entrance of their building, her arms crossed over her chest like she was trying to contain herself.

And most likely, Emma knew, she was. Regan's smile was full-wattage as she spotted Emma, lighting up not only her face but just... the area *around* her, if that was even possible.

"Like I said, perfect timing," Regan echoed her text as she walked closer, closing the distance between them. More like bounced closer, the frenetic energy coming off of her in waves. "Hi, Brynn."

"Hello to you, too, Regan. Great to see you again," Brynn commented, a sly grin on her face as Regan sidled up to Emma.

Much like when she'd picked Emma up from work all those weeks ago to go out to dinner, Regan settled right into Emma's personal space. Regan's arm pressed into hers, her hips angled toward Emma as well. Unlike the last time, Emma didn't put any space between them. She didn't feel the urge to, even with Brynn staring at them.

Being this close to Regan now felt... normal. She liked it, and she was in far too deep to deny that to either herself or Regan, now.

"I would love to stay and chat, but we have to head out," Regan informed Brynn with an apologetic wince. "But next time we run into each other, I'd love to chat more."

"Go, go," Brynn shooed them. "Have fun on your date."

Regan blinked after Brynn for a long second as Brynn started to walk away, before she looked up at Emma. Those dark eyes were wide, looking at Emma with surprise. "You told her?"

Feeling a twinge of embarrassment, Emma shrugged. "It's not a huge deal. We're... friends."

Slowly, Regan tilted her head, as that smile – even more wattage than before – returned. "You and Brynn are friends! And you told her that we're going on a date."

"That's what I said," Emma murmured, but she couldn't deny that Regan's joy was infectious.

Regan slid her hand down, lacing their fingers together. It wasn't the first time they'd held hands, not by a long shot. But it was the first time that they were doing it for *them*, and not because Regan was offering her comfort or because they were operating as fake-girlfriends.

They both stared down at their hands for a few seconds, and Emma had to believe that Regan was thinking the same thing she was. That this felt so... comfortable. Like they slotted together so perfectly, and they didn't have to brush it off or focus on playing a part.

Doing everything she could to try to stay grounded – this might be a date, but it was also a test run, Emma reminded herself – she cleared her throat to gain Regan's attention. "So... have you just been waiting out here or...?"

Regan laughed, leaning into Emma's side. "Only for, like, ten minutes. I didn't know when you were going to get out of the office today; if you were out at five, then I could have just met you at home. But once the clock hit five-thirty, I figured it was better to meet you instead."

With that, Regan used their hands to gently tug Emma, leading her down the street.

Amused, Emma stared at the side of Regan's face. "So, the mystery event tonight is on a schedule."

"Yes, it's scheduled," Regan confirmed, wiggling her eyebrows at Emma. "But that's all you're getting from me about it."

"Hmm," Emma hummed in thought. "It's kind of risky, given that I might not have gotten out of work until even later than this," she pointed out.

Because it was true. Yes, it was rare that Allegra needed her to be in-office until seven or eight, but it had happened.

Regan nodded. "It was risky, but it'll be worth it," she promised. "Besides, it's a Wednesday. You don't usually work later than six on Wednesdays."

Emma couldn't refute that, or even pretend to be surprised that Regan had noticed and memorized that fact.

"You're really hyping this date up," she quietly mused, still studying Regan's profile, as if she'd be able to read her mind.

"It's because I'm *prettty* confident about it," Regan shot back, and the grin that darted over her face was sharp and knowing and, indeed, confident. Something about it kick-started that sparking heat inside of Emma, similar to that feeling from Monday night in their apartment.

They'd been very good, very appropriate, for the remainder of Monday night, as well as all day yesterday. Emma was sticking true to her word – she'd see how the date went, but she *wasn't* going to indulge in anything else before this.

It didn't mean she hadn't wanted to, though.

They'd had dinner together last night, then had sat so close on the couch. No closer than they usually did, but... it was already different. The air around them felt so much heavier, and every single part of Emma was on high alert around Regan. Her body responded to every brush against Regan's as if it were Monday night all over again. As if she'd just heard Regan moaning and swearing as she neared an orgasm, as if they'd just shared the most intense kiss of her life.

She'd be lying if she said she wasn't incredibly relieved that Regan had announced their date would be so soon, because she wasn't sure how they'd push through with any boundaries intact if they had to wait even longer.

"Oh, wait," Regan paused, still holding Emma's hand, as she held out her other hand and gestured at Emma's bag. "Give me that."

Emma's free hand clutched at the strap of her bag, cautiously. "Why?"

"Because, you goof, I'm going to carry it for you. Because this is a date. Duh."

Emma chuckled, shaking her head. "I can carry my own bag."

"I'm aware of that. But..." Regan dug her teeth into her bottom lip, her eyes searching Emma's. "I want to be chivalrous. I've never been chivalrous on a date, before."

It was that freaking look in Regan's eyes, Emma thought, as she felt herself get caught up in them. The way she looked at Emma, like she would swear by every word she said. Like she wanted more than anything to make Emma... happy. It wasn't something she'd ever experienced before, and she didn't even register what she was doing until her hand brushed Regan's as she handed over her bag.

"You don't need to be *chivalrous*." She cleared her throat, drawing herself back to reality. "You just need to be you."

She could see how Regan swallowed, heavily, her gaze dipping to Emma's lips. The desire in Regan's expression was so clear, Emma felt short of breath.

Regan closed her eyes and tugged Emma's hand as she started walking again. "You said that to me before. When you were taking me to meet your grandmother."

"I remember." And she did. She remembered all of these moments they'd shared in the last several weeks, in vivid color. "And it worked. Because she really, really likes you."

Gram liked Regan so much, it was nearly overwhelming, and it was entirely, unbelievably appealing.

"No one's ever said something like that to me. That you actually *want* me to be my whole self," Regan admitted, softly.

"Well... people are stupid. It's why I don't like them, generally." Even though Emma knew she'd once been one of those people, someone that didn't know how to handle Regan's all-encompassing personality. But she'd been wrong. And other people were, too.

"Oh, Emma," Regan sighed, squeezing her hand a few times.

Emma felt that easy warmth flit through her. Regan didn't need to elaborate; Emma understood what she was feeling.

It didn't take long for them to arrive at their destination, and Regan used their interlocked hands to pull Emma to a stop.

"We're here!" She announced, buzzing with clear excitement, as she gestured with her free hand to the doors in front of her.

The doors to *By the Book*, apparently, a bookstore only blocks away from Emma's work. A bookstore that she hadn't even known about, which was enough to throw her off. Mostly, though, she felt herself already start to melt a bit.

She'd told Regan all those weeks ago that the best place to bring her was a bookstore. How was she supposed to keep any semblance of a level head on this date when Regan remembered every word she ever said, and brought her to one of her favorite places on earth?

Regan gasped, drawing Emma's attention. Concern welled up inside of her when she saw the undeniably upset look on her face, and she gripped Regan's hand a little tighter. "Hey, what's wrong? Are you okay?"

"No! I'm not okay!" Regan pointed to the window next to the door, where there was a flyer advertisement Emma hadn't yet noticed.

She, too, gasped when she saw *Alexis Levine – book signing and Q&A* on the ad. Only for the excitement that rushed through her to dampen quickly, when she saw at the bottom of the poster – *Postponed*.

Regan banged her knuckles against her forehead. "So stupid! I should have double-checked this morning that the event was still happening! I could have changed up the plans and done something else."

Frowning, Emma quickly reached up and grabbed Regan's wrist, stopping her from tapping her knuckles against her head again. "Hey, stop. It's okay."

"It's not!" Regan insisted, turning to face Emma, wide-eyed. "I have one date to try and solidify in your mind that we can really *be* something, together," she insisted, voice edging on desperate. "And – in typical Regan fashion – I didn't double-check to make sure everything was as it should be. I got swept up in how excited I was and rushed into getting ready, and I should have–"

"Regan, it really is *okay*," Emma interrupted, as everything inside of her demanded that she cut Regan off, here.

She reached up with her free hand, feeling compelled to brush her fingertips over Regan's jaw. A touch she'd never allowed herself, before, but right now, she had no reason to stop herself. It felt so... easy. So natural.

"I know who I'm on a date with," she gently informed Regan, a disbelieving smile pulling at her mouth. Because, yeah, it was hard to wrap her head around, but it was all true. "I know you. I know that when we go out to something you've planned with the best of intentions, there is a chance it might not go as planned."

It was an aspect of being in Regan's life even as her friend that Emma had already accepted.

A sheepish look slid over Regan's face. "Yeah... I'm working on it."

Emma shrugged, because at this point – it really didn't matter. She liked Regan's excitement and her energy and how willing she was to go along with whatever was thrown at her, and Emma couldn't pick-and-choose which facets of Regan to accept. Somewhere along the line, she'd bought in. "I know who you are. And I'm still here on the date."

"You are," Regan echoed, cautiously. "And you *do* know me."

"I'd say better than most."

"Me, too," Regan breathed in agreement. Still, she kept her eyes on Emma's, cautious. "So – you're not disappointed?"

"Disappointed that you brought me to explore a new bookstore on a date?" Pursing her lips in faux-thought, Emma shook her head. "I'd say it's *probably* one of the best date ideas anyone's ever had."

That mega-watt smile bloomed over Regan's face again, settling warmly through Emma's chest. Regan turned her head, placing a kiss to the center of Emma's palm that had been cupping her jaw in a move so fast, Emma hadn't seen it coming.

Her palm tingled from it, as her breath hitched, and she closed her fist tightly as she dropped her hand back to her side. "Uh." She cleared her throat. "Why don't we go in?"

There was a flush on Regan's cheeks, an undeniable energy that buzzed between them, as Regan reached out and opened the door. "After you."

As Emma walked in, her eyes widened as she took in the interior. The spiral staircase in the middle of the shop was entirely unexpected, leading up to a second and third floor. The shelves weren't all a uniform shape or size, with a variety of clearly new and used books mixed together. There was an organized chaos to it all, something so... beautiful, and Emma gaped.

"How did I not know this was here?" She asked, awed, as she stared up and around.

"Isn't it gorgeous?" Regan asked, bouncing onto her tiptoes next to her, squeezing the hold she still had on Emma's hand. "And there's a café in the back, too, that people *raved* about in reviews. They have a chef that changes the menu every month. It functions as a coffee house during the day, and they serve book-themed mixed drinks at night. I figured we'd have dinner here."

Emma's heart skipped a beat as she focused her attention back to Regan, who was staring up at her with a hopeful smile.

It might technically only be the beginning of the date, but Emma got the distinct feeling that she was done for. She'd attempted to tell herself all day that she needed to be as grounded as possible tonight. That she needed to be mindful of any potential downfall, to be wary of jumping into this head-first.

"That sounds great," she murmured, trying to stay as grounded as possible. "And, honestly, it's totally fine that Alexis Levine's Q&A was postponed. I can always keep an eye out and come back here to see her. But this way, you don't have to sit through something you don't really care about just for the sake of our date."

Even though Emma would be *thrilled* to listen to one of her favorite authors – obviously – she found that was the truth. She wanted to do something *with* Regan, not something Regan was doing for her, that she wasn't getting anything from herself.

Regan's eyebrows furrowed. "What? I care. I'm disappointed, too."

"About... Alexis?" Emma asked, confused.

"Yes!" Regan insisted, staring up at Emma as if Emma was the crazy one, here. "I read her *Escape* trilogy, and I really liked it."

Surprise filtered through Emma, and she shook her head with it.

"Uh-uh, wait. You told me – months ago – that you didn't read very much."

"Right, but that was before I followed your book reviews," Regan informed her, as if the was stating something obvious. "When you gave me your account info, I read through everything, and you were *so* into her books that it made me want to read them. So, I did. And I really like them."

Blood rushed in Emma's ears, making it so all she could hear was her own heartbeat, which thudded harder in her chest. "You read her books because I liked them."

"Yeah," Regan confirmed, plainly. "Obviously."

It was so clear that she had no idea what that information meant to Emma, what it was doing to her inside. How it made her stomach flutter with this feeling that Regan had increasingly inspired in her.

"And you did it before *we* were even a possibility," Emma pushed, unable to stop herself.

Even if Regan had read Emma's favorite books in the last two days, she would have been amazed and so, so pleased. But the fact that Regan had done it before, just when they were *friends*, it – it hit home on a deeper level, and Emma couldn't place why.

"Yes," Regan stated again, staring curiously up at Emma. "I wanted to know why you liked them so much, because you wrote your reviews about them so passionately. I wanted to understand, and... I mean, it was over a month ago; I wanted to know *you*, better."

No one had ever looked at her the way Regan did, the way she was right now. Like she wanted to climb inside of Emma's mind and know every single one of her thoughts.

Emma stared back, her breath catching in her throat, and she had the strongest, neediest desire to push Regan back against the bookshelf behind them, and kiss her. Though they'd kissed twice, Emma had never been the one to initiate one, and right now – in this very public, very inappropriate moment – she wanted to so badly, she had to clench her free hand into a fist and dig her nails into her palm as a sharp reminder that this wasn't the time or place.

Blowing out a deep breath, Emma got herself under control.

Grounded, she reminded herself, even though she could already feel herself floating into Regan's orbit.

~

She fell even deeper into that orbit over dinner.

Emma stared at Regan over her Gone-with-the-Gin cocktail, unable to take her eyes away from her.

Somehow, this was her life. Somehow, she was here, on a date with Regan Gallagher, and feeling more charmed than she'd ever felt in her life.

Regan glanced up from the menu she was perusing to catch Emma's eye. Arching an eyebrow, she asked, "Why are you looking at me like that?"

"I just..." She rolled her lips. "You read my favorite books."

There was an awed note in her tone that she still couldn't get rid of. And with it, a slow smile slid over Regan's face. "I did. And it was a great choice. The only other books I've read in the last five years were ones Katherine wrote, but I actually liked that this was a different vibe."

"Different genre," Emma mused, too entertained by Regan referring to the *genre* as a vibe.

"Right," Regan agreed.

Emma took a moment to reflect, before she sighed, wistfully. "I can't believe Katherine Spencer is Sutton's mom. When I found that out, after a few weeks of knowing Sutton, I almost peed myself."

Regan nearly choked on her own drink – a Tequila Mockingbird – with spluttering laughter. "Really?"

"Yes!" Indignance worked through her as she scoffed. "I mean, *the* Katherine Spencer is one of my favorite writers! And somehow, I happened into a friendship with her daughter? I've only met her a few times in the last couple of years, but I swear – each time, I've made a total fool of myself."

Regan chuckled, dropping her chin into her hand as she stared at Emma over the table. "How so?"

"I mean, the last time I saw her was in May, the week after I moved in. You were at work, and there was a knock on the door, so I answered it. And, there she stood." Emma could remember it vividly, and her stomach still churned in embarrassment. "As is par for the freaking course for every time I've interacted with this woman, I was awe-struck. When I was *finally* able to talk like a normal person, I stared at her like a total idiot and told her that Sutton wasn't home."

Emma groaned softly at herself. "And she stared at me with, like, the sweetest smile – like I was a moron, but she didn't want me to feel badly about myself or something – and said *I know that my daughter is in Rome; I'm looking for Regan.* Like, obviously, she knew her daughter was in fucking Rome."

Regan's guffaw of laughter forced a chuckle from Emma, even as she could feel herself blush.

When she looked back at Regan, she was taken aback by the soft, sweet look she wore. "Ahh, and the she came and saw me at Topped Off; I remember."

"And I think you went out to dinner with her." Emma's detailed recollection of Regan's comings-and-goings from months ago wasn't lost on her.

"I did," Regan confirmed. "I usually do when she's in town."

"Even if Sutton isn't," Emma slowly muttered, trying to put together the picture being displayed in front of her.

Regan nodded, easily. "Oh, yeah. I mean..." She rolled her lips, that smile on her lips fading just a bit. "I wasn't very close to my own parents, growing up. Like I told you. But I latched onto Katherine like a second mom, and I think she knew that I didn't really *fit* at my house, because she treated me like her sixth kid. Family vacations, holidays, birthdays – any time I could get away from my house, I would. And my dad worked for Sutton's dad and really respected him, so, they let me go to the Spencers *a lot.* I think..." Regan rolled her lips, her eyebrows knitting together in thought.

"I think they liked it, that way. They trusted I was in good hands with Katherine and Jack, and they didn't have to deal with, so it was a win-win. At least, that's how it always felt." Regan's tone turned pensive and heavy, as she shrugged. "Anyway, I think I spent literally at least fifty percent of my adolescence sharing Sutton's bedroom."

Much like the first time Regan had shared information about her past and her family with Emma, she found herself utterly riveted. It was the same feeling she had when she was reading a great book – she hated the idea of putting it down the same way she hated the idea of Regan not sharing every little detail with her.

Also much like that time, Emma felt this unfamiliar but undeniable anger well up at the idea of Regan's parents.

She didn't quite know what to do with that, honestly. She'd never felt so – so defensive over someone else, before.

Emma didn't actually need to process it right now, though, as Regan shrugged and pushed past it. "But, yeah. Katherine usually makes a point to check in with me when she's in town. She texts or calls me every few weeks, too. And she usually does like to swing by and see the apartment," Regan gestured at Emma, recalling her interaction with Katherine. "Which makes sense, since she pays a third of the rent."

Surprised and confused, Emma reeled back. "What?"

Regan slowly tilted her head at Emma, also looking confused. "You didn't know?"

"Like... she pays a third of the rent even *now*? When Sutton's not there?" Emma pressed, trying to wrap her mind around the possibility.

She'd assumed that Sutton's parents paid her share of the rent, given what a nice apartment it was, in a good neighborhood, and Sutton certainly didn't make enough to pay half of the rent from what she took home as a teaching assistant; Emma would know. But...

"Yeah," Regan confirmed, taking a sip of her drink. "When I moved to the city – freshly into the summer as a college dropout – I went out and got into an apartment. Kind of like your last setup; I found three randos online that were looking for a fourth person to rent out a bed. It was a *total* shithole. I think someone had possibly been murdered there? Not to mention the cockroaches." She shuddered.

Emma's attention snapped right back into riveted mode, as soon as the conversation turned back to Regan. That alone told her everything she really needed to know. And, of course, Regan shuddered in disgust at the *cockroaches* rather than the murder scene.

"I'd only been there for, like, a day when Sutton came over to check it out. She was... less than impressed." Regan's lips curled into a cute smile as she laughed. "Actually, the exact thing she said was, *no*. Then she packed up the only bag I'd unpacked and took me back to her dorm room. She had a single, and was staying here over the summer," she explained, "Taking a bonus lit. course for fun, the nerd."

"Sutton got on the phone with her parents and sent them the pictures of the apartment. We worked out a deal – I would pay a third of the rent, and Sutton's parents would pay the rest. When Sutton finished undergrad, she took over a third, too. I could afford my full half, after I got my promotion. And I offered," Regan was quick to inform her, as if still wanting to make sure Emma thought the best of her, clearly still thinking about how Emma had expressed her irritation at Regan's privileged upbringing. "But Katherine said she'd prefer it if I take some time to bulk up my savings. When Sutton comes back from Rome, the lease is going to be re-evaluated."

"I always assumed you had some sort of trust fund or whatever to fall back on," Emma's voice was quiet as she tried to wrap her mind around all of the new information she was being presented with.

A sharp smile flashed over Regan's face. "Well, I *did*, technically. You weren't wrong about what you said a couple months ago; I did grow up super lucky because money wasn't an issue. And both my sister and I had trusts set up for us from our parents. But as soon as I dropped out of college, my parents were very clear that I wouldn't ever be getting a penny of it."

Emma slumped back against her chair, heavily. Yes, Regan *had* grown up with wealth and privilege, but she didn't actually have it, *now*. And, if Emma was honest with herself, that would have changed the way she'd seen Regan a lot sooner.

As soon as the thought hit her, Emma gasped and sat at attention. "I let you pay my hospital bill!"

Oh, she didn't like this feeling that curled through her and sat like a stone in her stomach, not at all.

Regan's confusion was obvious, as was her shame. "I mean, paying your hospital bill was the right thing to do, since I sent you there."

Emma was already shaking her head, though, and she reached up, rubbing at her temples. "Regardless, I only agreed to let you do it because I thought you had, like, family money at your disposal. Even with my insurance, it was over a thousand dollars!"

Still, Regan stared across from her, undeterred. "And I was happy to do it; I owed you that."

"No, you didn't. I want to pay you back."

"I won't take it," Regan immediately returned, looking affronted. "Emma, I almost killed you. Literally. Paying the hospital bill was the least I could do. And I don't want to argue about it, especially on our *date*," she insisted, a steely tone under her typically relaxed demeanor. "It's been months; the statute of limitations has run out."

Emma felt it, again. That feeling of sliding deeper and deeper into this. "You, Regan Gallagher, have a lot of character." She almost wished she'd seen it sooner, but... honestly, she probably would have fallen for Regan a lot sooner, too, and she had no idea how *that* would have gone.

The look on Regan's face was pure radiance, as she hummed happily. "Why, thank you. Now, let's pick something for dinner – afterwards, we're going to do something I'm super excited about: pick out each other's next read."

Oh, yeah. It really was all over for her.

"All I'm saying is that vanilla gets a really bad reputation!" Regan ardently insisted, as they walked into the elevator of their building several hours later.

Emma shook her head, utterly amused. "I don't have strong feelings on it either way; I'm mostly just invested because *you* are so adamant."

Regan's heartfelt defense of vanilla ice cream had started two blocks over, when they'd stopped at the gourmet ice cream shop on the way home from the bookstore. Emma had gotten a mocha chocolate chip – a choice she stood by, wholeheartedly – and after she'd ordered, Regan had stepped up and gotten... vanilla.

Emma had given her a baffled stare, because out of any flavor she could imagine anyone but especially *Regan* choosing, vanilla hadn't been on the list of possibilities.

Admittedly, Emma had gotten a little lost in her argument, as she'd watched Regan lick her vanilla ice cream for the last few blocks. She'd gotten her own in a cup, a choice she'd been making since childhood.

And she was grateful for her decision as they'd walked, because her mocha chip had melted a bit from neglect, as Emma had gotten far too easily distracted.

"It's a classic, it goes with everything," Regan stated, firmly. "And I don't like vanilla slander, that's all."

Emma hit the button for their floor, before stepping back to stand shoulder-to-shoulder with Regan. "I've never heard someone be so intent about vanilla ice cream, but if anyone was going to do it, I'm not surprised it's you."

"Thank you," Regan accepted as if Emma's simple statement had been an outright compliment.

Even as her lips ticked into a warm smile at the response, Emma took a deep, bracing breath as the doors opened to their floor and they stepped out into the hallway.

"So..." Regan started, glancing down the hall at their door. "I think date etiquette states that the date is coming to an end, as we're coming to your front door."

"Your front door, too," Emma reminded her, amused.

Regan waved her off. "Yeah, sure, but this was *my* date that I planned for *you*. As your date, I'm walking you to your apartment door for the end of the night to close out our date, and then I'll become your roommate again."

"Ah, I didn't realize that you haven't been my roommate all along."

"Easy mistake to make," Regan murmured with a quiet chuckle. A chuckle that sounded riddled with nerves, which were reflected in Regan's face as she turned to face Emma in the hallway. Her hands were locked together in front of her, Emma's work bag still slung over her shoulder as she'd insisted that she carry it home, as well. The bag also now contained the three books Regan had bought for Emma at the store, and the one Emma had picked out and bought for Regan.

"So, how was it?" Regan asked, her voice soft, as her gaze searched Emma's. "On a scale of one to ten. One being that we need to forget this ever happened and you're back to not even liking me as a friend, four being that you were disappointed with the evening and don't see us working out romantically, but you still want to be platonic roommate-friends, seven being that you had a good time but you think there's room for improvement and you see possible pitfalls in our romantic future, and ten being that you had a great time and you'd love to do this again with me, because you see that we have something real between us."

An incredulous laugh bubbled up her throat. "You know, that's *quite* a scale. I've never heard someone ask me to rank something like that, before."

Regan shrugged, anxiety and hope clearly written on her face as those dark eyes glinted up at Emma. "Well, I'm an individual. Someone that's an acquired taste, that's for sure."

Emma stared intently at Regan, the smile on her lips fading slightly. "You are," she agreed in a murmur.

Their evening played on a loop in a blur in her mind, and what stood out the most was how Regan had taken such care to think about *Emma* every step of the way.

"I haven't really been on a date in over two years," Emma found herself admitting. "Which you know, since you know I haven't been with anyone since Felicity." It didn't make her feel any less embarrassed about it in a way she typically wasn't.

But Emma hadn't felt like this – desired and wanted, like she was more than a granddaughter and a friend and someone that needed to put her head down and bust her ass to get to the next step in her life – in the time since Felicity.

"And even then... well, the final months of my relationship with Felicity hadn't been exactly romance-central." Emma rolled her lips, wondering how much she wanted to confess. Normally, she wouldn't want to say any of this to anyone.

But this was Regan, and Emma felt so utterly comfortable with her, now. Comfortable enough that she *wanted* to tell her everything about her past relationship.

"Nothing in my relationship with Felicity was romance-central, actually. And part of that was on me," she admitted, accepting her role in it with a shrug. "I was caught up in her, sure, but she was very pragmatic, and didn't think very highly of people getting caught up in anything frivolous, which included romance. She referred to it as performative, and I really bought into that."

Emma had started dating Felicity when she'd barely been twenty,

Felicity had been a few years older and more experienced, and Emma had accepted so much of what Felicity said as truth. It had been a natural leap for Emma, too, because she'd seen all of Kimberly's relationships throughout her youth crash and burn on highs of infatuation, and she'd been so soured on the idea of being all caught up in another person. She'd liked what she'd perceived as Felicity's realism.

Regan's eyes searched hers, and Emma could *see* how actively Regan listened to her. Like she soaked in every statement Emma made, and it made those butterflies Emma had been trying to catch in an internal net all night trying to keep in check start to flutter again.

"So... did you feel like tonight was performative?" Regan slowly asked, nerves riddled through her tone.

"No," Emma breathed back, and the confession felt like it really was the final nail in the coffin. The coffin that held all of Emma's carefully-held logic and judgments and confliction about the what-ifs, and everything that could go wrong, here. "I feel like you listen to me, and care about my feelings and my thoughts. I feel like you put my interests first tonight, because you wanted to, and you wanted me to have a good time. But I felt like you had a good time, too."

Regan's answering nod was quick and eager.

"I feel like... I might be doing the most illogical, craziest thing I've ever done, but I can't fight against it, anymore. I don't know how I could," she admitted with a heavy shrug. "I've *tried*. Tried ignoring my attraction to you. Tried pushing it away. Tried reasoning that I just liked to spend time with you as a friend and tried to tell myself that it was enough. But I don't think it is."

She could hear Regan's breath hitch in her throat, and Emma's pulse quickened. She'd never imagined herself being able to say things like this without an ounce of self-consciousness, and maybe if she was saying it to anyone other than Regan, it would still be the case.

Emma licked her lips, dipping her gaze to Regan's mouth.

Her throat was dry and her heart skipped a beat, and she was going to kiss Regan. *She* was going to be the one to kiss Regan this time, and there was no doubt about it.

"Maybe you are an acquired taste," she acknowledged, her voice rasping out of her throat as she stepped closer. Putting herself into Regan's personal space, another role-reversal first.

With a mix of anticipation, uncertainty, and conviction, she lifted her hands to Regan's hips. The tantalizing curve of them in Regan's tight jean shorts had been distracting her all fucking night, and she'd been so good. Keeping herself on a tight leash and making sure they made it to the end of the date.

Flexing her hands, she tugged Regan forward a few inches so their bodies brushed together. Regan tilted her head up on a trembling sigh, her hot breath washing over Emma's neck and jaw, making her shiver.

"But you *are* – surprisingly but unquestionably – my taste," she finished, ducking her head to capture Regan's lips with hers.

Regan sighed, immediately into her mouth, and she swallowed the sound, tucking it into the back of her mind to a place she didn't think she'd ever forget.

She felt Regan's hands slide up her arms, her touch warm through Emma's long-sleeved shirt, and it was the only time all night that she wished she'd been able to change out of her work clothes before the date. Because if she'd work a short-sleeved shirt, she'd be able to feel Regan's touch on her bare skin, and she craved it. She wanted that touch so, so badly.

Groaning softly in the back of her throat, she slowly slid her tongue along Regan's. Tasting her and that fucking vanilla ice cream she'd just had.

"You're right," she muttered, not breaking their kiss, just speaking into Regan's mouth. "Vanilla goes with everything."

Now that she'd laid everything on the line, that she'd confessed the full extent of her feelings, that she'd stopped denying herself – denying either of them – of this, she felt ravenous for more.

She hadn't been with someone else in so long, hadn't been touched or been able to touch for *years*, and this intense neediness for Regan, specifically, far outweighed anything she'd ever experienced. It made everything feel so much *more*, and she gripped Regan's hips tightly, guiding them a few steps until Regan's back hit the wall.

Regan moaned – one of those low, throaty sounds that Emma had been convinced belonged to someone else the other night – and the vibration of it against Emma's lips was intoxicating. The sound went right to Emma's clit, making her pulse with need.

She felt Regan's hand claw into her hair, taking a tight fistful of it, and the bite – not too hard, but enough that Emma could *feel* her – only added to her arousal.

"It's why I got it," Regan's voice was so hoarse, so quiet, it barely registered over the way Emma's pulse pounded in her ears. "The vanilla. Mocha chip – anything coffee-flavored – is my favorite, too, but when you ordered it, I thought, *mm*," Regan sighed out a delicious groan, before she flicked out her tongue to slide over Emma's lips.

The sensation of it made Emma's knees quake, and she had to slap one of her hands onto the wall next to Regan's head to ensure she remained standing.

"I thought that I should get vanilla, because I knew they'd taste so good together, if this happened," Regan finished, before she used the hand in Emma's hair to pull Emma back in, decimating the scant centimeters she'd put between them.

God, Emma was vibrating with how strong this molten desire filled her veins. She slid her hand down slowly, relishing in the feeling of Regan's leanly muscled thigh under her fingers. Oxygen escaped her completely as her fingertips reached Regan's bare skin at the bottom of her cutoffs.

Regan keened, gripping Emma's shoulder so hard as she rolled her hips into Emma's.

Swearing into Regan's mouth, she rolled her hips back, harder, pinning Regan against the wall.

"Emma," Regan panted against her mouth, her lips brushing tantalizingly over Emma's, and something about it – about the way Regan's mouth felt on hers was so... so... insanity-inducing.

She'd thought about this mouth *so much* over the last few years. Back when she'd first had that fantasy crush on Regan, before she'd even known her. Even throughout their tumultuous relationship, when Emma hadn't let herself like Regan, she'd gotten so distracted by these full lips. The last several weeks – especially since she'd felt them on her own – had been torture.

And she didn't know how much self-control she could hold onto right now, she really didn't.

That fact made Emma feel crazy, mindless with this desire. Now that there was nothing holding her back, now that the final vestiges of Emma's hesitation were depleted, she just *wanted*.

It was that thought that had her breaking the kiss.

She gripped Regan's thigh tightly, stroking her thigh over the soft skin there even as she drew back a few inches, forcing herself to put some distance between them.

"I don't want to... to rush into anything," she managed out a whisper, through her panting breaths. "But it was a twelve," she breathed against Regan, tilting her head down and pressing their foreheads together. It took everything inside of her *not* to kiss Regan again, but she craved this closeness so deeply.

The hand Regan had gripped her hair with gentled and released, as she sifted her fingers through Emma's hair, and Emma could feel her hand shaking slightly. "Huh?" She hummed.

With every ounce of strength Emma possessed, she took a deep breath and lifted her head away. Regan's cheeks were flushed, her lips so pink and swollen, and she still had her eyes closed. Emma's heart skipped a beat, entirely unrelated to this raging heat inside of her, and all to do with how stupidly beautiful Regan was.

"On your scale," Emma murmured, finally feeling steady enough on her feet to take her hand off of the wall so she could stroke Regan's hair behind her ear. These dark waves she'd looked at but never touched were so, so soft under her fingertips. "The date was a twelve."

Regan blinked her eyes open, and... yeah. There were those tawny flecks around her irises in eyes so dark they were nearly black with desire. "Wow. I outdid myself so well, I didn't even know it was possible," she joked, quietly.

Emma nodded, entirely seriously. "Not surprising."

Regan took a deep, steadying breath and tilted her head back against the wall. "I know I need to walk you to the door and finish our date, but I also really don't want to. Because I totally respect that you don't want to rush into anything, but I don't want it to be over."

Emma very much understood the sentiment. "Unfortunately, Mrs.

Clemmons is probably going to peek out into the hallway to snap at loiterers any minute now."

The laugh that Regan let out was loud and full-bodied, and – in a feeling Emma had become increasingly familiar with – made her feel proud for causing it. "You're right."

Even though Emma knew it needed to happen, Regan sliding her hands away from Emma and dropping them heavily to her sides made her feel absurdly cold. Reluctantly, she removed her hands from Regan, as well, even though she knew that she'd still feel the phantom sensation of Regan's thigh under her hand for the rest of the night.

They slowly meandered the rest of the way to their door, lingering outside as Emma took her keys out of her pocket. "So, uh, I'd invite you inside," she started, clearing her throat as she sent Regan a conspiratorial smile. "But I have a roommate who recently told me that if I brought home a prospective new partner, she'd rip their hair out. You have really beautiful hair, though, and I'd hate to see anything happen to it."

Regan smiled, entirely unashamed. "I appreciate it. She sounds a little unhinged, though; you should be careful."

Emma shrugged. "Ehhh, you know, I've really come around to her."

twenty-three

REGAN WAS STILL VIBRATING with energy an hour later, as she lay on her back in bed.

Yes, it was nearing midnight. Yes, she'd had an extremely busy day; she'd worked an early morning shift, then had to cover half of Liz's shift she'd called out from, before coming home to prepare for her date. Then, had gone on the best fucking date of her entire life.

She couldn't believe it had gone so well, especially when she'd been a total idiot and hadn't double-checked the details for Alexis Levine's Q&A.

But... it *had*.

Regan was an acquired taste, but she was Emma's taste. And fuck, if that didn't both make Regan's heart skip a beat with sheer delight at the same time that it made her throb between her legs. What a feeling.

And then the kiss.

God, Regan had never been kissed like that, before. Like Emma had wanted to devour her whole, and Regan had felt the very same.

She totally understood and respected Emma's comment about not wanting to rush things, which was why she'd ended the date at their front door. She'd very deliberately not made any direct contact with Emma once they crossed the threshold into their apartment.

Because Regan had never in her life desired someone the way she did Emma, and right now, that desire felt like it was alive. Like a living, breathing need that had its own drive inside of her.

She knew without a single doubt that if she so much as accidentally brushed against Emma as they'd walked into their apartment after the official end of their date, that the tenuous hold she had on her self-control would snap.

Emma seemed to have felt the same, as she'd taken a deep breath and wished Regan a good night, and said, "It's probably... wise, if we go our separate ways for the evening."

"Probably," Regan had, unfortunately, agreed.

Admittedly, it was after ten o'clock and it *was* a worknight for Emma, so it made sense.

Emma telling Regan, after awkwardly shifting from foot to foot, that she was going to hop in the shower before bed was *not* helping Regan's state of affairs.

She'd resolutely made herself stay in her bedroom to avoid any temptation after that. Because she'd seen Emma topless multiple times, now, and if it drove Regan to the brink of wanting distraction *before*, she could only imagine what it would do to her, now.

And now, she very definitively knew that she was hungry to see more. Yes, Emma wore very sexy lingerie that showcased her ample chest, and Regan appreciated that. Very much. But she was desperate to see more. To see all of Emma.

And that desperation was what kept Regan awake right now.

She'd hoped that the fever born from their hallway make-out would fade, but it wasn't. At all.

Laying on her back on top of her comforter, stripped down to the comfy shorts and old t-shirt she planned to sleep in, Regan's eyes were wide open, staring up at her ceiling. She kept her hands tightly inter-locked over her lower stomach.

"You will not touch yourself," she sternly said, for the fifth time.

Honestly, Regan had *no* idea how else she was going to be able to relax enough to fall asleep if she didn't get any sort of relief. Her clit was pulsing and she was so wet, she could feel it, and if this were *any* other situation, Regan would have already had her vibrator out and made herself come at least once.

She supposed this was all wrapped up in the quandary Emma had about them going out in the first place. Fine, so Emma likely wasn't thinking about the sexual dynamics post-date, but Regan didn't know what was appropriate here.

Was it disrespectful or inappropriate or whatever, to work herself into a toe-curling orgasm with Emma, who was just across the hall, as the star of her sexual thoughts?

Sure, yes, Emma had been starring in Regan's fantasies for weeks now, but... it was *different*. Those were all just – literal fantasy. It was like reading a spicy story or something. It didn't feel like the same thing to think about Emma while touching herself after going on a literal date together, while Emma was, like, ten feet away.

Plus, after Monday, Regan was trying to be a bit more... conscientious.

"Conscientiousness sucks," she whined to herself, clenching her thighs tightly together, and then *immediately* regretting it.

The pressure gave her zero relief and – in fact – made the throbbing between her legs feel even more pronounced. She hadn't even known that was possible!

She swore she could still *feel* Emma's fingers on her bare thigh. Regan knew her shorts were the definition of short-shorts, and Emma's searing touch had made a home just under the hem. Inches away from where she was so desperately needing to be touched, to be filled.

No, she'd never do something like beg Emma to have fucked her in the hallway outside of their apartment – Emma would never go for it – but if Regan closed her eyes and let her mind drift the tiniest bit... there it was. The vision playing out as if that had happened.

Regan rolling her hips desperately against Emma's thick, perfect thigh and Emma pushing back into her, just as she'd done tonight. Only, it didn't end there, in her mind's eye. It –

Regan's eyes snapped open as she *swore* she heard... something.

The apartment had been so quiet, you could hear a pin drop for twenty minutes, since she'd heard Emma go into her room for the night. Regan had been tempted to put on music or a movie; anything to help drown out her thoughts. She *hadn't*, because she apparently loved pain, and didn't totally want to get rid of these thoughts.

She felt like a fucking bloodhound that had picked up a scent on a trail, holding her breath and tensing every muscle as she waited to see if she'd hear the sound again.

There! There it was again!

The faintest... moan? Was that a fucking *moan*?

Regan had – unfortunately – been the unwilling audio-spectator of the neighbor to her left having relations, and that quiet, almost imperceptible sound was not what it sounded like.

Her heart started to pound in her chest at the reality she was being presented with.

Those quiet sounds *had* to be coming from Emma's room. From *Emma*.

"God. Oh, god. Fuck," she swore, the heat she'd barely been able to slow to a simmer inside of her turning back to a boil in about two seconds.

Was Emma over there... ten feet away... touching herself, thinking about Regan?

Unable to help herself, she hastily grabbed at her phone where it rested on the bedside table. Her hands shook as she texted.

REGAN – 11:57PM

Are you awake???

She didn't breathe, didn't inhale or exhale a single fucking time, as she waited...

Emma looked at her message within seconds, but didn't answer for almost a minute.

EMMA – 11:58PM

Yes

Yes? That was all Emma was going to say to her right now?!

Deliberately crossing her legs tightly, giving into her need, Regan texted back.

And... what are you doing??

Swallowing thickly, she watched as those three little telling bubbles appeared, then disappeared, then appeared again. Disappeared. Appeared...

"Jesus christ," she moaned softly, because that hesitation in Emma's answer was all the confirmation Regan needed.

She knew Emma, now. Knew her very well. If Emma had been doing something innocent over in her room like reading a book or something, she would have simply said it.

Regan wasted no time, not a single second.

She rolled onto her stomach, sliding her hand down to wedge it under herself. Pressing her hand tightly between her body and the bed, angling her hips up so she could – "*Yesss,*" she breathed out, as she slid her fingers down into her shorts, brushing over her clit.

She used the lightest of touches, because she knew she'd come so, so quickly. Her very active mind had been operating film reels for an hour, working on the heady sensations that had flooded her system since that kiss.

When her phone vibrated in her hand and signaled a text, she whipped her head up in shock. She hadn't actually expected Emma to answer!

EMMA – 12:00AM

I'm not doing anything that I'm not allowed to do to and with myself, in my own apartment, in my own room, after a very intense kiss with a very attractive woman

Regan's breathing labored already, as she dropped her head into her pillow, and rolled her hips down into her hand. God. *God!*

She'd known Emma had been touching herself – probably – but the confirmation... it made Regan's clit pulse against the very light touch from Regan's fingertips.

What are you thinking about?

Texting with her non-dominant hand while balancing her phone against her mattress wasn't Regan's best skill, but she wasn't going to miss this opportunity for the fucking world.

Arching her hips up, she slid her hand further down, avoiding touching her clit directly. She was so, so sensitive and she couldn't let this be over so soon. A breathless cry caught in her throat as she pressed her fingertips against her opening, working her hips down against herself.

EMMA – 12:02AM

Obviously, I'm thinking about that woman

REGAN – 12:03AM

Me. You're thinking about me. Say it

Please

She dug her teeth into her bottom lip, sharply, waiting for an answer. Trying desperately to hold herself back from actually fucking herself – fingers deep inside, rubbing her clit, working to that orgasm that she knew would be within reach in mere moments – until she knew.

EMMA – 12:03AM

I'm thinking about you

Regan released her breath, and with it, an aching moan from the back of her throat. She hadn't even known, really, that the moan would escape, but without holding herself back... well, she couldn't say she was surprised. Nor could she say she cared.

They were *doing this*.

Without needing to restrain herself anymore, Regan slid two of her fingers further inside, feeling the slight stretch, and she groaned with it. The same kind of sounds she let out on Monday night, when she hadn't thought Emma was home.

EMMA – 12:04AM

What are YOU doing over there???

Already feeling herself start to pant, her hips canting down against her hand to ride her fingers, Regan attempted to type back. Only for her phone to fumble and fall face-down against her mattress, and, "Fuck it."

She flipped her phone over and hit the call icon, relieved that she didn't have to worry about maintaining enough sanity to text, anymore.

She knew she wasn't going to have the wherewithal to continue that soon, anyway.

It rang three times – far too many times, really, when Regan knew for a fact Emma was holding her phone in her hand – before Emma answered, "Why are you calling me?"

Emma's own breathing was labored, though it sounded like she was trying to get it under control for reasons Regan couldn't understand. Not when she was on the brink of completely giving herself into the flames dancing inside of her.

"Because – *ah,*" her breath hitched, and she whimpered as her fingers brushed against one of the sensitive places inside of her. Her entire body shuddered with it, and she could hear how broken her own words were, as she pushed them out. "Because you don't moan as loudly as I do, and I want to hear you."

There was a beat of silence and Regan wondered if she'd gone too far. Was the call pushing things? Emma had said she didn't want to rush –

Emma let out a deep, rasping groan. "Fuck, Regan. I – you're *killing* me."

"You started it," she shot back, pressing her hot cheek against her sheet as she rolled her hips down even harder, really starting to fuck herself, now. "I was being good tonight; I wasn't doing this. But then I could hear you, and I only have so much self-control."

She could hear Emma's breath hitch. "I didn't mean for you to hear me; that's never happened before. I just – I couldn't sleep," she admitted in a whisper.

"Me, neither," Regan eagerly offered, shamelessly. "All I could think about was you."

"I'm... I've never done this on the phone," Emma admitted, her voice sounding so deliciously guttural. "I've barely done it in text, but at least then I can think clearly about what I'm going to say."

"Don't think," Regan urged, feeling mindless herself. She slid her fingers as deep inside as she could, then held them there and grinded her hips down.

The sound that tore itself from her throat almost hurt, but it felt so... fucking... *good*.

"Fuck," Emma's answering moan only intensified this spiraling heat inside of her.

"If this is too much or too quick, then hang up. I won't be offended," Regan grit out, before she had to cut herself off for several long moments. She stilled her hips, swallowing thickly to try to maintain any possibility of a clear thought for Emma's boundaries. "I don't want to push you. I just – I want you, so badly. I've wanted you since that night in the bookstore. Maybe – probably – before. Every time I've touched myself since then, I've thought about you. About your body. About what you'd feel like on top of me. About how you'd taste. I've never tasted another woman, but–"

"*Regan*," Emma's voice was hoarse and reedy. "I – you..."

"Yeah, *me*. Even when I've tried not to think about you, you've kept popping up in my thoughts every time I touch myself. I can't help it, Emma. It's like a dirty obsession, and I can't stop," she confessed, wanting to confess even more.

Wanting to confess the detailed thoughts she'd gotten off to for weeks. Wanting to hear how Emma would respond to it, wanting to know how feasible they were.

"Hang up." She turned her head and pushed her entire face into her mattress, *hard*. Clenching her teeth as she tried to keep her hand and her hips as still as possible, even as she was shaking from the effort of holding back. "I'm seriously begging you, if this is a boundary for you, you have to hang up. Because I can't."

"I can't hang up, either," Emma admitted, her tone was so gravelly, it made Regan's eyes squeeze closed. Like, if she kept her eyes closed and heard Emma's voice sound like that right next to her ear, she could pretend Emma was here in her bed, instead of across the hallway. "I can't believe I'm doing this with you, but I don't want to stop. I was–"

Emma cut herself off on a hissed out breath, and Regan couldn't stop herself from slowly starting a new rhythm. Rolling her hips down against her hand, so slowly. Trying to make this last as long as she possibly could.

"You were what?" There was a tone in her own voice she'd never heard. Something that was a cross between demanding and begging, and that was exactly what she felt right now, when it came to Emma. She wanted to demand Emma tell her everything, to lay herself as open for Regan as Regan would do for her, and she also had no problem begging for it.

"I was so close, when you texted me. I didn't – *mm*, I didn't realize you could hear me. I'm... god," Emma broke off on a series of panting breaths. "I'm not usually a loud person; I don't usually make a lot of noise during... and I didn't think – I – I didn't *think*."

Regan whined, nodding wordlessly as she worked a third finger inside of herself, needing *more*. The fact that Emma wasn't vocal during sex, but she was tonight while thinking about Regan... yeah, that only served to drive Regan even closer to the imminent, orgasmic edge. She throbbed, clenching so tightly around her own fingers.

"I've never felt like this," Emma confessed, a whimper escaping her before she bit it off.

"What are you thinking about?" Regan breathlessly demanded. She just – she needed to know. She needed *desperately* to know.

"I'm thinking about your mouth on me. I – Regan, I think about your mouth all of the time; you have no idea." Emma's breathing was so ragged, and Regan knew Emma was so far gone. Because she couldn't imagine Emma ever saying that to her if she had all of her wits about her, and Regan's entire body felt like it was on fire from the inside out.

She licked her lips as if she could taste Emma on them, now, and they tingled. "I'd love that," she breathed back, groaning with it. "I love the idea of your thighs around my head, being able to slide my hands up them, gripping and touching *everywhere* that I want, and–"

Emma's breath caught in her throat, a ragged, high-pitched gasp ringing in Regan's ear. Followed by the quietest, trembling whimpers, and... Emma just came.

Emma came, for *her*. Emma came, thinking about Regan's mouth, listening to Regan talk, and – and...

Regan squeezed her eyes tightly closed, sliding her dripping wet fingers from deep inside of herself to rub desperately at her clit. She couldn't wait anymore. Physically, literally, she *could not wait*. If she denied herself this orgasm for any longer, she felt like she would die from it.

"I'm on my stomach," she hurriedly told Emma, wondering if her words were even coherent between the other cries she knew she was emitting. "Normally – fu-fuck – normally, I'd use a vibrator, but... but I didn't want to. I wanted to be able to imagine you were on top of me, and that it was y-your hand–"

She couldn't manage the rest of her sentence; she had no idea what else she'd been going to say. How was she supposed to know, when she couldn't think of anything, anymore? She could only think of the orgasm that rolled over her in waves, how her toes curled so tightly, and how best to rub her clit so she could draw out every last bit of pleasure.

In her head, that was exactly what she thought of, as she worked the orgasm from her body. She imagined Emma's voice not on the phone, but live. In her ear, her warm breath on Regan's cheek. She imagined it wasn't her fingers working over her aching clit, but Emma's.

Finally, when she had nothing left to give, Regan groaned – long and low – and fell, limply, to her bed. Completely wrung out, she collapsed, trying to catch her breath.

When she finally could, she lifted her hips up a few inches and whimpered as she slid her hand out from her shorts, before dropping her arm onto her bed.

She swallowed, wishing she'd had the foresight to get herself a glass of water. Then again, how could she have known this was going to happen?!

Blinking her eyes open, she glanced at her phone to see if their call was still connected.

And that hazy, post-orgasm pleasure dissipated immediately when she saw that the screen was black.

The liquid feeling that had made Regan's limbs feel pleasantly heavy and tired dissipated, replaced with a self-conscious gnawing concern. Quickly, she reached up and tapped at her screen, hoping that her phone was just being weird or something.

But... no.

The call was disconnected. That kind of – no, it *really* – hurt, and Regan's throat felt strangely tight. What had she done wrong? What –

The quiet knock on her door had her quickly pushing herself up, staring for several beats at it. Obviously, it was Emma, but Regan was feeling, uncharacteristically, unsure of herself right about now.

"I'm really close to just opening the door," Emma's voice was slightly muffled from. "But I don't know if you're wearing clothes or not, and I think – for sanity's sake – that clothing should be on, right now. Since we, obviously, don't have great self-control."

Still confused, but slightly less tangled up in knots, Regan glanced down at herself as if needing to double-check before she answered, "I'm wearing clothing."

Her door opened, then, and Emma stood in the doorway. She had a glass of water in her hand, and she had those stupidly sexy glasses on her face, as she hesitated after taking a single step.

"I, um, thought you might want this," she murmured, holding up the water. "Based on Monday... and the cries and moans you just let out, now."

If Regan were a betting woman, she'd bet her life that Emma's cheeks were blushing. She couldn't really tell, given that the only light filtering in came from the moonlight filtering in from her window, and the nightlight in the hallway behind Emma.

"You hung up the phone." She'd meant to sound either joking or accusatory – unsure which – but mostly, she could hear her own insecurity filter through.

Emma shifted from foot to foot, coughing slightly, before she answered, "I listened, first. To every single sound you made." There was that breathy pitch in her tone, again. Something that, along with her words, soothed Regan's worries. "I only hung up when your breathing started to even out, and I–"

Regan could see the way Emma bit her lip, and she tilted her head in curiosity. "You...?" She prompted.

"I just... I've never had sex with someone and not been *with* them," Emma admitted, sounding embarrassed. "It felt really impersonal, and weird, and wrong to not be with you, after. So, I just thought that I'd get you some water and come in here to see you. Which, ah, now that I'm doing it and seeing the way you're staring at me, I'm wondering if maybe I shouldn't have?"

Any of those cold, ugly feelings that had started to worm their way in were completely washed away, and Regan quickly shook her head. "You absolutely should have. Come in," she urged, waving Emma over to her. "Please."

She could hardly stop herself from bouncing on the mattress, feeling herself completely come alive all over again in Emma's physical presence. Especially as Emma walked, tentatively, closer.

She reached out for the water as soon as Emma was close enough, very deliberately sliding her fingers over Emma's, and relishing that feeling that buzzed through her at the connection.

As she brought the glass to her lips, she stared up at Emma in her dark room, and she could see how unsure Emma was, right now. She'd been able to hear it, when Emma had explained herself. And something about that made Regan feel so... endeared. Like she wanted to pull Emma down against her and hold her closely.

Because Emma was always such a commanding presence. Like she never doubted herself or how she felt or how she approached the world. But right now, in the middle of the night in Regan's room, after they'd essentially come as close to having sex with one another as they could without actually touching each other, she seemed off-kilter.

And because she knew Emma, she reached out with her other hand and grasped Emma's before she could walk away and gruffly excuse herself back to her own room.

"Do you want to sleep with me?" She asked as soon as she finished drinking her water. "Just sleep. I swear. No funny business... mostly because I'm all funny-businessed out," she added with a teasing smile.

She could both see and feel Emma's hesitation, even as she squeezed Regan's hand.

"I really liked sleeping with you the other night," Regan confessed in a whisper, and it was the utter truth. "I'd love to do it in my bed instead of on the couch." Internally, she forced herself to pump on the brakes. "But I get if you don't want to. We did go a little further than either of us had anticipated, already, tonight."

Still, though, Regan caught and held her breath. Wanting with every fiber of her being for Emma to take her up on her offer.

She'd never slept with another person in her bed. Never. Whenever she'd been sleeping with guys or dating, she'd stayed at their place, respecting this apartment as her and Sutton's sanctuary. But her entire body tingled with eager anticipation at the idea of sharing her bed with Emma. Especially after what they'd just done.

"Yeah. I'd like that," Emma agreed, her voice so, so soft.

Thrilled, Regan quickly placed her glass on her bedside table – so quickly, it rocked back and forth and nearly fell over – before she lifted herself up to scramble under the blanket, and then held the blanket up for Emma to scoot in.

Which, she did.

She sat, and then slowly reclined against one of Regan's pillows – the one Regan had pushed her face into a few minutes ago, actually, and *that* was a whole other rush for her.

Even as Emma laid back, Regan stayed sitting up for another minute, looking down at her.

"You're in my bed," she whispered, excitedly.

"I really liked sleeping with you the other night, too," Emma murmured, rolling her lips after, as she looked up at Regan. Slowly, she arched an eyebrow at her, and with it, she started to look far more like her typical self. "Are you going to lay down, or just keep looking at me like that?"

Regan shrugged, even as she shifted to snuggle down into her bed. "I just want to memorize it. You. Here."

She scooched in close to Emma, pressing their legs together. Emma was wearing shorts, too, and Regan shivered at the sensation of their skin-on-skin contact. She didn't stop, though, until she was pressed right into Emma's side, and she paused before she draped her arm over Emma's waist.

"Is this okay? It's how we woke up the other day, but–"

Emma's intent stare remained locked on Regan's face as she slowly nodded. "Yeah. I... I really like the way you feel, like this."

Oh, god. That hoarse tone to her voice had nothing to do with sex or lust, now, and everything to do with a shy confession, Regan could tell. And it made her heart skip a beat.

"Me, too," she reassured, needing Emma to know she was far from being alone in that.

She rested her head on Emma's shoulder, settling down snugly against her, before she took a deep breath and filled her lungs with *Emma*. She melted into it, feeling that post-orgasm exhaustion start to filter back.

"What we just did, for the record, was super hot," she whispered against the thin, soft fabric of Emma's shirt. "I have no regrets, and I hope you don't, either."

She felt a shiver run up her spine as Emma pressed her hand to the small of her back, sliding ever-so-cautiously under Regan's tank top. "I don't, and I agree."

Completely satisfied – physically and emotionally – Regan felt a smile tug at her lips as she closed her eyes. "For the record, I love your glasses. 10/10 think you should wear them more."

She could hear Emma set the aforementioned glasses on her night-stand, and Regan loved that she felt more than heard the soft, sleepy chuckle Emma breathed out. "I'll take that under advisement."

"Good, thank you." She sighed, that sleepiness she'd been begging for earlier finally hitting her like a ton of bricks. "Sweet dreams, Emma."

"Sweet dreams back."

twenty-four

EMMA WAS DEFINITELY NOT BABYSITTING her sisters the night after her date with Regan because she was nervous to be alone with Regan in their apartment.

Only, maybe she was. A little bit.

Granted, she was also doing it to help out her gram, which made her feel a lot better and a whole lot less crazy about the whole thing.

When she'd been winding down at work earlier, her grandmother had reached out to her. She'd informed Emma that there was an emergency at the women's shelter Kimberly ran, and that Kimberly was going to need to be on-site to manage it. Ted was out of town for work, and Kimberly had asked – apologetically, her gram was sure to tell her – if Gram could watch the girls this evening. Apparently, Kimberly had sounded very stressed, and she'd assured that she would manage to get Eva and Everly to Astoria "somehow" before getting to the shelter, so that Gram wouldn't need to figure out transport to New Jersey.

Gram, being Gram, had agreed to watch her grandchildren – coming as no surprise.

But she'd tentatively asked Emma if Emma would mind "being on-call" tonight, because, "*It makes me a little ashamed to admit it, Em, but you know it's been a long time since I've been in charge of watching any kiddos on my own. But I remember how tiring it was, even before my... health issues."*

Emma had frowned, disliking the idea of her gram possibly being run-down – especially as it had been less than a week since her heat exhaustion at the birthday party.

Her discomfort at that had warred with her discomfort at the offer to babysit, herself. Because she barely knew Eva and Everly, and in the limited time she'd spent with them, Emma hadn't figured out the magic trick to feeling some sort of sisterly bond.

Then, though, then... Emma thought about what her night might potentially look like, at home.

No, she didn't have any plans tonight. But neither did Regan. In fact, according to the calendar on the fridge, Regan was off from work by two in the afternoon and had tomorrow off.

So, ostensibly, the evening would just be the two of them.

Alone.

In their apartment, together.

She'd had no intention of taking things so far last night – after literally only *one* date! A date she was still trying to wrap her mind around – and they hadn't even gotten back to their apartment until almost eleven PM! She was very, very uncertain about what situation they'd find themselves in if they spent the entire night in closed quarters together, especially now that this chemistry between them had burst to life in screaming color.

Emma had put herself in a real pickle by volunteering to go to New Jersey and watch her sisters, though, because she'd immediately known she'd need Regan to join her.

No way in hell could she do it alone, without her. She didn't even want to try. That, alone, had been a jarring realization.

And, of course, Regan had gamely jumped on board.

Which was how Emma found herself sitting next to Regan on the couch in Kimberly's house, as they neared the end of The Game of Life with Eva and Everly. Everly had been the one to announce – as soon as they'd walked in – that it was board game night, and Emma had learned in the last two hours that board game night literally meant a night full of board games.

"Aha! Got another kiddo to put in the back of my car." Regan hummed in excitement, as she added a little pink "person" into her plastic van. "What do you want to name this one?" She asked Emma, fluttering her eyelashes, as she leaned into her.

Emma rolled her eyes, pushing back into Regan. It didn't push her away and, instead, it left them leaning heavily into one another, and she felt the entire side of her body tingle pleasantly with the connection.

She didn't know what to make of it, what to make of Regan. What to make of these feelings. What to make of... this. She certainly didn't think that she'd be figuring it out here, under the watchful eyes of her little sisters, in her mother's house, though.

"I want to know why you're so excited about adding kids to your van when you're, like, two turns away from retirement," Emma countered, gesturing to where Regan was on the board.

"Some grandparents raise kids," Eva muttered from where she sat on the opposite side of the coffee table. "I figured you would know that."

Emma pursed her lips as she narrowed her eyes at her sister. It was far from the first comment she'd made like that since Emma had arrived a couple of hours ago, and it was getting more difficult to ignore them.

"My turn!" Everly announced excitedly, pushing herself up to spin the dial.

Emma nodded encouragingly at her youngest sister as she counted out the spaces to move, and Everly beamed back at her, proudly.

Okay, so managing Everly was a lot easier than Eva. Emma could really appreciate that tonight.

She reached out and spun the wheel for her own turn, before landing on a space and receiving a "life event" card to read aloud.

"Your newest book release was a success," she read from the card. "Collect fifty-thousand dollars."

"I always knew you could do it," Regan's voice was jovial and light and teasing, but she squeezed her hand where it sat on Emma's thigh, and that sensation was very, very real.

Every brush against Regan's body made Emma think, without fail, about last night. About the sounds Regan had made while she'd orgasmed, about how she'd described – without an ounce of shame – what she'd been thinking about. What she'd wanted to do to and with Emma.

"Yeah, you get everything. Yay," Eva's voice cut in, scoffing with such gusto in a way only a preteen could.

Eva's comments *had* served a purpose, Emma supposed. Before she could get too caught up in any inappropriate thoughts about Regan, before any actual heat could take hold, her sister's acerbic statements cut straight to the quick.

So, that was good. That was exactly why she was here.

Only... being here also meant she was facing this ire from Eva all night. Truly, a double-edged sword.

"Ooookay," Regan muttered under her breath, shooting a glance at Emma as she darted her eyes toward Eva in silent acknowledgement. "I'm going to cut the brownies we cooked earlier. Does anyone need anything?"

Everly popped up in excitement. "I want to help! Can I help?"

Regan laughed, using the hand she had on Emma's thigh to push herself up.

Even *that*, the pressure from that innocuous touch, made Emma shiver and reaffirm that she had very much done the right thing by coming here tonight. By giving them a little... distraction.

"All right, kiddo, then let's hit it. But to be clear, I'm the one holding the knife," Regan commented.

"I never get to use a knife," Everly mumbled, sighing heavily, as she led the way out of the room.

"We all have our battles," Regan's sympathetic response came, making Emma grin as she stared after them.

"Ugh," Eva's quiet, disdainful sound grabbed Emma's attention.

Again – it was a *good thing*, cutting through this insane attraction and infatuation with Regan that seemed to be multiplying by the minute, now that Emma had allowed it out of the cage she'd kept it locked in.

But, still, she couldn't help the narrow-eyed look she shot at her sister. "What?"

Eva stared back at her, unwavering. "That *look* on your face. It's so sappy and...." She rolled her eyes, before muttering, "Whatever."

Emma rolled her lips, and told herself that it was fine. Eva could say whatever little comments she wanted to say; she was twelve. Emma wasn't going to confront a child.

And yet... all of these looks and the remarks – that she'd been on the receiving end of *all summer* – hit on something, inside of Emma. They bothered her. They *mattered* to her, in a way she hadn't anticipated.

With that in mind, she braced herself and asked, "Look, Eva, can you just tell me, if I've done something to you? There's clearly something going on, here, and–"

"I just don't like you. That's all," Eva cut her off, throwing Emma a pouty look.

Taken aback, Emma felt the remainder of whatever she'd been going to say completely disappear. She hadn't known a comment like that would cut so deep, either, but she felt the sharpness of it inside of her. "Ah... okay."

For a few awkward moments of silence, she wondered if she should just accept that. Eva was her own person; she had the right to feel however she felt.

Maybe, a couple of months ago, she would have left if alone.

But not now.

Because now, Emma felt the niggling need to push for more. It was a very different phenomenon for her, but she went with it.

"Can I ask why? What have I done to you?"

Because Emma was at a total loss. She wracked her brain, trying to think of anything she could have possibly–

"Nothing," Eva spit back, heatedly. "You haven't done *anything*. You've never done anything to want to be a part of our family, and Mom *still* acts like you're the center of the stupid universe."

Shocked by the honesty, vitriol, and the words themselves, Emma could only stare across the table.

It seemed like all Eva had been waiting for was Emma to give her an opening. "You never came to visit us in Miami. You never came to any birthday parties or Christmases or *anything*. I looked in Mom's Emma

Box, and she invited you to everything we ever did! And you never came."

"Her Emma Box?" She repeated, still trying to make some sense of this.

"Yeah. The box of everything about *you* that she keeps in her closet. And it includes little notes about every party and holiday and stuff that she's invited you to, and why you said you couldn't come," Eva explained, glowering at Emma. "We moved here so she could be close to you, and you still didn't even come over for *months*! You don't even care about our mom, and she still loves you the most!"

"That's not true," Emma immediately rejected the idea, reeling back as she shook her head. "She loves you and Everly more than anything; you have to know that."

Eva's bottom lip stuck out in a haughty pout as she sniffed angrily and angled her jaw up, and, *wow*.

Emma's stomach twisted with a feeling she didn't quite understand or recognize, but – this girl was her sister. That stubborn set of her jaw and the way her blue eyes glinted up at Emma with that attitude... Emma saw herself, there. She saw herself so clearly, it was startling.

"Fine," Eva snapped. "She loves us. But – but did you know that we only have our names because of you? *Eva* and *Everly*. She told my dad that she wanted to have something that tied all of her kids together, and she'd already used her favorite name on you. So, she picked E names for us, too. Did you know that?" She insisted, clearly not intending for the question to be rhetorical.

Emma blinked back, her stomach twisting in knots with the information. "I didn't," she admitted, quietly.

"And it's not even just Mom!" Eva hit the palm of her hand against the table, clearly worked up. "Gram also thinks you're perfect. She's *my* gram, too, but she loves you the most. And you don't – you don't even *care*."

Eva crossed her arms so tightly over herself, and Emma could tell she was holding herself together even as all of these clearly deep-seated feelings unraveled.

Emma had never once really seen herself reflected in her sisters in anything beyond the occasional physical resemblance, but she did right now. The pent-up frustration, the uncertain emotions flashing over Eva's face. The certainty that she knew everything.

Emma really felt that resonating inside of her. Spiraling through her veins, as she stared in awe across the table. This girl – this stubborn, grumpy twelve-year-old girl – was her *sister*. She was a part of her, in a ways Emma hadn't ever known they'd shared.

"I do care." Emma's voice was soft, and she'd never felt connected to Eva before in any way, but right now, she did.

Sitting here, with a board game about fake lives between them, she understood her little sister.

She didn't agree with her, but... life really *was* all a matter of perspective. And Emma didn't know if that had ever been more apparent to her than right now.

Other than, maybe, with Regan.

"I do care about you, and Everly. And our mom. And I care – a lot – about what Gram thinks about me." Emma reached up, scrubbing her hand over her face, as she tried to work through everything in her mind. As she tried to figure out how to sort out the complicated feelings inside of her. As she tried to figure out what made sense to discuss with her much younger sister, and what wasn't appropriate.

Ultimately, though, Emma found herself shrugging, heavily.

"I'm just going to be real with you, Eva, because I don't want to talk to you like you're a baby, and I don't know how else to say this, but – your relationship with our mom is very different than mine is." There. That made sense.

Eva rolled her eyes back at her, but didn't immediately shoot back a retort, so Emma pushed on.

"Honestly, I don't know how much Mom has told you about her life before you were born. About *my* life, when I was younger." She paused, again wondering how much was acceptable to say.

Because, in a shocking twist of events, she felt a little protective over Kimberly, right now. She really didn't know how much Eva and Everly knew about Kimberly's life, pre-Ted. And the reality Emma was facing in a rapid turn of events, was that... she didn't want to ruin the image Eva likely had.

Their mom had done a lot of work to get to the place she was in, now. Emma had a lot of issues with Kimberly, but she knew that without a doubt. She'd gotten her GED, gone to college, she'd started working at women's shelters. She'd become a model PTA parent. Maybe she hadn't been able to do that for Emma, but she'd done it for her little sisters, and Emma – she respected it. She was proud of her.

Eva's jaw was still set in a hard line, as she shrugged. "I know enough."

Emma couldn't help but roll her eyes, even as she felt her lips tick into a small, exasperated grin. Yep. This girl was her fucking sister.

"So, if you know *enough*, then you know that I lived with Gram. And you know that Mom wasn't... the same parent for me that she is for you," she spoke carefully, knowing she was toeing a line. "And honestly, Eva? Growing up, that wasn't always the easiest thing for me to deal with. So, that's why I didn't accept the invitations to holidays and birthdays."

Whew. God, saying that aloud to Eva was surprisingly... freeing, in a way.

Eva still frowned at her, but it was filled with slightly less anger. At least, Emma thought so.

"And Gram doesn't love me more than she loves you, either." Emma wouldn't – *couldn't* – not jump in to defend their gram in this. "But *she* was the one that did my birthday parties and Christmases. So... the relationship I have with her is always going to be a little different than the one you have with her. But it's not because she thinks I'm perfect; it's because she was – in most ways – my mom."

She stared intently across the table, hoping that she wasn't laying too much out for her sister. Hoping that she wasn't triggering a minefield in this situation and making it any worse, for anyone.

Eva's frown slowly melted into much more of a pout. "Do you not like me and Everly?" She asked, quietly, tilting her head at Emma. "Or is it just Mom?"

Oof. The quiet vulnerability in those questions packed far more of a punch than Emma had been prepared for.

"I just don't know you all that well," she answered, honestly. "And I meant what I said, before: I really do care about you both. *And* I care about Mom. It's just... hard," she admitted, her voice cracking unexpectedly on the word.

A little embarrassed, she cleared her throat and continued, "It's hard for me, too, sometimes. You see me and Gram being close, being a family that you don't feel like a part of, and it makes you feel badly. Right?"

Eva slowly nodded, dipping her gaze down to the board game as she reached out and toyed with her plastic van, idly. Looking a little embarrassed, herself, admitting vulnerable feelings.

"Sometimes... sometimes, it made me feel badly, to see you and Everly and our mom and your dad, as a family that I don't feel like a part of."

Eva swallowed as she pouted her bottom lip thoughtfully, staring down at the board game. "Does it still make you feel bad? To see us?"

Emma felt the question land, deep in her stomach, and she sat back as she mulled it over. She looked around the den, belonging to a happy little family that played board games and had movie nights – a family she was a part of, but not fully.

And while she still had a tug of that feeling she'd had a couple of months ago, the first time she'd come over here, she didn't feel sick from it. Her stomach clenched a little, but she didn't feel like she needed to cry or run away.

"A little bit," she admitted, softly. "But less than it did, before. And... I'd like to get to a place where it doesn't feel badly, at all."

She was surprised at the words coming out of her own mouth, but they were the utter truth. Somewhere along the line, she'd started to let this in as a reality, and it didn't make her want to die.

Eva blinked up at her, her eyebrows furrowed deeply. As if she was trying to assess how much she could trust Emma.

Emma felt that was fair; she didn't trust easily, either.

"Well... I wouldn't hate if you came to dinner more, then." Eva shrugged once more, the look in her eyes a little brighter. "Especially if you keep bringing Regan."

A loud cough from the far side of the room drew both of their attention, as Regan rounded the corner. She had a plate of brownies in one hand, with a few bottles of water tucked into the crook of her arm, and Everly skipped in behind her, already munching on a brownie.

"Dessert is served!" Regan announced, as she set the plate down with a flourish.

Emma felt like she'd run a marathon in the last five minutes, and she leaned heavily back against the couch cushions.

She didn't know if she was relieved or not to be interrupted before she found herself confessing to her twelve-year-old sister that she wasn't sure she'd ever want to leave Regan behind.

Emma yawned, widely, as she walked back into the den after triple-checking to make sure Everly was really in bed for the night.

If she'd wanted something tonight to help her see a similarity to Everly, it had come in the form of her doggedness to want to stay up as late as possible, telling Emma how much she hated waking up early in the morning.

Her footsteps came to a pause as her gaze landed on Regan.

Specifically, Regan's ass. As Regan was bent over across the room at the built-in shelves, organizing the mess of board games that had been picked over throughout the night.

Emma drew in a deep, calming breath through her nose, before alerting Regan to her presence. "I feel very grateful for my years of babysitting experience."

Regan didn't immediately straighten up – much to Emma's damnation. Rather, she sent Emma a look over her shoulder, dark eyes glinting from interest. "You were a babysitter?"

"Number one trusted call for everyone in my building, all throughout high school." Emma used her thumbs to point at herself. She tilted her head at Regan, curiously. "Did you babysit?"

Now – thankfully – Regan stood up and turned to look at her, incredulously. "Emma. Do you think people trusted *me* to babysit?"

"A couple of months ago, I'd say a resounding no, with a laugh for good measure," she agreed, easily, before she bit at her bottom lip and slowly shook her head. "Now, though, I'd say you're a far more trustworthy source than people think. More trustworthy than you let on, actually," she added on, speaking slowly.

But it was the truth, now that she really thought about it.

Regan played into being chaotic and flighty, and maybe she was – to an extent. But she noticed *everything*, and she was the best listener Emma had ever known.

Before she could push into that even deeper – and she very much wanted to – Regan shrugged. "Yeah, well, I also didn't know a lot of people with young kids. Anyway, back to the point here: I'm sure you've never run into the conversation you had with Eva while you were babysitting someone else?"

Regan's voice was light, tentative. She wasn't pushing, but the look in her eyes was hopeful, clearly eager to see if Emma would share with her.

Surprised, Emma's eyebrows lifted high on her forehead. "You could hear us?"

"Not the whole thing," Regan assured her, shaking her head. "I'd looped back to see if you two wanted something to drink and over-heard... a little. So, I skedaddled back to the kitchen. I tried to give you a little longer, but Everly was *rearing* to get back to the game, and I'd distracted her as long as I could in the kitchen. That's why I announced myself so clearly."

Emma breathed out a sigh, trying desperately to hold onto her sanity. Any semblance of sanity, really, that kept her from doing what she now desperately wanted to do. To walk closer to Regan, to be close enough to breathe her in.

With that sanity, she kept her hands tightly pressed to her sides, and stayed across the room from Regan.

Even if her sisters were no longer awake, they were still in the house. They were *all* in Kimberly's house.

There.

That thought served Emma a little dose of reality. Great.

"You're right, I've definitely never had that intense of a conversation with anyone else I've babysat," she agreed, warily, tugging her hand through her hair. "But... I think it was good."

She wouldn't say she believed she and Eva were going to be super close, immediately. Maybe ever – Emma couldn't read the future like that. But what she *did* know was that after they'd talked, Eva's eyerolls and comments seemed a lot more like a typical preteen and less like someone that hated Emma's guts.

So, that was a positive.

Regan's smile was so soft, so coaxing, Emma felt reeled into it. "Look at you, Emma Mystery-Middle-Name Bordeaux."

Rolling her lips, determined not to give into the smile that wanted to slide onto her face, Emma shook her head. "Yeah, I'm *still* not going to tell you."

Regan's mouth fell open in offense and she crossed her arms over her chest. "Emma! I took you on a date that you ranked as a twelve out of ten, and you still won't tell me your middle name?!"

She shook her head, unfailingly entertained by Regan even as she was charmed by her. The reminder of the damn date...

Regan seemed to perk up a second later, and she slowly tilted her head. "So... if you don't want to talk about your middle name, then why don't we address the elephant in the room?"

"The elephant?" She echoed, leaning back against the doorway and making herself comfortable there.

It was wiser, she thought, to stay here. Rather than potentially be convinced to sit next to Regan, where they would inevitably be right in each other's personal space, and Emma would inevitably find herself wanting.

Regan seemed to have none of the same concerns of keeping space between them, as she slowly started walking closer. "Emma. Are you going to pretend that you offering to babysit your sisters – for the first time *ever* – the literal day after we spent the night together is just a coincidence?"

Emma could only stare at Regan, her mouth falling open slightly at the sheer indignance. Because, "How do you do that? How?" She demanded to know.

That, at least, made Regan pause, leaving a solid four feet of space between them, still. "Do what?"

Emma tossed her hands in the air, exasperated. "How do you read me so well?"

"Oh." Regan shrugged, watching Emma intently. "I mean… it's not hard, I guess? You might think you're a closed book, Emma, but I think I have your number."

"I think you do, too," she agreed, distressingly.

"So, *are* you going to do us both a favor and admit that you were having us babysit so that you could pull back from what we started last night?" Regan pushed, that edge of raw honesty in her tone cutting right into Emma, right to the heart of everything.

Emma felt her heart thud in her chest, as she slowly shook her head. "I *did*," she admitted. "But – not because I'm trying to pull back from you. Or from this." She gestured between the two of them.

Regan's expression slid into something sweetly surprised. "Really?"

"Really," she confirmed, swallowing thickly, before she explained, "I'm just trying to figure out how to put some brakes on this – on us – so that we don't go careening forward too fast."

Regan took another step closer to her. Then another. And the look on her face, as she peered up at Emma was so *gentle*, in a way no one had ever looked at her before. "Will it make you feel better if I swear to you that I won't jump your bones when we're alone in our apartment? I know it might not seem like it," a self-deprecating smile flashed over Regan's face. "But I can control myself a little bit–"

"It's not you I'm worried about," Emma cut in, her cheeks burning with the truth.

That, again, stopped Regan in her tracks. Those gorgeous, dark eyes widened as her mouth fell open with surprise, and the gleam of excitement was clear. "Emma–"

"I'm worried about *me*," she added, even though she knew Regan already understood the unspoken implication. But Emma needed to say it. She had to get this out. "I want you, Regan. *I'm* the one that answered your text last night. I'm the one that didn't hang up the phone. And I'm the one that came into your room, after. It's not you I'm worried about."

Emma had never in her life been someone that didn't have some control over herself.

But that had been exactly how she'd felt when she'd gone into her room, post-date. She'd felt the ghost of Regan's hips rolling needily against hers while they'd kissed. She'd felt that kiss, burning through her. She'd felt... god, she'd felt so wanted and wanting in equal measure.

Emma had done very, very well to keep Regan from entering into her dirtiest, neediest thoughts. But the dam was had been officially broken, and she'd touched herself – feeling so wet, her clit so achingly hard – with a fervor she'd never had before.

She'd never been so turned on in her fucking *life* as she'd been when she'd come for Regan, and she'd felt desperate for more when Regan had orgasmed – loud and unashamed – for her. She hadn't even known what the hell she'd been thinking when she'd hung up their call and hurriedly gotten out of bed and went to get Regan a glass of water.

All she'd known was that she needed to actually, physically, see Regan after that.

"Do you regret last night? Either the sex or coming to sleep with me?" Regan asked, her voice an octave lower than before, and raspy. So raspy, it made Emma shiver.

And she found she couldn't be anything other than truthful, as she shook her head. "No. I don't regret it."

She'd tried. This morning, after she'd woken up with her face buried in Regan's soft, dark hair because of her alarm blaring in her ear – she'd tried. She'd told herself all morning at work that they'd moved too fast. That this wasn't the right thing.

But she didn't actually feel that way, and she was so, so tired of trying to pull herself back from Regan.

"This is all really new for me. Yes, I've been in a serious relationship, before. But it wasn't – it didn't feel like this," she could hear her own desperation in her voice. "It didn't feel so consuming. I didn't think about her all of the time. I didn't feel this need to check my phone to see if she texted. I didn't count down the time in my head until we were going to see one another, again. And it's crazy, because I've been doing all of those things for you, for far longer than the last few days."

There it was. The utter, most honest truth she had for Regan.

"You are so honest with the way you feel, Regan, that it blows me away. Oh, you're attracted to me? Well, then, you kiss me. Oh, you realize you have feelings for me? Well, then, you confess it to me. Oh, you want to know what it's like to be with me? Well, then you take me out on an incredible date and make it impossible for me to think straight. Do you know how crazy that is, conceptually, to me?" Emma demanded, needing Regan to understand. To see how different they were, how baffling she was to Emma.

"Do you not... like it?" Regan asked so quietly, uncertainly, as she bit the inside of her cheek.

Emma scoffed, scrubbing her hands roughly over her face. "I like it," she informed Regan, her voice gravelly. "I like it, and you, far too much. I liked waking up with you this morning. I liked going to sleep with you last night. I love how forthright you are, how you never make me wonder what's on your mind. How you never make me question where you stand or how you feel or what you think. It's never been my experience in dating, and I love it."

The wide, unabridged smile that broke over Regan's face was breathtaking, and she walked even closer to Emma. "Good, because I love it, too. I love that I can be my whole self with you, and I never hold back, and it's never been my experience, either! But I think it's a good thing. A really good thing."

"It is," she agreed. "But it's also something that makes me think – how soon is too soon? How are we possibly going to keep our wits about us when we're in such close quarters in our own apartment, all alone?"

Emma was entirely unsure if she *could*. Even now, in her mother's house, with her little sisters upstairs, she stared at Regan and she craved to be closer.

The sight of Regan – even the thought of her – filled Emma with this intense, needy feeling.

Not just her body, not just a sexually needy sensation – though, there was that, too. But something deeper, a place Emma had never really explored, before. Not even in the years she'd been in a relationship with Felicity. It made her feel giddy and excited and nervous, and like she couldn't wait for more.

Somehow, Regan had done this to her. She'd figured out how to slip into Emma's life and infiltrate all of her privacy settings.

Pressing herself back against the wall in a way that was reminiscent of her response to their first kiss, Emma shook her head. "Hence, the babysitting."

"You wanted little cockblocks around so that we didn't tear each other's clothing off," Regan surmised in the most Regan way possible.

Emma chuckled, unable to deny, "Yeah. Exactly."

Regan hummed quietly under her breath. "Okay, well, why don't we both just agree that we won't do anything – when it comes to sex – without checking in with each other about it, in-depth, first? You know, like, we can both keep each other in check. Make sure we're only doing what we think we're ready for?"

She took another step closer, leaving the distance between them only inches, as she clasped her hands behind her back and tilted her head up at Emma.

"I don't want to rush into anything with you. I just want to keep doing what we're doing," Regan's tone was so earnest, so open, and the sigh it elicited from Emma trembled out of her.

"I do, too," she agreed in a whisper. "We just... we have to be smart about it. We share the apartment and Sutton, and I still need us to make sure those things don't implode."

"Totally agreed," Regan promised, digging her teeth into her bottom lip as she rocked forward on her toes, pushing even closer... closer into Emma.

Their bodies brushed ever so slightly, Regan's chest pushing against Emma's, and Emma dropped her head heavily back against the wall.

"Regan," she breathed in warning or encouragement or... she didn't even know anymore.

"My hands are behind my back," Regan murmured back, her breath washing over Emma's neck, and the sensation made her shiver. "I'm not touching you. I'm not even going to ask if you want to sit on the couch, lest anything get too hot and heavy."

There it was. That *tone* Regan had, that made Emma so wet, so quickly.

"But haven't you ever made out while you were babysitting, before? Isn't that, like, a classic move?" Regan asked, remaining in that exact position. Brushing her body *just so* against Emma's, just enough to feel teasingly close, but not leaning in and giving her anything more. Anything substantial.

That unstoppable heat slid through her, and she shook her head as she grit out, "Nope. I believe that's the classic move for what *not* to do when you're babysitting, actually."

"Mm," Regan hummed, flicking her tongue out and licking her insanely full lips. "Right. Guess that's why I never got the job."

"Regan," she breathed again, unsure of what her tone conveyed other than a needy whine.

Somehow, Emma felt okay with that.

"I'm not going to kiss you. I *want* to kiss you," Regan husked out. "Because I've been unable to think about anything other than you since I woke up this morning. But if you want to kiss me, then I need to know it's what you really want. Because I don't want to have a repeat of last night, if you're going to try to put distance between us, after. I–"

Emma couldn't help it. Every breath that Regan exhaled, every word she spoke, washed over Emma and made this need inside of her grow higher and hotter.

It was fine, she assured herself, as she leaned down and captured Regan's perfect mouth with her own.

They weren't even on the couch, true to Regan's word. How caught up could they get if they didn't settle into a bed or a couch or even a chair?

～

Very.

They could get *very* caught up in one another.

Emma had made no such promise to keep her hands to herself, and she hadn't even registered when she'd moved them down to land on Regan's hips. She didn't recall any conscious thought to work them under Regan's t-shirt to feel her soft, warm skin.

She definitely didn't remember making the decision to slide her hands down even further so that she could cup Regan's ass in her palms. She didn't remember the decision to do so, but she'd done it.

And it felt so *good*. Regan's firm butt under her hands, as Regan

writhed against her. Emma was still pressed solidly against the wall –
leaning, really, as Regan leaned her entire body into Emma's.

Regan's hands hadn't remained behind her back, but Emma
couldn't fault her for it. Not when she'd been the first one to touch, and
definitely not when it felt so fucking *good* to feel Regan's hands on her.

Her deft, nimble fingers that had jerked Emma's shirt out of her
slacks – she was still wearing the same clothing she'd worn to work –
and slid up Emma's sides, before scratching to her back. Unsurprisingly,
Regan's hands never stayed in one place for too long.

Neither did her mouth. Her tongue moved actively and insistently
against Emma's, seeming to want to explore every part of Emma's
mouth. She traced over Emma's teeth, the seam of her lips, the tip of her
tongue. She worked those impeccably plush lips over Emma's bottom
one, sucking it between her own.

And now, she was working insistently at Emma's neck. She'd
dragged her lips down Emma's neck, before moving to the other side to
plant open-mouthed, wet kisses that were slowly driving Emma fucking
crazy.

Her head was back against the wall, her mouth open as she panted
out quiet sounds. Soft whimpers and choked-off moans, and –

"Oh, wow!" Kimberly's voice broke into the lust-addled haze that
had fully clouded Emma's mind.

Her hands tightened on Regan's ass, before she hurriedly released
her, dropping her hands listlessly to her sides. Regan's mouth on her
neck froze, before she whipped her head up, and they both turned
toward the large entryway.

Emma felt her cheeks burn as the mortification worked through her
veins, dampening the arousal that was thrumming through her.
"I... um..."

She could barely even catch her breath, still! What could she
possibly say in her defense!

Regan's dark eyes looked glazed over and her pillowy lips were red
and swollen, and – Emma immediately looked away, because looking
at Regan when she looked like *that* was not good for her nervous
system.

"And here I was, thinking you were a reliable babysitter; that's what your gram always proudly reported to me," Kimberly drawled, arching a look at Emma.

Guilt mixed with the embarrassment, and Emma dropped her head into her hands.

"Both Eva and Everly were up in bed before we did this!" Regan jumped in, somewhat helpfully. "We played board games all night; they'll vouch for us."

"I'm sorry," Emma finally managed to get out. She rolled her shoulders back and looked up at Kimberly, feeling the effects of this double-whammy.

Not only had she besmirched her perfect babysitting record, but she'd been caught by her *mother* making out like a teenager.

"I really am, I..." She trailed off, confusion taking over as she saw the wide smile on Kimberly's face.

"You don't need to apologize." Kimberly waved that off, clutching her purse with both hands as she grinned at Emma so excitedly, she'd almost think it was Christmas morning. "Emma Bo Bemma! I got to walk in and catch you making out with your girlfriend while you're babysitting your sisters?"

Her tone was awed, matching the way she perched one hand over her chest.

"I mean... I *never* thought I'd have this moment," she continued, and her eyes were so wide. Were there *tears* in them?! "And you felt so comfortable, to do it in my house?"

Regan let out a peel of laughter, before Emma saw her slap her hand over her mouth out of the corner of her eye. "Sorry. I just..." She cleared her throat, shaking back her hair. Which was a little tousled, because – apparently – Emma's hands had also worked through her hair, as well.

Emma couldn't believe the laughter she felt bubbling up inside, but there it was. She almost felt high, with the rush of endorphins and attraction still flooding through her, with the shock of being caught by Kimberly, and then the incredulity of her mom's reaction to this...

Yeah, she couldn't help but laugh at it, feeling her shoulders relax with it.

Kimberly sighed, staring at Emma like she'd made her dreams literally come true. "By all means, you can keep going. I won't interrupt again."

It made Emma laugh harder, even as she tried to get some control over herself. "Um, no. That's okay; we should go home."

"Well, if you ever need a place..." Kimberly shrugged, gesturing around them.

Emma couldn't believe her mother was offering her house as some sort of a hookup pad for her and Regan. She couldn't believe she'd actually just been walked in on by her mother. And, amidst it all, she didn't feel like she was going to be sick to her stomach.

She felt the tentative brush of Regan's fingers against the back of her hand, and she moved without thought to interlock their hands together.

"I think we're good. But thanks."

twenty-five

REGAN *HAD* to wonder if she was on some sort of practical prank show, as she pulled open the door to a bar that Audrey had asked her to meet her at.

Actually – no, she hadn't asked. She'd dropped Regan a pin along with the text:

Come and meet me . !

Even though they'd been on much better terms for the last month, Regan had never met Audrey to get a casual drink in their entire lives. Sure, they were texting more frequently, and it was amicable but there was no way she would have possibly anticipated Audrey wanting to meet up with her for a casual hangout after work.

Especially not when it seemed Audrey was possibly drunk?!

Cautiously, Regan approached the bar, where she could see her sister sitting on one of the stools.

Audrey's fine, silky blonde hair was pulled into one of those pony-tails that Regan often thought could only be accomplished by social media influencers or something. She wore diamond earrings with a matching necklace – jewelry that wasn't flashy but was definitely expensive as hell. The sleeveless dark blue dress she wore was undoubtedly designer, and the cream-colored blazer she'd definitely worn over it to work was draped over the back of her chair without a single wrinkle to be seen.

Regan had never seen Audrey at work at her fancy PR firm, but... yeah, this was exactly what she would have imagined her sister wore in her everyday life.

The wine bar itself was one that Regan would never have stepped foot in; she doubted she could afford to buy a bottle of anything in here. And, in her sports bra and overalls, she didn't exactly *belong* with the other clientele.

She cleared her throat as she approached her sister, alerting her to Regan's presence.

Audrey spun on her stool so quickly, she nearly fell off of it. Quickly, Regan jumped forward to try to help stabilize her, baffled by the fact that – *yeah*. Audrey really was drunk!

"Regan! Hey, you!" Audrey's cheeks were rosy, and her green eyes were a little glassy, and Regan felt like her world was flipped on its fucking axis.

"Uh, hey... you." Slowly, she removed her hands from her sister's arms, making sure that Audrey wasn't going to slip off of her stool again. "What's going on?"

Audrey ignored her question and turned to lift the briefcase that had been draped over the stool next to her, as if she'd been saving it. "Come and sit," she commanded, in that imperious tone. It was a little less imperious, though, when she was clearly not in full control of her faculties.

She turned sharply, waving at the woman tending the bar.

"Marlie, this is my sister, Regan. She'll have what I'm having." Audrey used one of her hands to swirl the red wine in her glass. Thankfully, there was very little left in said glass, or it would have sloshed right out.

Swearing she could hear horror movie music play in her head, Regan perched herself on the stool. "So–"

"Actually," Audrey started again, looking up at Regan with a considering frown. "Do you even like wine, Regan? Because, *ha*, I have no idea if you do. It's a Sangiovese, made and imported from a vineyard Armando and I toured in Italy last year." She laughed again, mirthlessly, as she tapped her fingertips against the bar. "*Actually* – only I went on the tour. But Armando had a ticket, so..."

She shrugged, as if to say *there you go*, and lifted her glass again, taking a large gulp to down the rest of the liquid.

Regan could only stare for several beats, finding herself at a loss for words. Mostly because what she wanted to say was *what the fuck*? But she bit that back.

"Um... wine is... fine. No punning rhyme intended." She smiled apologetically at Marlie as she poured a glass for Regan and refilled Audrey's, wondering exactly how difficult it had been for her to manage Audrey so far. God, Regan hoped her sister was going to tip well.

"Wine is fine. Indeed, it is." Audrey sighed in agreement, as she nodded toward Regan. "So – go on. Drink up."

Regan tugged the glass toward her carefully – this was the *last* place she needed to accidentally drop a glass and cause a scene – but kept her cautious gaze trained on her sister.

"Tell me what you were up to today," Audrey stated rather than ask, turning an expectant look at her.

Still feeling vaguely like there was a prank being pulled on her, Regan blew out a slow breath. "Nothing much. I'd just finished baking a batch of cookies when you'd texted."

"That's *right*. I saw on your Instagram that you do that, now," Audrey's voice dipped into something low and thoughtful.

Again, even though they'd definitely turned a corner, Regan couldn't help but be surprised that Audrey knew about her baking or that she kept up with Regan's socials. "Uh, yeah. These are for a retirement party, actually."

Emma's gram had not only gotten Regan a referral for this party, but two other potential events in the last week. Which Regan was still having trouble wrapping her mind around; people were *paying* her to bake? People liked the things she created enough to want her to cater parties?!

She was approaching this new avenue with as much caution as she could, but she was undeniably thrilled by it.

Audrey pursed her lips as she nodded decisively at her. "You know, Regan, that's great. That is really wonderful, that you have this passion."

Her eyebrows arched high on her forehead as she took a little sip of wine. "Thanks. It's been–"

"Now, tell me: are you dating anyone?" Audrey asked with as much laser-focus someone could have when they weren't sober.

Choking on her sip, Regan quickly sat the glass down; *that* was why she wasn't supposed to touch the wine glasses in fancy restaurants. "What? Why – Audrey, *what* is going on?"

There was a knowing glint in her sisters' eyes as she leaned back. "Ah, so you are dating someone."

"I'm..." Regan's cheeks heated, her heart skipping a beat at the very thought of Emma. "Yes. Yes, I am."

Her tone sounded just as awed as she felt, at the confirmation. Yes, she *was* dating Emma. How crazy was that?

"We've never talked about our personal relationships. Have you realized that? Never. Not once." Audrey frowned, her eyebrows knitting tightly as she shook her head. "I don't like that."

Good god, what had happened to set this off? She needed to know. "It's... I mean, we haven't talked about anything *real*, ever," she slowly said, with as much tact as she could manage. But they'd barely had any semblance of a relationship for most of their adult lives, which wasn't news to Audrey.

Apparently, her words didn't provide any sense of peace to her sister, whose frown etched even deeper into her face as she stared into Regan's eyes. "I *know* that. I'm telling you that I don't like it, and that it would be nice if things were different. And I know we – we bonded, or whatever you'd call it, at brunch, and we've texted a little. But I want to know more about you. All right?"

Yeah, Regan had not been prepared for this in any possible way. "All right," she warily agreed.

"So, tell me." Audrey waved her hand, imploring Regan to speak.

Regan chewed at her bottom lip, unsure of how to broach this topic with Audrey, given that she'd only ever shared it with Charlotte freaking Thompson. But also finding that she *wanted* to tell her.

She wanted to talk about Emma, badly. She wanted to gush about her and about them and their date and everything else that had taken place over the last week.

She wanted to talk about how Emma had surprised her with a little karaoke set up in their living room on Saturday night, when Regan had returned home from work. How Emma had shrugged that adorable little embarrassed shrug, as she'd murmured, "I just don't want you to feel like you're the only one that cares enough to plan dates, or that I don't listen to your interests. That's all. Besides, karaoke at home isn't the same as going out in public."

Honestly, it had been better. Because it was just the two of them, and Emma had done this entire set up for *her*. And she'd said *that's all*, like she wasn't being insanely sweet and more romantic than anyone else had ever been in Regan's life!

Then, best of all, Emma had – after two margaritas – finally let loose and started really singing, too.

She wanted to talk about how, on Tuesday, Emma had watched her work on her latest map for the D&D commission she'd received, and how it had made her feel important and sheepish and swept up, as Emma asked her questions and seemed totally, completely into it. Into *her*.

She wanted to share how they'd taken to cuddling in close on the couch while they watched tv together every night.

She... okay, well, she didn't really want to tell her sister about the sexual aspects, but she wanted to revel in it, still. In the hot, wanting, needy make-outs that always inevitably started after they were cuddling together. About how she'd never felt so fucking turned on in her life as she did when Emma's mouth was on hers or on her neck, feeling how their bodies slotted together so perfectly. How they grinded into each other like horny teenagers, and how Regan never wanted to stop.

She definitely did not plan on telling her sister about how the only reason they ever *managed* to stop was because she knew what would take place after she and Emma parted ways for the night. That they'd masturbated while on the phone with each other every night for the last five nights. How she was fucking *thrilled* to go to her own bedroom, because she was already so turned on and soaking wet from their cuddling and kissing and touching.

She'd never in her life imagined she'd have such an active sex life without actually *having sex* with someone.

And... okay, she *might* want to shout from the rooftops that she and Emma then slept together, in her bed, afterwards. That Emma was always the person that initiated their sleeping and cuddling together. That she'd woken up wrapped up in Emma every morning since their first date, and she'd never felt like her world was so on fire, before.

Blinking herself out of her thoughts, Regan reached for her wine glass and took a big sip. Hoping, somehow, that she could control herself from getting turned on by the mere thought of Emma while sitting across from her sister in this swanky wine bar.

"It's... kind of new," she settled on, darting her gaze at her sister. "But it's amazing." She inhaled deeply, wondering how this next part was going to go. "*She's* amazing."

Holding her breath, Regan waited for Audrey's response.

Which came in pieces.

First, Audrey's frown. Then, the widening of her eyes. Then the tilting of her head. And finally, she refocused on Regan, intently. "*She?*"

Regan exhaled the breath she'd been holding. "Yep. She. She who is named Emma."

"Huh. Okay." Audrey shrugged, taking another sip of her wine. "And she's your girlfriend?"

Flattening her hand on top of the bar, Regan leaned in, confused. "That's it? No other reaction to finding out I'm with a woman?"

Audrey narrowed her eyes. "What do you want me to say?"

"I don't know! Are you surprised?" She pressed, unable to quell how baffled she was at her strait-laced sister being so nonchalant about this. After all, it had thrown Regan, herself, for a freaking loop.

"Should I be?" Audrey challenged. "As far as I knew until one minute ago, the only deep and meaningful relationship you've ever had is with Sutton. So, no. I'm not surprised."

Regan slouched back, running Audrey's words over in her mind, and... "Yeah, okay. That makes sense." She rolled her lips, needing to ask, "And you don't care? You're fine with this?"

The scoffing laugh Audrey let out was so loud, Regan jumped back from it. Yeah, okay, that was the reminder she'd needed that her typically super reserved sister was drunk as a skunk. "What, like you're the only queer person I know?" The look in her eyes glinted, as she smartly tapped her glass against Regan's. "Like you're the only queer person in our family?"

Regan's jaw fell slack, shock rushing through her. "What?!" Her own exclamation was loud, but she didn't give a shit. "Is it Uncle Barry? Because I always thought–"

Audrey rolled her eyes as she cut her off. "It's *me*, Regan. Obviously."

Seriously, Regan could be knocked over with a fucking feather. Words escaped her, as she could only stare at her sister. Apparently, someone she knew even less about than she'd thought.

"How – and I repeat: *how* – is that obvious?" Regan finally managed to ask. "You've been with Armando since you were, like, in college."

"In business school," Audrey corrected, sharply. "I had a girlfriend in college. Kind of." She frowned, deeply, her bottom lip poking out, before she waved her hand, dismissively. "It was a thing, anyway."

Regan ran a hand through her hair, trying to make sense of it all. "Holy shit."

"Hmm," Audrey hummed, thoughtfully, in agreement.

"What happened with her?" Regan leaned forward, eagerly, ready to take in every detail. Because – what the fuck!

"Nothing. We... broke up, in a manner of speaking. Haven't spoken since," Audrey's sentences were disjointed as she shrugged, then drooped her shoulders down low. Clearly more affected by the memory than she wanted to verbally let on.

All Regan could do was sit back and try to wrap her head around this development, which was not an easy task.

"And *then*, I got with Armando. And he's... just, great. Really. So, so – *wonderful*," Audrey bit out, her tone dark, as she narrowed her eyes down at the engagement ring that glinted on her finger.

What in the world was going on?!

"Exactly forty-five days until the biggest moment of my life," Audrey continued, not taking her eyes off her ring. "Forty-five days."

Regan darted her eyes between the engagement ring, her sister's face, then back.

"Right. And you're... not... happy about that?" She slowly surmised. Maybe a little slower on the uptake than she usually was, but Regan didn't think that was her own fault.

"I'm ecstatic. Can't you tell?" Audrey pasted on a smile that was terrifyingly authentic looking, as she turned to face Regan again.

"Uh. I don't think I can tell anything about you, right now," she admitted, honestly. "I can't tell why you asked *me* to come here. I can't tell why you're getting drunk after work in a bar on a weekday, which doesn't seem to be your style but if this evening has taught me anything it's that I don't really know you at all. So, I have no idea about *anything*," she repeated, because it was the absolute truth.

"Join the club, Regan," Audrey muttered, as she picked up her glass and downed the remainder of it. "I texted you tonight because I felt like I was going to fucking explode, but I don't want to accidentally tell any of my friends about Armando treating our relationship like a business arrangement. Or about how he's more passionate about Dad's political connections than he is about me. *Or* about how we haven't had sex in over six months. We're not even married yet, and we're basically celibate."

She let out a harsh laugh, before she bit it off on a sharp breath and dropped her head into her hands.

"Forty-five days," she muttered, thickly.

Alarmed and filled with sympathy, Regan leaned in and tentatively wrapped her arm around her sister's waist, trying to comfort her.

It was something she'd never done, but it didn't feel as strange as she'd expected it would. In fact, it felt... kind of similar to when she comforted Sutton. Not the exact same, but she felt the same need to want to help figure out how to soothe over the pain.

"You don't have to do it, you know," she whispered, making sure to keep her voice as low as possible. She knew without a doubt that Audrey would never want someone to hear her say this; hell, maybe *Audrey* didn't even want her to say it.

Audrey didn't lift her head, even as she shook it in firm dissent. "Yes, I do. It's planned. It's paid for. The guest list is finalized. Armando's family is flying in from Spain. Mom and Dad have invited half of the country club. My friends and I are flying out for the weekend to Napa for my bridal party on Friday."

"So?" She refused to back down, because amongst that whole list, she didn't hear anything that sounded remotely like a real reason to get married. "Who *cares*?"

Audrey whipped her head up to stare at Regan with narrowed eyes. "Everyone cares," she hissed back. "Armando and I work at the same firm; he's – indirectly – my superior. Mom texts me every other day to remind me of what needs to get done before the wedding. *Everyone* cares, Regan."

"*I* don't care," she emphasized, holding Audrey's gaze with her own. "You're tying yourself to this guy for the rest of your life – or you're going to go through a divorce that is probably going to be lengthy and expensive. Both of which sound like really shitty options to me."

Audrey let out a trembling breath, her glassy eyes growing even glassier, before she blinked and turned away from her. "It's not that easy."

"I didn't say it was easy; I said you don't have to marry him."

Audrey dug her teeth so hard into her lip, Regan was concerned she'd draw blood. Still, she tightly shook her head. "No. I'm not that person; I'm not flaky or undependable. I'm not you. I can't just... just walk away from my commitments like that."

Regan didn't know why she was surprised by the statement, or why she was surprised it dug into her, sharply reminding her that she and Audrey still had a long way to go.

She slowly dropped her arm from where she'd still had it draped around her sister, in an obviously ineffective attempt to offer comfort.

"Maybe *that's* why you texted me tonight," she challenged, as she drew away. As she spoke, she grew more certain, though, because it was the only thing that made sense. "Actually, I think it is."

Audrey turned to face her, eyes red-rimmed, her expression drawn tight.

And Regan stared, the sharp bite of pain from Audrey's comment fading as she scanned her eyes over her sister's face. Mostly because it was replaced by... pity.

"I think you texted me because out of all of the people in your life, I'm the only one that isn't going to encourage you to marry some d-bag just because Mom and Dad think you should, or because he's attractive and successful, or because it already seems like a done deal." Emboldened, Regan knocked her knuckles lightly against the bar. "Yeah, I think that's exactly why. Because you had to know if you told me *anything* about Armando, that I'd tell you what I thought. And, on some level, you wanted to hear it."

Audrey hastily reached up, swiping her hand over her cheeks to wipe away any fallen tears as she shook her head. "*No*, that's not–"

Regan cut her off, on a roll. "You know, Audrey, you and I might be very different. I might not have Mom and Dad's approval in any way, but I'm happy with my life." She leaned in, imploring quietly, "Why do you still feel like you need to make them happy, when you know that they don't care if you are?"

Audrey's breath caught in her throat, hitching, before she hurriedly slapped her hand over her mouth in an obvious attempt to cut off any more threatening tears.

In yet another unexpected turn, Regan felt her stomach twist in sympathy.

"That's – I'm done," Audrey announced, her voice hoarse even though Regan could *hear* how much she tried for a steely tone. "I need to go home."

"Okay." Regan watched her sister shakily reach into her bag, pulling out her credit card.

She watched her for another long moment, wondering – for the first time – who in Audrey's life really cared about her true feelings, if *Regan* was the person she'd called tonight?

With that in mind, she unlocked her phone and tapped a few buttons, before locking it and looking up at Audrey, who was staring down at her credit card in utter consternation.

"I ordered you a car home. It'll be here in five."

Audrey's still-teary eyes widened, and she swallowed visibly hard. "You didn't have to do that; I – I'll pay you back."

Regan waved her off, as she slid off her stool. "I don't want your money; I just want you to know that I love you, whether you get married in forty-five days or not."

What a wild night.

Regan's thoughts whirred in an unstoppable loop as she walked down the hall toward her apartment.

> Sutton… I don't even have the wherewithal for adoring nicknames right now. I know you're sleeping, but you are the only person that is going to fully understand the magnitude of what I have to share. I HAVE to tell you about what happened tonight with Audrey. You would never in a million years guess what the developments are on this side of the ocean

She slid her phone in her back pocket with one hand as she reached for the apartment door with her other.

Even with all of the insanity with her sister, she could still feel the vibrating excitement inside at the prospect of seeing Emma. Even though – per her text to Sutton – Emma didn't necessarily know the gravity of what had happened with Audrey, she still couldn't wait to tell her. She couldn't wait to tell Emma *everything*.

"Hey! I'm home," she called out, quickly kicking off her shoes.

"I'm in the living room," Emma called back.

Regan grinned, nearly tripping over her own feet with the haste to get to Emma as quickly as possible.

"Do you just want to get a pizza or something for dinner? I planned on throwing some spaghetti together or something, but you wouldn't believe–" All of the words she could have possibly come up with escaped her as soon as she walked into the living room.

Nothing existed in her brain anymore.

The interaction with Audrey? Gone. Thoughts of dinner? Nope, what was that?

Because Emma was sitting on their couch wearing her glasses and one of her button-ups that she typically wore to work. But instead of how she usually wore it – appropriate for the office – the top five? Six?! Buttons were undone.

Leaving her breasts, encased in that sexy lacy red bra that Regan recognized from months ago, showcased for Regan's gaze to feast on.

Her throat ran dry – parched. She was parched. A woman in a desert kind of parched.

"Emma," she breathed, and she swayed where she stood. "What are you... you're just... what?"

Emma slowly raised an eyebrow at her. The look was both teasing and a little unsure, and Regan had no idea how she managed that combination. She had no idea why Emma would feel *uncertain* at all. "You mentioned last night when we were..." She trailed off, clearing her throat.

"Touching ourselves while on the phone with each other so we could hear each other come," Regan supplied helpfully, her voice raspy. "I find it so cute that you're so shy when we talk about it."

And she did. The dualities of Emma made Regan feel so soft. She was someone who was fearlessly sharp and had spoken her mind to Regan for years, yet became bashful when they talked about sex...

Regan loved it. Though, she wondered if she would love just about anything about Emma at this point.

Emma's exhale trembled on a visible shiver. "Yes, that. You said – not for the first time – that you were dying to see my breasts. And you've been very vocal about your feelings on my glasses, so..."

"Are you trying to *seduce* me?" Regan knew that was what was happening, because it was right in front of her fucking eyes, but she still couldn't believe it. Her blood rushed with delight and surprise and arousal – so, so much arousal.

Emma's lips pursed. "I guess I am," she answered, dragging the words out. "I don't really know; all I know is that last night, when we went to our separate beds and I came against my own fingers, I've never been so dissatisfied while still feeling sated. Because I... I want *your* touch. And I'm so tired of hearing you come, but not being the one to cause it. Not really."

She could see how hard Emma swallowed, across the room. "And it's all I've thought about, all day."

Regan was breathless with the heat that sparked through her, the need pulsing between her legs as if there was a switch Emma had flicked.

In a way, she supposed, there was.

How else was she supposed to react when Emma was sitting there, waiting for Regan to come home, so that she could make Regan's fantasies come true?

Still, she clenched her hands into fists so tight, her nails bit deeply into her palms. She needed that, to steady herself. To make sure she didn't run across the room and throw herself at Emma *right this fucking second*.

"I... you wanted to make sure we weren't going too fast," Regan cautioned, her breathing already growing erratic, and she couldn't stop staring at Emma's tits.

Her cleavage looked so incredible; Regan wanted to bury her face there and it was fine if she suffocated. She didn't really care – in fact, she could die happy.

"We're supposed to keep each other in check," she reminded Emma from their conversation last week. It took every single ounce of will power Regan had, to recall that conversation right now.

And that had been what they'd done every night.

When their kisses grew so heated, when they strained against one another so needily, one of them would pull back. When their hands started to wander and their touches grew more desperate, pulling on shirts and pants, they'd break away from each other.

It had become an unspoken agreement, really, that they'd quickly go their separate ways so that they could take things further, without *taking them further*.

"If you feel like it's too soon–" Emma started, but Regan couldn't let her finish.

"I don't!" She jumped in, vehemently shaking her head. Feeling crazed already. "It's not too soon, for me. Fine, it's only been like a week since our first date; big deal. We live together. Every night we hang out is a *date*. Dinner together, movies, tv shows, activities – we've spent more time together in the last few months than couples who have been together for a year. It's *not* too soon," she repeated, meaning every single word.

The relief was evident on Emma's face, as she breathed, "Thank god."

That was it. That was all the confirmation Regan needed.

She pounced at Emma, bounding across the room and jumping into her lap. Her legs bracketed Emma's thighs, and she settled on top of her, gripping her shoulders.

Immediately, she felt Emma's hands slide up her thighs. Maybe Emma was helping Regan catch her balance, but whatever the purpose of her touch – it didn't matter.

What mattered was that the sensation of Emma's fingers gliding up the backs of her thighs shot right to Regan's clit. She rolled her hips down against Emma's, before ducking her head to capture Emma's mouth with her own.

Several of their kisses in the last week had started off slow and soft. When they'd been cuddling on the couch just last night, and Emma had turned to look at Regan rather than the television, she'd felt hypnotized by the way Emma's blue eyes looked so... electric in the dim lighting of the living room. She'd been drawn in, gently cupping Emma's jaw as she'd pressed their lips together.

Right now, she did not have the patience for that.

Not when her thoughts were reeling, and she was pulsing between her legs, and she continued to roll her hips down against Emma.

There was so much she wanted to do. So, *so* much, she thought, desperately, as she sucked on Emma's tongue. One of her hands slid up to card through Emma's hair; something she'd learned was that she never tired of that. She never tired of feeling these long, soft strands between her fingers, or of the quiet whimpering sounds that escaped Emma's throat when she scratched against her scalp.

They'd managed to keep their heady make-out sessions relatively PG; she'd slid her hands under Emma's shirt, stroked them over her soft stomach, explored up her back, stroked down her sides. She'd slid her fingertips just under the cups of Emma's bra, had felt how stiff her nipples were against her palms through the material.

But she hadn't had the chance to really *see* Emma. To finally – finally! – get her shirt fully off, *and* her bra, too.

With that in mind, she broke their kiss. Regan honestly wasn't sure who let out the needy groan as soon as they were no longer kissing, but she wouldn't be shocked if it had been herself.

She flexed the hand she still had gripped in Emma's hair, watching in hungry amazement as Emma's eyes fluttered closed at the movement.

"I want to see you. God, I want it *so* badly," her voice was hoarse and rasping with need, and Regan wasn't going to hide it. She rolled her hips down, hard and intent, against Emma.

Dropping her gaze down very deliberately, she stared at Emma's chest. Flicking her tongue out, she licked her lips, and the move was entirely unintentional. She just really did feel hungry for more. Hungry for Emma.

She slid the hand she'd had braced on Emma's shoulder down, slowly. Moving over the thin fabric of her shirt until she made contact with Emma's soft skin. Hot to her touch, they both shuddered, as Regan drew fingers down over Emma's clavicle. She relished in every inch she touched, her breath ragged, as she stared down to watch her own hand on Emma.

For a moment, she paused. Holding still in the center of Emma's chest, so she could feel the pounding of Emma's heart.

She'd known – obviously – that Emma was attracted to her, that she was very affected by their kisses and touches. Hell, she'd gone to sleep every night for a week with the little sounds Emma made as she came, thinking of Regan, in her ears.

Still, it amazed her to feel Emma's heart racing the same way her own was.

Exhaling shakily, she inched her hand down...

Emma's chest was heaving with the panting breaths she let out, making the tops of her breasts rise out of the cups of her bra, and Regan didn't bother to bite back the keening whine that worked out of her, as she stroked her fingertips over the tops of Emma's breasts, before dipping down into her cleavage, and...

"I was staring right here when I registered how much I wanted to touch you," she whispered, reverently.

She could still visualize that moment, so clearly, in her head. Looking down at Emma as she'd been perched on the arm of the chair in the bookstore, starting at her face, before moving her gaze to her thighs, then – right here. And she'd wanted this – exactly this moment, as she stroked her fingertips over Emma's chest – so badly at that moment.

"Then touch me," Emma urged, her nails biting into the backs of Regan's upper thighs. Right under her ass, as they slipped under the hem of Regan's shorts.

Regan was itching to do just that, and her hands were shaking as she – reluctantly – dropped away from Emma's chest so she could undo the buttons on Emma's shirt. "I need this off. This, and your bra. I love your bras, I really do," she confessed, even though she was certain it wasn't a secret at all. "They're so sexy, but – take it *off*," she demanded, tugging down hard on Emma's shirt.

She couldn't completely undo all of the buttons herself, as she needed Emma to lean back so she could get to the bottom ones, and she needed it done *now*.

Emma hesitated, her breath catching in her throat. "I just... I'm just – a little self-conscious," she whispered, a rawness in her tone that mixed with the edge of arousal. "No one's seen me – all of me – in... a while. And even then, it was just one person, so..."

Regan squeezed her eyes closed, trying to reach for some semblance of calm. "I, um, I... we don't..."

God, she couldn't even find any words with how jumbled she felt inside, how the molten desire in her had twisted her up.

"I want to," Emma insisted, reminding her, "I decided to do this, remember?" She arched a teasing look up at Regan. Still, she swallowed, hard. "I just, I want you to know what I'm feeling."

That vulnerability in Emma's voice, that etched over her face, was the key to cutting through – a little – Regan's arousal. Making way amidst the heat inside of her for something soft, something that made her heart flutter in her chest.

"Thanks for telling me," she murmured, honestly. "I would never want to do anything you're uncomfortable with, I just..." She dipped her gaze back down, where her hand was resting just below Emma's bra, on her soft stomach. "I think you are so fucking sexy. Everything about you."

Emma nodded with her words, blowing out a low breath. "You've never made me doubt that."

Regan wondered, errantly, if Felicity had. Because – from everything Regan had gathered and been told – Felicity hadn't been the sweetest or most romantic or enthusiastic girlfriend. Regan was a much better one, in her own humble opinion.

"And, you know…" She lifted her eyes back up to meet Emma's, grinning crookedly. "I *have* seen you shirtless, multiple times. As you've said before. I've slept with your body against mine every night for a week. I know your stomach isn't flat, and that you aren't ripped, or whatever." She shrugged. "I want you exactly the way you are. Like… desperately," she admitted.

Taking a deep breath in attempt to stabilize herself, Regan reached back and grabbed one of Emma's hands. She guided it around, tracing Emma's touch over to the front of her thigh, as she pushed herself up on her knees. Even though it was her own hand moving Emma's, she shivered so intensely, her hips jerking with it.

She paused for a second so she could watch Emma's face and make sure she really *did* want to do this right now. Before she gripped Emma's wrist and guided her touch up her inner own inner thigh, until she felt Emma's fingers brush against her pussy through her underwear.

A moan rumbled through her chest, her eyes fluttering closed of their own accord, as she rolled her hips down and tightened her grip on Emma's wrist. Holding her firmly so her touch didn't disappear. Regan might die if it did.

Emma gasped, then groaned, "*Regan*, fuck."

Without Regan's hand guiding her, Emma flexed her fingers against Regan. Rocking against her, intently, as she breathed, "You're so wet; you're soaking my fingers and I'm not even *touching* you yet."

"I know," she panted back, rolling her hips down as she nodded, rapidly. "I know. I'm this wet for you every night. All of the time."

She released Emma's wrist, scratching her nails down her forearm.

"So, when I tell you that I *want you*, I mean it," she grit out, swearing as Emma slid her fingertips, knowingly, right over her clit. "You can feel how much I mean it."

Disappointment rolled through her when Emma's touch disappeared, only to be replaced by elation a moment later. Because Emma's hands went right to her own shirt, finishing the last of the buttons Regan hadn't been able to get to, before she reached back...

Regan's breath caught and held in her throat, the anticipation buzzing through her. Emma's eyes stayed locked on hers, as she undid her bra, and slid it off.

"Jesus," she breathed, and this truly *did* feel like a holy moment.

Emma's breasts were luscious and supple and immediately, Regan reached out, palming them.

They were much more than a handful; at least, much more than Regan could fit in her hands. She cupped, first, wanting to feel their weight, before she stroked her fingertips over the bottom curve.

"You're so soft," she breathed, mesmerized by watching her own hands map every inch of Emma's chest.

She circled her thumbs over Emma's nipples. Nipples that were so hard, and somehow, even softer than her skin.

"You have breasts, too," Emma murmured back, and there was a combination of amusement and heat in her tone. She could pretend Regan's touch wasn't igniting her inside the same as it was to Regan, but she could *feel* how erratic Emma's breathing was with every firm swipe Regan made over her nipples.

She shot Emma an admonishing look. "Not like *this*."

With that, she reached up to push Emma back against the couch, urging her to recline against the cushion. As soon as Emma did, Regan leaned in, so ready.

Ready to play out every want, every thought, every desire to explore Emma's body that she'd had for weeks.

Voracious, she captured one of Emma's nipples with her lips. Emma liked her lips; she'd told Regan multiple times. With that in mind, she wrapped them around Emma's nipple and sucked, before releasing... lightly brushing over the very tip with her bottom lip.

She both felt and heard the long, whimpering moan that escaped Emma, and it fed even deeper into Regan's hunger. She'd wondered for weeks if Emma was sensitive, how responsive she was. And now, she got to taste it. Got to feel it. The way Emma's nipple got impossibly harder against her mouth, how Emma's breath hitched and caught in her throat.

One of her hands roamed lower, stroking over Emma's perfect curves – finally, *finally,* unhindered by a stitch of clothing – as the other continued to toy with Emma's breast, rolling her nipple between her fingers, tugging on it. Testing out different things to see what got the best response from Emma.

Because Regan would be damned if she'd waited for so long – fantasized so many nights with Emma across the hall – and she didn't take full advantage of this moment. This moment to confirm for herself how perfect this felt, to show Emma how raw her hunger truly was.

She planted open-mouthed kisses over the inner curve of Emma's breast, before she licked up the center of her chest, every taste leaving Regan both satisfied and still wanting more.

Especially as one of Emma's hands tightened in her hair, gripping but not moving Regan's head anywhere. There was a neediness in her grip, the same that burned through Regan. She felt Emma's other hand as she dug her nails into Regan's shoulder, then scratched lower, over her shoulder blade, and Regan *knew* she'd have scratches on her back.

The idea made her groan against Emma, her clit throbbing. Yes, she wanted to be marked by Emma. She wanted the physical reminder of their night, in any way possible. Every way possible.

She tasted Emma everywhere she possibly could in their position. Every inch of her chest, alternating sucking and lightly dragging her teeth over Emma's nipples, feeling the way Emma's hips jerked up against her.

And no matter how forcefully Regan rocked her own hips down, it wasn't enough. She was aching and so wet, her underwear was so uncomfortable, and she wanted it all *off.* She wanted everything off, desperately. She wanted not a single stitch left on either of them. She wanted – no, she *needed* – to stop running into the waist of Emma's fucking pants, every time she stroked her fingers down, wanting so badly to be able to touch Emma's thighs.

With that in mind, she forced herself to pull back.

It was hard as hell, because she didn't want to give an inch of this closeness up.

Her lips tingled, craving Emma's skin, as she stared down at Emma. Whose eyes were heavily lidded, her cheeks flushed, her naked chest moving so deliciously with every ragged breath she took.

"Bedroom," Regan managed to pant out. "Sutton and I promised we'd never defile the living room couch, and I respect that promise, and I *need* us to go to my bedroom – now."

She'd never been more relieved, more turned the fuck on, than she was when Emma nodded with no hesitation.

Regan's knees were weak as she slid off Emma's lap and stood, and – wait, what?

As soon as gravity took over, her overalls slid off her body, pooling at her feet, leaving her standing in front of Emma in her sports bra and ruined underwear.

"When did you do that?" She asked, pointing down at her overall straps, which were – clearly – unsnapped. "I didn't even feel it."

"When you were biting my nipple, and I felt like I was going crazy needing to touch more of you," Emma answered, smartly, her voice hardly more than a rasp.

"You're perfect." Regan stepped out of her overalls and grabbed Emma's hand tightly, pulling her up. "Let's go."

Because she was seconds away from stripping them both down and pushing Emma back down against the couch, promises to her best friend be damned.

twenty-six

"*Emma*," Regan's breathless cry wasn't really all that loud, but Emma shuddered with it, feeling like it exploded in the dimmed lighting of Regan's bedroom.

Emma had Regan pressed against the doorframe, her own hands working fervently over Regan's body. She'd had such limited space to touch when they'd been on the couch, as Regan had been so determined to explore Emma's chest.

And she wasn't complaining, not by a fucking mile, because Regan's mouth had felt *so* good.

But, "You're not the only one that's desperate to touch," she rasped out, before nipping her teeth into Regan's throat. That sensitive place she'd found days ago, that made Regan melt.

As if on cue, she felt Regan's legs shake, and she pressed herself even more firmly against Regan, holding her up.

Had Emma *ever* felt so viscerally satisfied? She didn't think so; there was no way.

Regan was so responsive to her, to everything she did. And Emma wanted to touch everywhere she possibly could.

She hooked her fingertips into Regan's sports bra, tugging up slightly, urging Regan to lift her arms and let Emma take it off.

Regan complied, immediately, and that easy compliance shot another streak of heat down between Emma's legs. "I didn't – I didn't know this was going to happen," Regan panted, as Emma pulled off her bra. "I would have worn my own sexy bra, if I did."

"I didn't know, either. And you don't need a bra to be sexy," Emma informed her, before she slid her hands up the gentle curve of Regan's little waist and cupped her breasts.

She felt Regan shudder against her and watched how she dropped her head back against the doorway, before she leaned back in; the long line of Regan's neck was *begging* for her attention.

Really, though, Emma hadn't planned for this to happen.

Sure, she'd spent all day at work trying desperately to stay focused on the final Alton Fellowship interviews rather than letting her mind wander to Regan. To the sounds Regan made when she came, the sounds that reverberated in Emma's mind like an echo chamber. It only got more intense as the days went on.

It was as though every orgasm she experienced with Regan without actually being able to physically touch her simply made Emma's need even more urgent.

She'd tried to keep them on a fine line of satisfaction – she'd had to face the reality that they weren't going to be able to stay PG, not after that first night – without making any hasty decisions.

But when she'd arrived home from work, eager and wanting, so ready to see Regan after a long day of being apart from her, and Regan... hadn't been here.

She'd been so – ridiculously – disappointed. Regan had sent her a text, informing her that she had to go and see her sister at the last minute, but Emma hadn't seen it until she'd already arrived at their empty apartment.

And in that disappointment, in the too-quiet stillness of their apartment without Regan inside of it, Emma had far too much time to *think*.

She'd sat on the couch, trying to put something on tv to have some sound in the background... and all she'd thought about was the way she and Regan had ended up making out on the couch every night. She could see, so clearly, in her mind the different positions they'd found themselves in – Regan in her lap, the way they'd laid facing one another on their sides, the way Regan had pulled Emma to lay on top of her.

She'd groaned, forcing herself to get up, and – listlessly – had gone into her bedroom. Only to stare at the bed, thinking about her new bedtime routine. How she hadn't read before she'd fallen asleep in almost a week, because she was, instead, fucking herself with Regan's words and whimpers and moans in her ear.

She'd *tried* to keep a level head. She'd tried to tell herself that she should make them something for dinner. That she could get some reading done, now. That she could get a jumpstart on some emails for tomorrow.

All she'd managed to do was think more about Regan. About how the literal *thought* of Regan made Emma's blood pulse, heavy and hot, through her veins.

The longer she'd sat in their apartment without Regan, the more Emma had been left... wanting. The more certain Emma had become that she didn't want to wait any more.

Because – what were they really waiting for?

As Regan scratched down Emma's back, before gripping her hips and pulling Emma flush against her, she knew without a fucking doubt that she'd made the best choice.

She arched against Regan, her whole body shivering with the feeling of their stomachs and breasts pressed together. "Fuck," she groaned against Regan's throat.

"I know," Regan's voice was so throaty as she nodded, desperately. "I need – off."

She felt Regan reach between them, unsnapping the button on Emma's pants, before jerking down the zipper. Unlike with her shirt coming completely off, Emma simply let Regan do it. Those reservations, that zip of insecurity, had been decimated by Regan's undeniable arousal for her.

It made Emma's mind spin, the way Regan wanted her. She knew without a single doubt that she'd never been desired this way in her life, and that alone was the headiest aphrodisiac Emma had ever experienced.

She felt Regan's hands yank and tug down Emma's pants and

underwear – only low enough until Regan could completely slide her hands down and palm Emma's ass.

"Oh my *god*," Regan's words were released with a whine, as she gripped and pulled Emma against her. "You – I–"

Emma's eyes fluttered closed as she felt Regan dig her fingers into her ass, rocking Emma against her. In fairness, Emma didn't need the encouragement; her hips were already, subconsciously, rolling against Regan's.

"Bed," Regan bit out, scratching her nails into Emma for a sharp, delightful moment that left Emma gasping for air, before she released her. "Get in my bed."

Her words were a breathless command, and Emma was powerless to deny it. There was no part of her that wanted to deny it, in any way.

She breathed out a laugh – edgy and needy – as she rolled her eyes at Regan and slid her pants the rest of the way down her legs. "Well, if *someone* had taken my pants off completely..."

She trailed off, the teasing falling away from her lips and her mind, as Regan – without a hint of self-consciousness – hooked her thumbs into her own underwear and slid them down long, toned legs.

Jesus. Fucking. Christ.

Emma's gaze was affixed first to the center of Regan's underwear, which was so wet, the material was basically fucking translucent. She wasn't surprised, because Regan had urged Emma to touch her, already. She'd felt Regan's arousal coat her fingertips already, but seeing it...

Swallowing thickly, Emma ran her eyes up Regan's legs, between her thighs. Where she could *see* Regan dripping for her. Her thighs were wet, and Emma shuddered, clenching her own thighs together.

Regan wasted no time, stepping forward and pressing her hands against Emma's shoulders to guide her backwards. "In. My. Bed," she growled, dark eyes glinting up at Emma.

Something about that challenging look in Regan's gaze hooked itself inside of Emma, gripping her tightly. With it, she tilted her head and reached down, sliding her hands down Regan's sides. Beginning at the sides of her breasts – fine, yes, Regan was obviously right earlier; her chest was much smaller than Emma's, but she fucking loved it. She loved that she could cup Regan in her palms and feel all of her – she slowly, firmly, worked down until she gripped the subtle flair of Regan's waist.

"You. Aren't. In. Charge. Of. Me," she muttered back, narrowing her eyes.

They held each other's gaze for a beat, and it felt so – *them*. It was all Emma could think. That this moment, this give-and-take, this felt so right.

Wrapped up in that feeling, she spun them and used her grip on Regan's waist to push her down on the bed, first. Emma followed milliseconds later, laying her body completely on top of Regan's, and they both moaned at the sensation of bare skin on bare skin.

Regan's moan was louder, of course, and the fact that it was right here, right in Emma's ear from Regan's plush lips and not through the phone, had Emma whimpering.

Regan stroked her hands up Emma's back, surging up to connect their lips in a blistering kiss as she spread her thighs widely, fitting Emma perfectly between them.

Immediately, she felt Regan's hips roll into hers, intently. Searching.

"God, Em–" Regan breathed the words into her mouth, her fingers digging into Emma's back, hard. "I need... I *need*."

Emma was nodding already, because she needed, too.

She could feel how wet Regan was, how hot she was. Regan's pussy pressed against Emma's as she continued to try to find a rhythm and Emma's mouth fell open on a silent cry.

It felt *incredible* to feel Regan like this, bare and unashamed and needy against her. She'd never felt anything like this before, and she rocked her hips down, hard.

It felt so good, so fucking good, but Emma knew neither of them would ever be able to come from it. They were both so wet, there was no friction, and –

Emma couldn't wait.

She pushed herself up on one of her arms, working her other hand down between them. Sliding it down Regan's body – between her breasts, over the soft, pale plane of her stomach, over her bellybutton, and then... she paused.

Heart in her throat, feeling like she was choking on the desperation to touch Regan, she darted her gaze up from her hand on Regan's body to her face. Just to make sure –

And Regan met her gaze, nodding her head jerkily against the pillow. "Touch me. Fuck me. Emma, seriously, I *need* it. You have no idea."

Her words – demands, really – were delivered on halting, panting sentences, and it was all Emma needed to slide her hand lower.

She brushed her fingers over Regan's bare pussy for the first time, and Emma swore under her breath.

Regan swore out loud.

"Go inside, please. That's – that's what I want," Regan informed her, her hips rocking down against Emma's hand.

Still, she only worked her fingertips against Regan's entrance. It was mesmerizing, intoxicating, wildly, insanely arousing to be wanted like this. To have Regan's wetness coating her fingers, and she wasn't even really inside of her, yet.

"I know that's what you want," she found herself saying, not even recognizing her own voice with how gravelly she sounded. Her throat felt raw, and she wondered how many sounds she'd already let out that she didn't register. "I know, because you've told me every night."

Holding her breath, she pushed two fingers inside of Regan. Moving her hand slowly, pushing deep inside of Regan, and she didn't know what she wanted to watch more: her fingers, the way Regan arched her back, or the look of unadulterated relief on her face.

"You have no qualms about telling me what you want me to do to you. How you think about me touching you." Emma pulled her fingers out just as slowly, before working them back in, feeling Regan clench tightly around her.

She didn't even know where these words were coming from, honestly, because she'd *never* been much of a talker during sex. She'd have felt embarrassed, before; why did she need to talk, when her body was talking for her?

But she found, especially as she watched Regan's mouth tremble open with her words, that she really liked *this*.

"Why should I have qualms?" Regan rasped back, unevenly. She reached up and toyed with her own nipples, and Emma's throat went absolutely dry at the sight. "I'm not ashamed. I want you to know."

Emma nodded as she started truly thrusting inside of Regan, now. Pulling out slowly, pushing in faster and harder. Setting a rhythm that Regan settled into in moments.

"I know, and that's crazy to me. The way you want me, and how you want me to know." She moved faster, now, working in a third finger when Regan gasped *more*.

Emma rolled her own hips down, desperately, into the bed. It didn't do much for her, other than make her clit throb with an urgent and unfulfilled need, but she couldn't stop herself.

"Emma, *fuck*, my clit. Rub my clit – please!" Regan's tone was a desperate plea, her breath hitching as she stared up at Emma with a dark, needy stare.

And Emma didn't want to deny Regan. She wanted to give her whatever she needed, whatever she wanted, because more than *anything*, she wanted to feel and hear Regan come for her. She wanted to feel Regan pulse and throb around her fingers, to hear these moans right in her ear.

Just as breathless as Regan was, she buried her fingers inside of Regan as she slid her thumb up, rubbing at Regan's achingly hard clit. So, so hard against her touch, and Emma dropped her head to Regan's shoulder with a groan.

"Yes, *yes!*" Regan cried out, unabashedly, as she dug her nails into Emma's back and stared up at her with bleary eyes. "I'm going to – I'm–"

Her back bowed up, those unfiltered sounds escaping her and surrounding Emma, as she felt Regan come for her.

She watched Regan closely as she worked her through her orgasm, feeling every single pulse around her fingers, every twitch of Regan's clit. Emma's own clit pulsed with the same answering rhythm, and she was so close to coming without being touched *at all*.

Even when Regan melted onto the bed, gasping for breath, she still rocked her hips jerkily down against Emma, trying to wring every last ounce of pleasure. It was the most Regan thing Emma could imagine, and *fuck* if it didn't add to her own arousal.

Emma could feel her heart pounding in her chest as she stared down at Regan as she finally stilled, shuddering as she whispered, "Oh my god."

She nodded back, because... yeah.

In the quickest rebound from an orgasm *ever*, Regan's eyes met hers, and the blissed out look in them was rapidly replaced by something needier. Darker.

Before Emma could possibly prepare herself, Regan used the hand she'd had gripping Emma's shoulder to push her onto her back.

Within seconds, Regan switched their positions, pushing herself up to sit astride Emma. She groaned, unable to help herself, as she felt Regan's soaked core press against her hip, and her thighs *shook* with need.

Still, she felt dazed at the sight of Regan, who stared down at her, hungrily.

There was no other way to refer to that look in Regan's dark eyes, as she trailed her eyes over Emma's body splayed out for her. Over her breasts, her stomach...

And Emma didn't even feel – for the first time in her life – the slightest discomfort at being laid so bare for someone. Every last inch of herself on display, every curve, every stretch mark, every *everything*.

How could she, when Regan was staring at her like she was a five-course meal, and she hadn't eaten in days. Maybe weeks.

Trying to gather her wits – trying not to beg, demand, plead, order Regan to fucking touch her before she exploded – Emma managed out, "I know you've never–" She swallowed hard, a choked groan working out of her throat as Regan reached up and cupped both of Emma's breasts, firmly rubbing her thumbs over Emma's nipples.

Jesus... what had she been saying?

"That you've never been with a woman, before. So, I – *Regan*," she grit out, exasperated and so turned on, she could feel herself dripping.

"Yes?" Regan asked, her voice light and teasingly innocent.

Emma glared as best as she could in her situation. "Don't give me that *yes*."

Regan flicked her thumbs over Emma's nipples, before she rolled both of them between her fingers. Emma arched into the touch, feeling like she had a direct nerve between her nipples and her clit.

"I'm *trying*," she paused, needing to gather herself. "To tell you... that you don't have to do anything if you aren't–"

Regan pinched her nipples, *hard*, making Emma cut herself off with a whimper as she desperately rolled her hips up.

"Emma, be real," Regan's voice had fallen to that low octave, that one that Emma could have never known existed, before the last week. The one that worked to drive her *crazy*. "I'm going to make you come, and I'm going to do it with my mouth."

Emma's lungs fucking burned as she tried to take in a deep breath. The very idea of that... it shot through her like liquid pleasure.

"You love my lips," Regan continued, shifting her body and sliding down Emma's. She held eye contact with Emma as she moved lower... lower.

Emma widened her thighs for her, not giving a damn that she seemed as eager as she was. She was *more* than eager.

Regan settled on her stomach on the mattress, running her hands up Emma's thighs. "I already told you that I've thought about this, too."

Of course, Regan would continue talking even now. Even as she leaned in and pressed her perfect mouth to Emma's inner thigh, only inches from her pussy.

Emma's groan was so deep, so guttural, it *hurt* as it worked out of her throat.

"Regan," she moaned, encouraging and pent-up and reverent and wanting and... everything.

"I don't need to have done this before to know that I can make you come really–" Regan leaned in, drawing a long lick with the flat of her tongue up Emma's slit.

She couldn't fucking breathe, the spiraling heat already starting to tightly coil inside of her.

"*Really*," Regan whispered against Emma's core, before working the tip of her tongue up over Emma's weeping clit.

Emma was going to die.

"Hard," Regan finished, and she didn't give Emma another moment before she dove in.

Regan's mouth – those lips she'd fixated on for far too long – wrapped around her clit, as Regan's tongue lapped at it, and Emma reached down, sliding her hands into Regan's hair. Needing that contact, needing to touch her, to feel grounded in some way.

Regan was making hungry, needy sounds against Emma, and she could feel the vibration of them.

Fuck. Holy –

Emma had never been brought to the brink so quickly in her life, but she was already there, already on the precipice of falling into her orgasm.

And she couldn't make herself hold back, even if she wanted to.

Not when Regan's mouth was on her like she would die if she had to take a breath, when it seemed like Regan was getting just as much from this as Emma was. Not when it was so, so true – Emma *did* love Regan's fucking mouth, and her lips were so soft, and – and –

"Ah, *ah*–" Emma's breath caught, before she gasped, and she came.

So. Fucking. Hard.

Her thighs shook, clenching around Regan's head, and she gripped Regan's soft hair in her hands like a lifeline, because she wasn't sure she would survive this without it.

The pleasure that rolled through her was so blisteringly intense, and the only thing Emma could do was give herself over to it.

Regan didn't pause, continuing to move her lips softly against Emma's clit to work her through her orgasm and letting out those quiet whimpers of her own.

Eventually, Emma could feel the pleasure turn into a warning sensitivity, and she lightly tugged at Regan's head. "I – no more," she gasped, still unable to catch her breath.

Regan's groan of disappointment was unmistakable, but she removed her mouth from Emma as requested and stared up from between Emma's legs.

Her dark eyes were wide as she panted for breath, her cheeks flushed, and Emma could see herself coating Regan's lips and chin. Unbelievably, after coming so hard she was still clenching every few seconds, she felt another stab of arousal at the sight.

"That was... amazing," Regan's voice was awed, as she blinked up at Emma.

"It was," Emma agreed, softly. She slid her hand down to cup Regan's jaw, brushing her thumb over that fantasy-inducing pouty bottom lip, feeling her own wetness. Regan followed her touch with her tongue, and... god, Regan really might be the death of her.

"I can't wait to do it again." An exuberant, excited smile slid over Regan's face, and Emma felt a mirroring one tug at her lips.

"Okay, eager beaver–"

Regan scoffed out a laugh.

Emma rolled her eyes, even as she couldn't help but laugh, too. "Just get up here, please."

Regan pushed herself up and essentially hopped into her place at Emma's side, and she could feel Regan vibrating with renewed energy.

Emma turned onto her own side to really look at Regan, drawing her eyes down Regan's face as Regan draped an arm over Emma's side.

"This is crazy," she whispered, a disbelieving laugh bubbling up her throat at this reality.

She was having sex with Regan fucking Gallagher, and it was the best sex of her life, and she felt so *comfortable* here with her – more than she'd ever felt with another person – and...

"What?" Regan demanded to know, arching an eyebrow. "We're laying here, naked, after we just had the best sex of our lives – fine, an assumption, but the best sex of *my* life – and you're *laughing*?"

There was no real affront in her voice, and Emma... she could only shake her head.

It was absurd, but it was true. So wildly true.

"Keep it up, Bordeaux, keep it up," Regan murmured, as she surged up to press her mouth to Emma's again.

Emma knew she should probably be asleep.

It was after midnight and she had work in the morning, and her body was deliciously sore after the last several hours in Regan's bed.

And yet... she hadn't yet found the fortitude to drag herself away from the night with Regan.

A first for her, because Emma had never in her life not followed her internal rules around going to sleep at an appropriate time for school or work. She took those things very seriously, and did not mess around with them.

She would go to sleep soon, she idly thought, though she wasn't quite sure she believed herself.

She should be exhausted, but she wasn't. Even though Regan had worked her through another orgasm, and she'd fucked Regan twice more, she wasn't tired. Rather, she was wired.

She sat leaning back against Regan's headboard, as Regan had gotten up the energy to go and put their plates from the pizza they'd eventually gotten around to ordering in the kitchen. And she felt so... content.

She liked Regan's room. She liked the plants in here, how fresh and vibrant it felt. How comfortable Regan's mattress and sheets were.

Regan's phone vibrating on the bedside table cut into her thoughts, and Emma peered over at it, wondering who in the world was calling Regan after midnight.

And, ah. A nervous shiver worked through her as she saw Sutton on the incoming FaceTime call.

"Who is that?" Regan asked as she walked through the doorway, her hands falling to her hips. "I swear, if it's the café and someone called out tonight, I'm going to—"

"It's Sutton," she interrupted, tilting her head to the phone next to her. "She's requesting a video call."

Regan – standing a few feet from the bed, wearing Emma's discarded button-up that was too big for her and all wrinkled – blinked back at her for several seconds, before simply saying, "Oh."

Regan's eyebrows furrowed, obviously conflicted, as she shook her head. "Um, just – you can just... reject it." She cleared her throat, her mouth pulling into a small frown. "I can call her back in the morning."

Emma frowned back at her, her own stomach twisting with discomfort. Both at the clear distress Regan was feeling at concealing this from Sutton, as well as her *own* discomfort.

It was the first time Emma had felt like this, had experienced this niggling guilt about Sutton knowing nothing about what was happening between them. Sutton was a good friend to her, she'd never done anything to make Emma feel like she wouldn't be there for her.

And more than that, Sutton meant the world to Regan. She didn't want to be – refused to be, actually – the one thing in Regan's adult life that she felt she needed to keep from her best friend.

So, even though she still felt a little nervous – because the future was unknown, and she valued Sutton's friendship, and she didn't want anything to feel weird, ever – she glanced down at herself, making sure that she had Regan's sheet pulled up securely over her chest. Yep. She was going to do this.

With a deep breath, she braced herself for whatever reaction might be coming her way, and answered Sutton's call.

Sutton stared back at her from her own bed, looking as though she'd barely properly woken up before she'd called Regan. "Hey, I–"

Sutton abruptly cut herself off, confusion sliding across her face. "Emma! I'm so sorry." She reached up, carding a hand through her long, sleep-tousled red hair, as a small, apologetic smile tugged at her lips. "I thought I'd called Regan, but I guess I'm less awake than I thought."

Emma glanced at Regan, who was still standing a few feet away from the bed, staring at her with luminous, wide, questioning eyes.

"You did call her," Emma confirmed, pushing through that uncertainty. Through the twisting feeling that she was revealing too much of herself. This was *Sutton*, she firmly told herself, there was nothing she really needed to keep private from her, even if that demand for privacy inside of Emma still remained in the back of her head.

It was time to push past that.

Sutton's eyebrows knit together. "Um... okay?" She stared at Emma, obviously puzzled. "Did you accidentally swap phones or something?"

"No." Emma shook her head, but hesitated before any other words could leave her mouth. Where did she possibly even begin to tell Sutton about what had happened this summer?

Sutton got the conversation started for her. She squinted at the phone critically, leaning in closer. "Wait a second. Wait. Is that – that's Regan's headboard? And her purple sheet?" Sutton sat up sharply, her face so close to the screen that Emma's view of her was obstructed, as if Sutton were trying to crawl through the phone to investigate. "Why are you in Regan's room? Did you kill her and take over her space?"

Her tone was only slightly joking, but more urgently alarmed than anything, and Emma reeled back, unsure if she was more amused or offended. "*What*? Are you serious? No!"

Sutton still didn't look convinced. "With your track record with Regan, can you blame me?"

Emma glanced at Regan, gesturing helplessly at the phone in her hand to wordlessly ask Regan to do something, here. It seemed that was the only encouragement Regan needed.

"I'm alive," Regan confirmed, sounding breathlessly excited as she quickly crawled back into bed, slotting into the spot next to Emma. Their shoulders pressed firmly together, and Regan's face joined Emma's on the phone, to provide visual confirmation for Sutton. She grinned, beautifully and brightly, waving at Sutton. "Hey, babe!"

"Hey...?" Sutton drew out, slowly, leaning back from her phone, but her eyes didn't leave the screen. As if she couldn't quite connect the dots of what was being presented to her.

Because, presented to Sutton, was a very *obvious* picture. Emma stared, surprisingly fixated on their image together in the corner of the screen. They were both flushed with that post-sex glow that Emma had always rolled her eyes about. But it was real, and she saw it right now. Both of their hair was mussed, and it was very clear that hands had been gripping and pulling. They looked so... relaxed.

Which wasn't weird for Regan. Who looked relaxed almost always.

Emma was far more fascinated by how *she* looked. Leaning into Regan, she looked so... at-ease. More than that, she felt it.

Strange, how someone with so much energy, who was so vibrant, made Emma feel so calm. Yet, here they were, and her heart beat a little harder, a little faster at it.

Not the time to dive into that.

Clearing her throat, she refocused her attention on Sutton.

Who'd remained silent for nearly a minute, now, and Emma didn't know if she'd ever seen someone look so baffled in her entire life.

Finally, Sutton spluttered out, "You don't own anything that remotely looks like that shirt."

Clearly in reference to Regan, as Emma... wasn't wearing one.

Regan looked down at herself, before turning back to Sutton as she insisted, "Hey, I could have bought this!"

"No, you wouldn't." Sutton's eyes narrowed to little slits, as she looked between the two of them, shaking her head. "I... what the hell is going on over there? I need you to just – explain." She reached up and rubbed her fingers over her forehead, roughly. "Because what it *looks* like isn't – there's no way..."

Emma could feel the way Regan inhaled, deeply, and held her breath, and she turned to look at her.

Regan was already watching Emma, her gaze questioning and thoughtful and sweet, and Emma's chest filled with warmth at it.

Yeah. It was unbelievable to her, too, and she was living it. So, she couldn't blame Sutton's incredulity.

"It *is* what it looks like," she confirmed, quietly, turning her attention back to look at the phone.

Her stomach flip-flopped as the anticipation slid through her, because she honestly was clueless as to how Sutton would react to this. Sutton was protective over Regan, Emma knew that was true. She knew how staunchly Emma had pushed against Regan. And... well, she'd never even come out to Sutton on her own, before.

This moment really hit a lot of boxes for her.

That anxiety calmed, as she felt Regan's hand land gently on top of Emma's free hand where she'd had it clenched into a fist against her thigh. Instinctively, she flipped her palm upward to interlock their fingers.

"No," Sutton slowly drew out, making the short word last several syllables. "Because what it *looks like* is that you two are... that you just..."

"Had sex," Regan supplied, the words bursting from her lips, and Emma was truthfully shocked it had taken this long.

"And we did. Have sex," Regan confirmed needlessly, as she squeezed Emma's hand in hers, vibrating with that bountiful energy.

434

"You *what*?!" Sutton gasped, her eyes widening in shock in spite of having stared at them in bed together for the last two minutes.

"We had sex," Regan repeated, the pride in her voice was loud and clear. Like she wanted to puff out her chest and strut around, shouting it from the rooftops. Since this was Regan, it was quite possible she did.

Emma couldn't help but smile at it – why did she find that so charming? – even as she closed her eyes in wait for Sutton's response.

Sutton was silent for so long, though, that Emma opened her eyes in concern that she'd hung up on them.

But, no. Sutton was still there. Staring at her phone with her mouth hanging open, very clearly unable to form words.

The great news for all of them in this moment, was that Regan so rarely struggled with words.

"I know – you're shocked," Regan jumped in to fill the void. "And I totally get it; I was shocked, too! I mean, not tonight. This has kind of been building. But I *was* shocked when I realized I was attracted to Emma. You know, since we didn't know I was into women."

Sutton finally managed to speak. "And when was *that*?" She asked, still sounding so shell-shocked.

Emma couldn't blame her.

Regan's bright smile dimmed ever-so-slightly, as she winced. "Um... a while ago? Earlier this summer?"

Sutton shook her head, clearly trying to make sense of the information she was being given. "And Emma? You're into women, too? Obviously?"

"Yeah." She cleared her throat, pushing herself to be as open and honest as possible. "Though, I've known for a lot longer than this summer."

Sutton blew out a breath. "Sure. Right." Unsurprisingly, her attention turned back to Regan, a frown etched into her face. "Why didn't you tell me? You've been working through this for weeks – months? – and you didn't *tell* me?"

The confusion and hurt in her voice were undeniable, and she felt Regan's hand tighten on hers.

"I wanted to tell you," Regan said, with obvious guilt. Emma could feel the tension that worked through Regan's body. "I *really* wanted to tell you, but…" Regan worried at her bottom lip, clearly conflicted and a little distressed. "I didn't want to add to your plate, and I didn't want to stress you out, and–"

"You're my best friend! I've been way more stressed thinking that something terrible was going on for over a month," Sutton refuted, her tone inarguably steely, while still keeping that gentle edge she was so good at. "You were there for me every step of the way when I was figuring my sexuality out – sometimes, too much. I…" She rolled her lips, that wounded expression still on her face as she trailed off.

"I'm sorry," Regan's apology burst out, and her remorse was written all over her face. "I'm really sorry."

Sutton shook her head, as she stated, firmly, "I don't want to make this about me; because this *isn't* about me. I just… I'm – trying to figure out how to process."

Emma squeezed Regan's hand in support as she explained, "She didn't tell you because she knew I kept my own personal life so… guarded. And even though I wouldn't have been upset if she went to her best friend for support," she emphasized, needing Regan to know that was the truth. She turned to look at Regan as she said it, hoping Regan would be able to see how much she meant it. "She did it out of respect for me."

Yeah, that warm feeling filled her chest, again, and only grew bigger and stronger, at the tremulous smile that worked over Regan's face.

"Okay…" Sutton drew out. "I, conceptually, understand what you're saying. But… this…" She gestured at the two of them. Finally, she huffed out a breath and rolled her shoulders, as if forcing herself to get with the program. "So. You're having sex."

"Tonight was the first time… mostly," Regan supplied, sounding both hopeful and apologetic. "I'll tell you *everything* – because it's been a wild summer! – but you have to know that I would have told you if we were, like, in a real, official relationship."

At that, Sutton pursed her lips, a glint sparking in her eyes. "I see. This isn't a relationship, then?"

Emma didn't understand that tone; she didn't think she'd ever heard it before.

Regan groaned, though. "Why are you using Katherine Spencer voice on me?"

"I'm not," Sutton denied, but the voice was still there. "I'm just asking if this is a relationship. Because if you two are deciding to embark on some friends-with-benefits thing that could get really messy, then I'm not sure I want all of the details."

Regan scoffed. "Rich coming from *you*." She arched a look at Sutton.

Emma couldn't help but laugh.

Sutton blushed faintly, even as she remained firm in her stance. "Yes, ha-ha, fine. But if you two are doing something without any strings and are trying to keep things... light, then – for the sake of my friendship with you both – I'm not sure how much I should get into it."

That *tone* remained, and Emma didn't know why, but she got the distinct impression that Sutton was directing it at her?

She frowned, stomach twisting, as she stared back at Sutton. And, yes, they were communicating via video chat, but, "Are you looking at *me*, specifically?" She demanded to know, because it *really* seemed that was what was happening.

"Yes," Sutton confirmed, easily.

"Why?" Emma frowned, feeling very put on the spot. "We're *both* doing this."

"Because even on a phone call from across the Atlantic, I can read Regan like a book," Sutton informed her, and her tone gentled as she glanced at Regan. Slowly, she drew her gaze back to Emma. "It's – clearly – harder for me to read you. I mean. Obviously, this attraction is new. And I know how... tenuous things were in the beginning of this arrangement, so–"

"The attraction isn't new," Emma found herself stating, even as a rush of heat hit her cheeks.

She could see Regan's slow, sweet smile bloom, even as Sutton's eyebrows lifted high on her forehead. "Ah... huh."

"I think," Emma paused, her heart beating a little harder in her chest as her nerves buzzed to life. "It was always a lot easier – safer – for me to focus on any possible negative about Regan, so that I never gave myself the opportunity of feeling anything more, that I wasn't ready to feel."

She slowly turned to look at Regan, who was staring at her with those big, brown eyes. Those eyes that searched Emma's, amazed and thrilled, and Emma could only look right back and let Regan see whatever she was looking for.

Because that was the truth.

A distressing truth that Emma had to accept in the last month.

"Oh, wow. Okay," Sutton breathed, regaining both of their attention. "So, this is a thing, then. This is a real... relationship?"

Emma felt Regan's hand tighten in hers.

"I mean, uh, I *was* serious, Sutton, when I said this was the first time we've slept together." Regan breathed out a slightly nervous laugh, shooting Emma a look. "We don't need to–"

"It's a relationship," Emma interjected, as her stomach recoiled at the idea that it *wasn't*.

She turned to look at Regan, capturing her gaze with a steady, serious look.

"To me, this is a real relationship. I wouldn't want to do this," she gestured between them. "If it wasn't. I have real-girlfriend feelings for you," she echoed Regan's sentiment, when Regan had laid her cards on the table.

But – she needed Regan to know that. And she needed to make sure her own cards were laid out, too.

"I don't want you to be on dating apps. Or sleeping with anyone else." She recalled from the night Regan had told her that all Emma had to do was *say it* if she wanted this.

Regan quickly shook her head. "No, neither – uh, I mean, no. Me, neither. For both of us."

Satisfied, even as she felt exhilarated and a little scared, and definitely a little embarrassed at the fact that Sutton had witnessed this very personal moment between them, Emma exhaled a breath she hadn't realized she'd been holding.

"Wow. Just – all right. *Wow*," Sutton muttered, staring at them as if she'd never seen them, before. "So, this is what's been going on over there."

"I have a girlfriend," Regan announced, sounding delighted and shocked. She slid her bare leg along Emma's, clearly unable to keep still. "A real one, now."

Emma couldn't help but laugh, and...

She had a *girlfriend* – a real one, now.

"I'm sorry. What?" Sutton pressed.

Regan opened her mouth to start talking, and Emma could *see* how the excited explanation was ready to fall from her lips. Before she paused, looking at Emma for full permission to spill the beans.

Endeared, she nodded, inviting Regan to tell Sutton everything. It was about time, it seemed.

"The craziest thing happened," Regan started, and Emma leaned back against the headboard, gazing at her.

Everything felt surreal, but... not.

She was in a real relationship with this woman.

twenty-seven

REGAN – 5:37PM

Beth dropped an entire pot of coffee today. Literally SHATTERED the glass. It's great for me, because she's officially taken over as the most accident-prone person at the shop

I saw that guy on the subway, the one that tried to give me a ferret that one time. No ferrets, anymore, though. Wonder what happened to them all

OH and the biggest update is that I found this vibrator online that we tried out last night and when I tell you that they really mean MUTUAL PLEASURE – I'll send you the link

SUTTON, THE ONE AND ONLY – 5:38PM

When I said that I didn't need you to "make it up to me" I meant it. Really, I don't need the update on what time you peed this morning. I promise.

REGAN – 5:38PM

Are you sure? Because I am HAPPY to tell
you. EVERYTHING

I don't want you to worry that I replaced you
with Charlotte this summer

SHE CHUCKLED, utterly amused with herself for that one. Now that
Sutton was in the know about everything since their conversation nearly
two weeks ago, Regan had made it a point to text and call Sutton much
more regularly. Now that she didn't feel like she had to keep any secrets
or had any uncertainty about her relationship with Emma –

Because they were *in a relationship!* –

It was great! She got to gush about everything to Sutton. To ask her
advice. To tell her about how it felt so... perfect, like things just made
sense for her, now.

Being able to talk to Sutton and really talk to her, the way she was
used to, had soothed over the only remaining stress she'd had weighing
on her.

And she got to do that because Emma was her girlfriend, by Emma's
own admission!

SUTTON, THE ONE AND ONLY – 5:39PM

Believe me, I don't feel replaced

Regan snickered again, thinking about the relieved *FINALLY*
message she'd received from Charlotte the morning after she'd confessed
everything to Sutton.

REGAN – 5:39PM

I'm not relieving Charlotte of her friend
duties, though. I hope she still knows that

SUTTON, THE ONE AND ONLY – 5:39PM

You know, I actually think she likes it. Don't
tell her I said that

REGAN – 5:40PM

> Keeping secrets from your girlfriend AND telling me things she wouldn't want to tell me, herself?! Sutton, now that we are both relationship women, I think we both know that's not good…

SUTTON, THE ONE AND ONLY – 5:40PM

Oh my god

On that note, I'm going to sleep. I'll talk to you tomorrow morning <3

REGAN – 5:40PM

> I'll tell you what I had for dinner and what time I go to sleep, in the meantime…. :)

SUTTON, THE ONE AND ONLY – 5:40PM

I'm blessed, truly. GOODNIGHT

REGAN – 5:41PM

> Goodnighttttttttt

It was the perfect time for Sutton to bow out and go to sleep, really, because Regan had just turned down her hallway. She'd been at work for a *long* Saturday shift – she'd had to open this morning – and she was ready to discard her phone and bury herself in Emma for the night.

Emotionally, and – later – literally.

She looked up as she fished out her keys, and then froze in place, mid-step.

Squeezing her eyes closed, she shook her head – was she… hallucinating? She, admittedly, hadn't slept for more than five hours per night for the last week and a half, but she didn't think that was such a small amount that she'd start *hallucinating* from it.

In her defense, it was very, very difficult to force herself to go to sleep when she had Emma in her bed!

Regan had always loved sex. The closeness and connection, the indulgent pleasure of it. She loved expressing her affection for people with physical touch, loved leaning into people's energies, and sex was the ultimate form of that.

But her past experiences paled in comparison to this.

She had a whole new world to explore with Emma. She had a body that Regan really did feel very strongly could have been the perfect model for a classic sculptor, and Regan hadn't tired in the least in wanting to touch and taste her, everywhere. Sometimes to Emma's chagrin. But, in fairness, Emma seemed to feel the same way for her.

Even when she *tried* to act like she had more self-control or like she wasn't just as desperate as Regan was for their moments together, Regan could see the flush on her cheeks and the way her eyes lingered.

Pfft. Emma tried to play herself off all gruff and cool sometimes, still, but Regan knew better, now.

And she loved that.

Yes, okay, she was probably hallucinating, because she'd been too caught up in Emma lately – too caught up in the excitement, in something so good – that her mind wanted to remind her that there were some downsides to life, still. Before Regan got so filled with bright, fun times and simply floated away.

Blinking her eyes open, she found that – nope. The sight in front of her remained. Isaac and Dierdre Gallagher remained standing in front of her, their pinched expressions the same as Regan could always conjure up in her head.

"Mom? Dad? What are you doing here?" She asked, confused and a little scared, honestly. "Did someone die?"

Oh, god. Who could have died that was so important her parents needed to come and find her to tell her in person?! *Audrey?*

Her mother pursed her lips, shooting a dark look toward Regan's apartment. Following her gaze, she realized that the door was open, and Emma was standing there.

Her arms crossed over her chest, with a stubbornly serious glare that mirrored Regan's parents' expressions. Huh. Wow.

Regan remembered that look! It was crazy, really, to think that she'd so often been on the receiving end of a similar expression, because she hadn't seen that look on Emma's face in months.

"We'd *intended* to see your home." Her mother sniffed, haughtily, and gestured at Emma. "But when we arrived this woman – your... roommate? – refused to let us in."

"They arrived less than two minutes ago," Emma interjected, her tone exacting and sharp. "It's not like it's been an hour."

Baffled, Regan took a few steps closer. Only to stop as soon as she was within a few feet of her parents, feeling that awful, heavy sensation in her chest – like she was the world's biggest failure and disappointment – that only her parents knew how to bring out in her with just a look.

And, boy oh boy, were they giving her the look. A look she was, also, more than familiar with.

"But what are you doing here?" She repeated, because that comment hadn't really explained anything. "You never come here when you're in the city."

She knew her parents traveled to New York at least once or twice a year, coming to see shows, meet up with friends, have weekend getaways; they'd done it since she was a kid. She imagined they'd likely been in Manhattan a lot more frequently in the last year, too, since helping to plan Audrey's wedding.

But they never came to see *her*. If anything, they'd extend an invitation to join them and Audrey for dinner, but even that was a rare occurrence. The only time Regan was guaranteed to see her parents in a calendar year was over the holidays. So, this? Unprecedented and disconcerting.

Her father exhaled, impatiently. "We just had an early dinner with your sister. We hadn't even planned on coming into the city this weekend, but she insisted that she had to talk to us in person." He arched her a look. "Do you have anything you want to take accountability for?"

Confusion growing by the second – and that feeling inside of her, like she was the world's worst person, multiplied with it. God, how did they do that so well? – Regan slowly shook her head. "Um... no?"

She hadn't even spoken to Audrey in nearly two weeks, since the wine bar. So why in the world was she on the receiving end of their accusing stares?!

"Typical," her father muttered.

Ugh, Regan's stomach twisted, and she felt her shoulders slump at the tone. Still, she did her best to respond and push past the feeling, as it was the only coping mechanism she'd ever figured out in this kind of situation. Push through as fast as possible, so it could all be over. "I don't know what you're even talking about."

"Audrey told us that she's no longer planning to marry Armando," her mother informed her, in that classic icy tone she had.

Regan's mouth fell open, shock rushing through her. "For real?"

"Yes, *for real*," her mom echoed, disdainfully.

"Wow! That's wild." Regan should text her! Damn, she hadn't seen that coming at all.

Before she could go too far down that mental rabbit hole, though, she looked back at her parents, quizzically.

"Um... so, what does this have to do with me?" She slowly asked, pointing at herself. "Shouldn't you be taking this up with, like, Armando?"

After all, he seemed to be the cause of Audrey's unhappiness.

Her father – in his long-sleeved button-up, tie, and well-ironed slacks, despite the fact that it was the end of August, and the humid heat was still among them – pursed his lips. "Audrey – *very* atypically for her – was unable to give us a succinct explanation as to why she wants to try to call off the wedding. What she *did* tell us, in a ramble that was much more befitting of you than her, is that you are the only person she's talked to about this, and that you encouraged this behavior."

Regan shook her head quickly. "No! Well. I mean – yeah? But, only because she told me that she was unhappy, so–"

"So, you *did* tell her to call it off," her mother interrupted, eyes narrowing to a glare. "Why am I not surprised? Despite the fact that all of our friends and associates are invited to the wedding, despite the fact that we've already paid tens of thousands in nonrefundable deposits."

Regan crossed her arms over herself, tightly, as she set her jaw in defense. "Audrey's an adult! She can make her own choices – she *should* make her own choices, about who to marry."

"Out of all of the things you've done to embarrass this family, you have *never* tried to drag your sister down to your level." Her father always had this way of speaking – so quietly, but Regan swore she'd be able to hear his voice cut through the loudest crowd – with his tone being so scornful...

Yeah, even now, it made Regan feel about two feet small.

"You can't come here and talk to her like that," Emma cut in, her tone hard as steel.

Regan turned to stare at Emma so quickly, she felt like she had whiplash from the movement. Frankly, in the last five minutes, she'd forgotten that Emma had been standing there.

Her parents – despite all of the work Regan had done around managing her feelings regarding them – still had the ability to make her feel like she was a ten-year-old getting punished. Like her world was just that small.

"This is none of your business," her mother authoritatively stated to Emma. "And it's very rude to interfere in family matters that are none of your concern."

"It's also very rude to show up to your daughter's apartment and treat her like dirt when she hasn't done *anything* wrong," Emma shot back, staring down at Regan's mom.

Oh. Even when Regan had been on the receiving end of Emma's ire, she'd *never* been looked at like that. The way Emma stared at Regan's parents was very distinctly the same way she'd stare at a bug she'd just squashed. Absolutely disgusted.

Before either of her parents could say anything, Emma rolled on, "And I don't care if you don't think it's my business; you're saying it right in front of my face. I happen to know that Regan is sweet, and thoughtful, and a hell of a lot kinder than either of you seem to be."

Regan felt her heart skip a beat, and her breath caught in her throat, as she stared at Emma. Did Emma actually have a halo, or was it just the way she seemed to appear to Regan?

Emma turned to look at her, and the stone-cold look in her eyes immediately softened, as she tilted her head. "Come on. You've been at work all day, you should be able to come home and relax."

Even though she didn't look away from Regan as she spoke, she hard edge in her voice was so pointedly directed at Regan's parents.

It was as though that had been precisely what Regan needed. For some reason, she'd needed that to kick her into gear, to make her push forward and brush by her parents so she could enter her apartment.

Emma pushed the door open wider for her but didn't step back herself – much to Regan's delight. She brushed against Emma as she stepped in, hesitating for a moment as she turned to look up at her parents.

"Maybe if you actually *listened* to Audrey, you'd have heard why she's not getting married to Armando, and the fact that it has nothing to do with me."

She felt like she was finally able to take a deep breath for the first time since this whole... thing... started, especially as she was breathing in *Emma*.

Gripping the doorknob in her hand, she arched them a look, and she felt so emboldened, so ready to look them in the eye as she said, "Oh and Emma isn't just my roommate; she's also my girlfriend."

Immediately, she saw her parents' eyes widen, and that was all she needed.

She shut the door on them, satisfaction slotting through her with a rush, as she stared at the closed door for several seconds. She'd actually just done that!

Even when she'd gone against what her parents wanted and expected from her, she'd always just... ignored them. Waited out their commentary, and rolled through it.

"I can't believe you just did that," she breathed, exhilaration still rushing through her as she turned to look at Emma, her eyes wide.

Emma's jaw was still set, tight and angry, as she looked down at Regan. "I can't believe they have the audacity to show up here, like that!" She gestured to the door, scoffing in obvious disgust. "They came here to seek you out, so they could talk to you like you're a misbehaving child?"

Those electric blue eyes closed, as Emma lightly shook her head and took in a deep breath.

"I'm sorry, if you felt like I overstepped, thou—"

Before Emma could finish that statement, Regan surged up and tossed her arms around Emma. She wrapped her into a hug, slotting her body against Emma's in a way she was so familiar with and still, it gave her a rush. It was like the ultimate comfort, like there was no better feeling. Especially when she felt Emma's arms slide around her waist and hold her right back.

"No one's ever done that for me, before," she whispered, and – huh. Her throat felt thick with emotion as she spoke.

Closing her eyes, she didn't loosen her hold on Emma, not at all. Not giving a single inch, as she leaned her head against Emma's, gripping the shirt Emma wore in tight fists.

The backs of her eyes burned with tears, but they weren't sad, and her heart was pounding in her chest, and she breathed in deeply through her nose, wanting to feel surrounded by Emma.

"Thank you," she murmured, her voice thick. "Thanks for not letting them in. And for saying what you said."

Emma squeezed her waist, as she spoke softly back, "I mean, this is why it is very important to know who is persona non grata to your roommates."

Breathing out a chuckle, Regan nuzzled in closer to Emma, brushing the tip of her nose against the soft skin of her neck. "You're right."

Keeping her eyes closed, she whispered, "I want to tell you something, and I don't want it to freak you out, and I really don't want it to change anything we have going on between us. I really, really mean it – I don't want anything to be different, but I need you to know, okay?"

She loved that Emma hadn't released her, or even attempted to loosen this hold. She loved that Emma seemed just as content in this moment as she was.

She could feel Emma slowly nod. "Okay?"

Regan paused – for this one, heart-pounding moment – as nerves and excitement and comfort tangled together inside of her. Could Emma feel how hard her heart was beating?

"I'm pretty sure I'm in love with you." There. The words were out in the open, rather than just circling around in Regan's mind before she fell asleep with Emma at night, and... it felt right.

In fact, as soon as she said it, everything inside of her *settled*. Even as she felt Emma's surprised, sharp inhale.

Still, Regan didn't pull back from their embrace and didn't let Emma pull away, either. Even when Emma's arms went slightly slack around her.

"Now, I'm saying *pretty sure*, because I've never been in love before, so I don't have anything concrete to compare this feeling to," she explained, pausing to press a brief kiss to Emma's shoulder through the fabric of her shirt. "But the way I feel about you is exactly what I'd imagined being in love with someone would be like. Only better."

"Regan..." Emma's murmur of her name was halting, and throaty, and so quiet, Regan was fairly certain she only heard her because Emma's mouth was right next to her ear.

She shook her head, intently. "I know it's a little soon. I mean... kind of. I've known you for years, and we've shared an apartment for months, and I know everything about you, including your obsessive calendaring habits and the way you like to roll the toothpaste from the bottom of the tube–"

"It's the right way," Emma countered, sounding dazed, but – of course – she wasn't going to not make the comment.

And, yeah, Regan *loved* that. Her lips pulled into a smile, as she smoothed her hands down Emma's back, reveling in the touch.

"Anyway, I know it's technically kind of soon, as in we've only been dating officially for a few weeks. And I know you take more time to process your feelings than I do. So, I don't need you to say it back to me." She narrowed her eyes in thought, and, "Honestly, I'd rather you didn't. Not that I think you would ever say something of this magnitude unless you really felt it, but... that's not why I'm telling you."

"It's not," Emma faintly echoed, her breath warm against Regan's ear.

"No. I'm telling you because I want you to know how I feel. I like to be able to tell you everything." With that, Regan took in another deep breath of Emma's scent, pressed one more kiss to the side of her throat, and pulled back enough to look up at Emma's face.

Which, to her credit, didn't look like Emma was going to run for the hills, so that was great! Regan would take it.

Feeling a wide smile break over her face, Regan rocked up to her tiptoes and pressed a kiss to Emma's lips. Something soft but full. A greeting and gratitude and an *I love you!* in a brief moment.

She pulled back, gently sliding her hands down Emma's arms. She

449

wondered if Emma knew she was still gripping Regan's waist, or if it was just reflex, as she tried to sort through her thoughts after Regan's confession.

Studying Emma's face, the sharp planes and gentle curves of it – Regan felt an easy calm take a hold of her, reaffirming everything. "Yeah. I love you."

Emma's face flushed as soon as Regan said the words, and she was absolutely *delighted* by the way Emma seemed shocked and pleased and hesitant and so unsure of how to respond.

That was her Emma.

Regan reached up to stroke her fingertips over Emma's jaw. "Don't freak out, please."

"I'm not," Emma answered immediately, frowning down at Regan. "I'm just – thinking."

"Okay," Regan accepted, tilting her head up at her. "I mean, you had to know this would be how this moment would go."

"What's that supposed to mean?"

"You know." Regan arched an incredulous look up at her. "I kissed you, first. I told you I was attracted to you, first. I told you I had feelings for you, first. I got you to agree to go on a date." She shrugged, easily. "Me telling you that I love you first is the next step."

Emma's eyebrows knit tightly together indignantly and she shook her head. "What about the fact that I initiated us having sex first? Doesn't that count for something?"

Regan found her self-righteousness ridiculously cute.

"Only because I was respecting your boundaries and *not* initiating sex until you were ready! If you hadn't wanted to take things slower, I would have dragged you into my bed after our first date." Regan *dared* Emma to disagree; she knew she had the upper hand, here.

Emma's lips pulled into a pouting frown. "You can't prove that."

"The comeback queen," Regan teased.

"I thought you were in love with me," Emma groused. "Doesn't that mean you should be nicer to me?"

"I'm sorry. How about I go down on you until you can't remember that I ever teased you?" She offered, biting her lip as she looked up at Emma through her eyelashes.

450

And – *fuck*, she'd been saying it as a tease, but as soon as she voiced it, the very idea of that offer zipped through Regan like a wildfire.

Making Emma come in her mouth had been Regan's favorite discovery and was quickly becoming her favorite pastime. She had a very busy and active mouth, and what better way to put it to use?

It was also the most effective way she believed she would ever have to rendering Emma into an agreeable puddle, and Regan was absolutely in love with that.

Emma's mouth fell open with a trembling breath, her pupils dilating, and Regan was ready to drop to her knees right here and now. She wanted to, viscerally, especially on the heels of her love confession. On the heels of Emma sticking up to Regan's parents on her behalf.

Yes, after the last twenty minutes, Regan was fairly certain she wasn't going to be sated tonight until she'd rendered Emma a shaking, whimpering mess.

Slowly arching her eyebrow, she started to dip down to her knees...

Only to find herself stopped, as Emma reached out, her hands landing on Regan's shoulders. "Wait. Stop. I..." She closed her eyes and took a deep breath, clearly gathering her wits. "I *do* think that sounds incredibly appealing."

Her voice was low as she slid one of her hands up and rubbed her thumb over Regan's bottom lip, the touch sending tingles down Regan's spine.

Emma shook her head. "*But*, today has been – a lot. You worked all day, you accepted an offer to make that cake for Kimberly's neighbor's party, your parents, and then you – um, you telling me..." Emma rolled her lips, cheeks turning an attractive shade of pink. "Let's take a breather. You and me, on the non-defiled couch, and just – let me have a few minutes with you and decompress."

Regan's heart stuttered in her chest, as she nodded up at Emma. "I'd like that."

She reached out, interlacing their fingers together, and feeling the whirlwind of emotions she'd been through in a very short period of time today, calm.

Emma operated at a three, and she operated at a seven, and the two of them together gravitated toward a five, and Regan thought that was good for her.

"To be clear, though, I'm going to get to celebrate my being in love with you by making you come in my mouth later?" She asked, dead seriously, as they walked toward the couch.

"It's literally going to be my pleasure."

twenty-eight

Emma watched Brynn pack up her desk, feeling a very unexpected pang of sadness in her chest.

"I'm a little surprised at how much I'm going to miss you," she murmured, rolling with the feeling. If Regan had taught her anything, it was that making someone feel good about themselves could be as simple as sharing your true – positive – feelings about them.

Granted, it still made Emma feel a little too exposed, but she was working on that.

Brynn smiled at her, her eyebrows lifting with that expression that said she was a little surprised, herself. "Wow. From *somewhat friends* to you're going to miss me, in a month? Emma, you are truly a dark horse."

She rolled her eyes. "Don't make me regret it."

"That feels more like it." Brynn ran her hand over her forehead with faux-relief. Still, her smile gentled into something more genuine, as she returned, "I'm a little surprised at how much I'm going to miss you, too."

Brynn zipped up her bag. "I'm sure, in fairness, you're going to miss me a little more. Given that you're about to get a newbie to sit across from all day, and there is simply no way they're going to be as wonderful to share this confined space with as I am."

Emma scoffed out a laugh, shaking her head. "Yep, and there goes any potential sappy feelings from the goodbye."

Brynn grinned back, unashamed. "It's hardly a goodbye, anyway. I can't wait to come over to the inner sanctum for dinner next week. See where the love story has unfolded."

Brynn let out an exaggerated sigh, clasping her hands together and leaning her cheek against them.

She groaned, turning back toward her computer. "If I regret *anything*, it's when you and Regan managed to exchange numbers."

Regan had dropped by last week to pick Emma up from work and take her out to dinner – something Emma could never really bring herself to be upset about in any way. She'd tried, really, to tell Regan to at least give her a warning.

But Emma couldn't deny that she really enjoyed walking out of the office to see Regan waiting for her, that ridiculously bright, beautiful smile perpetually aimed at her. She hadn't even disliked it when Regan had done it the very first time, before they'd gotten together, and *now...*

Well, now, it made Emma's stomach flutter.

It was a kind of gentle spontaneity that Emma found she liked.

Last week, though, Brynn had left the office a few minutes ahead of her, and when Emma had walked out, she'd seen Brynn and Regan chatting like they were old friends.

Regan *had* asked Emma for explicit permission before she'd mentioned inviting Brynn over to their apartment for dinner, though, which she deeply appreciated. And even as she'd initially wanted to say no because it felt very... personal, having Brynn come over to her place, she'd found herself tentatively agreeing to it.

"Too late now," Brynn teased, waggling her phone at Emma, before she breathed out a sigh and looked around their shared space. "I'm all packed up; going to go say goodbye to Vicki before I head out."

Emma nodded in acknowledgement as she started working through Allegra's final emails for the day. It wasn't as though Allegra didn't have Emma stay on top of her emails throughout the weekend or that she drew a hard line between office hours at at-home hours; it was more that she wanted to make it clear to a certain echelon of people that she was a busy woman, and that she wouldn't be prioritizing their issues just because they'd decided to email her on a Friday afternoon.

"Emma?" Allegra called from inside of her office.

Glancing up, she could see that Allegra was already looking at her through the glass wall, expectantly. She was already standing even before her boss added, "In here, please."

Emma walked through the open doorway, turning on the tablet she kept notes on for Allegra as she went.

"I couldn't help but overhear your heartfelt goodbye to Brynn," Allegra commented, surprising Emma, as she looked up at Emma from over the top of her glasses.

Yes, and *there* was that feeling of exposure. Emma's stomach squirmed with it, before she forcefully reminded herself that telling Brynn she'd miss her wasn't wrong or inappropriate. "Like I said: surprising, but true."

Allegra's lips twitched into a grin. "Yes, I understand that. I do want to assure you that you won't be left to train someone brand new; I've officially poached Britney from health and fitness."

Narrowing her eyes, Emma wracked her brain trying to place a face with the name. "She handles their department admin."

Allegra nodded. "She's actually been doing much of the communications work that *should* be done by Lesley's assistant, as well as keeping the wellness department completely in check. I think you'll find that she'll be a more than adequate replacement."

"That's great," Emma commented, hesitantly. And, it *was* great; Emma definitely hadn't wanted to have to take it upon herself to show someone the ropes at *Olly*, get them familiar with their systems and policies. The fact that all she had to do was get Britney up to speed on Allegra's schedule sounded amazing.

She couldn't help but feel a little confused, though, at the fact that Allegra felt the need to call her into her office to discuss it face-to-face at the end of the day on a Friday.

"I thought so." The look in Allegra's eyes sharpened, as she pursed her lips. "Now, onto our actual business."

This made more sense, and Emma hovered her fingers over the screen of the tablet, at the ready.

"Now that Henry's been let go, I'm casting a wider net for submissions for next month. We have a gap to fill, and I'm not going to race to hire a new full-time staff writer. We'll obviously be looking at freelancers we've worked with in the past, but what I'm looking for is something new. Ideally, I want a writing voice we haven't featured, before."

Emma typed shorthand notes for herself as she nodded. "Makes sense."

And it should be simple enough; people constantly sent in submissions for human interest pieces. Combing through them to find ones that were actually well-written, that had some real meat to them... well, Emma supposed that was why they were starting now.

"I want you to feel free to submit a piece; you can send it directly to me."

Emma was in the middle of typing out Allegra's words before the meaning of them sunk in, and everything inside of her froze.

Gripping the tablet tightly so she didn't make a fool of herself and drop it, she whipped her head up to stare at Allegra.

Who was staring back at her with a sharply arched eyebrow, clearly waiting for Emma to catch up.

"I'm – sorry. You want me to submit a piece?" More than anything, Emma hated the idea of looking like a moron to Allegra. But she couldn't help but to press this, feeling a little sure that she must had misheard.

"I'm not guaranteeing you'll be published," Allegra's tone was firm as she held Emma's gaze, as if needing to make sure Emma wasn't going to walk away from this thinking that she was taking over Henry's job.

Not something Allegra needed to concern herself about, because Emma was having trouble believing this was real.

"No, I know that."

"I've read over all of your notes for our Alton finalists; the edits and critiques you made were saliant and astute. I'd have made the same comments on many of them."

A flushed pleasure worked through Emma, and she found herself unable to hold back her smile. "That's amazing to know. Thank you."

Allegra waved her off, her stare intent and direct. "I felt inspired to pull up the pieces you submitted for the Fellowship, when you'd been accepted. Your writing was good. Very good. On a couple of pieces, I'd even go so far as to say exceptional."

Yeah, Emma now had to try to contain how wide her smile grew, as surprise swept through her. "Thank you. Again."

"I know, however, that you were unable to accept your place in the program. Which is a shame. It could have very likely changed your career trajectory." She narrowed her eyes meaningfully at Emma, gesturing around her own office.

Emma knew what she was saying even without her saying the words aloud. And it was true; if Emma had been able to complete the Alton Fellowship, to take a crash-course in upping her skills, to make all of the connections that would have been available to her, there was a good chance she wouldn't be working as Allegra's assistant to get her foot in the door.

It was something she'd tried very gamely not to think about over the past couple of months, granting people access to what had once been Emma's own dream.

Luckily, she'd had everything going on with Regan to distract her from ruminating on it too much.

"I'd like to think I'm on a decent trajectory, still," Emma cut in, deferentially.

Even so, she did mean it. Working under Allegra wasn't something she took lightly, and she didn't want her boss to think that Emma believed she was better than this.

"So you are," Allegra agreed, an air of approval in her tone. "And I'd like to see you continue it. So, get me a piece by next Wednesday, and I'll give it a read."

"Yes. Absolutely. Thank you." How much had Emma thanked this woman in the last five minutes?! It didn't matter; she'd do it even more if she felt like Allegra wouldn't be irritated by it.

"You don't need to thank me; you'll earn any publication by your own merit." Allegra frowned down at her laptop screen. "Before you leave today, make sure you move up my meeting with Margaret Eddy to Monday morning."

Understanding that she was being dismissed, Emma nodded. "Absolutely."

She had to bite her lip to contain her stunned smile as she turned back to her desk.

～

What was she going to write about?

The thought had started to bounce around Emma's mind, obsessively, for the last hour and a half.

She had essentially three days to think of something good – something interesting, something moving, something that made Allegra respect Emma as not only an assistant with potential but as a real, prospective writer.

As she left work, she already had her phone in hand, unable to quell her amazement any longer.

EMMA – 5:42PM

I have giant news

REGAN GIRLFRIEND-MATERIAL GALLAGHER – 5:42PM

Good news??? Bad news? Scary news? What kind of news, beautiful?!

She still felt that slight hit of warmth on her cheeks at Regan's nickname. Granted, she'd heard the nicknames Regan had used to refer to Sutton over the years, so she couldn't say she was at all surprised that she was on the receiving end of her own nicknames. Given that they were in a relationship.

Given that Regan *loved her*.

Yeah. It had been a couple of weeks since Regan had dropped that L word on her, and Emma's stomach still fluttered at the idea. Regan wasn't shy about saying it, either.

She'd tell Emma she loved her before they went to sleep. She'd say it when they woke up in the morning. She'd pant it in gasping, moaning breaths when Emma made her come. She'd write it in little notes when she prepared Emma's lunch – something she'd only done a couple of times, but Emma found it damningly sweet.

Every time Regan said it, though, it made Emma pause. Made her *feel*.

She'd never been loved like this, before. Yes, her grandmother loved her unconditionally, and so did her mom, as different as they'd showed that love throughout her life. But *romantically*, it had never been close to this.

The only person that had ever said *I'm in love with you* to Emma had been Felicity. And it was not something she'd wanted to make a production out of, not something she'd given any fanfare.

That had been fine. Honestly, it had been what Emma believed she'd wanted. Something quiet, understated, and modest. Something that Emma had believed was just – real. No sappy, exaggerated gestures and meaningless fluff.

Though Emma had never had an easy time admitting when she was wrong, this was probably the easiest thing to be wrong about.

Because being loved by Regan wasn't quiet or understated or modest; it was loud and sappy and heart-pounding, and the realest thing Emma had ever experienced.

If someone had given her the hypothetical situation that her partner would tell her they loved her, but Emma wasn't ready to say it back, she'd have imagined it would make her anxious. That she'd feel pressured and uncomfortable and that she'd wished they'd waited longer to tell her.

She'd never have imagined that she didn't feel stressed at all by Regan's confession or repeated statements. It was purely because of Regan, herself. She didn't expect Emma to say anything back until she was ready, and Emma *knew* that.

And with that love came these nicknames. Most often, they were comments on Emma's looks – specifically, on how attractive Regan thought she was.

Again, something Emma was definitely not used to in any way. But... something she couldn't deny made her feel good. It felt wildly, unexpectedly *good* to be reminded how attracted to her Regan was. Emma hadn't felt better about herself in her entire life.

REGAN GIRLFRIEND-MATERIAL GALLAGHER –
5:43PM

?!?! the post-work rush is dying down a bit
and now I'm dying to know what your
news is!!

She couldn't even be upset about the fact that Regan had comman-deered her phone and changed her contact info. Something that would have once driven her crazy was now something she looked at with every text and *smiled* at.

EMMA – 5:43PM

Allegra is giving me the chance to submit a
piece

She paused, before correcting herself.

EMMA – 5:43PM

Actually, she asked me to submit something

Unsurprisingly, Regan's response was immediate, in spite of the fact that she was working.

REGAN GIRLFRIEND-MATERIAL GALLAGHER –
5:43PM

SHUT THE FRONT DOOR

That's so exciting!!!

EMMA!

I love you!!! You deserve this!

Biting her cheek, Emma shook her head as she walked toward the subway station.

EMMA – 5:44PM

There's a huge chance it's not getting
published

REGAN GIRLFRIEND-MATERIAL GALLAGHER –
5:44PM

> Not with that attitude!!

> Who cares, anyway! It's about the fact that she wants you to submit your writing!!!!!!

This was it.

Who else, in the world, would be so unadulteratedly, unashamedly, unassumingly thrilled for her, when she wasn't even published, yet. When she hadn't even *written* a piece, yet? Regan might even be more excited than Emma was.

REGAN GIRLFRIEND-MATERIAL GALLAGHER –
5:45PM

> I guess it's a good thing I'm working until late tonight, huh? I'll be out of your hair for you to get some real, focused, dedicated writing time

Emma lifted her eyebrows in consideration; she hadn't even thought about that. But Regan was supposed to be working until ten, which meant Emma had the apartment to herself to write. That was great.

It would be silent and still and she'd have time with just her thoughts. That was... great.

Emma's steps slowed, realizing that she didn't really *feel* like it was great. The idea of going back to their apartment and being there alone for most of the night made her stomach sink, the distinct feeling of disappointment sliding through her.

There was nothing appealing to her about going home to their apartment – even to write this piece – when Regan wasn't going to be there. When she wouldn't get to see her exuberant smile or hear the enthusiastic words Regan was sure to have or to feel the press of Regan's mouth against hers. Going home to their empty apartment right now felt just like that: empty.

Emma could feel her heart start pounding in her chest at the realization. Was she *crazy*? She'd never in a million years ever imagined this would her response, but it was undeniable.

That feeling stayed with her until she found herself not at their apartment, but at the entrance to Topped Off.

She took a deep breath, pulling open the glass door, as she heard the familiar jingle of the bells that signaled her entrance.

Even in the "lull" that Regan had described, the café wasn't empty. Topped Off was rarely ever truly empty. Regan was behind the counter, chatting animatedly with the only customer in line as she effortlessly made their drink order.

And... yeah.

Emma felt it, that feeling in her chest that she'd been experiencing for weeks now. That feeling that she'd written off in the beginning as the excitement over her new relationship. But if that were the case, it wouldn't feel the way it felt.

More intense, more insistent, as time continued passing. She felt it now, alive and buzzing inside of her, even louder than it normally was.

Coupled with it right now, as Regan handed the customer their drink and looked up across the café to meet Emma's eyes, was the tight spiral of nerves echoing through her.

Nerves, and excitement, and readiness, and *love*.

"Emma?" Regan's tone was tinged with wonder, her expression brightening with that smile Emma had never been able to dislike, even in their most antagonistic moments. "What are you doing here? Do you want to caff-up for the night of writing ahead?"

With a deep breath, Emma strode forward to the counter, and she had no idea what she was going to say, she just knew this was the time to say it.

"My middle name is Avery."

Confusion flit over Regan's face, even as a small, baffled smile tugged at her lips. "The way you've guarded that from me, I would have thought it was way more embarrassing."

Emma nodded. "It is. Because it's after Avery Wilder."

Predictably, Regan's eyes widened with obvious glee. "Shut up! Really? The actress?"

"Kimberly was fifteen, and her favorite show was *Here for Tomorrow*, so..." Emma shrugged, not even able to summon the kernel of embarrassment she'd normally feel when telling this fun fact to someone.

Especially not in the face of Regan's excitement, that gorgeous smile unfailingly making Emma's stomach flutter.

"That's so cool. Mine's Cady, by the way. After one of my mom's aunts. Boring origin story."

"And if I'd known you in middle school, maybe I'd feel differently about telling people my middle name. Because, yeah, the name itself is totally fine; as a name, I have no issues with it. It was people's reactions to finding out that my mom named me after an actress, when everyone in my private school was named after family members or other... respectable people, I guess, that made me embarrassed." She stared at Regan, thinking that if she'd known Regan earlier in her life, she'd probably feel very different about closing people out.

Regan's grin softened. "Well, kids can be really shitty. But I appreciate you telling me." The confusion from a few minutes ago crept back. "Is that why you came here?"

Shaking her head, Emma felt her heart start to pound – quickly and demandingly – in her chest. "No, I..." She drew in a deep breath, holding it in, and gathering strength from it to say, "I came here to tell you that I noticed you first."

Regan froze, her smile in place even as her eyebrows knitted together in confusion. "Uh... huh?"

Her breath came a little faster, and the words started to pour out of her. "A few months ago, the first time we went to my mom's for dinner and you called me into your room."

That memory was burned into Emma's mind, locked in.

Because, "It was the first time I'd ever seen you, undressed." And she'd tried so very hard not to let herself *feel* anything.

Regan nodded, slowly, as she placed her palms on the counter between them and leaned in. "Right. I remember that."

"You said that people always notice Sutton first," Emma prompted, and that sentence had sounded a little crazy to Emma, even then. "But I need you to know that I noticed *you* first."

Still looking confused, Regan's grin turned teasing. "Okay, sure, but only because I burned you with coffee."

Still, resolutely, Emma shook her head. "No, actually. If you recall, due to my gram oversharing, I'd already seen you in here and liked you, before that."

"Your crush, riiiight," Regan drew out, tilting her head up at Emma. "But–"

"The first time I ever saw you was also the first time I'd ever seen Sutton. She was in here; right here, actually." Emma gestured to the exact spot she was standing, right across from the register. "You two were talking, but I couldn't hear what was being said. And you made a comment, and you two both laughed. And yes, Sutton's beautiful – absolutely. But I noticed *you*. Your laugh and your smile and the way your eyes lit up."

She stared intently at Regan, hoping she understood what this meant to Emma. Not only the memory, but that she was telling Regan here. In public, in front of one of Regan's coworkers, who was only a few feet away, and was surreptitiously pretending not to listen.

And she only felt the barest amount of embarrassment, because she wanted Regan to know, and she wanted her to know, now.

The smile slowly faded from Regan's face, as she stared up at Emma with that look Regan sometimes wore when she stared at her. That soft, wide-eyed, *adoring* look.

"Emma," she breathed, and Emma shook her head.

There was more, and she needed to say it.

"I meant what I said to Sutton on that call; it was easier to lean into finding you irritating, rather than let myself give in to anything else. Because I *did* have a crush on you before we met. No, I didn't really know you. But I'd come in here for a few months, and I not only was attracted to you, but... I loved how funny you were. I loved that you never seemed daunted or overwhelmed during rush times. I loved that you were willing to give tourists recommendations, and that you remembered facts about your regulars. But I definitely was *not* ready to feel any more than that, so it was a lot safer to wall all of that away," she admitted, her cheeks heating, especially as she saw Regan's coworker turn and stare at her, all pretense of not eavesdropping forgotten.

"This summer has changed my life. And for someone who has never liked change, that's a scary thing. But it's all been... good. *Everything* in my life is better now than it was before, and it's because of you."

Wow, Emma felt a little breathless. She could hear it in her own voice, and she swallowed hard, as she whispered, "I'm in love with you, Regan. To the point that I don't even want to go home and take advantage of our empty apartment for the night. Because the thing I want to do the most when I have good news or even just when I leave work, is be with you."

She inhaled sharply with surprise as Regan hopped up from where she stood, bracing herself on the counter, and surged across to press her lips to Emma's.

Despite the emotion and the vulnerability and the public aspect of it all, she didn't care. She didn't care that they were in the café or that there were a few customers at the tables or that everyone was definitely watching.

She cared about the fact that she could feel the smile on Regan's soft mouth.

The moment was over within seconds, as Regan ended the kiss. As Emma blinked her eyes open, Regan was already in full motion. She made her way around the counter and grabbed Emma's hand in hers, tugging hard.

"Jackie, I'm taking my break," she informed her coworker, and Emma willingly followed Regan.

As Regan shoved open the door to the back room, she couldn't help but think about their first official meeting. Especially as Regan quickly turned and gripped Emma's shirt by the collar, and she teased, "Are you going to rip this one too?"

"Don't tempt me; you're lucky I didn't do it in the middle of the café," Regan growled, tugging Emma down to capture her mouth once more.

The kiss was hungry and searching and hot and sweet, and Emma gave into it, much like she'd given herself to Regan.

twenty-nine

SIX WEEKS LATER

EMMA SIGHED CONTENTEDLY as she blinked her eyes open for the first time of the day and snuggled in close to Regan.

Which wasn't difficult, given how they typically were wrapped up in one another upon waking up for the day. Unsurprisingly, Regan was an intense cuddler. Surprisingly, Emma didn't mind it.

Even more surprisingly, she often found herself cuddling in close to Regan, much like this morning. She was spooning Regan from behind, the contours of their bodies aligning, from their slightly bent legs, to the way Regan's butt was cradled in Emma's lap, to how Regan's back was pressed against Emma's front, with Emma's arm draped over her waist.

It felt so... normal. Alarmingly normal, to wake up with the fresh, minty scent of Regan's shampoo in her nose, the soft feeling of Regan's sheets surrounding her. Emma's own pillows were now in Regan's bed, because she had a very specific preference for neck support.

For the first few weeks into their relationship, she'd kept her own bedding in her own room, but in the last month she'd given in. The reality was that she hadn't slept in her own bed in... Emma didn't even remember, at this point.

She'd valiantly tried at the beginning to maintain some semblance of boundaries and distance, if only just a little. It was hard from the get-go, given that they lived together and – without Emma even realizing how intensely – their day-to-day lives were so entangled.

But she figured she'd probably still at least sleep in her own room at least a few days a week.

Even after the first few weeks, she'd deluded herself into believing it. It truly wasn't until after Regan had told Emma that she loved her that Emma had to just be honest with herself.

She wasn't going to sleep by herself at night in her own room. Definitely not after having sex with Regan. Not on the nights they didn't have sex, either. What in the world was appealing about walking away from being with her girlfriend to go to sleep in her room, alone, when Regan was a hallway away?

Contrary and grumpy as Emma could be, she wasn't stupid. Why would she want to punish them both?

Also, her room didn't have *that* –

The Modern Family – Mothers and Daughters by Emma Bordeaux

The printed and framed story that Regan had hung up proudly on her wall two weeks ago. Allegra had not only accepted her piece, praised it, and published it, but she'd also encouraged Emma to continue submitting to *Olly*!

And Regan had made a countdown that she'd hung up in their living room until the day Emma's piece had gone live, before immediately framing it. Oh, but not only did she frame *this* one, but also one for Gram and Kimberly, as well.

She dropped an affectionate kiss to the soft skin of Regan's neck.

Surprise filtered through her when she felt Regan shiver against her lips, and she drew back a few inches to look down.

Yep, Regan had goosebumps. She heard Regan sigh, before she felt the press of Regan's ass roll firmly backward into her.

Fascinated by her girlfriend's response to a kiss Emma had considered fairly innocuous – innocent, even – she dipped her head down to kiss Regan again, dragging her lips lightly over the soft skin of the side of Regan's neck.

"Emma," Regan breathed, rolling her hips back again. This time, more insistently. Deliberately pressing against Emma's hips.

"Are you awake?" She whispered, surprise filtering through her.

Regan sometimes woke up before Emma did, but she didn't usually stay all cuddled up and warm and languid against Emma like this. She almost always stayed in bed, but she would typically be on her phone and texting Sutton or scrolling social media or even making Topped Off schedules or typing out an idea for a recipe. She'd be quiet and respectful while letting Emma continue to sleep, but once Regan was awake, her mind was moving a mile a minute.

"Mhmm," Regan hummed, stroking her fingertips up Emma's forearm that was draped around her waist. She then scratched as she moved her hand back down, and Emma found herself shivering. "Been waiting for you to wake up."

"You're being awfully polite about it... very unlike you," Emma teased, speaking against the side of Regan's throat. The feeling of Regan's skin against her moving lips made them tingle, and she loved that feeling.

"I'm polite," Regan countered, an offended tone in her voice, circling her fingers around Emma's wrist, and squeezing. Not hard enough to hurt, but enough to remind Emma about the thrill Regan always got when she held Emma down.

Or when Emma held her down. Unsurprisingly, Regan liked to give just as well as she got, and she liked to get just as well as she gave. There was nothing – so far – they'd ventured into when it came to sex that Regan didn't want to explore.

"You are *not* polite when you want me to wake up," Emma disagreed, still. She couldn't help herself from nipping her teeth into Regan's neck – lightly, teasingly, but a reminder that Emma *knew* she was right about this.

Regan groaned, the sound husky and deep in her throat. "Well, that's because *usually* I'm not waking you up so that you can touch me and make me come; I felt like waking you up for that would be pervy."

Heat licked at her, starting between her thighs as her clit pulsed to life at Regan's words. "You've been laying here, awake, thinking about me touching you?"

She was no longer surprised by how forthright Regan was in saying how much she wanted her. She sometimes was surprised by how fucking strongly her body reacted to it, though.

"Mm," Regan hummed again, nodding against the pillow.

Anticipating Regan's next move, Emma rocked her hips into Regan's ass the next time she pushed herself back into Emma.

And, yeah, the pulsing between her legs was already strong enough that she *felt* it. Even though the contact wasn't right on her clit, the pressure of Regan's ass pushing against her provided Emma just enough to push the heat inside of her up to a solid simmer.

"I had this dream," Regan started, her voice raw and needy.

"What happened in this dream?" Emma asked, already feeling a little breathless, as she tightened her hold over Regan's waist and deliberately pressed into her ass.

Regan placed her hand over the back of Emma's and laced their fingers together. Then she used her guiding touch to work Emma's hand under the loose T-shirt Regan had worn to bed.

"*You* happened," she rasped. "You made me come over and over again, and I woke up so... wanting. So fucking wet."

As she spoke, Regan slowly slid Emma's hand down under the waist of the tiny, thin shorts she had on.

Closing her eyes, Emma reveled in the feeling of Regan's body under her touch. How warm she was, how soft. How Regan seemed to strain back against her, yearning for Emma's touch. How she always gave herself to Emma without hesitation, and how being on the receiving end of that obvious desire was the sexiest thing Emma had ever fucking experienced.

Her own breath caught in her throat as Regan pushed Emma's hand down, down, and finally, both of their fingers brushed against Regan's hard clit.

"You weren't kidding," Emma murmured, groaning at the feeling of Regan absolutely soaking her fingertips at the slightest touch.

"Would have been the worst joke ever," Regan grit back, her voice edging into a needy whine, as she rolled her hips back again.

This time, as her ass pressed against Emma, she swore she felt it right against her clit. Need sparked through her, as she worked her fingers over Regan's hard clit in slow circles. A move that she knew wouldn't make Regan come – she needed Emma to move a lot faster – but would drive her crazy.

Regan lifted her leg up to hook over Emma's thigh, giving Emma more freedom to actually touch her.

She slid her fingers down, pressing only her fingertips at Regan's entrance. She knew, now, that Regan did love to be filled, that she loved taking Emma's fingers inside of her. But that her favorite thing about it was right as Emma started to push inside, that initial feeling.

Pressing open-mouthed kisses against Regan's throat, she fucked her slowly and shallowly. She avoided Regan's clit deliberately, even as Regan started truly moaning.

It was Emma's favorite thing, the thing that made her absolutely, utterly *crazy* with her own need. Those sounds that Regan let out, loud and bold and unashamed, these sounds that told Emma just how much Regan wanted her. How lost she was in her pleasure.

Every time, it took her back to that first night. Every time, Emma thought about how these fucking sounds had gripped something inside of Emma and pushed her forward into their relationship.

Her own – much softer, but no less desperate – cries escaped the back of her throat as she rocked her hips against Regan. She'd never be able to come like this, but that didn't matter.

For Emma, right in this moment, it wasn't about coming. It was about the fact that she couldn't control this desire. That her clit was aching and needy, and Regan felt so fucking good against her.

"Emma, *god*, come on. My – you know what I–"

As the keening sounds Regan let out became more desperate, in turn making Emma more desperate, the thought struck her.

She pressed her body firmly into Regan's back, using her own strength to roll Regan onto her stomach, trapping her hand between Regan and the mattress.

Even though she had far less range of motion like this, it didn't matter. All she needed to do was be able to touch Regan's clit, exactly like she was now, slowly working her fingers over it.

Regan was so wet, she didn't have much friction, and she was pulsing so hard that Emma *felt* it, and she groaned, before biting at Regan's shoulder.

She felt Regan shudder, hard, under her, bucking her hips up at Emma. Then she immediately pushed back down, clearly seeking out as much pressure on her clit as possible.

"Yes, fuck, Emma, *yes!*" Regan pressed her face down into the bed, rocking down against the bed – against Emma's hand – so hard.

"I remember you said this was what you thought about, that first night on the phone," Emma panted out, bracing herself with her free hand. Using it to give herself enough leverage so that she could keep rolling her hips down against Regan's ass.

This angle wasn't only better for Regan, but herself. Balancing on her knees and spreading her thighs to bracket Regan, Emma's eyes rolled back with pleasure as she got the first hint of actual contact to her own clit.

Regan nodded, jerkily, as she gasped. "Yeah, this – you – uh-huh."

If Emma had any wherewithal, she might be amused at Regan's incoherence. But, as it was, she was almost just as far gone, herself.

"Fuck yourself against me, then," she demanded. "Just like you imagined."

Regan inhaled sharply, before she released a long, rasping moan, and erratically rolled her hips down. Harder, faster, and Emma's hand was *soaked* and –

"Yes! I'm – Emma!" Regan cried out, her throat sounding raw with pleasure, as she started shuddering under Emma.

She rocked down so hard that Emma couldn't move her hand at all, and she didn't give a damn. All she could possibly care about was that Regan was coming for her, coming on her, so hard.

She watched and felt Regan's orgasm start to subside, her movements becoming slower and more relaxed, until Regan finally sighed and melted onto the bed under her.

Emma's throat was dry, and her own clit was so hard, and she was so wet, she could feel her own sleep shorts sticking to the tops of her inner thighs. Thighs that were already trembling.

Not for the first time, she considered herself the luckiest woman on earth. Because Regan's rebound period after coming was almost nonexistent, and she'd come to learn that Regan was rarely ever exhausted by an orgasm. If anything, coming seemed to reinvigorate her.

So, so *lucky*, as Regan arched her hips up and let Emma slide her hand out, and then flipped herself over onto her back in the same breath.

Regan stared up at her, her face flushed, and her dark eyes bright and gleaming.

Emma couldn't even manage a cogent sentence right now, but she didn't have to. Because Regan moved so quickly, Emma could hardly register it.

But Regan slid her hand down into the waist of Emma's shorts, immediately seeking out Emma's clit.

Apparently, Regan wasn't in the mood for teasing or playing games this morning, and Emma was so fucking grateful for that.

She rolled her hips down hard into Regan's hand, already starting to shudder and throb from the way Regan rolled her fingers over her clit.

Still braced over Regan, she looked down at her. Watching Regan as Regan watched Emma's body.

She hadn't worn a shirt to sleep, her stomach and breasts were completely bare, and Regan stared at her, transfixed.

Emma moaned, tossing her head back as the need to come wound tighter and tighter inside of her. She felt no shame, not even the faintest hint of insecurity under Regan's intent gaze. It only made this hot, aching, *close* feeling build higher and higher inside of her.

She worked her hips harder, feeling viscerally satisfied at the way Regan's mouth fell open on a whimper.

Regan worked her hand down, pressing two fingers inside of Emma's clenching walls, as she firmly pressed her palm to Emma's clit, and –

"Fuck!" She cried out, her orgasm crashing over her.

All she could hear was the blood rushing in her ears, and her thighs shook, as the pleasure wracked through her.

Just before that pleasure turned to discomfort, Regan gently slid her fingers out of Emma. She jerked, then caught her breath as Regan lightly brushed against her clit – yeah, *that* was the last ounce of pleasure – before she pulled her hand out of Emma's sleep shorts.

She dropped down next to Regan on the bed, still catching her breath, as she felt Regan cuddle in close to her.

As her heart rate finally returned to normal, Emma let out a long, deep breath. She knew – knowing Regan – that *morning conversation* was due to start any second now.

"So, what's on the agenda today?" Regan asked.

Emma's lips curled into a smile – bingo.

Before that smile immediately faltered as she recalled the thought she'd very intently been pushing to the back of her mind for the last couple of days.

"I should probably start looking for apartments," she said, quietly.

She knew she wasn't imagining things when Regan took a second longer to respond than she normally would. "Oh. Right."

"I mean, it's officially November. Sutton's due back in December..." She trailed off, logic filling in the gaps.

The agreement had always been that Emma would find her own place at the end of Sutton's internship. She'd signed it in the roommate contract. *Obviously*, Sutton was going to need to move back to her apartment.

So, she needed to find a place to move into by December.

"Yeah," Regan whispered.

Emma's stomach twisted unpleasantly, and she drew in a deep breath. Taking in the scent of Regan's shampoo and laundry detergent, the way it had blended with Emma's in their bed. She slowly glanced around, looking at the organized chaos of Regan's room. At the map she had on the wall that she'd drawn, at that framed story Emma had written. At her plants. At her desk, where Emma's laptop was now perched. The desk chair, where Emma had draped Regan's Brandeis sweatshirt after she'd tugged it off before bed last night.

She licked her lips, her heart thudding, as she admitted softly, "I can't believe I'm saying this, but... I don't want to go."

Five months ago, she'd *never* have imagined she'd feel this way. If someone told Emma that the idea of not seeing Regan every day, of giving up this shared existence they'd created, would make her throat feel tight with emotion...

Well, she'd have laughed in their face.

"It's a great apartment," Regan's tone was so obviously glum, even as she tried to interject some levity into it.

Emma turned to look at Regan, who was worrying her teeth into that full bottom lip. "It's a great person in the apartment," she corrected. "A person I love."

Regan's smile was immediate, as she reached out and traced her fingers over Emma's cheekbone, all the way back to tuck hair behind her ear.

Then she froze, brown eyes widening, as she shook her head. "Why do you have to go?"

"What?" Emma frowned. "It's – that was the deal."

She could feel the energy vibrating through Regan, as she shook her head and refuted Emma's statement. "Deals change. *You* don't want to leave. *I* definitely don't want you to go. So – just, don't."

Emma couldn't help the exasperated laugh that bubbled up, even as she rubbed at her temples. God help her, she loved this woman.

"It's not just about what you and I want," she reminded her. "Sutton's going to *probably* want her room back–"

"Move into mine!" Regan excitedly cut her off, gesturing widely around the room. "It's bigger than Sutton's. You barely have that much stuff; we can fit your bookshelves over there." She pointed to the other side of her room, to her empty wall space. "And you can put your obsessive schedule on the wall in front of the desk! Clothing is the biggest issue, but I'll make you the space!"

Emma still frowned, shaking her head in disbelief.

Regan wasn't having it. "You basically already live in here, anyway, hot stuff."

"It's not up to *me*," she stressed, again. "It's – even if I moved into this room, we can't unilaterally just..."

Regan already had her phone in her hands, thumbs flying over the screen. "Asking Sutton now!" She needlessly informed Emma.

Sitting up, Emma scrubbed her hands over her face, trying desperately to wrap her mind around the turn this conversation had rapidly taken.

"Aha!" Regan's cry was triumphant, and she held her phone out for Emma to read it.

SUTTON, MY DARLING LADYBUG, I HAVE TO ASK YOU SOMETHING

What do you think about Emma... not moving out? Like, if you move back and you get your room back and everything. But what if Emma moved into my room? And we all were living here????

SUTTON, THE ONE AND ONLY – 9:59AM

You mean, another person in our home that thinks rationally and can help me corral you? Someone that has housebroken you and trained you to use a shared calendar? Sounds amazing, actually

"It sounds amazing!" Regan practically bounced where she sat.

Emma continued to stare down at the phone for several beats, as this rapidly forming reality started to set in. The weight of the dread and trepidation she'd started feeling in the last few days over the idea of having to move started lifting from her shoulders, and she turned to look at Regan.

Who was staring at her, questioningly, the bright smile on her face dimming ever-so-slightly. "I mean... I'm not trying to strong arm you into this," she quickly added, shaking her head vehemently. "Just, if you really meant that you didn't want to go, this is an option, and–"

"I think Sutton might be sorely disappointed," Emma interjected, softly but firmly. "Because I don't think that I think all that rationally around you, anymore. Somehow, you've made me think that me moving into your room is completely rational and makes the most sense, in a matter of minutes."

No, when it came to Regan, Emma didn't think logically; she'd been completely sucked in.

The wondrous grin that slid across Regan's face was absolutely gorgeous. "If you give me long enough, I'll grow on you. I should have warned you that from the beginning."

"The ultimate snowball effect," she agreed, leaning in to press her lips to Regan's and revel in the insanity.

475

epilogue

DROPLETS OF RAIN rolled down Regan's face, her hair was soaked, and she was wearing a rain jacket but even that clung uncomfortably to her body like a second skin, with how wild the weather was outside.

Even worse than how she felt on the outside, though, was how she felt on the inside.

Her stomach twisted so tightly with guilt and even heavier with disappointment. She was so, so fucking disappointed in herself.

"I'm *so* sorry," she apologized for at least the fifth time in as many minutes. And she would keep doing so, for as long as it took!

She rolled both her and Emma's suitcases down the gleaming hardwood floors of the inn, leaving a small trail of water behind. She'd apologized to the man at the front desk, preemptively for the mess it would leave.

Luckily, the hard side material of their suitcases had protected the contents. The purchase had been made by Emma two years ago, before they'd gone on a trip to London. Not *matching* suitcases, per-se, but the same brand, with complementing colors. "*It'll be easier to spot them, this way*," Emma had explained, as she'd given Regan's old, worn, cloth suitcase a disdainful look.

Regan couldn't disagree. Besides, much like everything Emma did, she'd researched the best, most durable and secure suitcases – this baby handled like a dream, compared to the one Regan had lugged around for the previous ten years.

She loved seeing her bright teal suitcase next to Emma's dark blue one, next to each other. It was a visual representation of them, as a couple, in a way.

"It's fine," Emma said over her shoulder, as she stopped in front of the door to the room they'd been assigned to and put in their key. It was a real key, too, not a key card, and it was designed to look like one of those old-fashioned skeleton keys.

This inn they'd managed to find was super cute, and Regan counted her lucky stars for that.

But, still.

"It wasn't what we'd planned, though. It wasn't what *I'd* planned, and I don't even know how everything got so messed up!" She lamented, resisting the urge to bang her palm into her forehead.

"Babe, it's fine," Emma stated, again, as she opened their door. But her tone wasn't totally *normal*; after being together for three years, Regan knew Emma's tones very well!

"It's not, and I understand if you're upset. You don't have to pretend." Regan followed Emma into the room, tugging their suitcases behind her, before turning to shut and lock their door.

"The room looks nice," Emma said, totally ignoring Regan's self-flagellation, as she looked around the room.

Taking a pause in berating herself, Regan looked around. It *was* really nice. Fairly large, with airy ceilings. An ornate dresser, a large television, and a cute old-fashioned working desk. The queen-sized sleigh bed had a solid wood frame, with a crisp white duvet laying over it. There were three large windows that Regan imagined might have a nice view... maybe when it wasn't storming, and there was some daylight coming in.

"At least there's that," Regan muttered, releasing her hold on their suitcases, as she flexed her hands to get some feeling back into them.

It was the middle of May, sure, but their walk in from the parking area had been chilly.

"I'm going to go to the bathroom and get situated," Emma

informed her, shaking back her own wet hair. She grabbed the duffel bag she'd brought in and started toward the adjoining door on the other side of the room.

"Great! Good!" She encouraged, trying to inject as much enthusiasm as she could into her tone. "Okay, I'll... try to figure out what the hell happened to get us so off-track," Regan muttered, mostly to herself.

Before Emma closed the bathroom door behind her, she pointed to the desk she'd just walked by. "Hey, there's a guestbook. Why don't you look through it and see if there's anything good to do around here if we're stuck for the weekend?"

With that, she shut the door behind her with a sharp *snap*, leaving Regan to herself.

Immediately, she took out her phone and pulled up the GPS. It just made no sense!

It was Emma's birthday weekend, and Regan had planned a little getaway to a cute little town a couple hours upstate. Emma had mentioned it a few weeks ago, because a farm-to-table restaurant had opened there that she'd wanted to try.

And she'd done *everything* right!

Regan knew herself; she knew that she was prone to potentially making small mistakes, to overlooking details that seemed insignificant but ended up with dire consequences. Since being with Emma, though, she'd changed.

True to what had just played out between them, Emma generally took it in stride when Regan messed up.

But being with someone that was so conscientious and well-prepared, in turn, had made Regan more conscientious and well-prepared. Now that she had her side business with her baked goods up and running, she'd needed to be a lot more organized. Keeping schedules and double-checking details was a game changer.

Sometimes things slipped through the cracks, but... Regan couldn't think of a single time in the last few years that she'd messed up *this* badly.

Thirty minutes ago, when the rain had started pouring so hard she'd barely been able to clearly see out of the windshield, she'd gotten a very,

very bad feeling in her stomach, and she'd pulled over so she could see what the hell was going on.

Because – from what she'd remembered – they were supposed to have arrived in the cute little town Regan had looked into at least an hour *before* the downpour was supposed to have started.

She must have gotten carried away during her drive with Emma, though, because she hadn't even registered that they'd been driving for far, far too long to be correct. But Regan had been focused on the road, and Emma had been reading aloud to her from a new book they'd both wanted to read – so of course, she'd been distracted!

By the time she'd tried to re-calibrate, they were in *Vermont*! Around them for miles was just... woods. No businesses, no people. Nothing.

Her GPS must have glitched or something, because it had been directing Regan to a small town in Vermont, rather than the one upstate. Again, all Regan's fault. Because when she and Emma had agreed on wanting to see more small towns around New England, Regan had put Green Ridge, Vermont on her list, and she'd put it in her GPS to check how far it was from the city.

Somehow, even though Regan had put their actual destination in her GPS *and* had Sutton check it over last night to cover all of her bases, though... this is where they'd wound up.

To make it all worse, it was Emma's *birthday*.

Feeling about an inch tall, Regan dragged her soaked rain jacket off and gingerly draped it over the back of the desk chair. Using the dry material of her shirt, she lifted it to dry off her face, before she blinked down at the guestbook Emma had referenced.

Reaching down, she flipped through it, finding that only the first few pages had been filled out.

"Bad luck continues," she shouted to Emma through the bathroom door. "This is a new book or something, because there are only, like, five entries."

Heaving a sigh, she tried to shake herself out of it.

When things like this had happened to her in the past, Regan had been able to take it in stride, to make light of it.

But... she'd just tried so hard for this weekend to be perfect.

Emma had officially been hired as a full-time staff writer at *Olly* a few months ago, and she'd been working so hard trying to prove herself, to make sure she lived up to expectations. Regan had been looking forward to this weekend as a little break, a little breath of fresh air for her, as well as a celebration.

Forcing herself not to go further down the road into the bad place in her mind, she focused down on the guestbook.

I've never had a bad experience with her! In fact, every moment I've spent with her since the moment we met has made my life a better place. She's helped my family come together in ways I never would have imagined. The girls keep trying to grab the pen to write their reviews, too - all glowing. - Kimberly Hayes

Frowning with confusion, Regan narrowed her eyes down at the book. What the hell?

"Um... has your mom stayed here?" She asked, even though it didn't make any sense.

She flipped the page.

All I've ever wanted was for someone to make Emma happy. Someone who loves her for who she is. Regan surpassed my expectations. Not only does she love Emma and make her happy, but she makes Emma an even better version of herself. Less... afraid of the world. Less scared to be herself. She makes me feel the same way, too. It's a very precious gift, and I'm honored to have her be a part of my life. - Sheryl Bordeaux

Okay, Regan wasn't seeing things. That was Emma's gram. That was *her* name.

She was no less baffled – maybe the most confused she'd ever been in her whole life – but her stomach tingled with excitement, nonetheless.

Who wouldn't love to walk into a room and be able to read people's – positive – thoughts about them?!

I spent a lot of my life not really knowing her. Not really wanting to know her, because I was so resentful. But I also spent a lot of my life feeling envious of her relationships with other people, the people Regan cared about. It wasn't until only recently that I allowed myself to see my sister for who she really is, and not who our family told me she was. Taking a page out of Regan's book was terrifying, but I think it was the best thing I could have ever done for myself. I think it - and she - saved my life. And I'm so grateful that I let her in. Because I don't have to be envious of the people Regan cares about and supports, anymore. Now, I'm one of those people. I've always loved her, but now I feel comfortable - feel allowed - to show it.
- Audrey Gallagher

Regan's breath caught in her throat, surprised. She stroked her fingers lightly over the page. She and Audrey were actually *friends* now, as well as sisters. So, this wasn't shocking. But... it was one thing to read this, to see it right in front of her eyes.

"Emma, what the fuck is going on!" She shouted, whipping her head up to look at the bathroom door. Still closed.

Regan *could* go and try to kick it down and get answers from the woman she was in love with. But... there was still more in the book, and she needed to read it.

I might not be Regan's mother by birth, but I'm a

parent to her by choice. As with all children - including all that I've given birth to - there have been issues. People are all flawed. But I'd be hard-pressed to find someone that cares so deeply about everyone else around her, than Regan. I knew from the day I met her - going to pick Sutton up from school, and being informed that my daughter had been pushed around on the playground, only to then be informed that the boy who'd pushed her had then been shoved to the ground by Regan - that she was a very special little girl. And she's grown into a very special young woman. Seeing her experience the last few years of true happiness and living her life for herself has given me the ultimate parental joy. - Katherine Spencer

Feeling her chin wobble, Regan sniffed. What the hell was this book?! Had she slipped on the rain outside and hit her head?!

I'm not always one for words, especially those from the heart. But I am one for being loyal to my ideals and to my favorite people. I'm someone that respects, deeply, people who follow their heart. I've always been someone to have many acquaintances, but few friends. And I'm someone that is truly lucky to consider Regan a great friend. - Charlotte Thompson

"You sappy bitch," she murmured, before flipping the page again.

I'll never have enough time to say everything Regan has been for me in my life. A constant confidante, support, reality check, defender, comedienne... a sister, in the truest, most meaningful definition of the word. I want her to have a lifetime of joy and love more than I want it for just about anyone else on the planet. - Sutton Spencer

P.S. Please forgive me, Regan, when you read this. I know you're probably beating yourself up about how wrong everything seemed to be going tonight. I'm sure you're going to understand, though.

P.P.S. You always take so much joy in saying that you get to be responsible for my finding love. I can't tell you how thrilled I am that I get to take responsibility for your love story, too.

Regan gasped as she read that – specifically, Sutton's apology. Suspicious and eager, she looked down at the final page.

Never in my wildest dreams did I imagine myself in a relationship with this woman.

Loud and messy and chaotic and gossipy...

And sweet and thoughtful and romantic and protective and hilarious and observant and talented and loving.

She has the most beautiful smile on the planet. She makes me feel calm and like everything is going to truly be okay, even in the most tumultuous of times. She's the best lover I've ever had (she'll appreciate that comment). Building a life with her feels as natural as breathing, and sometimes I look around at my life - in the apart-

ment we share - while she's baking or singing to herself or talking to me about articles I want to write or while we're going to visit my grandmother, and I think... this is it. I don't want anything or anyone other than this woman for the rest of my life.

10/10 would recommend. - Emma Avery Bordeaux

Her breathing was choppy, and the backs of her eyes burned with tears, and she *felt* like she knew what was going on, but she needed –

"What's going on?" She demanded, as Emma opened the bathroom door. She pointed at the book. "What is this?"

Emma's hair was dry, and she'd changed into the Brandeis sweatshirt that she'd confessed to Regan that she'd worn regularly through the years.

"Did you actually read the cover?" Emma teased, even as Regan could hear the edge of nerves in her voice.

... fair question.

Quickly, Regan closed the book and actually read the swirling font on the cover: *Regan Reviews*

Shaking her head, she blinked back at Emma. "I just... I don't..." She trailed off, dragging her hands through her hair. "I'm overwhelmed and amazed, and confused."

"I'm asking you to marry me," Emma clarified, biting her bottom lip as she lifted her hand up to show Regan the ring she was holding.

Oh. Wow. Okay. Regan had suspected it, and still, she felt her knees shake, and she jumped forward. Wrapping her arms tightly around Emma's neck, she held her so close, feeling Emma's heart pounding along with her own.

Unable to contain herself, she inched back enough to pepper Emma's face with kisses. Her perfect lips, her cheeks, her nose, her eyelids, her forehead, her chin, back to her lips.

Before she let herself get too caught up in kissing Emma, she pulled back to look at her. "Why did you torpedo this weekend trip that I planned?!"

"Because! When we talked about getting engaged, you said you'd prefer a surprise!" Emma insisted.

And... that was true.

They'd sat down together when Emma had gotten her promotion to talk about *the future*. Regan had indulged Emma in this conversation, coming prepared with her own notes. Emma loved to sit down together and make detailed plans, and Regan thought it was absolutely the most adorable thing.

"*This way, we'll never have another misunderstanding like the room-mate contract*," Emma had explained, the first time they did this – which had been the weekend before Emma had moved into Regan's room.

"I'm ready. To really think about marriage," Emma had started their conversation off, a couple months ago.

She'd listed off her reasons: her career was finally where she wanted it to be, Regan felt good about her own situation, Sutton had officially moved out of their apartment and in with Charlotte. All of these were things Regan knew mattered a lot for Emma to have in place, before taking any further steps in their relationship. Which was fine by her.

Because Regan had never really thought about marriage, before. She'd definitely never wanted to marry any of the guys she'd had *things* with. She wanted a future with Emma, and she loved their life, and she was happy to go at the speed Emma wanted to move at.

True to form, Emma had discussed her thoughts on proposals – she wouldn't want Regan to propose somewhere public or to make a big fanfare out of it, and she also didn't love big surprises. All of which were details Regan knew about her, already.

Regan... was the opposite.

So, they'd made an agreement that getting engaged was officially on the table.

Regan shook her head, trying to wrap her mind around it. "But – but it's *your* birthday weekend. I was going to propose to *you*!"

"I kind of figured that," Emma allowed, with a cute, small smile. "And I figured that I'd beat you to the punch, so what better way to do it than this? A complete and total surprise."

"I'll freaking say!" Regan's hands, braced on Emma's shoulders, squeezed as she bounced on her tiptoes. "Did you *have* to do it by making me think I totally fucked up? Also, *how* did you do that?"

"Sutton," Emma explained, easily, squeezing Regan's waist back. "She changed the destination in your GPS when she was "double-checking" it for you."

"That sneak!"

"She said – and I quote – this is a payback Regan will understand."

Regan could only laugh, before she remembered – the ring! She pulled out of Emma's embrace and grabbed her hand, where she still carefully held the ring between her thumb and index finger.

Feeling her own hands shake, she nodded, quickly. "Yes. Obviously, I want to marry you, Emma."

Carefully, Emma slid the ring onto her finger, and they both stared down for a long moment.

"And now, I get to say that amidst all of our firsts, *I* proposed to *you* first," Emma whispered, sliding her hand up to cup Regan's jaw. "It's a pretty big one."

"The biggest," she agreed, before leaning in and capturing Emma's mouth with her own.

She could feel Emma slide her free hand down and lightly stroke her thumb over the band of the ring. It was the perfect fit.

Somehow, they were the perfect fit.

about the author

Haley is an award-winning sapphic romance author. She lives in Massachusetts with her amazing wife and their dog, and spends 3/4 of the year waiting for the New England autumn. When she was little, she spent most of her time writing stories in her notebook, so being able to spend her adulthood writing professionally is a dream come true.

also by haley cass

Printed in Great Britain
by Amazon

51554292R00290